CATSEYE

Shattered Light™

3

CATSEYE

William R. Forstchen
&
Jaki Demarest

POCKET BOOKS
New York   London   Toronto   Sydney   Tokyo   Singapore

This book is a work of fiction. Names, characters, places and incidents are products of the author's imagination or are used fictiously. Any resemblance to actual events or locales or persons, living or dead, is entirely coincidental.

An *Original* Publication of POCKET BOOKS

POCKET BOOKS, a division of Simon & Schuster Inc.
1230 Avenue of the Americas, New York, NY 10020

Copyright © 1999 by Catware, Inc.

ISBN: 0-671-03268-2

First Pocket Books printing August 1999

10 9 8 7 6 5 4 3 2 1

POCKET and colophon are registered trademarks of Simon & Schuster Inc.

Cover art by David A. Cherry

Printed in the U.S.A.

CATSEYE

Chapter 1

RAF CAME INSTANTLY AWAKE AS SOME-thing pelted him. With a sharp hiss he rolled off his cot and came up in a single smooth motion, throwing knives in hand. He was trembling in every limb with the sudden rush of adrenaline.

"Who's there?" he whispered, feeling like an idiot for asking. "Pellar, is that you?"

"Wakey waaaakey time, my lovelies!" a cheerful feminine voice announced, a voice with the faint but distinctive twang of Tycor's northern provinces. Tazira. It could only be Tazira. Raf's green-gold eyes adjusted quickly to the darkness of his chamber, and he could just make out a tall, black-furred, infinitely familiar shape against the whitewashed wall. Tazira.

"Good morning, Captain," Raf saluted her dryly, replacing his knives and recovering his accustomed dignity. "Or is it still evening?"

Pellar, the chamber's other occupant, snorted derisively at that. "You ask that as if it mattered, Raf," he yawned. His cream-colored fur rippled as he stretched, and Tazira narrowly suppressed a jealous sigh. She would have killed for fur like that, or for those detestable sky-blue eyes of his. Not that she'd ever admit as much to him, but Pellar was easily the most beautiful mrem in Tycor.

With another luxuriant yawn, Pellar picked up his thread of pontification where he'd left off. "Ever since the Great Fall, there's been at least one sun in the sky at any given time. I really don't know why we persist in keeping up the artificial, old-fashioned distinction between morning and evening." He pulled back the heavy, dark red drape from the chamber's sole, narrow window to accent his point; the green sun was high in the sky, and the blue was dawning.

"Perhaps we persist in our illusions because the Old Ways still bring us a sense of continuity, fluidity, and dignity in a blasted world—" Raf began placidly, but was cut off by a low growl from Tazira.

"As much as I *love* listening to your philosophical debates," she drawled, "we don't have time. Varral Romney is asking for us."

"Val?" Pellar asked, frowning. "At this hour? Any idea what's up?"

"Other than us? No idea." Their captain shrugged with disheartening honesty. She started to pace the small stretch of bare wood floor between the cots and the door, her long white-tipped tail lashing with nervous energy. "But whatever it is, it's bad enough that he's summoning all three of us into the presence chamber in the middle of the night, rather than trusting it to anyone else. And judging from the mood in the palace halls,

I'd say no one else has heard about it, whatever it is."

"We're summoned to the presence chamber? Not the great hall?" Raf frowned, his short gray fur bristling slightly. Tazira glanced up at him, nodded, and resumed her pacing. "Not the usual form," he murmured. "Definitely something he wants kept quiet. What should we bring?"

" 'Civilian clothing' was all the messenger said. So, as much as I'm enjoying the view," she purred, giving them both a lazy, amused perusal, "I'd suggest you dress. I'm going armed to the back teeth, myself."

She made a slow, exaggerated pirouette for comic effect, mimicking the high-fashion models of the pre-Fall era. True to her word as always, she was indeed armed to the back teeth, and beyond if possible. There were throwing knives in both her knee boots, two francisca hand axes at her hip, and a large pouch of spellstones on her belt. And her great axe, the improbably named Black Bessie, was strapped across her back for that final bit of overkill.

Her garb was a nondescript ensemble of blacks and grays. Surprisingly close to tasteful, coming from a woman whose usual civilian wardrobe ran a narrow gamut from bold to garish. She couldn't be trying to blend with the locals; no mrem could hope to blend too closely with a largely human population. She might have been anticipating a potential assignment outside the safety of the city walls. Whatever the case, Raf planned on following suit, figuratively and literally. Gray and black were about the only colors he ever wore, anyway.

As for Pellar, Raf doubted he'd be able to resist his usual apparel: something that accented his eyes or highlighted his pale fur, something in the first stare of fashion. The older mrem's whiskers arched with amusement, but he kept the thought to himself.

"My dears," Tazira sighed, "I honestly have no idea what we're about to walk into. All I can suggest is that you be ready for absolutely anything. Now, you won't have any room to dress with me in here, so I'll just take myself out into the hall, where I can pace to my heart's content."

"Will your tail be lashing majestically as you pace?" Raf teased her laconically.

"Love, only for you." She smiled as she walked out. For her, it was an oddly subdued response, and one that betrayed her worry more than any words could have done. Raf and Pellar exchanged a knowing glance at that, and dressed quickly.

A contingent of four Guards awaited them at the door to the presence chamber. It was the usual number, and did not suggest that anything was out of the ordinary. Dano, Hallir, Alima, and Cain were on duty that night, exactly as they should have been. Tazira made a brief study of their faces; the three new recruits seemed a bit on edge, and Dano looked positively furious. Oh, yes, they knew something was going on, and they were undoubtedly being kept out of it.

"Captain, Lieutenants," Sergeant Dano saluted the trio crisply. "You're expected. If you'll please follow me?" He bowed and led the way in as the tall, dark wood door opened before them.

"Any idea what's goin' on, son?" Tazira asked him under her breath, quirking an eyebrow at him.

"No idea, Captain. I'm sorry," he whispered. "There's obviously a problem, but no one's seen fit to tell the Guard about it." The stubborn set of the human's jaw told her exactly how he felt about that, if she needed to look. She closed one large golden eye in a conspiratorial wink, and Dano grinned in spite of himself. The sergeant saluted the trio and headed back out to the corridor, and the heavy door was closed behind him. For the moment, they were alone.

The presence chamber was a small, intimate room with plain white plaster walls, high, dark wainscoting, and a fraying burgundy carpet. It was Varral Romney to the core, functional and unprepossessing, a room in which a soldier would be comfortable. A large, rectangular, highly polished creothwood table dominated its surroundings, and the only decoration the room boasted was a pre-Fall personal computer, a graceful, useless beige thing with softly flowing lines.

Tazira's gold eyes darkened as she contemplated that relic and the soft, sane world it had been a part of. She'd never known that world. She was thirty-five, born in the fifteenth year after the Fall. To her, Raf, and Pellar, life had been nothing but a constant struggle to survive, a battle against nightmares made flesh in a world no longer theirs to command. For her part, the life suited her well enough; she was a soldier, and she doubted she would have been at home anywhere else, even in a softer world. But she'd often caught herself wondering what Raf and Pellar might have made of themselves if the Fall hadn't come, if the monsters and the magic hadn't come, if technology and physics hadn't failed so utterly.

The graceful and clever Pellar could have been a diplomat, a detective, a spy, a jewel thief. An actor. Something exotic that took advantage of his polish and address. And Raf, what might he have become? A professor at one of the great universities, she realized, glancing over at him. He was standing at perfect attention, waiting calmly for Romney to appear, the picture of elegance, poise, and long-whiskered dignity. Raf would have been a philosopher, reading, writing, lecturing, and pontificating to his heart's content. The corners of her mouth arched downward in a wry grin, silently betraying a sudden surge of affection for them both.

Then again, she thought, without a trace of bitterness, *humans created mrem to be soldiers. I suppose there's no sense wondering if we might have been anything else.*

"I honestly don't know why Val keeps that relic," Tazira sniffed at last, flicking the tip of one ink-black ear in the computer's direction. "It's not like it'll ever work again."

"I think I can tell you exactly why he kept it," Raf murmured. Just as he was about to elaborate, the small door at the other end of the chamber swung open, admitting Varral Romney, Third Lord Tycor.

"Truth be told, that particular model didn't work too well even before the Fall," Romney admitted in the harsh, strident voice that had once belonged to a captain of the Tycor Guard. The position, and the strident voice and manner, had long since fallen to Tazira.

"Val!" the woman laughed delightedly, and they met in a great bear hug, throwing propriety to the winds as usual.

"Tazira, my girl, you look well!"

"So do you, Val, so do you!" she lied with a bold laugh. Oh, Val was attractive enough, at least as far as humans went: tall and barrel chested, dark skinned, with a shock of close-cropped silver hair and piercing black eyes. He bore his fifty-eight years extraordinarily well. But he'd been drinking more heavily of late; that and the pressures of command were beginning to show themselves.

"How are these ruffians treating you?" He gestured toward Raf and Pellar with comic expansiveness. They bowed in unison, much more concerned with the social niceties than either Tazira or Romney.

She shrugged "Same as usual."

"That bad, eh?"

"Oh, they're wretched," their captain sighed dramatically, fighting off a grin and not succeeding. "I mean, look at 'em! They let *me* come in here looking like an old gray dishrag, while *they* got dressed for court!"

Pellar looped his tail in amusement, and Raf's whiskers arched wryly on one side to acknowledge the left-handed flattery. Pellar's ensemble was a flawlessly chosen taupe, practical enough for the streets and roads, but a subtle complement to the darker points of his ivory fur. And Raf . . .

well, Raf would have had that same effortless elegance no matter what he wore. But his civilian garb, a slightly darker gray than his fur, was every inch as well chosen and beautifully tailored as Pellar's. Tazira looked at them, then looked down at herself, sighed, and gave up for the moment. Romney took one of her black-furred hands in his and kissed it gallantly.

"Foolishness, madam!" he chided her. "You'd be the most beautiful woman at any court in Delos. I'm fortunate enough to have you in mine."

"Flatterer!"

"Temptress!"

"I wish you were mrem, Val," she rolled her eyes at him teasingly.

"I wish you weren't," he quipped, completing the oldest in-joke that existed between them.

"Oh, but enough of this," Tazira said, half smiling and half growling. "You and I could flirt all day, but I'm sure you didn't call us in here for our charming company." With that, she shot him a searching glance. Raf and Pellar continued to watch him impassively.

"True enough, my friends," the human admitted grimly. "Though the company is always welcome. The fact is, we've got a problem. No . . . I've got a problem. It doesn't affect Tycor, just my ability to rule it." He paused, half expecting a barrage of questions. When the three of them had served under him in the Tycor Guard, they'd all been about twenty years younger, and wet behind the ears. Their patient silence now was all the difference between the brash kittens they'd been and the seasoned professionals they'd obviously become. Romney smiled to himself and continued.

"Tonight," he said as calmly as he could manage, "someone walked off with the Great Seal of Tycor."

Pellar nodded as if he'd been expecting something like that, Raf arched an eyebrow, and Tazira drew in a short, sharp breath. She laced her hands behind her back tightly, itching to pace the chamber, but forcing herself to stand at attention.

"Can't you have another one made, in secret?" Pellar suggested.

"Even if it were possible, and I doubt we still have the technology, I couldn't do that without admitting that the original is gone," Romney muttered. "And some might be inclined to take that as a sign that it's time for the Cycle of Houses to change. Worse, anyone presenting himself at court with it will be proclaimed Lord Tycor instantly, no matter who he is or how incompetent he is. The Great Seal is a pre-Fall symbol, one of the few we have left, and I have no doubt that the people will cling more tightly to that symbol than they will to me. Go ahead and pace, Tazira; I can tell that you want to."

"Thank you, sir," she breathed, tail lashing as she walked briskly back and forth. Her pacing and tail lashing were hallmarks, and a source of endless affectionate teasing from her friends. Even her soldiers tended to call her Old Lash, partly for her tail and partly for her taskmastering. The "Lash" part she didn't mind. The "Old" part she pretended not to mind. Raf smiled to himself as he watched her, but didn't tease her for once.

"I don't think I need to tell you, my friends, that I have no intention of stepping down gracefully in the event of a challenger." Romney sighed. "I worked too damned hard to free Tycor from the Tyrant's rule, and so did you, for that matter. I'm well aware of the fact that I owe my current lofty title to the three of you. And now, I need you to help me keep it."

"We will, milord," Raf said quietly.

"Any clues as to who took the shardblasted thing, and how?" Tazira asked, steadily wearing down the burgundy carpet with her pacing.

"Actually, we do have a sketchy physical description. Tall and muscular, with shoulder-length dark brown hair and blue eyes. Bit of an unkempt beard. Lanky and provincial. Answers to the name of Jain Riordan."

"Well, that's something, at least," Pellar looped his tail almost cheerfully. "It's much more than I was expecting, this early in the game. If you know who he is and what he looks like, you must have some idea of how the theft was accomplished."

"We do, at that." Romney nodded, lacing his hands behind him. "It had to have been done by a wizard, or by someone who had magical assistance. The safebox I kept it in was locked and heavily warded."

"Who created the wards?" Pellar asked him, one eyebrow arching in graceful contemplation. There was nothing on Delos Pellar enjoyed so much as having a puzzle to solve.

"Daman Najendra, one of my court wizards," Val replied. The Guardsmen nodded at that; they all knew him, if only in passing. "In fact, when the wards crashed, he was immediately alerted, and he managed to trace the Seal to an address in the city. It's currently resting, with its *temporary* owner, at the Gryphon Inn in Southgate."

"Damn it, Val, that takes all the fun out of it," Pellar grumbled. Raf shot his friend an amused and sympathetic glance.

"Can wizards really trace items that way?" Tazira's ears perked up suspiciously.

"Shards, woman, *I* don't know," Romney growled with affectionate exasperation. "I'm no bloody wizard. I have a few spells at my beck, like everyone else. But the wizards, they're another matter. Raised in the craft, most of them, proud of the fact, and close with their secrets. I suspect that, like the rest of us, they're still discovering what can be done with the new influx of magic on Delos. But as to the limits of their abilities, if any, I have no choice but to take their word for it. Soon enough, they'll get tired of supporting those of us in power, and they'll take it for themselves, and there won't be a flaming thing we can do about it. I just hope, selfish wretch that I am, that it doesn't happen in my lifetime." He sighed, suddenly looking old, as if that simple admission had exhausted him.

"It won't happen in *my* lifetime, I promise you that," Tazira said quietly after a moment. "Not in Tycor, and not to you. But for the moment, let's settle for solving the current problem." Her friends nodded their agreement, and Raf picked up the thread of her thought, as he often did.

"You said the seal was at the Gryphon Inn, with

a man calling himself Jain Riordan?" the mrem prompted gently.

"There, and likely to stay there until red dawn, according to Najendra," Romney nodded. "That should give you about another six hours."

"I don't know that it's worth depending on that assessment," Pellar murmured thoughtfully. "We'd better move out. Can we bring Najendra with us?"

"Unfortunately, no. He began a leave of absence about an hour ago."

"Convenient," grumbled the ever-suspicious Tazira.

"He'd asked for it weeks ago, and I have no reason to suspect him of any wrongdoing," Romney sighed, shaking his head. "I'll admit, it would be easier if we had him with us, but at least he left us a spelled ring capable of tracking the seal. The jewel will glow redder as you get closer to your target. Which one of you wants it?" he asked, holding it up. The oval, unfaceted jewel was a softly shining pale pink, for the moment.

Raf and Pellar glanced at their captain expectantly. After a brief thought, she took it and gave it to Pellar.

"You're the best tracker," she admitted. "Wear it in good health. Val, we'll be back as soon as we can manage this, and I promise you, it'll come out all right. Let's move out." Her long tail lashed as she headed for the door. Pellar followed in her wake, but Raf hesitated.

"Captain, permission to stay on a moment with Lord Tycor?" Raf asked her. She paused at the door, considering the request, and turned back to lock eyes with him.

"A moment, Lieutenant, no more," she said gruffly, and she and Pellar exited the chamber. Raf took no offense at her brusqueness; he never did.

"What is it, Raf?" Romney regarded him with undisguised curiosity. "And will you *please* call me Val? The others seem to manage. Humor me."

"This once, milord . . . Val," the mrem corrected himself, "I will. Because what I have to say to you, I'm saying as friend to friend, ignoring the impropriety of addressing one's liege lord this way."

"All right, I'm listening, son. But you're beginning to worry me."

"I don't think it's anything to worry about—yet. But it could be. How much have you had to drink tonight?"

Romney froze, and his face became stonily impassive. "I don't think that's any of your concern, Lieutenant," he said coolly.

"How much?" Raf pressed him. The human flushed with anger and started to pace the chamber as furiously as Tazira would have. "And what about yesterday? And the day before that? Enough to relax you? Enough to be a problem?"

"Enough to—" Romney began loudly, caught himself, and seemed to think better of his answer. He stopped his pacing, closed his eyes, and took a deep breath, mastering his temper. "You know, Raf, if you were anyone else, even Pellar or Tazira, I honestly think I would throttle you right now. But I can't lay one finger on all that shard-blasted dignity."

With a sigh of frustration he sat himself down in front of his pre-Fall computer. He stared numbly into its depths for a long moment, studying the soft reflection of his face in the darkened screen. The lines were blurred, but it wasn't the face of the boy who'd wasted good hours there, playing computer games before the Fall. It was the weathered face of an aging man who'd made hard choices, hard compromises with life and his integrity. Raf, with any luck, would never have to know what that was like.

"Hard choices aren't the sole prerogative of rulers, my friend," Raf said softly, as if in response to the other man's thoughts. Romney stared at him, unnerved, and he continued. "Believe me, I've known enough of command to know what it costs. I know the shifts you make, the choices you have to live with. But that's what life is. In the end, that's all it is, and all we are is the sum of the choices we've made, some good, some regretted. I've lost count of the number of times I've killed, to save myself, to save an innocent. To shield a friend. Each death is a choice. I'm choosing who lives and who dies. I'm choosing to continue to live, when death would be easier. You and I, Tazira and Pellar, your people, we've all made that choice. To live. To fight. You've had to become hard beyond anything you imagined you could be, when you used to play on that computer as a boy. That's what you're seeing now in your own reflection. And that's what you have to accept, if you want to live. *That*, ultimately, is the choice you have to make."

There was a long pause as the human looked up at him, considering him carefully.

"You know, Raf," he sighed at last, "I think that's the most I've ever heard you say. You were always the quiet one."

"Yes, I suppose I was. But it didn't mean I wasn't thinking."

"Clearly. I just didn't realize you were one of my wizards, all this time." He smiled a bit in spite of himself, and the tension in the chamber finally started to break. Raf arched his whiskers wryly, acknowledging the compliment.

"I'd better go join the others, sir," Raf said calmly. "Tazira will be spitting shards by now."

"Undoubtedly. And pacing her way through the floor." They shared a grin at that, and the lord of Tycor Keep rose from his chair and offered Raf his hand, in the Old Way. Raf took it, deeply honored by the gesture. "Good luck, my friend," Romney whispered.

"And to you, milord." The lieutenant bowed and silently left the chamber. The closing door had a dreadful finality about it, a hollow sound, like the sealing of a tomb. Romney stood and stared at the door for a long time, alone with his choice, and the blurring edges of his vision.

Chapter 2

JAIN RIORDAN CAME INSTANTLY AWAKE AS something pelted into him. A pillow, he discovered groggily. He pried his eyes open with some effort and peered out at the darkened bedchamber around him.

"Who's there?" he mumbled. "Lucian, is that you?"

Silence. Unnerved, he started to reach for the great axe by his bedside. It was no Black Bessie, to be sure, but it would serve well enough, he hoped. His eyes adjusted slowly to the darkness, and he could just make out three towering dark shapes against the peeling white plaster wall. With a panicked, incoherent cry he started to struggle to his feet, tripping himself up in his musty wool blanket.

"Jain Riordan?" a feminine voice asked almost casually. Her voice had the twang of the northern provinces, and he wondered if someone had been sent to fetch him home to Uppervale.

"Who's asking?"

"I take it that means yes," the woman said

dryly. "Jain Riordan, I arrest you in the name of
the lord and the people of Tycor."

"What? But—"

"If you surrender what you stole, your sentence
will be lessened. My word on that."

"Ohh," Jain gasped, mortified. He'd stolen a bit
of bread off a street vendor's cart that morning; it
was the first time he'd eaten in two days. Suddenly the boy was glad of the chamber's darkness;
here he wouldn't have to look a more honest man
in the eye. Arrested by the very Guards he'd run
away to Tycor to join . . . He didn't know how
he'd ever get over the shame of it.

"I'm sorry, I really am," he began contritely. "I
didn't mean to, but I was so hungry—"

"And someone promised you a great deal of
money if you stole it for them?" a soft, cultured
male voice inferred gently.

"No, I was just hungry," the boy corrected him.
"And I can't return it, because I ate it."

"*You ate it?*" the woman bellowed incredulously. "You *ate* the Great Seal of shardblasted
Tycor because you were *hungry?*"

"What? No, I . . . wait . . . what's the Great Seal
of Shardblasted Tycor?"

"Well, I guess we'd better open him up and get
it over with," the woman sighed.

"Wait, you . . . What? Open me up?" Jain tightened his grip on his axe, hoping against hope that
he'd get a chance to use it before he died.

"That's right, son," she purred dangerously. He
could see the flash of sharp white teeth against
dark skin. No, he realized with a sharp intake of
breath, not skin. Fur. *Mrem.* He shuddered convul-

sively. The mrem were killing machines. *But they would never intentionally kill a human. They were genetically programmed to protect us . . . unless something's gone horribly wrong . . .*

"You see," the woman continued conversationally, opening the heavy black curtains to admit the suns' light, "I don't believe that any human, even you, has a big enough mouth to fit the Great Seal into it. I think it's still here, somewhere in this room, if you haven't pawned it already. Pellar?" she asked, gesturing at a large ring he was wearing on a chain. Pellar glanced at the ring, and it was glowing faintly pink.

"The seal is somewhere nearby, but not in the room."

"Son, I'm gonna give you this one last chance to cooperate, 'cause I'm so generous," she smiled, showing a chilling number of teeth. "Where's the seal?"

"I don't know, ma'am, I swear!"

"But you just admitted to stealing it," the man's voice corrected him.

"I stole a loaf of bread! I don't know anything about a seal, and that's the truth, and no one's opening me up!" Jain swung his great axe in a panic. The woman sidestepped its arc with terrifying ease, as graceful as a dancer.

"Oh, I'm *so* glad the boy wants a fight," she sang joyfully. "Here I was afraid this was gonna be dull!"

The human managed to scramble to his feet despite the tangle of the blanket, and he swung again with a roar. The black mrem, thwarted again, reached over and casually plucked the axe out of his hands, which were too loose on the shaft. Jain's mouth fell open and stayed there for a moment.

"That's not fair, madam," the third mrem protested, folding his gray hands behind him placidly. "Give the nice boy his axe back."

"Oh, if I must," she sighed.

"You must."

"Very well. But I still don't think he should be using a great axe in a cramped space like this. He's more likely to embed it in the ceiling or his own leg than he is to tag one of us with it. Do you have any other weapons, boy?"

Jain was well ahead of the Guardsmen on that score. He waded through his dark green knapsack until he found his short sword, and he tugged it out with something less than grace. But he brandished it threateningly in front of him and waved it around in the broad, showy figure-eight flourishes that had never failed to amaze the folks back home. If he was ever going to become a Guard, well, he'd better start by impressing them.

"Perfect choice of weapon, lad!" the light-furred mrem congratulated him. "We may make a Guardsman of you yet!"

"That's why I came to Tycor," the boy admitted cheerfully, placing himself en garde with a low ward.

"Really? Splendid! I couldn't *possibly* recommend a better career choice, my good man," the light-furred one beamed, wrapping his elegant brown short cloak twice over his left arm and letting the rest drape in front of him. Jain couldn't imagine what the mrem was doing, and his confusion was apparent.

The Guardsman unsheathed his rapier, struck a high ward en garde stance and instantly snapped it into a flawlessly graceful thrust. Jain parried and made a head cut, but the mrem wasn't where the human had expected him to be. Rather than stepping back and recovering, the mrem carried his motion forward with a passado into a punta reversa, slapping Jain on the backside with the flat of his blade. Jain's blade, meanwhile, sliced harmlessly through the air to his opponent's right.

"Oh, by the way, I was talking to Lira the other day," the light-furred mrem called over his shoulder to his comrades as he and Jain recovered and came back en garde. "It seems she and Sergeant Dano have become an item."

"No, *really?*" the woman gasped, clearly delighted with the gossip.

"Can you pay some attention to *us*, please!" Jain cried, exasperated by his opponent's evident lack of interest in their duel. He tried another head cut, which the Guardsman parried without looking. The motion of the parry carried with seeming effortlessness into a stinging reversi tap on Jain's right shoulder, again with the flat of the blade. He wasn't even taking this seriously, damn him!

"Yes, really!" The infuriating bastard nodded cheerfully. "Apparently they'd been keeping it secret for a while, and they finally decided to get serious about each other!"

"That's wonderful!" The woman beamed. "Anyone care to start a betting pool for dates on the wedding?"

"Anyone care to bet on a funeral?" Jain snarled. He tried pressing in with some of the fancy figure-eight loops Owen Parden had taught him back in Uppervale. The mrem retreated, watching the motion of the blade, feeling out the boy's rhythm. Just after the third turn of the corkscrew, he lunged in and, with surgical delicacy, sliced off a good-sized lock of the human's dark hair. Jain paused, shocked, and felt at the place where the lock of hair had been.

With a roar he lunged, and the mrem, with a left circular pace opposing, sliced a lock off the other side to make it even. Jain bellowed incoherently and swung again. The mrem thwarted left, tossed his elegant cloak over the boy's newly shorn head, and kicked him in the backside, toward the other two Guards. The human went sprawling, and his short sword slid across the room and under the bed.

"I must say, humans have *such* tempers," his opponent sniffed. "I'll never understand why they get this upset over trifles."

" 'Bout time you decided to share with the rest of us," the woman growled. Jain shook the cloak off his head, pulled himself painfully to his feet, snarled, and lunged at the black mrem. She thwarted right and used the motion of his lunge against him, hurling him into the yellowish white plaster wall behind her. He groaned and struggled to his feet, shaken, but still game.

"I taught them everything they know," the gray mrem said conversationally.

"Must be why he has so little left," the woman quipped with obvious affection.

"That hurt, Tazira," he chided her.

"I know, dear."

At that point, two things occurred to Jain almost simultaneously. First, the woman and the gray mrem seemed to be in love, though it was just possible that they didn't know it themselves. And, second, the woman's name was Tazira. How many black mrem named Tazira could possibly be members of the Tycor Guard? Unfortunately, he didn't realize any of this fast enough to stop the kick he was aiming at her head.

"Tazira?" he asked her incredulously, trying too late to pull the kick. At the point when both his feet had left the ground, she swept him, and he crashed backward in an ungraceful heap. "Tazira Goldeneyes?" he grunted faintly. "Of the Three Furies?"

"Of course, son." She shrugged indifferently, as if it were the most natural thing in the world that she should be a legendary warrior and one of the heroes of his childhood. "Now, what you don't realize is, those flying kicks look real fancy, but the reality is, you let both feet leave the ground, and you deserve everything you get . . ."

"But . . . you're *the* Tazira Goldeneyes!" he stammered incredulously.

"Yes," she said patiently, waiting for his point to arrive.

"And you, you must be Raf Grayfur! And Pellar Longclaw! You're the Three Furies!"

"Last time I looked," she said less patiently, still waiting for his point to arrive.

"The greatest blades in all Tycor!"

"I begin to like this boy," Pellar looped his tail

in amusement. Jain thought about getting to his feet, but realized that he *hurt*, just about everywhere. No, on second thought, just lying here seemed to be a good idea. If he was going to be arrested, or killed, at least it would be by one of the Furies, he thought to himself proudly.

"That's right, son, just lie there for a few minutes and try not to move too much," Tazira said gently, kneeling down next to him.

"But I haven't gotten to fight Raf yet," the human groaned, struggling to rise.

"I'd say that's probably for the best," she drawled, laying a delicate and surprisingly strong black-furred hand on his chest to keep him pinned.

"No insult to your own abilities, of course," Pellar said diplomatically, and his kindness only made the matter worse. Jain flushed hotly with the greatest shame he'd known in seventeen years of life. Somehow, he had to prove himself to them.

"Now, then. Let's take this from the beginning," Tazira sighed. "What did you do with the seal?"

"Ma'am, I don't think I've done anything with the seal. I guess I could've done something to it without knowing, but I've never heard of any such thing before tonight."

"What was it that you confessed to stealing and eating earlier?" Pellar asked him.

"A loaf of bread," he admitted, flushing again with the shame of that. "I arrived in Tycor this morning, with eight coppers left in my pocket. It'd been two days since I'd eaten anything. There was a street vendor selling bread off a cart, and it was there, and I took it. I promised myself I'd pay him back out of my salary as soon as I became a Guardsman, and I will," he added earnestly.

"With only eight coppers in your pocket, how could you afford a room at an inn?" Pellar raised a skeptical eyebrow at him. "Even one as run-down as this?"

"Oh, I lucked out there. For exactly eight coppers a night, they'll let you sleep in the common room downstairs."

"Did you tell the innkeeper that was how much you had on you?"

"I did better than that," Jain said proudly. "I showed him." The three mrem rolled their eyes, and the boy continued. "The cook let me wash a few dishes in exchange for a bowl of stew, and while I was eating in the common room, I made my first friend in Tycor. His name is Lucian Alander. He said I could use his room while he wasn't here, and he'd be gone tonight. He left by the window, actually, about two hours after blue dawn. I drifted off to sleep right afterwards. It seemed a little strange, but I got a bed and a room out of it, so I wasn't arguing."

Tazira pursed her lips together thoughtfully, rose, and started to pace the chamber. "I dunno, gents. What do you think?" she muttered.

"I think it's too bizarre not to be true," Pellar admitted. Raf smirked at that.

"The innkeeper can verify every bit of it," the boy insisted. "Everything except the bread."

"Lucian Alander *was* the name the innkeeper gave us for the occupant of this chamber," Raf pointed out. "And everything else checks out with what the innkeeper already told us about Jain."

"At best, then, the kid's an accomplice," Tazira growled. "At worst, he's a thief looking at a death sentence for lifting the Great Seal."

"But I—" Jain started to protest.

"Whatever the case," she continued, ignoring him, "someone's gotten away with the shard-blasted thing, and chances are this boy can identify that someone. Thief or dupe, he's coming with us." She stopped pacing and favored Jain with a piercing gaze. "Do you want to live?" she asked him sharply. He nodded, trying not to show the slightest trace of fear. "Good. That'll make this a whole lot easier. Where I go, you go. Quietly. No fuss, no tricks. At the first sign of treachery or cowardice, I'll kill you myself. Let's move. Pellar, you're on point."

"Umm . . ." Jain spoke up hesitantly.

"What?" the woman snapped, her tail lashing impatiently behind her.

"Can I get dressed first?"

She sighed and rolled her eyes. "Hurry up, kid," she said, giving him a meaningful glare as she pulled him to his feet. Jain hastily threw his clothes on and prepared to follow her. It was a chance to prove himself, if not in quite the way he'd hoped. Pellar started out the window, and Tazira paused and turned back to Jain for a moment.

"Oh, and Riordan?" She smiled, a dangerous, soft, almost seductive smile. "Stay quiet. One word from you to warn your new friend, and I'll give you to Raf to play with. He's a lot meaner than I am, and he doesn't like humans much." She smiled sweetly at Raf, who was standing just past Jain's right shoulder, and she made her way out the window after Pellar.

Jain glanced back at Raf, unable to help the impulse. The mrem grinned at him evilly, baring needle-sharp white teeth. His green-gold eyes glittered with sheer malevolence. The human shivered and followed Tazira meekly out the window, wondering if it was too late to go home to Uppervale.

Chapter 3

PELLAR HELD THE RING OUT BEFORE HIM once they'd all hit the trash-filled alley behind the inn. He moved in a slow circle, studying the color changes in the jewel.

"South," he hissed after a moment. "He's probably headed toward the gate and out of the city. But I don't think he's made it that far yet."

"Odd," Tazira frowned. "If he left two hours after blue dawn, he's got about an hour on us. He should have been able to make it out by now, if that's where he was going."

"This is the Southgate," Raf reminded her. "A lone traveler, moving through these streets at this time of night? He's probably been waylaid."

"Possibly," she admitted gruffly. "Jain, did he say anything to you about where he might be headed?"

Jain hesitated for a moment, glancing down at his worn leather boots. Lucian was the first friend he'd made in Tycor, and he hated the thought of betraying him. On the other hand, the man had apparently stolen something important enough that the Furies had been sent to retrieve it, and him.

"I . . . I overheard him talking with the innkeeper in the common room," the human admitted after a brief bout with indecision. "He was asking for the fastest route out of the city. The innkeeper told him to take something called the Shadowed Way, and it would lead him directly to the gate." He lowered his eyes, afraid he'd just made a terrible mistake in telling them.

"Good work, son," Tazira remarked, choosing to trust him because he had indeed named the fastest route to the gate. Interesting that the innkeeper hadn't mentioned that conversation. Very interesting. "Come on, let's move," she growled. "The Shadowed Way is a few blocks in that direction." She bowed Pellar into the lead, and he moved intently and silently, obviously cheerful to be stalking his prey at last.

Jain was anything but cheerful, Tazira noticed. At the moment, all he seemed to be was downcast. The captain narrowed her eyes and pursed her lips in thought, as if trying to decide whether or not to say something.

They reached the mouth of the alley and walked out into the refuse-laden street. The Guards' eyes slowly swept the scene, taking in barred and shuttered windows, shadowed doors, alleys, rooftops, and civilians with cool, professional thoroughness. There weren't many people out on the streets of the Southgate at that time of night, but anyone they *did* encounter at that hour was potential trouble.

"Don't feel too bad about betraying this Lucian

character, son," the captain said under her breath after a moment. "He betrayed you first, by the sound of it."

"What? But . . . how?"

"We were given your name and physical description," Raf said quietly, forgetting that Tazira had cast him as a slavering baby-eater not two minutes ago. "One of the court wizards told us that the trail ended at the Gryphon Inn, with a man named Jain Riordan. Your friend was never named or even mentioned. Innocent or guilty, you were still set up to take the fall alone."

Jain pursed his lips and nodded; he might have been young and inexperienced, but he wasn't stupid. He instantly lost the illusion that Lucian had ever been remotely interested in his friendship. And that would make this easier.

"Never, *never* make Raf the evil Guard," Tazira muttered to herself, shaking her head.

"I'm sorry?" Jain blinked innocently.

"Nothing," she growled. "Don't talk. Just move."

They continued on in silence, keeping to the widest and best-lit streets until they reached the Shadowed Way.

There was a perpetual gloom that clung to those streets, a gloom the three suns together couldn't seem to penetrate. It was the gray and dingy pall of despair, futility, and hopeless rage. The Southgate was the last resort of thousands who were unlikely ever to be able to improve their circumstances enough to leave: ragged, half-starved children, begging for bread; diseased women, selling their bodies because they had no skills to offer a shattered world; addicts; lunatics; petty thieves; humans preying on other humans, because the monsters outside the walls and the wards were a worse nightmare. Here was the refuse of humankind, the ones who could not or would not adapt to the Fall. Every city-state had its slums. Tycor had the Southgate.

It was a cramped, gray collection of high, ramshackle buildings, created with little skill and less care from the salvageable ruins of older places. The tenements were a uniform three stories high, shutting out much of the eternal sunlight. Not infrequently, they collapsed and were replaced by something equally tenuous. But they were the closest thing left to the Old Ways. This was what the pre-Fall cities had apparently looked like, and the residents of the Southgate clung to that image with fevered tenacity.

"We're definitely close, Captain," Pellar said quietly. The ring he held glowed a lurid red. "We're practically right on top of it."

Tazira and Raf scanned the street, one in each direction, while Pellar made a slow circle, watching the ring's color changes carefully.

The Shadowed Way was almost abandoned, and unnervingly quiet. There was a girl of about twelve or thirteen sleeping in a doorway, a group of three men sitting out on a stoop passing a drinking horn, and one old man clutching his cloak tightly around him and shambling down the street in the opposite direction, muttering to himself. No one seemed to pose an immediate threat, but you never knew.

"It's in that alley, or one of the two buildings

next to it." Pellar pointed grimly at a dark, relatively broad gap between two tenements about thirty paces away.

"Fodder for the theory that he was attacked and robbed on the way to the gate," Raf murmured thoughtfully.

"Possibly," Tazira muttered. She scanned the darkened windows inside, around, and just across the street from the alley. One inside and one across the street had been left open about a handspan, just enough to shoot an arrow through. Her eyes narrowed.

"I have another theory for you," she drawled. "Look at those windows just inside the alleyway, and that other across the street. Partially open. Perfect spot for an ambuscade."

"Lucian shouldn't know we're coming, should he?" Jain frowned. "He undoubtedly thinks you arrested me, and he's gotten off free as a bird."

"He's not the only player, son," Tazira whispered. "The one who actually set you up is a court wizard named Daman Najendra. He's running a very deep game, and right now we're the only ones who have any sense of that. If I were him, I would have planned on taking us out as soon as we left the inn. Raf, get your bees spell ready. Pellar, we'll need smoke from you. Fill that alley with them on my mark."

"Are we flushing them out, or trapping them in?" Raf asked, adjusting a large blue stone on one of his rings.

"Flushing them out," she said, adjusting a ring of her own. The red jewel started pulsing with a soft, ominous light. "And bees and smoke won't

do irreversible damage to innocent civilians, such
as they are, if we're wrong about the ambush. Jain,
you're behind me."

"Can I have a weapon?" he whispered.

"No, you can't," she growled. "You're still
under arrest, remember? Now, Raf, Pellar, are you
set?" The mrem nodded calmly. Tazira took a
deep breath and began. "Start walking, nice and
casual, fifteen paces. Stop. Three. Two. One. Fire."

Smoke and a swarm of hundreds of yellow jack-
ets poured out of the lieutenants' spellstones. At
the same instant, Tazira set off a grand fire shield
about twenty handspans over their heads. The
shield blanketed the alleyway and the street
around them for about twenty paces in each direction. Whoever was in that alley would now be
trapped within the perimeter, and they wouldn't
be getting any help from the outside, including
any snipers in the windows.

Three arrows sizzled harmlessly into dust
against the flame wall. Definitely an ambush, and
they would have been mown down rather quickly
if they'd rushed in there unprepared.

"Nice call, Captain," Pellar saluted her, the gray
smoke from his jewel finally exhausting itself.

"A glowing tribute to her eternally suspicious
nature," Raf nodded, solemnly teasing. The last of
the bees shot out of his ring, and the alley started
to echo with screams and scuffling.

"Let's not get too cheerful yet," she muttered,
tensing and readying the next spellstone. More
arrows sizzled harmlessly against the shield, and
one by one, Lucian's hired killers stumbled out
of the alleyway, choking. They brandished their

weapons and tried to keep to their feet, but it was obvious that the bees and the smoke had done their work.

Tazira fingered her next spellstone anxiously; it was set to throw a wide-dispersal flame strike. It would take out up to a dozen men if she timed it right. But she knew Raf hated it when she did things like that; it went clear against his very strong sense of fair play.

The captain had no such compunctions; if it was the fastest, most efficient way to take out an enemy force, she tended to do it without counting the cost. That much she'd learned from Romney. She'd learned to be hard, and she'd probably won the captaincy on that trait alone. If Raf hadn't been along, Tazira wouldn't have hesitated; she could admit that much to herself.

The stone was warm in her hand. She didn't know if she could use it in front of him.

More and more mercenaries poured out of the alley, over twenty, all told. Too many. Tazira raised the stone and fired, and eight of their number disintegrated in a white-hot sheet of flame. She wouldn't let herself look at Raf; she couldn't afford the distraction now.

The other men hesitated, demoralized, and after a few seconds one shakily pulled a spellstone out of a weathered brown belt pouch. One of Raf's throwing knives vaulted through the air and hit him in the throat. The human dropped the stone, and it rolled harmlessly away without firing.

"Well, boys?" Tazira called out to them with every semblance of laconic cheer. "Are you just gonna stand there, or are you gonna charge us?"

She pulled her franciscas out of their belt loops, balanced them firmly in her hands, and braced herself in a fourth-position stance. Pellar took two throwing knives in hand and loosed them, taking down one more of their would-be assailants. Raf stood en garde with his quarterstaff and waited calmly for his opponents to come to a decision. And Jain looked around desperately for anything he might be able to use as a weapon, even something in the stinking refuse that littered the unpaved street.

There were thirteen of the enemy remaining. They started to move forward hesitantly, and Raf and Pellar each took a step backward, tightening the protective semicircle around Jain. A cluster of five assassins concentrated on Tazira, leaving four for Raf and four for Pellar. The mrem growled low in their throats, an inhuman sound that chilled Jain to the marrow.

The boy thought he'd seen all the potential uses of Pellar's elegant half cloak, but as he watched him now, he realized that he'd seen only a fraction of them. Pellar snapped the cloak up in a smooth cast, blinding his first opponent for the crucial half second it took him to follow the cloak's motion with a rapier cut. The human fell, clutching at his opened throat and trying to scream with a voice he no longer owned. The second fell almost as quickly as the first, pierced through the heart by an unnervingly swift thrust.

One of Tazira's opponents made the mistake of coming within Pellar's range, and with her back turned. Pellar took full advantage of the fact, turning and slashing at the nape of the mercenary's neck and coming swiftly back en garde. The mercenary collapsed in a seemingly boneless heap, screaming.

Jain plucked the dirk out of the woman's hand, trying to decide whether or not he had the nerve to slit her throat for her. It would give her a swift and nearly painless death, but he'd never killed a human before. Trembling, he raised his hand to try. He hesitated for another instant, and the mercenary's eyes rolled back in her head. With a last choking gasp, she died, sparing him the choice.

Now that he was armed, the boy sneaked out of the protective semicircle of mrem, skirted the combat, and went in search of the spellstone the first mercenary had dropped. With that, he might be able to do some *real* damage.

Raf was waging a largely defensive battle with his opponents, calmly baiting them and waiting for them to make mistakes. His staff was a blur, creating a physical ward around him that his opponents couldn't penetrate. One woman, frustrated, tried to hack her way in with a broadsword. If she'd struck at his hands or wrists and instantly withdrawn, she might have gotten somewhere, but she let herself stay too long. Raf took advantage of her awkwardly narrow stance to sweep her with one end of his staff, and the other end swiftly shot around and struck her head as she fell. She was unconscious, and he was back in a flawless defensive posture before she hit the ground.

Jain glanced up from his search to watch the Furies in action; he couldn't resist the impulse. The mrem were so fast that their weapons literally blurred in front of them. They were living legends, and they'd earned the sobriquet.

Tazira in particular was clearly having the time of her life. Two of her opponents were down, and she practically danced over them to come after a third. The mercenary raised his brown buckler in front of him and lifted his broadsword to swing at her. The axe in her left hand blocked the swing and forced his arm down. Her right axe thrust over the buckler and twisted down and inside with a sharp flick of her wrist. She wrenched the buckler down and finished the job with a clean stroke, burying her left francisca in her opponent's chest. Hissing her triumph, she turned to search for her next victim. Jain shuddered at that and forced himself back to his own search.

Pellar was so focused on the man in front of him that he didn't see the woman sneaking up behind him. Tazira did, and without thinking she hurled her last francisca, full force. It hit the woman in the back and dropped her like a stone. Pellar flashed her a grateful look and went back to fencing with his last opponent.

One of Raf's attackers disengaged to take on the disarmed captain. She glanced down at the hand axe she'd left in her last opponent's chest. It was too deeply embedded; she wouldn't be able to retrieve it quickly enough. Retreating over the corpses of her fallen enemies, she drew her last throwing knife from her boot and hurled it.

The mercenary thwarted swiftly, and the blade barely nicked his ribs. He continued to advance, his rapier glittering in the light of the fire shield. Tazira drew her last weapon, Black Bessie, off her back, already knowing it would be next to useless against this particular opponent. His rapier would be faster, and that would be all that mattered unless she could somehow outwit him.

He opened with a simple thrust, which she parried with a broad, two-handed grip on the shaft of the great axe. She brought the blade down at his head in a swift short chop, and he thwarted and retreated. The man feinted and thrust again, overextending himself in his confidence. Tazira thwarted right, caught his blade in the curved upper edge of her axe, and twisted. The rapier broke, and the upper half spiraled off uselessly through the air. She swung again, and ended it.

Raf's last opponent danced out of range of his staff, and he pursued, sensing an end to the battle. Behind him, Tazira had just downed the last of her would-be assassins, and Pellar was steadily finishing his off. He wondered where Jain had gotten to, but he didn't have time to worry about that just now. The mrem stalked his last opponent, resting the staff lightly in his right hand at its balance point and maneuvering it from the back end with his left. He moved the tip in small, lazy circles, menacing.

"You'd be better off surrendering now," he purred, assuming his best evil Guard look to frighten the last mercenary into peaceful compliance. "You can tell us what we want to know, and you can survive this night. Or not. I assure you, I don't care one way or the other."

Without a word she raised a glowing spellstone and fired a bolt of lightning at him. Raf dropped his quarterstaff and dodged, but the lightning followed him and laced him with searing, white-hot energy. Howling in pain, he reached for one of his throwing knives.

"Raf!" Tazira shouted, sprinting toward the female mercenary with Black Bessie raised. She had no more distance weapons, and it was all she could do.

Pellar drew a throwing knife from its thigh holster, already knowing it would be useless from that far off.

Suddenly the mercenary jerked and spasmed, dropping her spellstone. The lightning cut off abruptly, and Raf gasped with relief. Pulling himself painfully to one knee, he picked up his staff with trembling hands. The tip of the staff shot into the mercenary's stomach, knocking her back into the fire shield. She flashed out of existence before she could scream, leaving a brilliant white silhouette on the flamewall behind her, and then nothing.

Tazira dropped to her knees beside Raf, gently prying the staff out of his trembling fingers and pressing him down on the ground. Pellar scanned the area, throwing knife at the ready, tail twitching in agitation. Jain was the only human left standing, and a spellstone was smoldering in his hand.

"What did I do to her?" Jain asked, bewildered.

"I honestly don't know," Pellar responded shakily, forcing his breathing to slow. "I've never encountered that particular spell. But it was certainly useful enough. Well done!" he saluted. The human positively beamed, delighted that he'd managed to impress at least one of the Furies. "Do you want to do something else useful?" Pellar asked him archly.

"Sure," Jain nodded cheerfully. At that moment, if the mrem had asked him to jog seven times around Tycor, he would have done it.

"Collect the weapons. And hurry; we don't have much time."

Jain nodded again, more sharply this time, and set about the grim task of extracting weapons from their victims' corpses.

He started with one that was close to where Raf lay. Making sure he was unobserved, he pulled out his healing stone and held it tightly in the palm of his hand. It was the only spellstone he'd possessed before tonight, and he'd left it in the pocket of his dark brown breeks as he'd dressed to leave the inn.

If he used his healing talent openly in front of the mrem, they'd force him to join the Healers' Guild, and he'd never be allowed to become a Guard. He'd be shut away in a monastery with other healers, and his life would be over at seventeen. But at the same time, Raf couldn't be allowed to go into shock. If he did, he was as good as dead, and Jain would be responsible for that. The boy spat out a mild oath, the strongest of which he was capable, and risked a light healing spell. Mercifully, they all seemed too distracted to detect it.

Pellar walked to the mouth of the alley, took out his tracking ring, and spat out a brief but effective string of soldiers' oaths. The stone was pale pink again.

Chapter 4

"DON'T BOTHER WITH THE KNIVES UNLESS you find them on the ground, Jain," Pellar called over to him. "We just ran out of time. Get Tazira's axes and get ready to move." He turned his attention to Raf, who was sufficiently recovered to be fussing right back at Tazira.

"Don't give me that, my girl," Raf was blustering in his best impression of Romney. It was extraordinarily good, and Tazira laughed although she was trembling faintly with the aftershock of the battle.

"Raf, can you move?" Pellar asked him with just a shade of impatience. Tazira glanced up at Pellar, caught his grim expression, and rose gracefully to her feet.

"The seal?" she asked him, already sensing the answer.

"Gone," he spat. "Fading as we speak."

"I can move," Raf nodded, letting the others pull him to his feet. He swayed a little, and Tazira looped an arm around his waist to support him before he could protest.

"I really want at least one of these people for questioning," Tazira growled, almost to herself. She glanced down at the bodies and spotted one that was still breathing.

"You! Jain!" she bellowed. Jain pulled the last francisca free of its victim and glanced up inquiringly.

"What a delicate flower of womanhood you are," Raf murmured to his captain with mock admiration.

"Hush your mouth, boy," she smirked and turned her attention back to the human. "That unconscious woman, there, do you think you can carry her, son?"

"Sure." He shrugged. "Depends how far, though . . ."

"May be quite a ways, though it won't be farther than the gate. Give me those axes, pick her up, and follow us. Raf, Pellar, get ready to dispel the smoke and the bees. Lucian went out through the back of that alley, which I couldn't cover with the fire shield because I couldn't see it. We're going the same way."

"What about the snipers?" Pellar asked.

"They're a problem," Tazira admitted. "I'll leave the fire shield up until we're safely out the back, but that's as much as I can do. We don't have time to take them out individually."

"And the bodies, what happens to them?"

"Leave 'em," she said coldly. "A warning to anyone else who might decide Guards look like targets. Drop the spells in the alley, and let's go."

In any other section of Tycor, a grand fire shield and a fight would have drawn a crowd. In the

Southgate, nobody wanted to be bothered. There were even fewer people in the streets than there had been before, and the Guards sped silently along with their two human prisoners in tow.

Jain was gasping for air, struggling under the weight of the unconscious mercenary he was carrying. He paused just long enough to shift her over his other shoulder, and he ran to catch up with the Furies.

"You gonna make it, son?" Tazira raised an eyebrow at him. He nodded, not wanting to spare breath for speech. She turned her attention forward again and smiled to herself approvingly. The kid was doing pretty well, for a raw recruit.

An old drunk staggered around a street corner, got one good look at the group in front of him, and hastily decided to be elsewhere.

"We must look like death's swift ministers," Tazira murmured, glancing over at Raf with concern. He looked better, and he was now walking unassisted, but he still moved somewhat stiffly.

"You do, anyway," Raf teased her, looking her over from head to foot. "Do you realize you're positively covered in blood?"

"Disgusting, isn't it?" she said with a grimace. "I feel like a walking country breakfast for vampires. I should have taken up the quarterstaff instead of opting for a career as a professional axe murderess."

"So, just how much of that blood is yours, this time?"

"More than I'd like, but not enough to kill me."

"Anything bad?" he asked her, trying to sound

casual about it. Tazira had a bad habit of ignoring potentially fatal injuries.

"No, nothing bad. Now don't you start fussing at me."

"That's a pretty nasty cut on your upper arm," he began.

"You need to take care of your *own* wounds, soldier," she growled irascibly, secretly amused. "Don't worry about mine; they'll heal in a day or two."

"Oh, don't worry about me," Raf rolled his green-gold eyes at her comically. "I'll just sit here bleeding in the dark . . ."

Pellar laughed, and Tazira shot them both an acid glare, the effect of which was utterly ruined by the grin she couldn't entirely suppress. Her long tail flicked back and forth, finally looping around in open amusement.

"I love you both very much," she growled, half laughing. "And then there's now. Pellar, are we getting any closer to the seal?" she asked almost plaintively, just managing to shift the subject away from her. Pellar glanced down at the ring, which still glowed faintly pink.

"No," he replied with disheartening honesty. "Lucian's got to be out the gate by now. We seem to be keeping pace with him, but we're not catching up." She nodded and pursed her lips, but said nothing. There was no way to speed up for any appreciable length of time, not with an injured Guard and an unconscious prisoner.

Jain was lagging farther and farther behind them, and he finally gave up his burden with a heavy groan, setting her down on the street. The mercenary's blue eyes were open, but utterly vacant; Pellar had spelled her with a mind riven to keep her from giving them any trouble on the way to the gate. Jain sank to his knees beside her, gasping for air, trembling and nauseous with exhaustion.

He glanced up as a shadow fell across him. Pellar stooped and lifted the woman, tossing her over his broad shoulder as casually as if she were weightless. He, Tazira, and Raf turned and started down the street again, and Jain pulled himself a bit unsteadily to his feet and forced himself to follow them.

"I'll tell you, these young people today," Raf murmured, shaking his head. "Good out of the starting gate, but not much for staying power." The human shot him a low-lidded glare, but couldn't take in enough breath to form a suitably scathing retort.

"Oh, I'd say he's done enough for one day," Pellar said cheerfully. "He's run away to Tycor, fallen in with criminals, been arrested, and quite probably saved the life of the famous Raf Grayfur in a lowly street brawl. Yes, it's been a busy day."

"He did *what*?" Raf and Tazira chorused.

"You owe me an ale," Tazira muttered distractedly to Raf. "What did you do, Jain?"

"I . . ." He paused, fighting to get his breathing back under control. "Umm . . . while you were all fighting, I . . . grabbed a dirk off one of the bodies . . . and I snuck off to find that spellstone the mercenary dropped . . . before the fight began. When I saw that woman shoot the lightning at Raf . . . I aimed the stone at her and fired. I'm still not sure . . . exactly what it did to her." He found he was breathing even harder after he finished.

"That was a jolt spell," Tazira murmured. "Raf, I thought you fired that."

"I thought you had," he replied calmly. "Jain, it seems I owe you thanks."

"Good work, son." Tazira clapped him on the back companionably. "Of course, you really shouldn't fire off a spellstone unless you know what it'll do."

"Of course . . . I mean, of course not," he stammered, secretly delighted by her praise.

"And none of this ever would have happened if Raf wasn't getting so old," Pellar teased him. "Three years shy of forty, and falling apart already . . ."

"Nice to see the famous Pellar Longclaw diplomacy in action, isn't it?" Raf inquired dryly of the wide world.

"You're *never* living this down, Raf, you do realize that," Tazira grinned wickedly.

"Jain, you should have let me die," Raf growled, a hint of plaintiveness creeping into his voice.

"I believe I'll compose a song about it," Pellar looped his tail cheerfully.

"Please don't."

"You're safe enough for now," Tazira said, her tail stiffening to seriousness. "There's the gate ahead."

It loomed in front of them at the end of the Shadowed Way, a massive, ugly structure built of several different types and shapes of stone blocks.

Functional rather than attractive, like everything else since the Fall. The Great Wall of Tycor bounded the gate on both sides; it was an excessively glorious name for the ten-foot rubble barricade that surrounded the city. That was another eyesore, but with the wards in place, there'd never been a need for Romney to replace the barricade with anything more solid. Tycor still managed to survive and even thrive in the midst of ugliness.

Tazira sped up her pace, and the others matched it. They were practically running by the time they reached the gate. There were six Guards stationed just inside. Sergeant Lira was the first to spot them, and her jaw dropped for a fraction of an instant before she remembered herself and saluted them. She hastily unlatched the iron grating of the inner gate to allow them into the high stone arch of the entrance.

"Sergeant," Tazira called, her voice echoing wetly in the archway, "we're pursuing a man who's probably been through the gate and out by now. Jain, describe him for us."

"His name is Lucian Alander," the human spoke up. "He's a bit shorter than average . . . about Pellar's height—"

"Diplomacy in action," Pellar sighed.

"Not now, Pellar," Tazira growled.

"Sorry, Captain."

"Blond hair, about shoulder length," Jain continued doggedly. "I think his eyes were sort of green. When he left, he was wearing a dark green padded doublet and breeks. Do you remember seeing him?"

"Yes, I do," the sergeant replied grimly. "I'm sorry, Captain, but I let him through."

"Of course you did." Tazira shrugged. "You had no order not to. Shards, but I miss communications devices . . . How long ago did he come through?"

"About half an hour, I'd say."

"We'd better be after him," Jain said tensely. "Come on!" He was about to take off through the gate full-tilt when he felt a friendly arm being draped around his shoulders—a friendly arm with sharp claws at the end of it. Tazira smiled at him, one of those frightening mrem smiles with a lot of teeth.

"Where you headed, son?" she inquired curiously.

"We have to catch Lucian! He's getting away!"

"Yes, he is. And half an hour out there isn't like half an hour in the city. He has a lot more options and directions to take out there. We're not equipped or prepared to follow him out into the marches, and only a passel of fools would rush out there blindly. Forethought, my son, is the difference between live professionals and dead adventurers."

"So, here's what we'll need," she said, releasing Jain and turning back to the assembled Guards. "Sergeant Lira, I want you to assemble teams and start a search for Lucian Alander, quickly. No more than five leagues out, and you probably won't find him. But if I can spare myself that journey, I will, because I'm lazy," she winked. The others laughed, and she continued. "Bring him in alive, directly to one of the three of us. No one else sees him or speaks with him. If you fail to find him, send orders to the other gates to apprehend him if he tries to reenter the city. Good luck, Sergeant."

Lira saluted crisply and bowed herself off, taking that for the dismissal it was.

"Private Tamar, we'll need a healer for Raf," Tazira continued without missing a beat, gently pressing Raf down to a sitting position against one of the stone walls. Raf didn't fight her, which showed her just how badly he needed that healer.

"Once that's done, take three Guards to the Gryphon Inn on the corner of Broken Street and Vine. Get Jain Riordan's belongings out of Lucian Alander's room and send them to my quarters in the Red Tower for safekeeping.

"Private Kalan, raid the storage room for us. We'll need provisions for a one-week journey. A medkit with alcohol, linen strips, needles and thread. A food pack with water, dried beef, hardtack, flint, tinder, and an iron skillet for cooking. Four blankets and cakes of soap. Three bows, arrows, as many throwing knives as you can get your hands on, and a good length of rope with a grappling hook. A change of clothes for me if you can manage it; the others aren't too bad, but I'm likely to scare the locals. And finally I'll need a quill, ink, and paper, and a volunteer to run a message to Lord Tycor for me. Have you both got all that?"

They nodded, saluted, and disappeared quickly inside the building. The other Guards settled back into their positions and turned their attention to the Shadowed Way.

"What are *we* going to do?" Jain asked her, itching for something useful to occupy him.

"We're going to stand watch for the three Guards we just dismissed," Pellar replied before Tazira had a chance to. "And I'm going to take this heavy woman off my back." He grunted a bit as he lowered her to the ground. "Now that we've carried her all this way, what do we do with her?"

"I want answers out of her before we go haring off after this other idiot," Tazira grumbled. "I don't suppose anyone's discovered anything as convenient as a truth spell?" The three men shook their heads, and she smirked in spite of herself. "Never easy, is it? All right, we do it the old-fashioned way."

"What's that?" Jain asked warily, already afraid of the answer.

"We bluff shamelessly," Pellar admitted with a grin. "Can I be the evil Guard this time? I love being the evil Guard."

"And you do it so well." Tazira punched him on the shoulder with affection. "All right, get that mind riven spell fired up. If she gives us any problems, I want you to use it."

Pellar nodded, plucking the stone out of a pouch at his waist. "Everybody ready to be intimidating?" he asked, looping his tail in amusement. Jain nodded, though he wasn't sure what he'd really be able to do to help. A soft, brief dispel flare fired out of Pellar's stone, and the mercenary came back to consciousness, gasping and looking about her wildly.

"Where am I?" she blurted before she could stop herself. She ran a hand nervously through her pale blond hair, looking so lost and fragile that for a brief moment Jain actually pitied her.

"Where you are is of no consequence, girl," Pellar informed her coldly. "Answer our questions honestly, and we'll let you live. Lie to us, and this jewel will flare red," he murmured, dangling the tracking ring in front of her by a long, sharp claw. "If it does that, I'll pluck out your eyes. Now . . . who hired you?"

"L-Lucian Alander," the woman responded.

"And who is he, exactly?"

"I don't know much about him. He lives in the Southgate, he sometimes hires mercenaries and assassins to do his wetwork, and he sells dreamdust."

"What did he hire you to do?"

"Tonight was supposed to be simple. We were supposed to take out three Guards. You. No bodies, no traces. You were supposed to disappear quietly."

"Any idea why?"

"I don't *care* why," she snapped, getting some of her courage back. "A good mercenary doesn't ask too many questions. I don't know who you are or why you were singled out for assassination, and I don't care. It didn't work, anyway. Congratulations. Can I go now?"

"No. Who hired Lucian Alander?"

"I don't know."

Pellar glanced ominously at the ring, but of course it would have told him nothing in any case.

"Did Lucian have any more work for you after tonight?"

"He said there'd be something spectacular

when he got back, but he didn't have time to give us details. That's all I know, I swear," she said sullenly. Pellar and Tazira exchanged a look that seemed to communicate a world of unspoken things, but Jain couldn't be sure what they were thinking.

"One more thing. Do you recognize this man?" Pellar asked her, flicking the tip of an ivory ear in Jain's direction.

"The dupe," she sneered. "We had a good laugh about that one."

"Thanks," Jain said dryly, getting truly tired of having his nose rubbed in his gullibility.

"I have a question for you," Raf said quietly from his perch against the opposite wall, his green-gold eyes boring steadily into hers. "How do you justify murdering humans?"

"You aren't humans," she sneered. "You're mrem! You're animals, freaks, genetic constructs! You're—"

A jolt spell cut her off and blasted her against the wall behind her. She twitched, and passed out cold.

"You're unconscious," Jain growled, pocketing his new spellstone. "No one talks about Guards that way in my hearing."

The three mrem and the human Guards around them turned to stare at him for a long moment. The humans broke out into broad grins and saluted him. And Tazira finally smiled at him.

"That's my boy," she said softly.

Chapter 5

VARRAL ROMNEY REREAD TAZIRA'S MIS-
sive, committing it to memory before he committed it to flame. The abstruse formality of its tone
contrasted sharply with her usual brash honesty,
but, then, that was probably wise enough. Any
messenger could have heated the wax seal just
enough to open it. And after what he'd just finished reading, he wasn't particularly inclined to
trust anyone at court.

Milord, it read, *The object of our quest continues
to elude us. The plot is far more vast in scope than we
had first imagined. The escape was well planned and
well timed, undoubtedly aided by the absent friend who
first warned you of the danger and sent us after Jain
Riordan. Jain is safely in our custody, but only because
he's seen the real thief, a Southgate druglord named
Lucian Alander. I have little doubt that Jain is innocent
of the affair.*

*Alander set up an ambuscade meant to take us out
on the Shadowed Way. The three of us, specifically. It
obviously failed, but it bought him the time he needed
to leave Tycor. We've questioned one of his mercenar-*

*ies, and it seems he's planned "something spectacular"
for his return. Have left standing orders for his arrest
if he tries to reenter the city, but strongly recommend
that all travelers be turned away at the gates until the
object is safely recovered and returned to its rightful
owner.*

*Alander is clearly going to meet his co-conspirators
out in the provinces. We will be pursuing, to learn
who they are and what they intend, and then to recover
the item. If possible, we'll eliminate the threat
ourselves.*

*Beware the friends of your absent friend. Suns illu-
mine the Lord Tycor.*

"Suns illumine you, my own," Romney whispered to the flames as he watched the letter burn.
Hard choices, he thought bitterly, remembering
what would probably be his last conversation with
Raf. The Furies were badly overmatched this time,
and Romney seriously doubted he'd ever see them
again. But they were the best people for the assignment, the logical choice. He wondered if that
would make it any easier for him when he got
the word that his best friends, his only friends,
were gone.

The beaten dirt path seemed to stretch out before the Guardsmen endlessly, over wild and
shifting terrain that had no logic left to it. One
league was a forest; the next, a lush, moist swamp,
followed shortly by a blasted desert where nothing grew. The Marches were constantly changing
with the flux of wyld magic, and there were re-
markably few reliable landmarks this far out of
the city. Technically this land was a part of the

Du'unmor Province of southern Tycor, and under Tycoran protection. But in truth, it was difficult to hold this land, and not many tried. A few scattered farmers, traders, and frontiersmen held and defended the villages this far out, but frequent raids by monsters made doing so more difficult still.

In all his seventeen years, Jain couldn't remember ever being this utterly exhausted. They'd been on the road two days already, with no sign of Lucian or anyone else. Tazira forced them to sleep in shifts at each blue dawn, always leaving one man awake to guard the rest. But the sleep shifts were only four hours, and Jain didn't yet have the soldiers' gift for falling instantly asleep no matter where they were, or how uncomfortable the damned shifting ground was. Twice now he'd fallen asleep in one place and seemed to awaken in another. The dirt path was the only constant, and he found himself clinging to that for comfort, for sanity.

"You know what's really funny about all this?" He laughed, a little surprised by the sound of his own voice after hours of silent travel. "I walked for three days to get to Tycor, through shifting terrain a lot like this. I got to the city, where after hours of looking, I finally found an inn I could afford. There was a reasonably comfortable bed there, which I got all of an hour's use out of before I was arrested. And less than twelve hours after my arrival in the city, I'm back out in the Marches. What are the odds, I wonder, that I'll ever sleep in an actual bed again?"

"Welcome to the life of adventurers everywhere, kid," Tazira said dryly. "Sure is glamorous, ain't it?"

"Sleeping on the soft earth under a blanket of stars . . ." Pellar began with teasing romanticism.

"Waking up cold and stiff as a board," Jain griped right back at him.

"A meal of crunchy, delicious hardtack at the end of the day, baked two or three months ago only for you . . ."

"Picking out the weevils inside them," the human added peevishly.

"Why bother picking them out? They're perfectly good protein," Tazira said matter-of-factly.

"You actually *eat* them?" Jain asked her, horrified.

"Of course, son. You'll have to eat a lot worse than that on the road, believe me. Once you've learned to eat grubs and large insects, you'll never go two days without eating again."

"I'd rather starve."

"That's certainly an option," she acknowledged. "Very sensible of you. Tell me, kid, is this griping some new magic power I'm not yet acquainted with, or did you find a guildmaster to study under?"

"Oh, and you *never* complained when you were his age." Raf rolled his eyes at her. Jain smirked, but cut the look short when Tazira caught him at it.

"Not like this boy. I'm sure I never gave Captain Romney this much lip." She nodded sharply, agreeing with herself, and Raf and Pellar doubled over with laughter.

"Unsupportive bastards," she growled, trying

very hard not to grin. Her tail alternately lashed with anger and looped in amusement. She licked her shoulder at them, an obscene gesture in a mrem, and they laughed even harder at that. "When you're quite composed," she said icily, "we're walking."

"Ahoy for adventure," Raf snickered, and Pellar completely fell apart. Even Tazira finally laughed at that. Jain stared at them all as if they'd grown new heads on their shoulders.

"Sorry, son," Tazira chuckled, wiping tears from her eyes as she started down the path. "You're just coming into twenty years' worth of bad inside jokes. It's something one of our old lieutenants used to say to get us moving, back when we were raw recruits." The others continued down the path after her, Pellar stepping into the lead with the tracking ring. "He clearly thought he was being inspiring," she continued. "We didn't. And I had a hell of a time keeping a straight face whenever he said it."

"We didn't help, either," Pellar admitted. He looked like he was about to elaborate when his expression suddenly sharpened. His ears and whiskers quivered. "Do you smell what I smell?" he growled, holding up a hand to halt the party.

Tazira and Raf sniffed the air around them and unsheathed their weapons.

"What's going on?" Jain asked, drawing the short sword they'd allowed him to carry.

"Dire wolves," Tazira hissed. "Can't you smell them?" Jain sniffed the air experimentally and shook his head in the negative. The mrem spread out a few feet into the same protective triangle they'd formed around him in the Southgate, but this time Pellar was at the head of it. They kept walking forward, but more cautiously, ears straining to catch every sound.

"They're moving off down the road," Pellar growled. "Bad sign."

"Come on!" Tazira snapped, breaking into a run.

"What's going on?" Jain asked, running to catch up with her. "Why is it bad that they're moving away from us?"

"It means they've found a more tempting target," Raf told him. "Probably a human."

A scream tore through the air to emphasize his point. Human male, by the sound of it, and not far. They ran faster, spotting a merchant's cart that had tumbled off the road about a hundred feet ahead. The merchant was trying to climb the nearest tree. One of the wolves had the edge of his cloak in its mouth and was trying to pull him back down. The other wolves were piled at the front of the cart in a feeding frenzy, ripping the burden ox to shreds. It screamed and struggled feebly, but couldn't regain its feet.

The mrem leaped into battle, not bothering to waste their throwing knives. Those wouldn't have done anything but irritate dire wolves. Raf rushed to save the merchant, leaving Tazira and Pellar to deal with the rest of the pack in unspoken agreement. His staff whipped around three times in rapid succession, each blow hitting the wolf squarely on the head. It paused and turned, stunned, and one more blow left it slumped on the ground. Raf swept down and ripped its throat out with his claws before it could regain consciousness.

One of the wolves broke away from the burden ox to leap at him, and the tip of his staff caught it squarely in the chest. The impact knocked both of them back, because Raf hadn't had time to brace, and the staff was knocked out of his hands. The wolf leaped again, snarling, and mrem and monster hit the ground in a vicious tangle of claws and fur. Raf hissed, seeking the creature's throat as it sought his.

Jain ran forward, sword in hand, looking for an opening. The mrem and the wolf were moving with inhuman speed, and Jain didn't dare swing wildly for fear of hitting Raf. The mrem sunk his claws deep into the wolf's back, and his hind claws splayed through his leather boots. He started ripping out the creature's stomach with rapid-fire kicks. It howled in pain and frenzied rage, straining to reach Raf's throat. Jain risked a thrust, and it connected. The creature howled again and glanced back to see what had wounded it. It was all the opening Raf needed to sink his sharp teeth into its throat and tear it out. The wolf convulsed and stilled. Raf rolled the gory corpse off him with some effort, grabbed his staff, and launched himself at the next creature.

Tazira and Pellar were fighting back to back, and Raf started tagging wolves at the perimeter of the battle. Jain followed suit, after sparing a glance at the merchant behind him. The man was cowering on a tree branch, making no attempt to join in his own rescue. *Ah, well, at least he isn't underfoot,* the boy supposed. He shrugged and turned back to the wolves, skewering the nearest with a single well-placed thrust.

It was almost over. One of the wolves launched itself at Tazira, and she swung her left axe, catching its throat in mid-flight. With a right circular pace opposing, she thwarted and freed her axe, widening the wound. The creature hit the ground, twitched, and stilled. The last of the wolves tried to run for the safety of the forest, and Tazira hurled her axes in rapid succession. One hit between the ribs, and the other buried itself just behind the creature's ear.

Pellar hissed and growled low in his throat, casting wildly around for his next opponent. His weapons were on the ground, and something about that unnerved Jain just enough to make him shout a warning to Tazira.

"Oh, shards," the woman hissed, bracing to defend herself. Pellar was in complete frenzy and didn't seem to recognize her. He growled again, baring his teeth and beginning to circle her. His ears were laid back flat against his head.

"Pellar, it's me, Tazira," she murmured in the most soothing voice she could manage. "The battle's over, Pellar. It's over. The wolves are gone."

Raf edged toward them quietly and waited, readying his staff. After a long, tense moment Pellar howled and sank to his knees, his vision clearing. The sound was unearthly, and Jain shivered convulsively. Tazira walked to Pellar, knelt, and folded her arms around him, and Raf drew Jain gently away from the scene. They busied themselves righting the merchant's cart on the other side of the road.

"What happened?" Jain whispered. "Why did he do that?"

"It was a killing frenzy," Raf whispered back. "Rarer than artifacts, and incredibly dangerous. Pellar might have shredded us all before he had a chance to come out of it."

"Shards and ashes," Jain breathed.

"Dire wolves slaughtered his entire family when he was a child," Raf said quietly. "He saw the whole thing, and he was powerless to stop it. He doesn't talk about it much, but it drives everything he does."

Jain felt the unexpected sting of tears at that, and he turned and blinked them away in irritation. More proof that he was a healer, not a warrior, as if he needed any more proof.

"Your compassion does you credit, Jain." The older mrem smiled wisely. "Never be ashamed of it."

An incoherent bellow of pure outrage from behind them startled Jain out of any reply he might have made to that. He spun wildly, raising his short sword in front of him. The merchant gasped and clutched defensively at his own cloak, and Jain lowered his sword again and sighed with relief. Truth to tell, he'd forgotten all about the man.

The plump, balding, gaudily dressed tradesman sank to his knees beside his burden ox, checking it desperately for signs of life. When he found none, he bellowed again and started to pummel the animal's lifeless hide. Few beasts of burden had survived the Great Fall, and their scarcity made them terribly valuable. The ox was probably worth three or four times the contents of the cart it had been pulling.

"How am I supposed to get these goods to Tycor?" he fulminated, hitting the dead beast a few more times for good measure. Jain took an instant dislike to the man—not that he'd really expected anything else. "You've ruined me!" he snarled, glaring at Raf and Jain.

"We've *what?*" Jain snapped, not sure he believed his own ears.

"I'm sorry, my young friend and I seem to have misheard you," Raf said dryly, interposing himself between the two humans. "We *thought* we heard you say we'd *ruined* you, when what you undoubtedly *meant* to say was, 'Thank you, kind sirs, for saving my undeserving life.' "

"*Thank* you? For *what?*" the merchant shouted. "Did you save my burden ox?"

"What about your escort? Where were they during all this?"

"Do you have any idea how expensive it is to hire an escort?" the man sneered.

"I give up," Raf sighed, throwing up his hands and starting to walk away.

"Probably best," Jain grumbled in agreement. If he'd had a mrem tail, it would have been lashing. Then he spotted the blood on the merchant's sleeve, and he frowned with concern. "You're wounded, sir," he pointed out more gently. "Do you need help?"

The merchant paled and swooned at the sight of his own blood. Jain knelt beside him, pushing the man's sleeve gingerly off the wound on his forearm. It was an ugly gash, a terrible patch of torn flesh that would certainly scar, perhaps even limit the motion of the arm and hand if it went untreated. He felt the healing stone's coolness in his pocket. He could do something about that wound, and he knew it. One simple spell, a little energy, and it was done.

It was done, and so was his life in the Guard— his childhood dream, his reason for leaving Uppervale. Healers were too rare to risk in combat. If he used the gift in front of the Furies, he'd be shut away in a monastery with other healers. For his own protection, they'd say. For his own good. Jain felt the healing stone in his pocket, cool, accusing . . . and he knew he wouldn't fire it. He cursed, despising himself.

Raf blinked down at him with a question in his eyes. Jain couldn't answer it.

"Hold him down for me," Jain instructed the mrem curtly, fishing a needle and thread out of his pack. "I'm going to stitch him up, and I don't want him struggling if he comes to in the middle of it." As he prepped the wound with alcohol, the merchant awoke with a gasp and struggled wildly. Raf finally had to sit on their unwilling patient to get him through the stitching, and the man railed and wept and cursed both his rescuers roundly.

I could spare him this, Jain thought. *I could spare him the pain.*

He wanted to vomit.

Chapter 6

"NO, NO, NO, SON, NOT LIKE THAT," TAZIRA growled, shaking her head at him. "Think of the weapon as an extension of your arm. Does your arm move like that?"

"But—" Jain started to reply.

"No, wise and mighty Tazira, it doesn't," she finished for him, cutting him off as usual. "How clever of you to point this out to me."

Maybe, just maybe, she'd let him finish a sentence someday.

They talked as they walked, Pellar in the lead again. The mrem hadn't said a word since the incident with the dire wolves the day before, and even Jain was concerned about that. Tazira, Raf, and Jain had kept up a steady line of patter since the attack, hoping to find a subject that interested Pellar enough to get him talking again. Right now, the subject was weapons: how to hold them, swing them, and ward with them. Jain would have found it fascinating, if he hadn't been getting the "you incompetent fool" end of the lecture.

At the moment, the path they traveled was surrounded by dense, lush growth. It was enough to give them much-needed shade; the red sun was at its zenith, always the hottest part of the day. Jain was still sweating and short of breath, and he couldn't imagine why the mrem weren't dying in their fur coats. But they seemed perfectly comfortable. He found himself peevishly wishing one of them would complain about something.

"Here, son, give me your short sword for a minute," Tazira said a little too cheerfully, casting a worried glance at Pellar's back. Jain handed it to her carefully by the hilt, expecting her to humble him with a brilliant demonstration of how to use it. She surprised him by sheathing it in her pack, and reaching over to take his off his back.

The human flexed his aching muscles gratefully, feeling positively liberated.

"Now, I want you to swing your arm around. Just let it swing, don't think about it," Tazira insisted.

"Brilliant," Raf murmured, meeting her eyes. She winked at him and arched her whiskers in amusement. Jain had no idea what was supposed to be so brilliant about this, and he felt more than a little ridiculous, but he did as she asked, swinging his aching right arm around for all he was worth.

"Good!" Tazira nodded at him. "So what are you doing, exactly?"

"Umm . . . swinging my arm around? Like you told me to?"

"Swinging your arm around in . . . ?" She left the query dangling, regarding him with a raised eyebrow.

"Circles?" he guessed, fearing the answer because it was too obvious.

"Exactly! In circles!" She beamed at him as if he'd just said the cleverest thing on Delos. He stared at her, mystified, and she explained. "That, my son, is the natural motion of your arm. Not just your arm, but your whole body. Everything in combat is built on circles, from attacks to wards. With a short sword, and especially with that great axe of yours, you'll have a lot more success if you complete the circle, following through the motion of a strike rather than trying to cut it short and recover. That's a typical beginner's mistake, because it seems to make more sense to cut an attack short if it misses, and come back to a nice defensive posture, where you're safe. But the half second it takes you to do that leaves you completely vulnerable, and it takes an expert only a half second to take advantage of that and nail you."

"Like Pellar did the first time we fought," Jain said. He looked hopefully at the man's back, but the dispirited slump of his shoulders was Pellar's only response.

"Exactly!" Tazira grinned, clapping him on the back. "The boy's a fast learner!"

"He is that." Raf arched his whiskers in agreement. He'd noticed Jain's attempts to get Pellar talking, and he'd appreciated as well just how competently the boy had stitched the merchant's arm up. Jain had all the instincts and compassion of a healer, if he could learn not to fight those gifts.

"Now," Tazira continued, "go ahead and shake your arm out, as if it ached."

"It does," Jain admitted, half smiling and half growling in the same way Tazira tended to. He obeyed, shaking the arm out.

"Where does the arm bend when you do that?"

"At the elbow, mostly."

"And?"

"The wrist."

"And?"

"The shoulder."

"And?"

"Ummm . . . there's nothing else to bend."

"Gotcha," she winked. "Always make sure they're paying attention. So, you've got movement, circular movement, in three joints: your shoulder, your elbow, and your wrist. How are we doing up there, Pellar?"

"Getting closer," she startled him into replying.

"Any idea how close?" Her tail tip quivered with tension; she needed to keep him talking if she could.

"Difficult to say, really. But the stone has been getting steadily darker." He held it up and showed her, and it was a light shade of fuchsia. "Can I take over the lecture and give you point for a while?"

"Absolutely," she breathed, trying not to show her relief too openly. She, Raf, and Jain shared a quick glance of subdued elation, and Tazira took the ring from Pellar and stepped out in front of the group. Pellar stepped back to Jain's right side, and Raf took his left in unspoken agreement. Watching the Three Furies move together was like watching a dance, a choreographed, graceful, wordless agreement. It was mesmerizing, and Jain wondered if they had some sort of telepathic link he didn't know about. He wondered, but he was afraid to ask.

"So," Pellar continued without preamble, "you've got three joints on the arm to initiate strikes with: wrist, elbow, and shoulder. Which do you think would give you the best point control?"

"The wrist," Jain answered without hesitation.

"Right you are. In a lighter weapon with easier point control, like a small sword, your wrist is your best friend. But your wrist is also the weakest joint in your arm, and can't strike with the force of the others. When you're using a heavier weapon, like your great axe, you'll need to strike with the force of the whole arm, or you won't get any strength behind the blow."

"That makes sense," Jain agreed.

"For the most part, it will," Pellar said quietly. "A lot of these basic rules seem perfectly obvious, and they are, if you're willing to sit down and think about what you're doing. But most people don't put even this much thought into the process." He paused just long enough to pluck a berry off a branch and pop it into his mouth.

"Fighting is a philosopher's art, my boy," the mrem continued thoughtfully. "The first step is to think about your own body, how it moves, what it can do. That's the first spiral in the Masters' Wheel. The next is to put a weapon in your hand, to extend your reach. And after that, you extend the circle out again to admit an opponent, multiple opponents, small units, armies, bringing in limitless combinations of attack and defense. And from which *direction* can those opponents attack you?"

"Well . . . from any direction, I guess," the human shrugged. His head never hurt like this when Owen Parden was teaching him, back home in Uppervale . . .

"Precisely, my boy," Pellar nodded. "Another circle. The Masters of the pre-Fall, Goshen Ilendr in particular, referred to that concept as the eight-pointed star. Four points for north, south, east, and west, and four points to cover the areas between them. When you fight, you need to own *all* the space around you, not just what's in front of you. You need to be able to attack and defend from all points of the compass, especially in melee combat. When you've fought in the past, did you feel the world narrowing, as if you were in a tunnel?"

"Sure, I felt that once or twice," Jain remembered. Shards, he was almost feeling it now, he was so tired.

"Perfectly natural; we've all done it. Also extremely dangerous. When your world narrows, you lose sight of every other point of the compass. And that's when you'll fall to a sneak attack. I've found that when I've gotten that tunnel vision, I've actually started fighting better, against the opponent in front of me. But I've been much, much more susceptible to attack from any other quarter."

At that moment Tazira hissed and bristled, startling Pellar right out of pontification mode.

"Speaking of being aware of our environment," she growled, "look down at the path, just ahead of us." Imprinted in the rain-softened mud of the road were large tracks.

"Ogres," Pellar said sharply. "Four of them, headed in the same direction we are." He stooped down and sniffed the tracks, his hackles rising. "The tracks are fresh, not more than an hour old."

"Close, then," Tazira murmured thoughtfully. "Odd to find two bands of monsters traveling this close together outside the Badlands . . . very unusual."

"Where'd you put my sword, Tazira?" Jain asked, starting to rummage through the packs she was carrying. Without a word she handed him the sword and his pack. "Come on," he snapped, throwing the pack over his shoulders and starting to move down the road. Tazira was instantly at his side, a friendly claw-tipped arm draped around him.

"Where you headed, son?" she inquired lightly.

"I have the strangest feeling we've done this before," the human answered dryly. "I'm going after the ogres."

"Why?"

"Well, because . . . because they're ogres," he concluded lamely. "And they might hurt someone."

Raf shook his head. "Highly unlikely." They're headed away from the city. If we leave them alone, they'll probably just head out of the Marches and back to the Badlands."

"And if we kill them, they won't head anywhere," Jain insisted, struggling to get out from under Tazira's draped arm. Her claws tightened into his shoulder just short of drawing blood, and he gasped and quit struggling.

"If we kill them, they'll be resurrected in a matter of hours," Raf sighed. "They're bits of wyld magic given flesh by human imagining; they're living nightmares. You can't kill nightmares permanently, but they can kill you, believe me. Unless they're hurting someone when we encounter them, there's absolutely no sense in taking them out. All we'll do is slow them down."

"It might be worth it," Jain said stubbornly.

"You think so, son?" Tazira snarled, quickly tiring of the argument. "Will you still think so if one of my men gets injured fighting those things? There's no point, and it's not a mission objective. It's a dangerous distraction. You're on a mission, not a training exercise. Stay focused on the mission."

"But—"

"Stay focused. One more difference between live professionals and dead adventurers, kid. Add it to your growing collection," the captain said flatly, tabling the discussion. "We skirt them if we can. I want to make it to that mountain range before we camp tonight." She pointed a claw-tipped finger at the high, bluish snow-capped peaks ahead of them. Without another word she eased her axes out of their belt loops and started moving silently forward.

Jain sighed and followed her, not really understanding.

The rest of that day passed in silence, a silence the human found uncomfortable. Pellar would periodically pause to study the tracks in the road, ogre and human. They couldn't afford to be spotted by either; they had to let Lucian lead them to his co-conspirators before they could take any action against him. They skirted the ogres' encampment easily enough, and if Jain had any regrets about the fact, he managed to keep them to himself.

Around red dusk they reached the base of the mountains, and the road cut a thirty-pace swath through the thick of them. Looking at the high ridges around them, Jain started to worry about the prospect of another ambush. But this was clearly the path Lucian had taken, and there were no other options.

The path led slowly upward, and the climb grew steadily more difficult. An hour or two before blue dawn, Tazira called a halt, and they found a small ravine to set up camp in. Jain had the uncomfortable feeling that he was the reason they'd stopped; he'd been finding it more and more difficult to breathe as they went.

They risked a small cooking fire in the hollow of the ravine. Tazira set out the kills, herbs, and wild vegetables they'd hunted and foraged along the path that day. She hummed as she worked, and Jain sighed, stretched, and allowed himself to relax somewhat. This had quickly become his favorite part of their days together; there was a routine about their camping that he'd started to take comfort in. Pellar would skin the kills and clean the vegetables, Tazira would cook something surprisingly wonderful, and Raf and Jain would post guard over the camp and clean up after the meal. Every night, it was the same, a reminder of the home and family he'd left behind him.

Tazira's beautiful, soft singing was painfully like his mother's.

He watched her as she worked, unable to help himself. Tonight, she was frying thin slivers of snake, spicing them with wild onion and herbs he didn't know the names of. She threw herself into the process with a love and creativity he found surprising in a warrior. Her tastes were exotic, sometimes too exotic for him, but he could still appreciate the artistry and passion behind her work.

Jain glanced over at Raf, who seemed lost in watching her. The wonderful, sharp, almost sweet smell of frying onion began to fill the ravine. Jain stepped outside to post guard, wanting to leave Raf alone with his thoughts, but the mrem followed him out.

"Starting to smell awfully good in there," Jain remarked conversationally. It was a take-it-or-leave-it line, one Raf could ignore if he wanted to think, or take up if he wanted to talk.

The mrem recognized it for exactly what it was. He had a knack for seeing people, often more clearly than they saw themselves, and he sensed the same gift in Jain. A fledgling warrior and a budding healer, innocent and wise beyond his years. Frankly, the boy intrigued him.

"Of course it smells good in there, soldier," Raf teased him. "That's our captain cooking."

"I wonder why she does it. Every night, I mean.

It would be so much easier to just order one of us to do it . . ."

"Answer your own question, Jain. Why do *you* think she does the cooking?" Raf regarded him with arched whiskers, half in amusement and half in contemplation. Jain closed his eyes for a few seconds, thinking before he spoke. He was being tested again, and he knew it.

"She said to me once that anything worth doing is worth doing well. I'd guess she cooks the same way she does everything else, with passion and ability."

"That's a good part of it," Raf admitted softly. "Tazira was born in love with the world, and she devours life like no one else I've ever known. But there's more to it than that—"

"Will you two stop gossiping and come eat?" Tazira growled at them both from just inside the mouth of the ravine. "Honestly, what a pair of old women!" She stepped outside and threw an arm around each of them, guiding them in. "What am I going to do with you?"

"Feed us?" Raf inquired innocently. The captain snorted, swatted the tip of his ear and walked over to the campfire, where Pellar was setting out the thin metal plates. Jain sighed contentedly, settled in, and started eating ravenously. He watched the Guards' faces in the firelight as they talked, telling old stories, sharing inside jokes he didn't yet understand. He would, though, he promised himself.

This is home, he thought. *All the home I have left. All the home I want.*

Chapter 7

ALL OF TYCOR WAS BOWING TO HIM. THE cheers in the great hall were deafening. *Riordan! Riordan! Riordan!* His name echoed throughout the keep, vibrating in the stone walls themselves.

The ancient and infirm Lord Tycor, Varral Romney, rose unsteadily from his throne to greet the hero of the Battle of Southmarch. With a trembling hand, he presented his daughter, the Lady Taziralendra. *The most beautiful woman in the world,* Jain thought with simple honesty. *Just like I've always heard.* Her eyes shone like emeralds, and her long, night-black hair waved in the gentle breeze. Jain wondered how a gentle breeze could get into the enclosed great hall, but quickly decided it didn't matter.

"How like you this man, daughter?" Romney croaked, his voice reed thin. "Would you take him in marriage, this great hero, and share the throne of Tycor with him?"

Riordan! Riordan! Riordan!

Her ruby lips parted in a smile, and she said . . . she said . . .

"Wakey waaaakey time, my lovelies!" in a strident, excessively cheerful voice. Jain's eyes flew open. Tazira Goldeneyes was standing over him, burying the last of the campfire. No wonder it was so damned cold this morning.

"Another beautiful day in the Guard," the madwoman crowed. "Every pay sack is a fortune, every meal a royal banquet, every day a new adventure! I *love* the Guard! Isn't it a wonderful morning, Riordan?"

Jain groaned and threw his blanket over his head, hating the world, particularly the Tazira Goldeneyes part of it.

The other mrem were no better, Jain decided sullenly. As the group made its way through the mountain pass and out the other side, they kept up a cheerful line of banter, occasionally breaking into a jog which he was expected to keep up with. He wondered why he couldn't stop shivering. Every joint and muscle he owned was in full, aching rebellion, and all Jain wanted to do was set down his pack and sleep for a while. And every time he tried, the damned mrem were there, cheerfully pulling him along.

"It has to be the fur," he slurred at last, forming something like a conscious thought. Raf and Pellar exchanged a look he couldn't decipher, and Tazira smiled at him. A little false, that smile, a little forced. Were they worried about him?

"What has to be the who, son?" Tazira blinked at him.

"Your fur. It must keep you a lot warmer than

my clothes and blankets keep me. You must be better suited for a campaign like this."

"You're doing fine, dear," was all she said. "Come on, you'll be warmer if you run." She broke into another jog, and the path shifted again from rolling fields to rocky terrain, as abruptly as that. They ran. It felt like forever. Jain stumbled on blindly, conscious of nothing but the determination not to fail.

The terrain shifted again; Jain didn't know how long it had taken them to cross the barren rock. Another forest sprang to life around them, and the air was suddenly filled with the cries of birds, the shimmering of insects, and the pale, delicious scent of the trees. Tazira paused to gather herbs for that night's meal, glancing back at Jain occasionally to make sure he was resting. The boy sank to his knees, gasping for breath, still cold in spite of the oppressive heat of the lush forest. Pellar studied the tracks in the road, frowning.

"We must be close to a settlement," the mrem called out to them. "There are more footprints in the road, and wagon tracks as well. Someone around these parts is wealthy enough to own a burden-beast. Are there any towns nearby?"

"Blackstone is a little ways to the south," Tazira answered thoughtfully. "We've already passed the roads to Woodenbridge and Greenvale."

"Blackstone?" Raf asked, his eyes widening. His tail lashed with sudden emotion. "I'm an imbecile," he muttered. "I can't *believe* I didn't think of it before . . ."

Tazira looked up at him, forcing calm over her

features. When Raf of all people got this agitated, it was bound to be bad. "What is it, Lieutenant?" she asked him neutrally.

"Blackstone," he said grimly, almost to himself. "Do you remember the days just after the revolution? Jain, this would be a bit before your time, but Tazira and Pellar will remember it well." They nodded, hackles rising a bit, and Raf continued, falling into pontification mode for Jain's benefit. "About twenty years ago, Tycor was ruled by the Tyrant. His name was Dzinjael Osska, but history will scarcely remember that. For eleven years he ruled, and his emotional instability gradually deteriorated into madness. He proclaimed himself a god, and his wife and daughter goddesses."

Jain nodded; he'd heard that much of the story, at least.

"Naturally," Raf murmured ironically, "that didn't go over too well. Delos hasn't *had* a sanctioned religion in almost four millennia, because of the destruction wrought by the Holy Wars. There was outrage at the proclamation, and that was when the public torture and executions began. Some eight or nine hundred of them, over a course of six months. The people were terrified. Thousands took the risk of leaving, because there was a worse monster inside the barricades.

"We were young Guards then, about your age, serving under a brilliant and ambitious captain named Varral Romney. The four of us arranged a near-bloodless coup, taking the palace and imprisoning the Tyrant. Osska was tried and executed for his crimes, and Val ascended the throne as third Lord Tycor. But we were too soft on the

Tyrant's widow and child, and that was my fault. Do you remember what happened to them, either of you?" Raf asked the other mrem with a raised eyebrow.

"I seem to remember that you said you'd take care of it," Tazira murmured. "At the time, I recommended that Lady Varna be imprisoned or exiled. Illana, I thought, should be raised at court to guarantee her mother's behavior. In retrospect, it was cruel, but those were hard times. What did you do with them?"

"The worst of all possible things. I let them live, and in peace. I had them set up in a comfortable castle keep, just outside Blackstone. It would seem to be exactly where Lucian has headed with the seal," Raf sighed.

"Damn your conscience, old friend." Tazira swore quietly, starting to pace. "Did Romney know?"

"He knew," Raf nodded. "One of the few times I've seen him choose mercy over practicality. We extracted an oath from Varna that she'd live quietly and seek no retribution for Osska's death, and I'd believed she would have kept that oath. Varna was a sensible woman, and in truth I think she was relieved to be going. But Illana was more like her father, from the beginning."

"She was," Pellar agreed. "The same instability, the same fevered hubris. Whatever the case, we're a lot closer to the seal," he said, pulling the ring out of his shirt and showing it around. It was a brilliant fuchsia.

"You know, one thing really bothers me about that," Jain interjected quietly. "You were given that ring by the same wizard who set me up. Now, you might not be convinced of my innocence yet, but I am. So, assuming I'm innocent and whatsisname is a liar, how do you know that ring is tracking the seal?"

"We don't," Tazira shook her head. "Doesn't matter, either. In order to set up that ambush, Najendra had to give us a ring capable of following his man. The spell didn't lose its capability when the ambush failed, possibly because no sane man would have expected that ambush to fail. Najendra's ring is still the only lead we've got, and we have no choice but to follow it. Even another trap will tell us more about our opponents than we know right now. Besides, look at that color, boy. We're close enough to spit on 'em." Her smile was feral. "Are we ready to move out?" They nodded wordlessly and gathered their packs. Pellar took the lead again.

"Ahoy for adventure," Raf said quietly. They smiled grimly, but this time no one laughed.

The wagon tracks and footprints branched off onto a smaller dirt path that led east. Pellar took them a good thirty feet off the path to minimize their chances of detection, and they continued through the woods for about another mile before they spotted the castle keep. Pellar's ring glowed a soft red, and he flashed it at the party silently before concealing it. They crouched between a large boulder and a group of thick hedges. It was a good vantage point, and one that was unlikely to give them away. The mrem set down their packs, settled in as comfortably as they could, and waited. In unspoken agreement, Pellar and Raf watched the keep, and Tazira watched the woods behind them.

"Well, now what?" Jain whispered.

"Now, we wait, and we study the keep's defenses," Tazira hissed back, so softly the human had to strain his senses to the utmost to hear her. "This is the part that takes a while, son. Two or three days, if need be. So you might as well get comfortable." She didn't seem inclined to continue, but Raf felt it was a lesson the boy would need. He picked up where she'd left off.

"We're watching the guards," the mrem whispered, putting together a device with a long leather tube and two round bits of glass. A spyglass? Jain had read about these in one of his mother's pre-Fall novels, but he'd never thought to actually see one. It must be very old; technical knowledge of glassmaking had all but vanished with the Fall.

"We need to study their patterns, numbers, armaments, habits, weak spots," Raf continued. "When do they change out, how often do they change out? What about the doors? Who's entering? Who's leaving? What are they bringing with them? We're looking for the best time to strike, and we can't afford to fail. We have no reinforcements, no hope of rescue, and no second team to try for the seal if we don't make it back."

Raf finished piecing his spyglass together, and he peered at the keep, allowing Jain to do the same after a moment. Jain was astonished at just how effective the thing was. They had to be about two hundred paces away from the castle, but with the glass, he could make out minute details and individual faces.

"In an ideal world, we'd at least have a floor plan," Tazira hissed, her whiskers arching downward in chagrin.

"We have a floor plan," Raf grinned. "I supervised the design of the keep, and I built in a back door, just in case we ever needed to do this. I'm not a completely trusting soul."

"I love you, Raf Grayfur." She beamed at him.

"That's because you're an infinitely sensible woman." He nodded approvingly, arching his whiskers in amusement. "Ordinarily, Jain, we'd waylay a merchant or a wealthy farmer with a cart, and we'd bribe or frighten him into sneaking us inside. It's a bit of a cliché, but still effective. In our case, however, we need to rely on the memory of a very old mrem."

"Oh, *now* we're in trouble," Pellar teased quietly.

"Ye of little faith," Raf chided him. "I'll be looking for a tunnel entrance that will let us in through one of the sewer drains. I have a rough idea of where they would have put it, but I haven't actually been here before, and it's been twenty years since I looked at the bloody plans." He pulled up his staff and rose slowly and silently, glancing around for guards or scouts. Not a soul in sight. "I'll be back in about an hour," he whispered.

"Be careful," Tazira and Pellar hissed in chorus. He nodded wordlessly, arching his whiskers in sardonic amusement, and swiftly blended out of sight.

"You owe me an ale, Lieutenant," Tazira whispered out of absent habit.

"Anytime, Captain." Pellar turned his full focus back to the castle keep, studying it intently. Jain peered up around the boulder, joining him. "Take a good look at the keep, Jain," Pellar said softly. "What kinds of defenses are we likely to run into?"

The human's eyes narrowed as he considered the castle. It had been built for beauty rather than defensibility, that much was obvious. It looked like nothing so much as a candycake, of a kind self-indulgent nobles sometimes had baked for them—the ultimate sin against the starving, in these hard times.

The stone walls were a soft milk white, with light blue roof tiles and lattices. The moat was too narrow to be anything but a decoration; it certainly wouldn't keep ladders off the walls in the midst of a siege. Nor, Jain thought, would it be especially good at keeping monsters out. But the moat had been riddled with narrow wooden spikes.

Four guards were posted at each of the corner towers, and they were armed with short swords and longbows. Four more guards paced the walls. There were iron cauldrons lining the south and west walls in three places each, and Jain guessed that they could be filled with pitch or hot oil and dumped over the side.

The tops of the walls had been liberally laced with twisted glass and metal shards, scraps of sharp refuse from the Fall. That, to be sure, hadn't been in the builders' original plans. Nor had the spikes in the moat. Someone with a bit of actual military acumen had readied that lovely, fragile candycake for defense. Jain said as much to Pellar, and was rewarded with the delighted arch of the mrem's white whiskers.

"Excellent, lad! Truly outstanding. Now, what did you leave out?" Pellar whispered as soon as Jain's recital was finished. The human pursed his lips thoughtfully and went back to considering the castle. Windows? Large, open, and difficult to defend. No glass, of course; window glass hadn't been available for the last fifty years. Guards he'd missed? He counted again. No, it wasn't that. Outside defenses? He couldn't see any at all. Damn.

"I give up," he hissed after a moment. "What am I missing?"

"The wards," Pellar said quietly. "Romney's single greatest contribution to Tycor, and to mankind as a whole. They've made it possible for us to survive on this planet, creating safe havens where no monsters can enter. The entire city of Tycor is warded. So is this keep."

"But if the wards are only set to keep monsters out, then what—"

"Ordinarily, they would be," Pellar admitted, cutting him off. "But that might not be a safe assumption to make. If they have the aid of a wizard, and we know they do, a wizard might be able to alter those wards. For example, the wards might fry a mrem. Just something to think about." He shrugged. "Always include contingencies in your assessment if you can."

"Good idea," Tazira hissed behind them. "That way, your captain will know to take point."

"How did I know *that* was coming?" Pellar asked wryly.

"Possibly because we've campaigned together for the last nineteen years. Don't even mention the possibility to Raf. We'll worry about it only if it becomes a problem."

Pellar nodded in agreement, and they lapsed back into silent waiting.

Raf returned within the first hour, having found the entrance to the passage. In silence he took a stick and sketched in the dirt all he could remember of the floor plans. The other three committed the drawings to memory, and after that there was nothing to do but wait and watch.

The real, insidious enemy, Jain discovered, was boredom. Several times he caught himself daydreaming, and he shook himself out of it with increasing frustration. The mrem had no such problem. They continued to watch their prey for hour after hour, with an exquisite, predatory patience that the boy began to find just a little unnerving after a while. With nothing better to do, he drifted off into a fitful sleep. The mrem joined him in shifts.

When he awoke, he dove into his pack and pulled out some of the dried beef. Eating the hardtack would make too much noise, and he was in no mood for weevils tonight, or today, or whatever it was. What he really wanted, more than anything else, was a good night's sleep in a soft bed. And a bath. And a change of clothing. And . . .

"Looks like we've got visitors," Raf whispered,

breaking Jain out of the wonderful self-pity banquet he'd been working up.

Jain joined Raf and Pellar in peering over the boulder. A group of about thirty armed men were just arriving at the castle's main gate. Jain didn't recognize any of them, but apparently the mrem did.

"There's Najendra," Pellar hissed. "Congratulations, Jain, you're now officially off the hook."

"About time," Jain growled softly. "Which one is he?"

"That's right, you don't know him, do you? He's the one just behind the leader. A little on the short side, blue robes?" Pellar glanced at Jain, handing him the spyglass. The human nodded, took the glass, and carefully etched the wizard's features into his memory, in case they should ever meet.

Najendra looked young, maybe not too much older than Jain. Jain had never seen a wizard before, and somehow he'd imagined they'd all be terribly old. The man in front of Najendra looked a good bit like Akan, a childhood friend of Jain's back in Uppervale. The same short, curling dark hair and sharply square chin. Najendra's nose was hooked, giving him the appearance of a bird of prey, at least from that distance. His clothing was everything Jain would have expected of a wizard: long dark blue robes bordered in gold trim. Expensive looking, and completely impractical for travel. There was another wizard with him, who was wearing equally absurd robes in an even more pretentious royal white.

Those robes might have been laughable on a less

imposing figure. But the white-robed wizard was almost a full head taller than the tallest of his guards, and he towered over Najendra. His shoulder-length white hair shone around him in a halo, fired pale red by the light of the setting sun. A close-trimmed beard and moustache softened the sharp, square line of his jaw as much as anything could. White hair notwithstanding, nothing about him suggested age or frailty; he looked more like a bricklayer or a druglord's enforcer than a wizard.

Raf plucked the glass out of Jain's hands and peered through it for a moment. "Pellar, do you recognize the leader?" he whispered, handing the glass to the other mrem.

"Taran Vesh. The plot thins," Pellar answered dryly.

"Who in the name of the Triune Suns is Taran Vesh?" hissed Jain, who was getting awfully tired of being out of his depth.

"The boy sounds more like Tazira all the time," Pellar drawled.

"Doesn't he, though?" Raf agreed with an amused arch of his whiskers. "Taran Vesh, for the blissfully uninitiated, is a scheming malcontent. He was one of Romney's court wizards until he was banished last year for plotting against the throne. The usual penalty for treason is death by beheading, but for some reason Romney was lenient with Vesh. I suspect he didn't want to provoke the other wizards into rebelling; I know he fears them."

"Banishment is supposed to be a sort of unspoken death sentence," Pellar interjected quietly for Jain's benefit. "It involves a journey through the Badlands to another city-state, and no one should be able to survive such a journey alone and unescorted. But Vesh obviously did, and that surprises me. I'd always thought he was somewhat overrated, and not nearly as powerful as he claimed."

The castle drawbridge lowered to let the humans inside. Clearly, they'd been expected. They filed in silently, and one of the guards in the armed escort glanced back at the road behind her. The mrem recognized her instantly.

"Private Alima," Pellar hissed, appending to her name a few quiet but very creative curses.

"*What?*" Tazira hissed from behind them. "*Our* Alima? I don't believe it!" She pulled herself up beside them on the boulder, and Pellar switched out with her to watch the forest. "Son of a bitch! Najendra I can see, but I *trusted* Alima!" Her tail lashed violently behind her, hitting Pellar in the head. He glanced up at her, and she whispered a quick apology, altering her tail's trajectory a bit before she continued her quiet rant.

"How many of our own have been corrupted by this?" she wondered aloud. "Shards, we can't even take it for granted that Romney knows anything! He may never have gotten my missive! We may have been pronounced dead, and a coup could be taking place as we speak!"

"Possibly, but probably not," Raf said with his usual implacable calm. Tazira's claws splayed and dug into the rock. Her ears flattened. She took a few deep breaths, and after a long, tense moment she finally forced herself to match his coolness. When he saw that the worst of her temper had passed, he continued. "They're clearly planning a coup, but it hasn't happened yet. There are too many armed men still inside those walls, and another contingent just arrived. I'd say this is somewhere in the 'late planning' to 'early implementation' stage. We've caught it, Tazira. Now all we have to do is find a way to stop it."

"Just the four of us, eh?" she quizzed him ironically, some of her humor returning in spite of her mood. Jain wasn't sure whether he should be delighted or concerned by the fact that she'd included him in her assessment.

Raf shrugged. "There doesn't seem to be anyone else, at the moment."

"True enough, old friend. How quickly can you get us in there?"

"Through the sewer tunnels? Twenty minutes or so, if we're lucky. More if we run into opposition."

"Are we going to run into opposition?"

"Unlikely, Captain, but always a possibility."

"All right, let's get in there as quickly as we can. They're about to have a meeting I *really* want to listen in on. Can we sneak in and hear a conversation in the great hall, then extract without running into the guards?"

"Yes, I think we can," Raf said after a moment's thought. "We should be able to follow the sewer tunnel into a hollow above the kitchens. It connects with an area between the gallery and the great hall. If memory serves, we'll be able to get in and out again without being seen."

"Then let's do it," she whispered, rising slowly and cautiously to her feet and looking around. She nodded to the others after a moment, and they gathered their packs, unsheathed their weapons, and slipped silently through the shadowed wood.

Chapter 8

"THIS STINKS," JAIN WHISPERED.

"Figuratively, or literally?" Raf regarded him with a raised eyebrow that bespoke volumes of irony.

"Yes," Jain answered emphatically and continued to trudge through the mire. The sewer tunnel was dank beyond anything the human had ever imagined. The air was moist and fetid and clung heavily about them, weaving its stench into clothing, fur, and skin. Every step they took into the soft and questionable contents of the wet ground brought up a waft of sickening decay.

Jain essayed a brief and ill-fated experiment in breathing through his mouth. It didn't take him more than a breath to decide he'd rather smell this place than taste it.

The slick, round tunnel was about five feet in diameter, not nearly tall enough to allow them to stand fully upright. They crept swiftly along it, a weapon in one hand and a small torch in the other. Once they got close enough to the castle, they'd have to douse the torches and hope they'd be able to relight at least one later. But for now, they were the only illumination in the seemingly endless tunnel.

"Raf," Jain whispered sweetly, "do you suppose that the next time you plan a secret tunnel, it could lead into something *other* than a sewer outlet?"

"Quit whining, boy," Tazira hissed. "I mean it. Hush." The glint of her eyes convinced the human of the wisdom of temporary silence. He might have been mildly annoyed, but then he took a good look at her. Her tail stood out a good six inches in diameter, a long, twitching spike of pure fear. Her breathing was erratic, though she was doing a good job of hiding it. Tazira had a problem with enclosed spaces. And she'd deliberately taken the rear guard position to conceal the fact. Jain slowed his pace a bit, just enough to let him keep an eye on her without crowding her.

There was a faint rumbling sound in the tunnel before them, and Tazira's fur spiked out. She glanced up at the stone ceiling as if she expected it to collapse on them. A low growl rose in her throat before she could stop it, and she hastily smoothed down her fur and assumed an indifferent mien. Raf and Pellar glanced back at her quizzically, and another, louder rumbling echoed in the tunnel, snapping their attention forward again. The sewer tunnel widened about ten feet ahead of them into what looked like a large stone vault. The chamber was filled with the most enormous giant spider Jain had ever seen.

The damned thing had to be at least twenty handspans high. Its eight gray-brown legs were each about as wide around as Tazira's waist, and it must have had a hundred black eyes in a great cluster above its gaping mouth. The thousands of hairs on its body were long, glistening spikes. Jain glanced down at his short sword, thinking it might as well be a toothpick for all the good it would do against *that*. He hastily shifted the pack off his shoulders and started rummaging through it, looking for last-minute inspiration.

"No chance of stealthing around that, I suppose." Pellar shrugged lightly.

"No spells, unless you have to use one to save a life," Tazira hissed in warning. "The wizards are bound to detect any magic use." The other mrem nodded, and Tazira handed Pellar her franciscas. His rapier and cloak wouldn't do him much good against a giant spider. Raf pinned a large, sharply spiked spearhead onto one end of his staff, turning it into a corsesca polearm, and Tazira took Black Bessie down off her back and balanced it firmly in her hands.

Jain had sneaked out in front of them with his chosen weapon before they'd even had time to notice him. He tested the heft of the grappling hook, fingering it nervously as he crept into the room. The spider fixed most of its eyecluster squarely on him and hissed.

"Oh, don't *you* look happy to see me," he whispered, trembling. He paused, then realized that waiting wasn't going to make the task any easier. With a last, deep breath he launched himself at the monster's right foreleg, sinking the grappling hook into it and pulling it taut with the rope. The spider screeched, and Jain started to run around behind it with the rest of the rope, with the hope of binding all its legs and tripping it up. The Furies rushed into the chamber, Tazira spitting curses.

"What in the name of the Triune Suns do you think you're doing, Jain?" the captain hissed at him emphatically. The sight had her somewhere between anger and laughter: Jain was trying to run a rope around the spider, and the bloody thing was chasing him almost as quickly as he was running. The pair of them sped around several times, neither really getting anywhere.

"Son, when I told you all combat was built on circles, this wasn't precisely what I meant," Tazira drawled with a dry hint of buried laughter in her voice. "Do yourself a favor and go tie off the other end of the rope by the entrance there. We'll get him tripped up for you."

Jain nodded with more than a little chagrin, and went to do as he was told. The mrem went to work.

Tazira scrambled up one of the spider's hind legs and got herself onto its back, wrapping her legs around it tightly and grabbing a huge fistful of its hairs for balance. It spun wildly, trying to throw her off, and began to tangle itself in the rope. Pellar danced swiftly in and out of its range, hacking at the creature's legs with bold, broad sweeps of Tazira's hand axes.

Raf stayed on the fringe of the combat, stabbing at the spider's body with his polearm and leaving great gouges. The thing began to screech in a way that set Jain's teeth on edge. Aware that the noise might attract attention from inside the keep, which they couldn't afford, Jain began to pull on the rope for all he was worth. The spider scrambled madly to keep its balance on the slick stone floor. The rope frayed and snapped, causing Jain to stumble backward.

"Finish it!" Raf hissed, driving his polearm deep into the spider's soft underbelly and twisting the staff. Another screech. Shards and ashes, they'd be lucky if the guards didn't hear this. Tazira balanced herself as carefully as she could on the squirming spider's back, tightened her grip on its hairs, and swung the heavy great axe with her other arm. The creature's eyecluster was shorn away, along with most of its face, such as it was. With a hiss of triumph she dove off as the thing collapsed.

It rolled over onto its back, and its massive legs shriveled up around it. Raf plunged his corsesca into the spider's belly for the coup de grâce. It didn't move.

Tazira rolled to her feet and bared her teeth. She swung Black Bessie into the spider's body over and over, with a savagery that bordered on hysteria. With a final hiss she shook herself out of it, shuddering.

"Are you all right?" Raf asked her quietly, his eyes darkening with concern.

"Fine," she whispered curtly, cleaning her axe and strapping it onto her back again. She grabbed her franciscas back from Pellar, holstered one, and freed her torch from its crevice in the wall.

"Any injuries?" she asked them more calmly. The men shook their heads, and she forced a bit of a smile. "Very creative thinking, Jain. The rope was a good idea, even if it didn't quite work out like you'd expected it to. Good going." She winked, clapping him on the back with a teasing glint in her eye.

In that moment, the human had more respect for Tazira than he'd ever had for anyone in his life. For all the world, she seemed to be back in complete control. If it was an act, it was a necessary act, and a good one. She wasn't letting her claustrophobia endanger the mission, and she wasn't turning to her friends for the comfort they would have provided.

She couldn't, Jain suddenly realized. It was a luxury she didn't have. Everyone else was allowed to falter, to fear, to need, and occasionally to fail. Not her. If she did, she could never show it, and it must have placed a terrible boundary between her and her friends. The loneliness of her life and her choices suddenly overwhelmed him.

Tazira squared her shoulders and glanced over her men. No injuries, and they looked ready to go.

"Let's move out," she whispered, taking point. They were getting close to the keep, and they'd be running into the wards within the next thirty or forty paces. She wanted to be the first to do that. Keeping her shoulders squared and her tail smoothed down very consciously behind her, she led the party through the vault and into the tunnel on the other side.

Jain squirmed a bit, trying to find a more comfortable position. He didn't succeed. They'd secreted themselves in a small hollow in the ceiling, a space between the long, narrow wooden gallery and the spacious great hall. There was a small crack between two of the floorbeams that gave a limited view of the hall and provided what little light there was in the alcove.

The small space seemed even smaller for the stench they couldn't help bringing with them. The odor of the sewers had clung to them, seriously limiting their ability to move around the castle keep undetected. They'd used the water supply in the secret passage off the kitchens to clean themselves up a bit, but it really hadn't made any appreciable difference.

Jain's left leg began to cramp severely. He took the risk of straightening it slowly and massaging it. The murmuring from the great hall grew louder, then suddenly quieted. Raf's ears quivered as he leaned down to peer through the crack. The meeting was about to begin.

"All rise and reverence her ladyship, Illana Osska, Lady Tycor by right of blood and seal!" a deep male voice boomed, and Jain heard the rustling of dozens of courtiers, soldiers, and functionaries rising to their feet. He also heard Pellar curse very, very quietly.

"Enter the court wizards, Taran Vesh and Daman Najendra!" the same voice rumbled impressively.

"Enter this, you pompous ass," Tazira grumbled softly, licking her shoulder contemptuously at the proceedings and grimacing at the rancid taste of her fur. Jain bit back a smile.

"I, Taran Vesh, swear fealty to the Lady Illana! My blood to hers, my life to hers, my hands to her service!" the first wizard cried in an equally grandiose manner. Tazira and Jain rolled their eyes at each other comically, and Jain leaned over to whisper in her ear.

"At this rate, they'll probably bore each other to death in five or ten minutes, and we'll be able to grab the seal and leave," he hissed softly. He was rewarded by the amused arch of her whiskers and an almost inaudible snort.

There seemed to be a long moment of awkward silence in the hall, and the court began to rustle and whisper restlessly. Then Najendra's voice rang out with the same oath.

"Our forces are gathered at Blackstone," Vesh continued, "and to those forces I will add armies of my own when we begin the assault in nine days' time. Your men will enter Tycor in small groups, peacefully, and mine will attack the city in force at green dawn on the Festival of Light. The Tycor Guards will be too busy fighting off the external threat to be able to protect the palace adequately. The usurper will pay for his crimes at last, and the House of Osska will be avenged! Death to Tycor!" A cheer rose in the great hall, then was suddenly, awkwardly silenced.

"I know the plan, wizard," a woman's voice snapped out, a whiplash of cool contempt. "I made it."

"Of course, my lady," Vesh murmured obsequiously, confirming Jain's guess that the woman must be Illana. "It is as you say. With your permission, I will send Lord Lucian Alander to lead the mercenaries at Blackstone."

"As you will," the lady said indifferently, apparently placated. "Go, Alander, and bring the men back to the keep with you tomorrow morning. Suns illumine you all."

There was a great rustling, as if a sizable number of people were rising to leave. Raf pulled himself away from the crack in the floorboards and gestured for Jain to look.

"Is that the thief?" he hissed softly. Jain glanced around the room and saw Lucian bowing to the throne. A beautiful, willowy creature with long, straight blond hair nodded regally in response, and Lucian bowed again and walked out. A handful of men followed him, and the heavy doors finally groaned shut behind the last of them. Jain looked up and nodded a wordless confirmation at Raf. The mrem nodded back and turned his attention to the crack in the floorboards. Jain shifted a bit and tried to massage his cramping muscles.

"You have the seal secure, my lady?" the wizard inquired in that same simpering voice. That voice sounded ridiculous, coming from a man of his size; it sounded as if he were laughing up his sleeve at all of them, in no subtle way.

"Of course," she replied coldly.

"How secure?"

"Judge for yourself, Taran," she answered with a mocking laugh. "It stays in this chest. This small, plain, rather ugly steel chest. But this chest can't be moved or opened by anyone but me, I'm afraid. The protection spell is so simple that the greatest of wizards couldn't break it, and it revolves around a riddle. *By the Triune Suns I speak it: I can hold but never touch it.* The wrong answer, naturally, brings death. Would you care to try?"

"Thank you, no, Lady."

"I rather thought not," she laughed. "When I march into Tycor, I'll have the seal tightly in my grip. No one will be able to challenge my right to reclaim my throne. No one!"

"And how many lives will it cost to secure your 'right,' do you think?" a male voice challenged her with cool irony. A rustling whisper of pure shock broke across the chamber.

"Najendra, you go too far," she warned him icily.

Jain blinked in surprise. Najendra? What was that ratbastard doing with a conscience?

"I have indeed gone too far, Lady," he shot back. "I've allowed myself to become a party to mass murder and the destruction of Tycor. I never bargained for this."

"You're an Amaran spy!" she spat contemptuously. "What possible loyalty do you owe to Tycor?"

"I owe it to them not to see them slaughtered."

"And what precisely did you think would come of stealing the Great Seal and passing it off to Alander?" came another voice, a soft, male voice. Vesh. "You're in this with us, now, Daman, up to your neck. Your only possible redemption is success. So why not share a glass of wine with us and try to relax? Tomorrow, we march for Tycor, and history."

"History does tend to favor the victor, doesn't it?" Najendra murmured ironically. "I'm sure it will never record the tenth part of your petty deceptions, win or lose. And as for these famous armies of yours, I've certainly never seen them. I wonder if they even exist."

"*Enough!*" Vesh roared, and there was a fantastic rush of energy. Jain couldn't see what was happening, exactly, but Najendra's screams were testimony enough. After a moment, everything stilled, and the only sound in the room was Najendra's tortured breathing. "I *own* you, Daman," Vesh said softly, a whisper of chill, exquisite malice. "Body and spirit, you've signed over to me, and I will give you power for them. Such power," he sighed, "if you obey me. It's too late now for regret."

Najendra tried to respond, but couldn't seem to manage the words.

"Carry him out," Vesh ordered, and there was a rush of men apparently anxious to obey. "Carefully," the wizard crooned, almost tenderly. "Be very, very careful with your master's possessions."

The doors at the other end of the hall groaned open, then closed again as Vesh and his men departed.

And there was a long, long moment of terrified and breathless silence.

Chapter 9

"I DON'T SUPPOSE THERE'S ANY WAY TO follow the wizards?" Tazira hissed softly to Raf.

"Not easily, and certainly not smelling like this," he answered with a grimace. Tazira nodded, not really expecting any other answer. The deathly silence in the room beneath them finally broke like a wave, giving way to hushed whispers and frightened clamoring. The captain sighed and changed position to listen again. She didn't really think there'd be that much more useful information to gather, but a few more minutes would buy them all time to think, digest the problem, and hopefully solve the riddle that was protecting the seal.

"Be silent, all of you!" Illana finally snapped irritably at the whispering courtiers. "This changes nothing!"

"Vesh is mad, milady!" a male voice cried, and the sentiment was quickly echoed by others.

"Vesh is powerful, you imbeciles! And he is under my sway. He swore fealty to me, as did all of you," she finished coldly. She clearly expected the matter to lie there.

"Milady, we are honorably sworn to your service," a woman's voice rang out across the chamber. "But there can be no greater danger to you or to any of us than a mad wizard!" The clamor at that was deafening, and it was only silenced at last by an enraged scream from Illana, almost a howl.

"Cowards!" she railed. "Frightened children, all of you! Have you forgotten Romney? Forgotten your families, dishonored and cast off their lands by him and his minions? My mother died in exile, my father at the block! You have all sworn fealty to me, and I will be obeyed! Vesh is powerful, and I can control him! I *need* him, damn you! With his power and his armies, I will reclaim my father's throne! It is mine by right, *and I will have it!*"

There was another brief silence, followed by the loud slamming of a door.

"She left," Raf announced quietly and unnecessarily, with his typical mordant humor.

"Nice to know some things never change, eh?" Pellar whispered. "She used to scream that way as a child, too."

"Well, now what?" Jain asked them.

"That depends on the three of you," Tazira whispered. "Has anyone solved the riddle yet?" They shook their heads in the negative, and she cursed softly. "Neither have I, not that I was expecting to. Illana could have been lying about the fact that a wrong answer will kill us, but that's not a hope to pin your cloak on. Our best option at this point is probably to hightail it over to Blackstone tonight and see what we can do to disrupt or scatter the forces gathered there. In the morning, we'll come back here to the mad ward and see what we can do about the seal, the wizards, and one tyrant-in-training."

"Just the four of us?" Jain teased.

"Just the three of us, son," Tazira corrected him quietly. "This is over all our heads, and the best thing we can do is give you an option out. You're free to go, though I wouldn't suggest heading back to Tycor just now. Try for Woodenbridge or one of the nearby villages."

He shook his head without the slightest hesitation. "I can't do that, Captain. I ran off to Tycor to join the Guard, and that plan didn't include backing out to save my own skin. I want to stay and help, if you'll let me. And if you won't, I'll still find a way to help."

"Sounds like you've made up your mind," she whispered dryly. He nodded stubbornly. "Well, then, Private Riordan, welcome aboard," she drawled with an amused arch of her whiskers, clasping his hand in the Old Way.

"*Private* Riordan?" he asked, delighted and disbelieving.

"You heard me, boy. If you're going to risk your life in this gloriously hopeless venture, you might as well die a Guard. Let's go, gentlemen," she hissed, rising slowly to lead them out. Their muscles were knotted with cramps, at least the ones they could still feel. They ignored the pain and forced their legs to carry them.

One step at a time, Tazira, my girl, she thought to herself in imitation of Romney. *Each step brings you that much closer to the light.*

*　　*　　*

"Boy, will you quit being so virginal and get in the water already?" Tazira spat testily, splashing him. They'd followed the road out to Blackstone, and the first order of business after that was finding a good, isolated spot on the local river and getting clean. The mrem, Jain discovered, were more fastidious than most of the humans he'd known. They were also a lot less shy than anyone back home. He started to peel off his rancid clothing, hiding behind a convenient hedge as he did so.

"Shards and ashes, Private!" Tazira laughed at him. "If I see anything I haven't seen before, I'll just grab Black Bessie and hack it off!"

She probably would, too, though somehow it wasn't an image he found remotely comforting.

Jain couldn't imagine how Pellar and Raf put up with the distraction. Tazira was rather emphatically female, and not at all shy about her body. But they seemed absolutely accustomed to her, and utterly unfazed by the whole thing. *Maybe after you've campaigned together for twenty years or so, it doesn't matter,* he thought to himself. He shed the rest of his clothing, grabbed his cake of soap, and made for the water hastily.

The mrem were engaging in a free-for-all splash fight in which they seemed to change sides frequently and without warning. When Jain got in, they triple-teamed him for a few seconds before everyone turned on Raf in one of those unspoken agreements they seemed to have. Raf splashed back with his usual calm efficiency, somehow managing to look dignified and aristocratic in the middle of it all. After a minute or so they went right back to bathing and washing out their clothing, in another of those unspoken agreements. They watched each other a bit suspiciously, but no one started up the fight again.

"I thought you'd hate the water," Jain blurted without thinking. The mrem turned to him and blinked in surprise, and he instantly regretted the words.

"We're humans, Jain," Raf said quietly, turning meticulous attention to scrubbing his gray doublet. "Humans born and bred with some felinoid genetics, but still human for all that. We're not cats, or house pets. We even like water."

"I'm sorry," Jain murmured, reddening with mortification. "I can't *believe* I just said that . . ."

"Don't worry about it, Private," Tazira teased him, splashing him lightly to break up the sudden tension. "We hear worse all the time."

"I know," Jain sighed. "Doesn't make it right, though."

"Think nothing of it, my good man," Pellar sniffed, bringing out his best foppish courtier routine with a comic flourish. "Already forgotten. Now, onto a genuinely important subject. Your hair. What on Delos do we do about the boy's hair?"

"What's wrong with my hair?" Jain frowned, running an unconscious hand through it and stopping when he remembered exactly what was wrong with it. Pellar had sliced two locks off the sides in their duel, if it could be called a duel.

"You'd forgotten all about it, hadn't you?" Pellar teased him.

"Completely," Jain admitted sheepishly.

"Come on. I think I might have a small pair of scissors in my pack." The two of them climbed out of the water and went off in search of the perfect hairdressing implement, and Tazira silently blessed Pellar for his tact. Jain, at least, seemed to have quickly forgotten the entire exchange.

She turned to Raf, expecting to have to defuse his half of the situation, but he appeared to have forgotten it as well. He wrung the excess water out of his clothes and draped them over a rock on the shore to dry in the heat of the red sun, which was at its zenith. *So adorably efficient*, she thought. Tazira was just going to hang her clothing over a tree branch, but the rock idea was a better one. She swam ashore, found a broad, flat boulder, and copied him unashamedly.

"So, how angry are you, really?" she asked him as she laid her clothes out. "It's hard to tell, with you."

"Angry with Jain, or the world at large?" he sighed, spreading his blanket on the hard-packed dirt by the shoreline. He lay down on it with his hands laced behind his head.

"With Jain, pest," she teased him, sitting down beside him on the blanket.

"Not at all. It was a harmless, offhand comment."

"You might do me a favor sometime and make sure *he* knows that. He strikes me as a rather sensitive lad."

"He does, doesn't he?" Raf murmured with that quiet, thoughtful intensity he usually saved for interesting philosophical dilemmas. He propped himself up on his elbows and drew a breath to speak.

"Oh, no," Tazira rolled her eyes laconically heavenward. "I feel a pontification coming on."

"You do," he nodded unapologetically. "I think the boy might be a healer."

"You *what?*" she hissed, unconsciously glancing around them to make sure Jain wasn't in hearing distance. "Are you sure? Wait a minute, Raf . . . Could he be a healer without knowing it, or one who has the potential to develop it in later life, maybe?"

"Possibly, but probably not. It seems to be a talent that develops around puberty, and Jain's a bit past that. If he's a healer, he already knows it, and he's running away from it."

"Damn," she breathed. "He really, *really* wants to be a Guard. And he's *good*, Raf, he's got such potential . . ."

"Healers are more useful," Raf shook his head. "Warriors are twenty for a silver piece; we just can't do what healers can. Jain should be encouraged to go with his best gifts. If he *is* a healer, you need to discourage him from joining us. It's in his own best interests, really."

Tazira pursed her lips thoughtfully for a long moment. Finally she sighed, lay down, and curled up next to him affectionately.

"You're wrong, you know," she said at last.

"I feel strangely certain you're about to tell me why."

"Yes, I am. You're absolutely right that he needs to go with his best gifts. But he's been given the talents, drives, and cunning of a warrior as well.

He can't ignore all that and still be complete. There has to be a way to let him combine the warrior and the healer."

"But if the boy really is a healer—"

"Then he'll decide how best to use those gifts, in his own time," she cut him off gently. "If he *is* a healer, and he *knows* that, then he must have fled Uppervale to avoid being shut away. I don't blame him, Raf. The boy's seventeen years old, too young to be sacrificing everything that makes life worth the living."

"But the sacrifice is for humanity."

"So is the sacrifice of mrem," she said with quiet fierceness, rising on one elbow to look at him. Her gold eyes flashed soft fire at him. "Did you become a Guard because it's what you truly feel called to, love? Or did you become a Guard because war is what you're conditioned to? What might you have been, if you truly had the exercise of your own free will? We can't deny that to Jain, just because we don't have it ourselves."

She stared down into his eyes, and he was breathless for a moment, conscious only of the fact that he suddenly wanted her. With effort, he forced away that impulse. It would do neither of them any good.

"Damn," he finally swore with a shade of amusement, carefully contemplating the trees overhead. "I don't have a good answer for that one. You don't pontificate often, but when you do, it tends to make an uncomfortable amount of sense."

She laughed and licked his cheek affectionately, then pulled back almost shyly when the rush of mutual desire made the moment an awkward one. They'd been lovers, long ago, and then they'd been friends, and sometimes it was difficult to remember how or why it hadn't worked between them. *Times like this, mostly,* he thought; moments when Tazira looked dreadfully torn between the desire to take him and the desire to run.

"Tazira, are you sure we shouldn't just scramble back to Tycor and warn them about the invading army?" Raf asked her at last, easing the tension between them somewhat. Talking strategy always seemed to relax her.

"We will," she replied, more calmly, "at least, one of us will. But first, I want to see if we can't somehow neutralize the threat of Illana's forces at Blackstone, for one very good reason. We have no idea what sort of a conspiracy is going on inside the walls. I'm afraid that if the three elements of the plot are allowed to come together, Illana's forces, Vesh's armies, and the conspirators inside, there'll be no stopping them no matter how quickly we can get word to Romney. But if we can somehow prevent at least one of those elements from ever reaching Tycor, we should be able to shut down the other two. I hope." She sighed, rolling over onto her back and watching the branches sway in the light wind.

"If their plan has one great failing," she continued pensively, "it's that the effort won't be coordinated beyond this morning's discussion. Vesh's army will be counting on the fact that Illana's forces are inside to do the actual dirty work, but they don't seem to have set up any lines of communication that will let them be sure of that. I'm betting that if we can scatter Illana's forces tonight, Vesh won't know they aren't in place until it's too late. And if that female mercenary we talked to was telling us the truth, Alander hadn't yet bothered to coordinate anything with the conspirators inside Tycor. If he and the Blackstone forces never show, the whole plan should fall apart. I'm not sure I'm making the right decision, here, but it's what my gut is telling me."

"Then that's what we'll do." He nodded, arching his whiskers forward. "Any plans as yet for how to deal with the force at Blackstone?"

"I have a few ideas. We'll need to do a brief scouting run, just to see how many we're looking at, but I honestly think we can throw a good scare into them. Depends on how good an actor our new private is," she said, raising her voice for the benefit of Jain and Pellar. The two of them returned to the makeshift campsite, Jain with considerably less hair than he'd had before. He was running a hand through it a bit nervously, as if he wasn't sure he'd wanted it quite that short.

Tazira had to admit to herself, though, that the boy cleaned up nicely. With all that scraggly hair and several days' worth of beard gone, he was downright gorgeous, at least for a human. He'd be beating the female population of Tycor off with a stick. *Matter of fact . . . if I were human myself, and maybe half a lifetime younger . . . Bad Tazira! Bad! No catnip!*

"Looks good, Private!" she winked at him, biting back a laugh at the evil course of her thoughts.

"Of course it looks good," Pellar sniffed proudly. "I did it."

Jain briefly considered the way Tazira and Raf were lounging together on the blanket, and he grinned to himself. "You owe me an ale, Pellar," he murmured.

"Only because you said it first," the mrem-turned-barber replied dryly, and the two of them shared a secretive smile.

"Care to share it with the regiment, boys?" Tazira asked them with a raised eyebrow.

"With the regiment? Certainly. With you? Not on your life," Pellar teased.

"Conspiracy," Tazira growled, appealing to the heavens. "Everywhere I look, conspiracy and insubordination."

"It's a captain's lot, ma'am," Pellar nodded with an unsympathetic grin.

"So it is," she agreed, with that subtle shift of energy that always seemed to mean she was about to start discussing business. Even Jain had learned to recognize that pattern.

"Now, gentlemen, let's settle in and get to work," she said crisply, rising to her feet and starting to pace. Jain wished he'd had time to place a bet with Pellar on that. Pellar and Raf were still mysteries to him in a lot of ways, but he'd already learned to read Tazira like a book.

"First, we're going to scout out the enemy encampment," she continued, "and hopefully come up with a plan so earth-shatteringly brilliant that it can't possibly fail."

"Optimistic, isn't she?" Pellar smirked.

"Never paid to be anything else." She shrugged cheerfully. "Next, plan allowing, we settle in and get as much sleep as we can. It may be the last chance we have for a couple of days, depending on how it plays out with the forces at Blackstone. And while you sleep, my loves, I want you to dream me up an answer to that shardblasted riddle. Any questions?"

They shook their heads, and she began to shrug into her still damp but at least clean clothing. The others followed suit, and Raf began to ponder the riddle. *By the Triune Suns I speak it: I can hold but never touch it . . .*

Watching Tazira, he feared he had his answer to that.

Chapter 10

THEY DID THEIR INITIAL SURVEILLANCE from the cover of a high, heavily wooded escarpment. Tazira would have had scouts up there, but, then, Alander wasn't Tazira. He was a druglord trying to perform the office of a soldier. The Guards shook their heads almost pityingly at the lack of intelligent defenses.

There looked to be about a hundred and twenty men down there, few of whom could truly be called professionals. Those that could were undoubtedly city-based assassins, unfamiliar with this kind of fight. The rest looked to be simple farmers and tradesmen who'd let themselves be seduced into rebellion. Tazira resolved to spare as many as she could, but it wouldn't be easy. She might have to kill a few of the mercenaries in order to get the rest to panic into desertion.

To that end, she started to consider the sentries. Alander clearly didn't trust the competence of the tenant farmers; his sentries were all of the hired killer variety. *Good*, Tazira smiled grimly to herself. *That always makes it easier to do what you have to.*

There were two sentries posted at the makeshift gate, and three more border guards pacing the camp's perimeter. That was it. It wouldn't be a difficult operation, just a less upright one than Tazira wanted her men involved in.

"Well?" Jain whispered at last. "Does anyone have an idea?"

"Oh, yes," Tazira purred dangerously. "The three of you are going to pull sleep shifts while I lay the groundwork. I'll be back at blue dawn, and we'll plan our attack from there."

"Tazira—" Raf started to protest, but she cut him off with a sharp hiss.

"That's an order, Lieutenant. Sleep; you'll need it."

"Tazira, you can't simply put me to bed every time one of the more unpleasant aspects of this job comes up. If I couldn't handle it, I wouldn't be here," the mrem said grimly.

"You're no assassin, Raf," she said softly. "You're better than that, better than I'll ever be. Do me a favor and stay that way. Besides, what I'm going to be doing over the next six hours is a one- or two-person job at best, and I want you rested for the fight."

"And what are you going to be doing while we rest?" he asked her a shade testily.

She considered him for a moment, clearly not wanting to tell him. Finally she sighed, flicking the tip of a pointed ear in the direction of the camp. "You see those sentries and perimeter guards? In less than an hour, they're going to turn up dead. So are their replacements. Soon, nobody will want to post sentry duty, and they'll be disheartened and afraid. They might not desert initially, for fear that whatever's out there would kill them if they left the security of the camp. But at the least, they'll be off balance and fighting among themselves."

Her eyes hardened thoughtfully, and she continued, "There are obviously two distinct factions in the camp, as well, and that might be turned to an advantage. The mercenaries don't trust the farmers, that's clear enough. With a little manipulation, that could blow up into open conflict."

"It could," Raf agreed, "though a lot of them are likely to die if that happens. Isn't there any way to spare more people than that?"

"I don't know," she admitted. "The only other way I've thought of is a lot more gruesome than that, and it would finish off the lot of them. I could set off a grand fire shield around the camp and close it down on them."

Pellar whistled appreciatively. Effective. Grisly, but effective. By comparison, the first plan didn't sound too bad.

"We could always try to scatter them with a deception," Tazira continued thoughtfully. "Set off a few fire spells and convince them there's an invisible dragon flying over the camp. Or send Jain in there screaming that Vesh has gone mad and is coming to kill them all, or that Romney's discovered the plot and ransacked the castle . . . Only problem there is that if the deception didn't work, at least one of us would be trapped in the middle of an enemy camp. A hundred and twenty or so of them, four of us. Those odds make it just a bit difficult."

"Those odds do one very good thing for us, though," Pellar murmured thoughtfully. "One man alone is reasonably bright. A hundred and twenty men together are a stationary herd of dumb, nervous animals waiting to be stampeded. Panic is very contagious, especially when it's enhanced by a mass confusion spell. Seems there's one sitting here in my pouch, just waiting to be fired off . . ."

"That'll help," Tazira approved, suddenly grinning. "That'll help a lot. But a deception would hinge on Jain's acting ability, because he's the only one of us who could begin to pass for a conspirator. There are no mrem in their ranks. Private, how well can you act?"

"How . . . how well can I act?" Jain sobbed, summoning tears to his eyes. "Captain, after all we've been through together, how can you ask me that?" The three mrem snickered, looping their tails in amusement.

"Son, that's really pathetic," Tazira teased, punching him in the arm. "Cut that out! I won't have my private sniveling! Where on Delos did you learn to do that?"

"Uppervale," he admitted sheepishly, wiping his tears away. "We used to put on plays in Jed Sandol's backyard. Tears were a useful trick when I was a kid, but after a while I got too old to get away with it."

"Sad when that happens, isn't it?" Pellar grinned. He had the same ability, and he'd often wished he could have been an actor himself. "Of course, as you get older, you'll find that trick works on women—"

"Really?" Jain asked, suddenly fascinated.

"Pellar, I don't believe you!" Tazira chided him. "You will *not* teach Private Riordan how to take advantage of the opposite sex!"

"Wouldn't dream of it, Captain," Pellar said smoothly. "So, now that we know Jain has all the makings of a perfect con artist, what do we do with him?"

"Unfortunately, the initial part of the plan remains the same," Tazira said quietly. "We need to take out as many of their elite fighters as we can before we try to scatter the rest. Alander's made my job easy for me by putting so many of them on sentry duty. I'll spend the hours until blue dawn whittling down the mercenary element, and when I get back, we'll put Jain to work."

"Doing what?" the human asked.

"Panicking."

"Oh, good. I can panic. I like panicking," he teased, and Tazira snorted soft amusement.

"First, we're gonna have to mess you up a bit . . ."

"But I just got clean!"

"Never lasts long in this line of work, son," the captain sighed ruefully. "You need to look like you've been in a fight, and I don't want Alander recognizing you. That haircut should help, actually. Once you're sufficiently unrecognizable, we'll send you running into the camp with the news that Vesh is a few arrows short of a quiver, and he's turned on his employers. Everyone at the castle is dead, and now he's headed this way. Think you can manage that?"

"I think so." Jain nodded earnestly.

"Next, Pellar, I want you to hit the largest group of 'em with that mass confusion spell. I'll let it sit for about five seconds, and then I'll unleash a flame strike. At that point, Jain, I need you to bolt like a rabbit, yelling at them all to run. You get yourself out of camp and head back up here, and we'll take it from there. Hopefully, they'll panic and desert in droves, and we'll go in and clean up the rest. Raf, I'm holding you and your best spells in reserve, so you can pull our tails out of the campfire if this doesn't go as planned. Sound good?"

"Sounds good," Raf agreed grimly. "Everything except the part where you go off and take out the mercenaries while we sleep."

Tazira sighed, and her tail started to lash with frustration. "Raf," she said with all the patience she could muster, "if I don't take them out now, they might manage to rally the farmers out of the scare we're trying to throw into them. If that happens, we're dead, Val Romney's dead, and Tycor's at the mercy of Taran Vesh."

"That's not what I'm arguing, Captain. Why go alone? You could bring one of us to watch your back—"

"No, I can't, and that's the end of it," she said firmly. "I need the three of you well-rested and thinking clearly tonight. And Jain's not ready to start killing humans; it's a far, far cry from killing monsters. I need the two of you to watch him, let him sleep, and sleep yourselves. I *will* be back at blue dawn. If this goes sour, our rendezvous point is the river ford where we bathed this morning. If it goes well, we rendezvous here. All clear?" They nodded, and Raf dropped the argument with obvious reluctance. Tazira started unstrapping her franciscas and leaving them on the ground next to her pack.

"Why aren't you taking your axes?" Jain frowned.

"Because if I get myself into a bad enough situation that I need 'em, I'm dead anyway," she shrugged indifferently. Raf's tail lashed ominously, but he managed not to say anything. Tazira checked her throwing knives, put one between her teeth to keep both her hands free, and started making her way down the hill with a last, breezy salute.

"*That* is an incredibly brave woman," Jain breathed after a moment.

"More than you know," Raf agreed, his tone half angry and half tender.

Jain settled down and started unrolling his blanket. "Who gets first watch?"

"I'll take it," Raf muttered. "I doubt I could sleep anyway." Pellar nodded, unrolled his blanket, and soon fell asleep. Jain tried to do the same, but found that he couldn't. Curiosity and confusion kept pulling him back to the world. He watched Raf pace for a few minutes, and then he risked a question.

"Why are you so angry with Tazira?" the boy whispered, to avoid waking Pellar. "If you don't mind my asking, that is."

Raf considered that for a minute before he decided that, no, he *didn't* mind. He walked over and knelt next to Jain, so that they could talk quietly.

"She and I have been having this argument for more years than you've been alive, Jain," the mrem sighed. "I'm not angry with her, exactly, but I think she takes too much on her own shoulders. There's a dark side to this job; it's not all parades and white uniforms. Sometimes—times like this—we have to be prepared to do things that aren't easy to live with.

"Tazira is like a mother duck, and was long before she made captain and had the excuse to be. She tries to shield her people from that side of life by doing as much of it as possible herself. And she has violent nightmares because of it. I've slept beside her, and I've felt her having them. *That's* why we have this argument."

"Because you want to protect her, as much as she obviously wants to protect you," Jain interjected shrewdly. "Because you love her, maybe?"

Raf started pacing again, unable or unwilling to answer that. After a minute or so, Jain gave up and drifted off to sleep, knowing it might be for the last time. And all he felt about that was a curious sense of detachment.

"Run!" Jain bellowed for all he was worth, dashing through the forest toward the camp. "Run for your lives! It's all over! He's mad, the wizard's gone mad! He'll kill us all! *Run!"*

There were no sentries standing guard, so Jain breezed right into camp.

"Run!" he shouted at the nearest soldier, grabbing him by the arms and shoving him away.

"Get out, now!" The man took to his heels, without having any particular idea what he was running from. A few of his comrades followed him, then a few more. And panic started to spread through the camp like wildfire. One of the surviving mercenaries ran up to Jain, grabbed him, and slammed him up against a tree.

"What in the name of the Triune Suns are you talking about, soldier?" she snarled. "Run from what, exactly?"

"It's Vesh!" Jain sobbed, letting his nervousness play into hysterics. "Vesh is mad! He killed Illana, killed everyone at the castle! And now he's coming for us! *Run for your lives!*" he howled, shoving the mercenary away. By now, the panic was becoming a rout, and Illana's men were fleeing in droves. It was Jain's tears that convinced the mercenary he was telling the truth.

"Oh, shards," she hissed, looking around her wildly. *"Run!"* The woman dashed off, shoving people before her and taking up the cry. "Get out of the camp! *Run!*"

Tazira's flame strike filled the air above them, and screams of mindless terror followed it. Pellar's smoke went off, slowly and ominously flooding the ground. Realizing that there was nothing more he could do, Jain started running back toward the hill position.

Someone grabbed him by the tunic as he ran, and he gasped and froze in his tracks. Lucian Alander took a good, long look at him, not letting go of his collar.

"I know you," the druglord frowned, obviously trying to place him. Jain didn't intend to give him the chance to piece it together. Seizing Lucian's shoulder, he shook him roughly.

"You have to get out of the camp, *now!*" he bellowed. "Vesh has gone mad and killed the others, and now he's coming here! For the love of your own skin, *run!*" Jain gave him a rough shove toward the fleeing soldiers and started to take off in the other direction, quickly. Lucian, after the barest hesitation, ran after him.

"Riordan!" he snarled. "You shouldn't have risked speaking, Riordan!" He tackled the boy to the ground, and they rolled down a small escarpment.

"The bruises and the haircut hide you well, boy, but that Uppervale twang of yours is unmistakable!" Lucian growled, reaching for the long, razor-sharp dagger at his hip. Jain spotted the movement and forced Lucian's hand away, pinning him to the ground. The druglord struggled for a moment, but quickly saw that it would be a wasted effort; the farm boy was considerably stronger. Not that that would save him.

Lucian smiled suddenly, and a look of smug challenge settled over his features. "*Guards!*" he bellowed for all he was worth. "Stop running, you idiots! It's a trick! *Guards!*"

In a moment's blind, unthinking panic, Jain snatched the dagger from Lucian and slashed him with it. It connected with flesh and sliced through—a sickening hardness, a wet warmth, a tearing. The blade bounced and scraped along a collarbone as the boy jerked it free with a gasp. His victim tried to scream, but the sound died in his opened throat. Lucian rasped as his mouth filled with blood, and he flailed with one hand while trying to hold his flesh closed with the other.

Jain scrambled away from him, reeling with horror. The world seemed to slow around them, and they locked eyes in a communion more intimate than lovemaking. Lucian's head lolled to one side, and his eyes glazed over as blood poured out of his mouth.

Murder. I've done murder. Shards, I've done murder . . .

Two mercenaries arrived at the top of the escarpment, saw their leader's blood on the boy's dagger, and charged him. Jain tried to raise the blade to defend himself, but it was like moving through lead, through dream. The world around him was white and slow and shaking.

Murderer. Killer. Lucian's blood was soaking through Jain's tunic to his skin. The boy tried to focus on the battle in front of him, but all he could see was his victim, flailing, rasping. *Killer.*

The mercenaries dropped in their tracks, suddenly and seemingly for no reason. One was clutching a throwing knife that seemed to have blossomed out of his throat. The other, face down, simply didn't move at all. Jain turned, bewildered, to find Raf at his shoulder, unsheathing more throwing knives. Nothing, not even the mrem's calmness, seemed real.

"A life for a life," Raf said solemnly, arching his whiskers. "Now, go on, get out of here. Get out, Jain!" He gave him a good shove in the direction of the hill. "Go!"

Jain ran, not knowing what else to do. The

sounds of a skirmish rang in his ears. After a moment of running, he turned and forced himself to look back, in case he was needed. He wasn't; the Furies were just polishing off what little resistance they found. Most of the camp was scattered, the foliage trampled in the general haste to escape. Pellar killed the last mercenary, and as soon as the area was clear the three of them began picking over the ruined tents and broken furniture.

What they hoped to find, Jain had no idea. He had no idea of anything anymore. *Murderer. I killed Lucian*, he thought. *I took a human life. I even have a name for my victim, if that was his name.*

I think his eyes were green, after all.

At that remembrance, Jain sank to his knees and was suddenly, violently sick. Afterward, he lay there for what seemed like an eternity, too weak to move, too disinterested. The sky moved overhead, mundanity and unreality folding and unfurling in the slowly tumbling clouds, like a bit of white bottle glass he remembered finding once. This was what it felt like to look at the world through white glass, he thought. It felt like this, soft edges, slow, languid detachment, wordless grace. A whispered prayer to a silent god. He retched again, and suddenly someone was holding him through it, murmuring kind and empty things.

It occurred to him only after a moment to care who it was. He glanced back, and Tazira pulled him close and stroked his hair comfortingly with a gentle, black-furred hand.

"Let it go, son," she whispered. It was only then that he realized he was crying. He buried his head in the crook of her shoulder and howled, a sound of rage and loss as inhuman as anything he'd ever heard issue forth from the throat of a mrem. And all at once it occurred to him that he was a killer, that his innocence was shattered, and that he was being petted by a giant cat. Even that only made him cry harder, where he should have laughed, or smiled at least.

All the griefs of the last week combined and overwhelmed him. The homesickness, the exhaustion, the merchant he should have healed, the man he'd just killed. The rough, scraping feel of a blade slicing into flesh and bone. Tazira held him through it all, and finally his sobs subsided a bit.

"That's it, Private," she said softly, and he heard her as if from a great distance. "What you just lived through is the hardest, most hateful part of what we do. We've all been exactly where you are now, and we've all done exactly what you're doing. It gets easier with time, though it's never easy."

"I'm sorry," he whispered, over and over, hating himself.

"Hush your mouth, boy," she stopped him. "No shame, and no apologies for being human. The only time I'd worry is if you *weren't* feeling this."

He nodded and forced himself to stop crying, taking a few deep breaths to fortify himself. Later would be time enough to grieve, he suspected. Later, when he could stand it.

"Thank you," he said simply after a moment.

"Anytime, son." She smiled at him, punching his arm lightly. The quiet levity felt out of place, almost vulgar, but he knew it was well intended.

"Think you might be ready to move out?" she asked him, cocking her head to one side in the way she tended to. He didn't want to move, not ever, not really. But he managed to nod anyway, and they helped each other up.

As they made their way up the escarpment to the rendezvous point, Tazira made idle conversation about the next phase of the mission, letting him talk if he wanted to or lapse into silence if he needed to. He was silent, mostly, thinking about Lucian, wondering where Tazira and the others ever found the courage to keep doing this.

And at the same time, he couldn't shake another feeling, one that horrified him. He had killed. There was no worse thing he could do. If there was a black place after death, he was going there for this day's work. That wasn't real to him yet, but it would be. Shards and ashes, it would be.

He'd killed a man. He'd done the single hardest thing he would ever have to do, and he'd survived it. Worse, he thought he could probably do it again if he absolutely had to. It changed him, in a way nothing else ever had or ever could. Not the discovery of his healing talent, not the loss of his virginity, not the night he left Uppervale. This made him dangerous. This. Jain Riordan, the healer, could kill.

Now, in a terrifying sense, he mattered.

Chapter 11

THE FOUR OF THEM MADE THEIR GRIM AND silent way back toward the castle, following the main road. Jain hadn't said two words during the last hour, but that was pretty much to be expected.

Tazira told herself she wasn't worried yet, but she still found herself babbling stories of her girlhood in Haymarket, to see if they would elicit some response from him. So far, nothing. No glimmer of familiarity or shared experience. She wasn't even sure it was a good idea; the boy had to be homesick, and Haymarket wasn't ten leagues from Uppervale. But she was trying the only thing she could think of, and for once Raf's quiet wisdom and Pellar's diplomacy seemed to be at an equal loss.

After an hour or so they found the tunnel entrance, and they sneaked in exactly as they had before, even encountering a resurrected form of the giant spider they'd already killed. They defeated it easily enough and moved on, finally entering the first of the secret passageways into the keep itself. It was quiet. It was dreadfully quiet.

They cleaned themselves up and dressed quickly and in silence, abandoning their ruined clothing in favor of fresh tunics and breeks they'd managed to scavenge from the enemy campsite. Not exactly the first water of fashion, but at a glance, they could pass for a group of Alander's mercenaries. And that half second was all they'd need to dispatch anyone who spotted them.

The quiet in the castle got more and more unnerving as they moved through its walls. There should have been something: a lovers' tryst, a servants' quarrel, a whispered conversation between plotting courtiers. The clatter of pots and preparations in the kitchens below, at least. But there was nothing but the raw wind whispering through the seemingly empty corridors, and the distant scent of blood. Raf and Tazira exchanged a concerned glance, but didn't dare even to whisper the observation. The Guards made their way to the listening space between the gallery and the great hall, and Tazira peered down into the crack between the floorboards.

"Shards," she hissed. "I was afraid of something like this!"

"What is it?" Raf whispered.

She shrugged. "Have a look for yourself. But I warn you, it's not pretty."

That turned out to be an understatement.

Even nominally prepared for the sight, he gasped. Everyone in the castle was dead; he'd already guessed that much. Vesh—it had to be Vesh. But he didn't see how a single wizard could manage quite that much devastation. Courtiers and soldiers alike had been crushed like insects, smashed against the walls, perhaps two or three dozen of them in all. Many of them had been torn limb from limb, probably before they'd been allowed to die. Those who still had faces had died with uniform expressions of terror and anguish. Raf's claws splayed reflexively, and he growled low in his throat. Not even traitors should have to die like that.

Oh, Light . . . *one of them was still moving* . . .

With an inhuman yowl, Raf bolted out of the crawl space, leaving the others to follow him. He led them down through the abandoned kitchens, across the gallery and into the great hall. Pellar froze at the sight and growled low in his throat before he recovered himself. And Jain paled with intense sympathy and started checking some of the less brutalized victims for signs of life.

Illana Osska was beyond hope. She'd been nailed to her throne at the wrists, elbows, knees, and ankles, and her torturer had finally buried a warhammer in her skull when he'd tired of the sport. A hideous end to a brief and bitter life, one in which she'd probably never known a moment's honest contentment, for all her obvious and lavishly displayed wealth. He closed her eyes as gently as he could and swept her hair over the gaping head wound. She would probably have taken a farm boy's pity as the final insult, but she had it, nonetheless.

"Jain!" Raf called to him from across the room, breaking the course of his thoughts. He wandered over a bit absently, half convinced he had to be dreaming all this. Raf was kneeling over Daman Najendra, who was twitching slightly. *Still alive?*

Jain knelt down and hastily felt for a pulse at the man's throat. It was there—faint, but there. Raf had ripped a tapestry off the wall and was using it to try to stop the bleeding, but it was unlikely to help. The floor around them was a pool of the man's blood already.

Jain's healing stone glowed faintly in his pocket, a cool, reassuring presence in a sea of blood and savaged flesh. It was Najendra's only hope now. His enemy's only hope, and the end of Jain's life in the Guard.

A life for a life, Raf had said to him after Lucian, though this wasn't what he'd meant. A life for a life for a life, Najendra's life for Lucian's death. Najendra would never have done as much for him, he knew. And, somehow, it didn't matter a damn. Here it was, he realized dimly, the ultimate fusion of the warrior and the healer, an opportunity for redemption that might never come again.

Heal your enemy. Do it. Now.

The voice was his, and not his. The voice belonged to him, to every teacher he'd ever had and every teacher he had still to encounter. *Do it, Jain.* The healing stone glowed, fiercely, insistently, and this time the force of it wouldn't be denied. It was in his hand, and the energies were rushing through him as the stone fired.

All his power sharpened and intensified, became a spear's point seeking Najendra's life force. It was there, a dim, raw, vital essence, humorous, cynical, clever. Fading. Death was dragging him relentlessly, hungrily, toward the precipice, and if he was allowed to tumble off, no healer could pull him back. If that happened, and Jain didn't or couldn't disengage, he'd die with Najendra. No one had ever told him that, but he sensed it instinctively.

Reaching out with everything he had, he bound the wizard to him with tendrils of white energy, pulling him slowly and steadily back to consciousness, pain, and the light. He could feel the other man's fear rush him in an overwhelming wave, and he let it wash over and through him, leaving no mark.

In this place, he was unafraid. He knew this place, knew the satisfaction of cheating death and dancing away unscathed. Not forever, but for now, and for every day he could. For every soul he could. Here, there was triumph, and sweet, limitless power, and confidence that must never quite become arrogance. There was silence and peace and a tempting end to pain. There was no regret, here. Fighting past his own sudden and terrible longing, he pulled Najendra back and away, back from the precipice, back from the darkness.

The light gradually surrounded them and flooded through them, and sounds began to return. The soft murmured conversation of his friends, their worry. Scents: the sweet, faint perfume of Tazira's soft fur. She must have been holding him. Jain's eyelids fluttered open, and he gasped, his body fighting against the shock of a near-death experience. Najendra breathed deeply and evenly beside him, still unconscious, but very much alive. His wounds had closed. Jain closed his eyes and breathed a long, flooding sigh of relief.

"How do you feel, Jain?" Raf asked him gently.

"Like the morning after a three-day liberty," the human admitted. His voice was weaker than he'd expected it to be. Raf's whiskers arched in wry amusement, and Tazira laughed aloud with joy and relief. "Am I . . . am I still a Guard?" the boy asked hesitantly. Tazira and Raf exchanged a look he didn't quite understand, and then she smiled at them both.

"Private, as far as I'm concerned, you're a Guard for as long as you want to be," she said, a shade of Haymarket stubbornness lacing her voice. "If you ever decide to leave us and pursue the healers' art, well, it ought to be your choice and nobody else's." She nodded firmly, agreeing with herself, and for once Raf didn't argue with her.

They were willing to let him stay. Thank the Light, they were willing to let him stay. Jain was too exhausted to bellow his excitement as he wanted to, so he settled for a contented sigh.

His head, he noticed, was being cradled in Tazira's lap. Ordinarily he would have teased Raf and Pellar about his luck, but for the moment, all he wanted to do was sleep for about a hundred years. He closed his eyes, giving in to the temptation.

"That's right, son," Tazira purred. "Just lie still for a few minutes while we figure out what to do from here."

"What's to do?" Jain rasped, opening his eyes again. "We find the seal and get back to Tycor. Mission's over. The conspirators are either dead or scattered."

"Oh, I wish it was that simple, Private, I really

do." Tazira laughed mirthlessly. "Can you lift your head enough to get a good look at where I'm pointing?" He complied, though he'd had an easier time lifting fifty-pound bales of hay. His eyes followed the gleaming tip of her claw to a corpse about ten feet away. A corpse much, much too large to be human.

"Shards and ashes," he whispered dully, the shock not quite registering yet. "Ogres. How did they get in past the wards?"

"You got me, son." Tazira shrugged. "That's what we've got to find out. Wards are all that's kept the monsters from overrunning Delos completely, and if they don't work anymore . . . well, this just got a whole lot bigger than seals and conspiracies. This just became a potential threat to humanity. It might not be as damaging as it looks, but I wouldn't bet a week's rations on that."

"Indeed," Raf concurred with a sour downward arch of his whiskers.

There didn't really seem to be a whole lot left to say, after that revelation. They lapsed into a grim and thoughtful silence, and after a moment Pellar burst back into the room.

"What did you find?" Tazira asked him sharply.

"Sorry it took me so long, Captain. I had to dig one of the Catseyes out of its casing and show it to you."

Pellar sounded breathless, and Jain didn't think it was just because he'd been running. The boy struggled to lift his head again, and he looked over at the wardstone in Pellar's hand. It was blackened, burned, cracked. Useless. Someone, or something, had used magic to fry it. It no longer looked remotely like a Catseye, or any other type of stone.

"Shards," Raf and Tazira breathed together. For once, they were both too distracted to quibble over who owed whom an ale.

"Any sign of Vesh?" she asked.

"None. And no sign of any of the guards I could specifically identify as his, from the initial surveillance we did outside the keep. But there are fresh tracks outside the postern gate. Probably about twenty men, though it's impossible to tell, really. I'd guess that Vesh did his worst here, and now he's moving on."

"To Tycor?"

"Probably," Pellar nodded. "That was the direction they were headed in, at any rate."

"He could be headed to Tycor with those mysterious armies of his, or he and his men may simply have beat a fast retreat," Tazira murmured thoughtfully, tapping a single translucent claw against her cheek. "We won't know until Najendra comes to and we get some answers out of him. Can you wake him up, Jain? Kid?"

Jain had long since passed out from exhaustion.

Chapter 12

THE MONSTERS WERE COMING. HE FELT them coming for him in their thousands, thirsting mindlessly for his blood and the blood of his city. The wards would no longer protect it. He felt the creatures, waves of them, leagues and legions that stretched as far as the eye could see. And beyond them all, another presence, scrabbling, chitinous, malicious, and infinitely, exquisitely patient. Watching. Suddenly it was aware of him, a fly in the artfully arranged web of a spider. Curious, and curiously exultant, it turned to study its prey more closely . . .

Jain bolted upright with an incoherent cry. Raf was instantly beside him, quieting him, and pressing his damp forehead to check for fever. The human took a few deep, ragged breaths to shake off the dream. *A dream, that's all it was*, he told himself. Even in his own mind, that sounded hollow. He wanted to tell Raf about it, but decided it was a stupid idea. Just a dream, and one best kept to himself.

"Where am I?" he asked after a brief hesitation.

"We put you and Najendra in what I assume must have been Illana's room," Raf responded calmly. Jain glanced around him and decided the mrem was probably right. It was a large, light, airy chamber with graceful lilanthwood furnishings and brightly woven tapestries. The portieres and counterpane were a sumptuous royal white silk velvet; the material alone would have cost more than most families saw in a decade. Everything about the room smacked of indolence, luxury, exquisite taste, and an utter disregard for the suffering of the common run. In its own way, the room was a defiance of the Fall. It was beautiful in a way that nothing was beautiful anymore— nothing anyone of Jain's social class was privileged to see, at any rate.

In both its complacent selfishness and its beauty, this had clearly been Illana's chamber.

Najendra, he noticed, had been summarily tossed into a soft-looking white armchair by the fireplace, where he still dozed fitfully. *Probably having worse nightmares than I did*, Jain thought to himself. He couldn't quite bring himself to pity the man, though, not after all the trouble he'd caused them.

"How long was I out?" Jain asked Raf after a moment.

"Oh, about eight hours," the mrem smiled at him.

"Eight hours!"

"You needed to rest and recover. We all did."

"But Vesh's armies—"

"Might not even exist," Raf finished for him, cutting him off as abruptly as Tazira usually did.

"There's a rogue wizard on the loose, and we want to apprehend him, but right now we need to focus on the problem with the wards. Unless Najendra wakes up and informs us these two problems are related, we might just have to settle for letting Vesh go, for the moment."

Jain nodded, seeing no sense in arguing. Raf was right; everything hinged on Najendra's confession. Pellar chose that moment to appear in the doorway.

"Jain!" he called brightly. "You're awake! How do you feel, lad?"

"Alive," Jain said, smiling back at him. "Beats the alternative." That, of course, made him think instantly of Lucian, and his smile faded abruptly.

"So I've heard," Pellar concurred breezily and a bit absently, glancing around the sumptuous chamber. "Oh, will you *look* at that counterpane! And those curtains! You won't be needing these anymore," the mrem informed him stoutly, snatching up the coverlet and beginning to fold it. "I'm claiming these before Tazira gets her grabby paws on them."

"Don't tell me you and Tazira have been ransacking the castle," Raf groaned in a pained voice, holding his suddenly aching head in his hands.

"All right, I won't tell you," Pellar shrugged good-naturedly. "But if we didn't put a few things in that crawl space for storage—just to preserve them, mind you—the local Blackstone farmers would eventually come and strip the castle bare. It's simple human nature. All we're trying to do is preserve the beauty of—"

"Yes, yes, all right," Raf cut him off with a long-suffering sigh. Jain couldn't help but laugh, in spite of his mood. The noble Raf would never dream of stripping a castle like this, but to the romantic, luxury-loving Pellar and the earthy, practical Tazira, it was clearly irresistible. Jain might have been tempted to set a few things aside himself—after all, he'd never be able to afford any of this on a Guardsman's pay—but the fact that their previous owners had died such a hideous death would likely keep him from enjoying anything he might have taken. In a few years, when he was as inured to death as the Furies, he just might feel differently about that. He might feel differently about a lot of things, including Lucian.

"When do you think we can safely roust Najendra?" Pellar asked Jain, changing the subject as he took the curtains down and folded them.

"We should probably try it soon." The human frowned thoughtfully. "If Vesh was the one responsible for frying the wards and letting the ogres in here, we'll want to be after him before he gets too much farther ahead of us. But Najendra still looks pale. We have no idea what he must have lived through, or what Vesh might have done to torture him. I want to let him sleep for another hour, if you think we can spare it."

Raf and Pellar exchanged a glance, then nodded.

"Another hour," Raf agreed. "After that, we really need to bring him around."

"Understood," Jain said crisply.

"Well, I'm off." Pellar bowed, taking up his ill-gotten gains. "Time to go stand a watch for Tazira before she keels over from exhaustion."

"Are you telling me the woman *still* hasn't slept?" Raf yowled angrily.

Pellar shrugged. "She slept a little, but she looks like she could use a bit more, and in a comfortable bed for a change."

Raf nodded, more calmly. "Do me a favor and relieve her. Knock her over the head if you have to, but see that she sleeps. I'll be here keeping an eye on the wizard."

Pellar grinned, shouldered the curtains and counterpane, and saluted the other mrem broadly. He made his way toward the door and stopped dead in his tracks about halfway across the room. "Oh, I'm an idiot!" he exclaimed suddenly, startling the others. Raf's ears flattened, and his thin gray tail flicked before he calmed it.

"Sorry. I just figured it out," Pellar explained sheepishly. "The answer to the riddle."

"Wonderful!" Jain beamed. "What is it?"

"You know, I don't think I want to tell you," the mrem said ruefully after a brief bout with indecision. "It's just too horrible. I'll see you later." He waved, dashing off in a hasty escape. Jain laughed softly, shaking his head.

Raf shrugged. "I suppose we'll find out eventually."

"I suppose we will," Jain agreed, "though if it's as bad as he's making it out to be, we might not want to know."

"Jain, you're going to find that *nothing* is either as good or as bad as Pellar makes it out to be. He's a romantic, and just a bit prone to exaggeration."

"If you say so, I'll trust you on it." Jain smiled.

"You knew I was a healer, after all, without my ever telling you. How did you find me out?"

Raf leaned back in his cane-backed bedside chair, closed his eyes, and thought for a moment.

"It was little things," he said at last. "Your compassionate streak, your perceptiveness . . . and there was something that nagged me about the way you patched up that merchant we met on the road. You did a perfectly good job with those stitches, but the whole time, you looked guilty. Either you hated the thought of causing him pain, or you thought you should have been doing more. And either way—"

"I *should* have been doing more," Jain admitted grimly. "The man might lose partial use of that hand because I was selfish, because I wanted a life in the Guard so badly—"

"Jain, that man can count himself shardblessed to be alive. Anything beyond that is an added bonus."

"Not that he seemed particularly grateful."

"No, a lot of them don't, really," Raf sighed. "But we still do what we have to."

"Why?" a voice asked them from across the room. Najendra. They turned slowly to face him, embarrassed that he'd awakened without their noticing, but determined not to show that. The wizard seemed to be completely recovered from his injuries and looked the perfect picture of calm self-possession in spite of his ruined robes.

"Why what?" Jain asked him coolly.

"Why bother? Why bother healing me, for example? I set you all up for assassination, I stole your precious seal, and I made it possible for a mad wizard to claim the throne of Tycor. I assure you," Najendra said dryly, "I wasn't worth saving."

"What say we start from the beginning and get through this as quickly as possible?" Raf sighed, considering him carefully. "It'll go a lot easier on all of us if you cooperate."

"I have every intention of doing so. I never thought things would go this far, and because of me . . . well, as you say, let's start at the beginning. Vesh was exiled, you may recall, and for months we didn't hear from him. I didn't much care one way or the other. As a spy, I'd made myself privy to the details of that first plot, but I hadn't been stupid enough to take part in it." The wizard shook his head ruefully.

"Very sensible," Raf agreed. "So why take part in this one?"

"I'm coming to that."

"Eventually."

"Anyway," Najendra sighed with a perfect expression of martyrdom, "Vesh reestablished contact with us about three months ago. He'd been traveling in the Badlands, and he claimed to have had some great spiritual revelation there. He's certainly gained a great deal of power, more than I would have imagined possible, but as to the nature of the spiritual revelation, he managed to be vague and grandiose at the same time."

"It seems to be a common failing among wizards," Raf said dryly.

"Do you mind?" Najendra regarded him with a raised eyebrow.

"Not particularly, no."

"Right," the wizard muttered, "back to selling

out my fellow conspirators. Vesh mentioned something about a creature called the Dark who approached him and gave him all that power in exchange for his service, his soul, the usual."

"The Dark?" Jain asked quietly. Something about that sent a chill down his spine, in spite of the late summer warmth.

"I think that was it. Why, does it sound familiar? I'd never heard of it."

"Raf, I think we need to talk," the boy murmured. "Later."

Raf nodded, eyeing him quizzically, but saying nothing. Jain tried to force the details of his dream from his mind and focus on Najendra, but it was difficult. He had dreamed of a great presence behind it all, malicious, subtle, weaving plots for its own amusement—plots that would take generations to cultivate. Jain shuddered and forcibly banished those thoughts for the moment.

"So, Vesh approached me with an offer," Najendra was saying. "A new conspiracy. At first, I let myself be drawn in so that I could be privy to the details of the plot. Spies really do need to know these things. Vesh was tight with his secrets, and the more I wanted to know, the further in I had to let myself be drawn. Finally, he ordered me to steal the Great Seal and pass it on to Lucian Alander. And I was to fashion a ring capable of tracking it.

"According to Vesh, the whole plot was intended to take out Romney's close support structure, and we expected him to send the Furies. You were supposed to walk into an ambush no one could possibly hope to survive, except, of course, that you did survive. He never bothered to check on that, by the way. If he has one great weakness, it's that he believes himself and all his plans to be infallible."

"We'd noticed that," Raf arched his whiskers. "So, you planned on weakening Romney and Tycor by taking out his support structure. A good way to keep him off balance. Logical enough."

"Thank you."

"I didn't say it was admirable; I said it was logical. So, next you came here in the company of Vesh and his guards, only to find that the seal was being put to a different purpose than they told you they'd intended. And faced with the prospect of being a party to mass murder, you rebelled."

"How did you know that?"

"I'm damnably clever; ask anyone." The mrem shrugged. "So what happened after you voiced your noble objections?"

"They *were* rather noble, weren't they?" Najendra inquired ironically. "After that, Vesh tortured me. Jolt spells. Lightning spells. After a while, I lost track." He paled, losing his sardonic air for a moment. Jain actually pitied him; he'd made a terrible mistake, and clearly paid a price for it.

"He promised me power like his, if I followed him, and something much, much worse than death if I didn't," Najendra continued quietly. "I agreed to do whatever he wanted, and he released me. I never said I was brave. I would have promised him a year of nights with my sisters, just to make the pain stop."

"You were brave enough to question him in the

first place." Jain shook his head. "I didn't hear anyone else doing that."

"Stop, you'll turn my head with flattery," Najendra drawled. "I'm a coward, my friend, and unlike most people I have a refreshing lack of illusions about that. So, I screamed my fool head off, sobbed, promised him anything, and he released me. Afterwards I actually tried to tell myself I'd been pretending to be cowed, but I have to be honest. I *was* cowed. You will be, too, if you're fool enough to follow him."

"Perhaps after you're finished debasing yourself and confessing your cowardice to the world at large, you'll be kind enough to return to the point and tell us what happened next," Raf suggested archly.

"I like him," Najendra said to Jain. "He's unkind. A bit stuffy, but definitely unkind."

"I'm gratified that I meet with your approval." The mrem drawled. "Now, moving on, what did you do next?"

"I staggered back to the great hall. There just didn't seem to be anything better to do. The courtiers were there, whispering to each other, and a few of them pumped me for details of the torture session. They wanted to know what I'd meant when I'd said Vesh's armies might not exist. Well, I still wondered about his armies, but I no longer doubted his power. Just as I was saying that to my rapt audience, Vesh stormed back in. He had a servant summon Illana and all her palace guards. She came in a few minutes later, understandably miffed, and they threw temper tantrums back and forth at each other. It was amusing right up to the point where he summoned the ogres."

Raf actually coughed in shock. "He *summoned* them? A human mage *summoned* ogres? No human would do that!"

"I'm not so sure he's human anymore," Najendra shuddered. "Whatever he is, he's a wizard capable of summoning ogres, and actually willing to do it. He told us our only option was to follow him to Tycor, and to a man we refused. Deposing Romney was one thing, but unleashing monsters on a defenseless human population was another. Even I wouldn't countenance that. I threw my lot in with them, and Vesh turned the ogres on us. Not too surprising, but definitely unfortunate. I didn't even acquit myself particularly well. I killed one with a flame strike, but the next one flattened me with his club. All the magic in the world won't save you from an unsympathetic ogre who's faster than you are. Maybe I should have taken up the sword, instead."

"Maybe you should have," Raf agreed. "It might have kept you out of mischief."

"And miss all this entertainment?" Najendra sighed lavishly. "Not in a million. Not to mention the fact that wizardry pays better. So, there's my story in its simplest form. I had an unexpected attack of nobility and was clubbed for my pains. You found me under the club, healed me, shards know why, and here I am. Next, I suppose, you'll need to decide what to do with me. Actually"— he hesitated for a brief second—"I'd like to come with you."

"You'd *what?*" Raf sputtered, completely taken

aback. Of all the strange turns this story could have taken . . .

"If I hadn't stolen the seal, none of this would have happened. I need to find Vesh and undo the damage I've done, preferably before he gets to Tycor."

"Actually, you didn't do that much," Jain pointed out helpfully. "The seal's still here in the castle, and everything else that happened probably would have happened with or without you—"

"Hush up, boy," Tazira said a bit tensely from the doorway. She and Pellar entered, taking up standing positions just inside the door. Their weapons were unsheathed, and they both looked fully ready to kill. Najendra paled and sank back in his chair. "What makes you think I want to take a wizard with me?" she asked mockingly, favoring him with a piercing gaze.

"I could be useful," Najendra offered. "You'll need a wizard when you move against Vesh."

"Oh, I dunno," she murmured, carefully considering Black Bessie's razor edge. "Brute strength seems to have taken *you* down just fine."

"I'm not V-Vesh," he stammered. "And I have a lot to make up for."

"You certainly do. But I can't trust you, boy. And I'm not taking a wizard I can't trust along with my soldiers. If you really want to do something useful, go back to Amar and warn your queen about Vesh. Then, if *she's* feeling useful, maybe she'll send along a few troops to help us wipe out his armies."

"But I still don't know if he has any actual armies—"

"He has 'em," she said firmly. "Bank on it. The only question is, when are they gonna round on Amar? You're the closest city-state to Tycor. Once he finishes his conquest of Tycor, I'd imagine he'll move on to the next target. You. And your wards won't protect you anymore."

"But the wards . . ." The wizard came to a halt, thinking.

"How did the ogres get past the wards, Najendra?" Tazira asked him quietly.

"I honestly don't know. I hadn't even thought about it. I'd assumed that since Vesh summoned them—"

"The Catseyes were burned out," she cut him off. Jain was privately, quietly, and maliciously delighted to see her doing that to someone besides him. "Show him, Pellar."

Pellar pulled the cracked wardstone out of his pouch, and Najendra whistled appreciatively.

"You see why solving this takes precedence even over the pleasure of slitting your lying throat?" She smiled. It wasn't a pleasant smile.

"Yes, I see," Najendra breathed. "That's why you should take me with you."

Tazira rolled her eyes in exasperation. "Look, kid, we've been over this already—"

"I know, I know, you don't trust me. And I can't think of a single reason you should. But if there's something out there capable of frying wardstones, that's a threat to humankind, and when last I looked, I was a human."

"Debatable, but I'll let it go."

"Thank you. Yes, we have personal and political differences; yes, I set you up to be assassinated—

my job, you understand; nothing personal—yes, I'm a spy, and you don't like spies."

"You're damn right," she growled, her tail thumping an ominous tattoo against the door.

"We're not all terrible people," he chided her. "Isn't that right, Pellar?"

"I'm sure I have no idea what you mean." Pellar sniffed haughtily, giving Najendra a long, quelling look. The wizard let the matter drop without any further explanation, and went back to groveling.

"Anyway, my point is, I need to solve this problem as badly as you do. And I'm going after Vesh, with or without you. Wouldn't it be easier to keep me under your eye than to be constantly wondering where I was?"

"In that outfit? I wouldn't have to wonder," Tazira snorted, rolling her eyes at his heavily gold-trimmed dark blue silk gown. "If you do come with us—and I'm sayin' *if*—you ain't wearin' that."

"No, ma'am."

"And I'll be holding on to your spellstones, for safekeeping."

"Of course."

"And if you disobey or choose to ignore a single order I give you, I'll tear your guts out."

"Completely understandable."

"And you get to be on clean-up detail."

"Perfectly acceptable."

In tribute to his easygoing submission to her dictates, she was unable to think of any further concessions to gouge out of him.

"All right," she growled, "we can argue it out on the road. Go find yourself something decent to wear, and we'll see what we can do about freeing the seal."

Najendra nodded, pushed himself up out of his chair with a quiet groan, and left the chamber. He still moved a bit stiffly, but there was nothing more Jain could do for him. Tazira watched him limp down the corridor for a moment before she turned her attention back to her men.

"Jain, do you think you're ready to move?" Tazira asked him briskly. He nodded, and she smiled. "Good to have you back among the living, Private. How about the riddle? Any solutions yet?"

"I think I have it," Pellar admitted sheepishly, "though, I'll warn you, it's bad. It's really bad."

"I love you, dear," she purred at him.

"I know," he preened, fluffing his ivory fur proudly.

"Are you sure it's the solution? You know what's supposed to happen if you're wrong . . ."

"I know." He shrugged. "I'm sure enough that I'm willing to take the risk."

She nodded, wanting to talk him out of it, but realizing that they really didn't have much of a choice.

Wordlessly they followed Tazira down to the great hall. The bodies were gone, the walls and floors scrubbed clean.

"When did you do all this?" Pellar asked his captain, instinctively knowing she must have taken care of it all.

"You were on sleep shift." She smiled wanly. "I didn't do much, just piled the bodies, said a few words, and brought a fire shield down over them."

"And when do *you* go on sleep shift?" Raf asked her, trying to keep his tone light and not succeeding.

"I'll sleep when I'm dead," she chided him.

"Keep saying that, Intensity Lass, and it'll be here before you know it."

"I know, dear. But I don't have time to sleep just now. And speaking of not having time for anything . . . Pellar, if you're sure you're up to it, we should pick up the seal and get out of here. The casket is over there, behind the throne."

Pellar nodded wordlessly and knelt before the casket. It was unprepossessing, to say the least. Actually, it was downright ugly, a small, dull hammered-steel chest about the size of a footstool. There were no markings anywhere, but it glowed faintly and ominously with a malignant sense of purpose. The light around it reddened and shimmered, and Pellar nervously touched the lid with a single translucent claw tip. A silvery, feminine voice—Illana's voice—responded.

By the Triune Suns I speak it: I can hold, but never touch it, the voice crooned. Tazira shivered and dug her claws into her palms, praying to long-forgotten gods to give her friend luck. She approached him softly, steadily, climbing the three steps to stand beside the heavy creothwood throne. If he failed, maybe she could pull him out. Maybe.

"A breath," Pellar responded a bit shakily, half expecting to be charbroiled on the spot. There was a long moment when all he could do was listen to the sound of his own heart pounding. A single bead of sweat trickled down his forehead and into his eyes. He didn't move. Slowly . . . painfully slowly . . . the heavy lid creaked open. Tazira breathed a heavy sigh of relief and started forward.

"You know," Pellar said shakily, "I'm not sure whether to be relieved or ashamed that I knew the answer to that."

"*I'm* relieved," Tazira growled, embracing him just to assure herself of his solidity. He purred his own relief and licked her cheek affectionately.

Raf and Jain pocketed the spellstones they'd been preparing, just in case, and joined Pellar and Tazira on the dais. They all peered cautiously into the casket.

The Great Seal was inside—at least, after all this trouble, Jain bloody well *hoped* that was what it was. The maybe-seal was a hand-sized, clever contraption of some silvery metal, probably steel or aluminum. It had small black rubber wheels on it, and the wheels had numbers on them. The numbers could shift as the wheels did.

"That's it?" Jain asked, a little disappointed.

"I'm afraid so, kid," Tazira grumbled, smiling in spite of herself. "A date stamper. Sure is an elegant symbol of power, ain't it?"

"A who stamper?"

"A date stamper." Pellar shrugged, almost defensively. It might not look like much, but it was still a symbol of majesty and pre-Fall cunning, at least to the city he'd always called home. "You see, you've got these little wheels that—"

"Oh, I see," Jain interrupted, not even pretending to take an interest. "And people were really willing to heave Romney out on his ear if someone showed up and waved this date stamper around?"

Tazira nodded laconically. "Yup. Such is the ephemeral nature of power, son. And the vast majority of Tycorans really are that dangerously attached to the artifacts of a softer and easier past. It's something you'll need to understand and accept, if you're gonna spend your life protecting 'em."

Jain nodded pensively and glanced down into the box again. "What's that?" he asked, pointing to a rolled slip of parchment wrapped in a red ribbon. Pellar removed it gingerly, touching it only with his claws. Nothing happened, so he put his gauntlets on and took the risk of unfurling it.

" 'Smash, strike, stab . . .' " Jain began to read it, frowning thoughtfully.

"Not out loud!" Pellar cautioned him in a hasty whisper, almost as if the parchment could hear him. *Well, maybe it could, at that,* Jain thought. He continued to read the rest of the list to himself silently: *smash, strike, stab, sally, scar, scuffle, seize, shackle, shame, shock, suck, swarm . . .*

"Kinky," Tazira drawled after a moment. "What is it?"

"You got me," Pellar murmured. "Anyone else?" Raf shrugged an elegant disclaimer, and Jain looked at him blankly. "Passwords to something, I'd guess," Pellar concluded.

"That, or the latest dance steps for vampires,"

Tazira said dryly. "Keep it; it seems harmless enough.

"But what is it?" Jain frowned, devoured by curiosity.

"I suspect we'll never know, kid. If life has taught me one thing, it's that there are a lot more questions than answers out there." The captain sighed, draping an arm around his shoulders. For once, her claws were sheathed.

Chapter 13

TAZIRA CALLED A HALT TO THEIR LIGHT
run, and Najendra fell gasping to his knees on the
broad dirt path. Wheezing somewhat melodramatically, he crawled to a shady spot beneath a
large tree; the lush forest terrain hadn't yet given
over to the next shift. Raf and Pellar took off in
opposite directions to scout the woods on either
side of the road. The wizard fumbled for his waterskin and downed his drinking water in hasty
gulps. After a few seconds, Tazira walked over to
him and snatched it away.

"Don't waste it, Najendra," she snapped, holding
up the skin in front of him. "It's fresh well water. Difficult to come by, this far out in the provinces. And
the next terrain shift could be desert. You can have
this once you've got your breath back, and you can
drink it more slowly, savoring every precious drop,"
she smiled wickedly, taking a luxuriant swig from her
own waterskin. She licked her black whiskers in obvious and somewhat overplayed enjoyment.

"You're a cruel woman, do you know that?"
Najendra informed her in pained tones.

"I try," she purred with a particularly feral grin. Najendra's breathing finally slowed a bit, and she tossed him his waterskin and turned to Jain. She found him sitting on a broad, flat gray stone, in the shade of another tree. "How you holding up, son?" she asked him, dropping down to her knees beside him.

"Not too bad," he said, and for a change he actually meant it. The running wasn't killing him. And if he had any doubts about the matter, he had only to look at Najendra to feel like the pinnacle of human fitness. The wizard was lying down on the road, spread-eagled, the waterskin draped over his face to shield him from the suns and from the cruelty of mrem. Jain tried to hide a smirk at the sight, and didn't succeed.

"You feel good enough for your next combat lesson?" Tazira grinned up at him.

"Always," Jain said cheerfully.

"You're mad, both of you," Najendra moaned, and his words were muffled by his waterskin. "It's much too hot to do anything but expire gracefully."

She shrugged indifferently. "Don't let us stop you."

"That was unkind, Captain," the wizard protested.

"It was, wasn't it?" She smirked, suddenly much more cheerful for having insulted someone. "Now, Jain, I think we'll start you off today with the basics. Simple hand-to-hand combat."

"There's probably nothing simple about it," Jain quipped.

"That's where you're wrong, son. Unarmed combat is *about* simplicity. An attacker strikes, presenting you, in the simplest possible terms, with a problem. As you learn forms, blocks, and counterstrikes, you'll find that the best solutions to those problems are usually basic ones. There's nothing I like better than a showy, overconfident opponent; they're easier to take down than most novices."

"Why?" Jain couldn't help asking.

"Try launching another kick at my head, kid, and I'll show you." She winked. "But in all seriousness, novices can be more dangerous because they're harder to read. You don't know exactly what they're going to do, and for that matter, neither do they. An awful lot of embarrassing training accidents happen when novices get overenthusiastic."

"Why bother learning at all, then?"

"If you learn right, the skills will serve you well for a lifetime. But in some ways, you're better off not learning at all than you would be if you learned wrong. In the beginning, see, I learned wrong. I was trained by a warrior who'd given up the life and retired to Haymarket to farm. He taught me all sorts of high kicks and flying leaps. They looked great, and they probably would have gotten me hammered if I'd ever used them in actual combat. In the real world of 'we could bloody die out here' battle, you want to go with simpler, faster choices that don't put you as far off balance. You don't want to risk anything more than a short, sharp waist-high kick unless you're willing to bet your life on being able to get away with a higher one. And as for a flying kick, forget it. When you're in the air, you have no balance, and minimal ability to shift. You've just eliminated

ninety percent of your choices and made it easy
for an opponent to sweep you.

"Mercifully, instead of finding all that out the
hard way, I joined the Guard, and Raf, my first
sergeant, took me aside and completely retrained
me. That first night we met you, when he said
he'd taught Pellar and me everything we know,
he wasn't kidding. He really did."

"She only admits it when I'm not around." Raf
sighed melodramatically, emerging from the trees
to stand beside Tazira.

"Say, what's that down there on the path?" She
smirked, peering down at the dirt road with comically exaggerated interest. "Looks like the tiniest
acting troupe on Delos is playing out your life as
an ancient tragedy."

"Well, *someone* should, damn it," he sniffed, the
amused arch of his whiskers belying his wounded
tone. Jain barked a surprised laugh at both of
them.

Tazira smiled, throwing an arm around Raf's
waist affectionately, "Anyway, back to the boy's
lesson. A few days ago, Jain, Pellar started telling
you about the first spiral in the Masters' Wheel:
learning your own body, finding out what it can
do. You also need to find out what it *can't* do,
because that knowledge will allow you to disable
an opponent without killing him. I'll show you
exactly what I mean. Raf, you get to beat me up
today."

"Oh, good." The mrem grinned evilly down
at her.

"Knees, elbows, shoulders, and wrists all have
vulnerabilities that can be exploited," the captain

continued, studiously ignoring him. "They all have limited motion, and there are ways they aren't able to bend. For example, your elbows and knees don't bend backward or to the side. That makes it easy to lock an elbow, or sweep and take out a knee.

"If I go to grab Raf like this," she said, slowly bunching a solid handful of the front of his tunic in her right hand, "all he needs to do is take my hand, like this, twist it inward at the wrist, and my whole arm will follow it. Now he's got my elbow locked straight, and he's forcing it down, and I have no choice but to let my whole upper body go with that motion. From here, he's locked me in, and I'm pretty much immobile. I can't reach him to strike with my other arm. But he should force me all the way down to the ground, because if he doesn't, I can still take out his left knee with a good sharp kick."

Raf forced her to her knees, completing the motion, and gently let up the pressure on her arm. Pellar chose that moment to rejoin the group, and he smirked at the proceedings.

"Kinky," he pronounced cerebrally. Najendra snickered beneath his waterskin.

"I'm enjoying it," Raf smirked. "After all, I still owe her for shedding blood in my kitchen."

"Raf, I've already apologized for that about a hundred times," the woman growled a bit plaintively, picking herself up and dusting herself off.

"You shed blood in his kitchen?" Jain blinked innocently, sensing a good story there.

Raf nodded sagely. "Yes, and it wasn't hers. You see, I was hosting a small dinner party at my house in town and— Never mind," he concluded sheepishly as Tazira glared him into silence.

The captain sighed, grabbing her pack and strapping it over her shoulder. "I have a small, forlorn dream that someday, maybe, they'll let it drop, or at least stop writing songs about it and teaching them to the regiment—"

"Oh, we couldn't *possibly* do that," Pellar protested.

"Especially when it was all that Amaran warlord's fault, anyway." She bristled, glowering at her lieutenants. Her tail lashed impatiently. "He could've waited until I'd sobered up before he challenged me."

"Whatever you say, dear," Pellar smirked.

"Jain? Do me a favor, son. Don't ask about this one. Just don't even ask." Tazira sighed.

"But I'm sure Jain would *love* to learn a good campfire song," Pellar volunteered innocently.

"No songs. No singing. No humming. No whistling. That's an order. And *don't* ask, son." She growled at Jain, holstering her franciscas and starting off down the path again with an agitated lash of her tail. Jain shrugged and followed her, figuring that if there was something the irrepressible Tazira Goldeneyes was too embarrassed to talk about, it really probably was better not to ask . . . her.

The tracks led them down the path, league after league without ending. They ran when they could, and walked when the terrain allowed for nothing else. Jain was beginning to show the effects of exhaustion, and Najendra was periodically visiting roadside bushes and gracing them with dry heaves. Jain gave him a certain amount of credit for managing to keep up, actually; most people would have given up trying to follow the Guards, at the pace they were setting.

He couldn't say he liked Najendra, exactly, but he didn't entirely dislike the man, either. That odd combination of cynicism, selfishness, and self-effacing humor might even have had a certain charm, if Jain could have managed to overlook small details like seals and assassination attempts. Najendra was complex, and more difficult to read than anyone Jain had ever encountered. Odd, that the man was his fellow human in this adventure, and he had an easier time understanding the mrem.

Tazira came to a halt and knelt down to sniff the tracks in the road. The group slowed down behind her, finding logs, flat stones, or bare earth to collapse on. The terrain around them had shifted for the fourth time in the last hour, and they were relieved to find themselves in another forest, after the swamp, and the icy tundra before that. The trees were vast and golden, and the road was almost completely in their dappled shade.

Herbs and wildlife were plentiful here, and Tazira began to regret stopping off at that farmhouse off the road to buy potatoes and game hens. They were an unnecessary expense, as it turned out. But perhaps it was for the best; it would spare any of them having to hunt tonight. They'd managed to refresh their food supplies a bit at the castle keep, but Tazira still wanted a solid meal in them all after this day's running.

Najendra was busy being lavishly sick behind the nearest tree. Tazira couldn't manage even the slightest grain of sympathy, not that she was trying, really. They had to catch up with Vesh, and Vesh had half a day's journey on them. Less, now. Considerably less, she realized as she scented the tracks. At the rate he was moving, they'd catch up with him tomorrow. She began to study the tracks more closely.

About twenty humans, and an equal number of ogres, traveling together, as incomprehensible as she found that. They were taking their time; the footprints they left behind suggested they were walking, not running. They'd stopped often enough to mill about, forage and rest, but they didn't yet seem to be gathering numbers. Najendra might have been right to doubt the existence of Vesh's army. But, somehow, she just didn't expect any of their lives to be that simple.

Tazira listened to the labored breathing of the men around her, and decided to halt here for the night. It seemed to be as good a place as any, and she was as exhausted as they were. *Maybe more*, she admitted, but only to herself.

"We're getting close," she announced, taking them all in with her eyes. "We'll catch up with Vesh tomorrow—early afternoon by the look of it. I want to make camp here tonight. Raf, do you feel up to scouting a good campsite for us?" He nodded, picked up his staff, and disappeared into the brush. "Pellar, Jain, can you start plucking and gutting the game hens? I want to gather a few herbs, hopefully alanthe and imita, and then I really need to crash out under a bush for an hour or so before I start dinner."

"Do you want me to cook tonight?" Pellar offered.

"I'm tempted," she admitted. "You're a marvelous cook, and I'm wretchedly exhausted. But if I don't occupy myself with cooking tonight, I'll sleep so long that I won't be able to wake myself to eat. And this is the last solid meal we're likely to have before we engage Vesh."

Pellar nodded and started pulling the game hens out of one of the packs on the ground. "Can we afford longer sleep shifts tonight?" he asked a bit pointedly.

"Oh, yes," Tazira drawled. "As slowly as Vesh and his men are moving, we can afford to sleep until red dawn tomorrow. Tonight, your lazy old captain gets ten hours of unconsciousness, and I leave the rest of you to set shifts as you need 'em."

Without another word she pulled out a small knife and began foraging for herbs. Alanthe and imita both grew wild near the roadside, and charrh as well. Tonight's meal would be positively wonderful, if she could rouse herself long enough to cook and eat it. Tazira snorted and shook herself at that thought. *No pity banquets, my girl*, Romney's voice sounded in her head. *You'll feast and slumber like a lord tonight.*

I wonder if all captains talk to themselves in the voices of their old commanders, or if it's just me. I wonder if Jain, when he's captain, will hear my voice in his head at moments like these.

Now where in the name of the Triune Suns had *that* thought come from? Tazira shook herself with increasing irritation. She caught herself about to drift off to sleep while leaning against a tree, and began to realize with a little fear just how dangerously far she'd been pushing herself and the others. Tonight, she'd make damned sure they all slept. Swaying a bit on her feet—she assured herself it was only a bit—she made her way back to the roadside with her herbs. She fell instantly asleep under a bush near Najendra, and she was too exhausted to care for any of the dangers of that, magical or natural.

By the time Raf rousted her out from under the bush, the others had set up the campsite about fifty feet off the road, started a small fire, and set the hens roasting over it. Pellar's blanket was strung up a few feet over the open fire, to disperse the smoke to near invisibility from a distance. The potatoes were cooking in the small, lightweight, hammered-steel pot Tazira had scavenged from the castle keep.

She'd managed to pick up a few other things in the keep as well, and without a word she set to work with them, braising the hens lightly with honey butter and a good liqueur. A faint sprinkling of finely ground charrh finished them off; there was nothing left to do with them but let them broil. Jain set about turning the spit with all the earnestness and diligence he seemed to attach to everything.

Tazira added her herbs to the potatoes, along with a few clear drops of nolok for flavor. Attracted by the scents, Najendra came over to the fire and started poking through her herbs and jars.

Like a curious kit, he had to sniff out every one of them. Tazira sighed with irritation, but otherwise let it go. Finally, though, he started getting into the small bottle of liqueur, and without turning to look at him she smacked his hand away with her tail.

"But that's nolok," the wizard protested. "Aged at least twelve years in a creothwood barrel; I can tell just by smelling it. Dinner smells *very* good, by the way." He smiled, trying to soften her up. Tazira was a woman, and like other women, she was bound to be susceptible to flattery.

She disappointed him by snorting soft amusement at him and pulling the bottle away with her tail.

"For cooking purposes only, son," she drawled. "Until this mission is over, I don't want anyone's judgment clouded by drink." She set the bottle down next to her.

Pellar launched into a sprightly battle song about an Amaran warlord and a kitchen, and Tazira glared him into silence, her tail whipping around her wildly in a full semicircle.

"No singing," she growled.

"No singing," he agreed lightly, turning his attention back to sharpening his rapier.

Raf came down out of the tall tree he'd climbed to survey the territory. Tazira glanced up at him, smiled, and turned back to her cooking.

"Road's quiet," he announced. "Vesh and his men aren't visible yet, but that's just as well. If we could spot him, he might be able to do the same to us."

"And surprise is the one serious advantage we

have right now," Tazira murmured a bit absently, concentrating on salting and seasoning her hens. "Besides, I want one night of solid, uninterrupted sleep if I can get it. Was there anything else we should know about?"

"There was, actually." Raf frowned. "It might be nothing. But I saw what looked like stone giant tracks about half a league up the road. No idea how fresh they are, obviously, and they're headed in the other direction."

"Toward the city?" Tazira frowned. "That *is* strange. You don't often find them this close to Tycor Keep. Something else Vesh has summoned, maybe?"

"That, or something attracted to their stronger scents. Either way, it doesn't look like it'll be a problem tonight. Something to watch out for tomorrow, at worst."

Tazira nodded and let out a yawn she couldn't suppress. Her fur rippled as she stretched, and her claws splayed. She shook herself, peered at the hens almost suspiciously, and finally pronounced them done.

Pellar instantly appeared over her shoulder with the thin steel plates and started passing them out. Tazira doused the campfire, and Jain and Raf concentrated on burying it carefully before they all settled in to dinner. They propped themselves against rocks, trees, or their packs for as much comfort as they could provide themselves, and soon they were sprawled out lazily, contentedly enjoying the best meal they'd had in quite a while.

"If this is the usual fare for soldiers, I'm joining the Guard," Najendra said with a grin. "We don't eat this well at court. This really is wonderful, Tazira." He saluted, waving a drumstick at her.

"You're unduly kind, my boy. It was nothing at all," she lied pleasantly. Inwardly, of course, she was preening, but she wasn't about to let this shardblasted wizard think that she was even marginally susceptible to flattery. After all, he was plainly used to dealing with women who were.

"Nonsense, madam," he chided her. "Between cooking this and steering me away from the various pots and jars, you put a lot of effort into tonight's masterpiece. I thought you deserved a bit of fawning adulation."

There was nothing she could do but laugh and succumb gracefully to that overkill.

"So, Jain, what made a healer decide to join the Tycor Guard, if you don't mind my asking?" Najendra inquired lightly, obviously more for conversation than sincere curiosity. Jain thought about it for a second or two, then decided there was probably no harm in telling him everything. He already knew the worst.

"I grew up on a cotton farm in a small town called Uppervale." The boy shrugged, pausing to take another bite of his game hen. "Not much went on there, so I was weaned on stories of other places. The Tycor Guard, the Three Furies, flashing blades and high adventure."

"Cut it out, kid, you're embarrassing me," Tazira chuckled.

"Anyway," Jain continued, flushing a bit, "I've always known exactly what I wanted to be. I lived for it, trained for it, and everything I did went into preparing me for the day I'd finally leave home, head to Tycor, and join the Guard. Then, about two weeks ago, I found a spellstone out in the cotton fields. My first spellstone. You have no idea how excited I was. I took it straight to Elder Valerian, like you're supposed to. He studied it for a few minutes, and then he sort of laughed softly to himself and shook his head. It was a healing stone, he said."

"So you haven't known for very long that you could do this," Raf murmured thoughtfully.

Jain shook his head ruefully. "Not long at all. By way of a test, Valerian made me heal a neighboring farmer who'd been dying of nalakra. Needless to say, it worked, and my whole life began to change." He paused, thinking for a moment.

"Turns out it's not the stone that makes me a healer," he admitted, grimacing a bit. "The stone only works if you have the potential to use it, and I do. The stones are rare, and the people with the talent to use them are apparently just as rare. The elders wanted to ship me off to the monastery right away, but I bargained for a few days' time. My pa was gonna need to get someone to replace me in the fields, I said, and they agreed.

"That night, I packed up a few belongings in a bag, said good-bye to my family, and ran off to Tycor. I was planning on doing it as soon as I turned eighteen, anyway; this just speeded things up a bit."

The group fell thoughtfully silent for a moment, no one knowing exactly what to say to that.

"You have a remarkable gift, Jain," the wizard finally edged carefully into the silence. "To say nothing of the fact that I owe my life to it. Are you sure you want to waste it?"

"I have no intention of wasting it," Jain snapped. "But I also have no intention of letting anyone lock me away for what I can do. Valerian and the other elders tried to tell me that it was for 'my own good.' My own good . . . *shards*, I hate those words," he growled in exasperation. "I want the power to decide that for myself. No one else knows what's best for me. No one *can*. Sorry to get preachy on you, but it's an argument I've been having with myself every night for the last couple of weeks."

"No apologies," Najendra said smoothly, "unless I'm the one offering them."

"You win, Tazira," Raf said quietly.

"I understand rebellious teenagers better than you do, that's all," Tazira teased him. "I was one."

"No argument there," Raf agreed with the ghost of a smile, remembering.

"What does she win?" Jain asked, half curious and half defensive. Raf sighed, wondering whether or not he should tell the boy, and finally he decided it was best.

"The day Pellar took you off and cut your hair, Tazira and I had a talk about you," the mrem admitted. "I'd begun to suspect you might be a runaway healer. I told Tazira I thought she should discourage you from joining us; it's a dangerous life, and it's a rare and valuable gift you're putting at risk. But she argued with me that it was your life, your gift, and your choice. After a little thought, I agreed." He paused for a second, toying absently with a drumstick.

"I once told Varral Romney that all we are is the sum of our choices, some good, some regretted," he continued. "I believed it then, and I still believe it, and I almost made a terrible mistake in spite of that belief. If your power to make your own choices is removed or denied, you lose an essential part of your humanity. And that's far, far worse than anything else I could ever do to you."

"I couldn't have said it better myself," Tazira said with a grin, slurring a little from exhaustion. Raf draped an arm around her, and she rested her head against his shoulder. A few seconds later, she drifted off to sleep there. He propped himself up against the small boulder behind him, finding a position he could hold for a while, so as not to wake her.

"For my part," Najendra began a bit pretentiously, "I won't ever breathe a word to anyone about your talent. I'll just be grateful that you chose to use it on me, even if I'm still mystified by that."

Jain shook his head. "Don't be mystified. Just be worth it. Earn it, Daman. Someday, soon, I want you to be able to look at yourself in the mirror and tell yourself I did a good thing by saving you." His gaze was piercing. Najendra looked away, visibly unsettled.

"I won't breathe a word to anyone, either," Pellar assured Jain quietly. "But, then, I hope you already knew that."

The boy nodded. "Of course I did. Thank you, all of you. I don't know what else to say."

"Then sleep on it, lad." Pellar smirked. "It's

past time the four of you did that. I'll take first watch, since I slept last night."

"I'll take the second," Jain offered.

"Well enough," the mrem agreed, turning to climb the tall tree Raf had initially used to survey the terrain. It would give him an excellent vantage point from which to keep watch. Jain pulled out his blanket and was instantly unconscious, and Najendra collected the dishes and went to wash them in the stream, as he'd promised the captain he would.

Raf carefully pried his arm out from under Tazira, and she remained dead to the world. He brought back their blankets and laid them out quietly.

Not that I really need to worry about disturbing her, he realized with a sudden smirk. *An army of giant spiders with loud musical instruments wouldn't faze her right now.* He lifted her gently and rolled her blanket around her, astonished as always by how light she was. Tazira was so boisterous, so full of life, so damnably stubborn, she should have been as immovable as a boulder. There was something incongruous about her lightness. Something incongruous about how fragile she looked as she slept, all that drive and boundless energy stilled. Odd, how he'd never really noticed that before.

He'd noticed everything else about the way she slept, over the years. The slight determined frown that never faded from her brow, the breathing that almost but never quite became a snore, the nightmares that left her thrashing and mewing. But he'd never really seen her quiet and still like this. Awake, of course, she was anything but.

Shaking his head with a soft huff of quiet laughter, Raf lay down on his own makeshift pallet and closed his eyes. Tazira stirred in a dream and rolled closer to him, and he folded an arm around her gently, unable to resist the impulse. In her sleep, she purred.

Oh, I'm going to enjoy this, Jain thought gleefully. The whole camp was asleep beneath him, particularly the Tazira Goldeneyes part of it. He bounded down out of the tall tree, stretched out his aching muscles and watched the world come to life with the hazy radiance of red dawn.

Mornings, he decided, were wonderful things, as long as you'd stood second watch and were reasonably awake to see them. They were wonderful in direct proportion to how miserable you could make your comrades.

He saw to it that the dishes and his blanket were packed, and everything was as ready as he could/make it. Then, with a fierce grin, he took a deep breath and bellowed, "Wakey waaaaakey time, my lovelies!" His reward, he told himself, for all his hard work, and all those wonderful interrupted dreams.

Tazira cracked open her eyes and shot him a low-lidded, satisfying glower.

"I thought I heard a game cock crowing." She yawned, digging thin furrows into the earth with her claws. "But it's just an overzealous private who's looking to be busted back to KP. Let's go back to sleep." She flopped her head down onto Raf's chest and pretended to snore.

"What, and miss this lovely morning?" he sang

cheerfully, plucking the tousled blanket off her and rolling it up. "The red sun is dawning, a glorious death awaits us! I love the Guard! Every meal is a banquet fit for a lord! I'd say every pay sack is a fortune, but I've never actually gotten paid yet!" Tazira threw a boot at him, and he dodged it handily. "But who needs to get paid? I'd live this marvelous life of adventure for free!"

"I'm gonna remember the fact that you said that, Private, next time I stamp the expense chits," she drawled lazily.

"Is he always this insipidly cheerful?" Najendra groaned, pulling his blanket over his tousled dark head.

"Naw," Tazira muttered, "usually he's complaining about something. But I suppose I deserve this." She pulled herself to her feet and dusted herself off, grimacing a bit and wishing distantly for a bath and a change of clothes, which weren't going to happen. *If I survive long enough to see my house again, or even just my quarters in the Red Tower,* she promised herself, *I'm ordering up a bath. A hot one, scented with thahla petals. And I'm going to soak for an hour and a half, and read a trashy pre-Fall romance novel. Damn it.*

The thought was enough to warm her through the rest of a cold morning.

They downed a small bit of hardtack and ran for a few leagues, and the terrain shifted from golden forest to harsh white desert, and back to forest after a while. Najendra was lagging behind again and gracing the local landscape with dry heaves and half-consumed hardtack, but he was still doing an admirable job of keeping up with them, all things considered.

They finally came to a reasonably defensible hill position with heavy concealing brush, and Tazira held up one black-gloved hand and called the group to a halt. The wizard collapsed gratefully, too exhausted even to throw up anymore.

That was part of the captain's strategy, actually; she still didn't trust Najendra, and she didn't want a full-strength wizard changing sides on them in the heat of battle. Dealing with Vesh would be difficult enough, and if he truly had an army with him, it would be impossible. Either way, if Najendra chose to add his powers to that, Tazira and her men would be lucky if they were afforded the dignity of a grave site.

Najendra was a dangerous variable in a dangerous game. The only reason she was allowing him to follow her at all was that it truly was easier to keep an eye on him than it would have been to wonder what he was up to. The fact that he might be able to bring Amaran reinforcements into a battle was keeping him alive, for the moment. But Jain's innocence and Raf's sense of fair play be damned; if Tazira found it necessary to gut the bastard in order to save her men or Tycor, she'd do it. Swiftly and efficiently, and without much regret.

Without sparing him another thought, she knelt down to sniff the tracks. Vesh was less than three hours down the road. Closer if he'd chosen to stop, as she had.

Pellar went on ahead to scout, but he didn't have to go any farther than the next ridge. The others watched him as he froze in his tracks for an instant, backed away slowly, then retreated to their hill position at a dead run. His fur was spiked out from pure terror. He was breathing heavily as he rejoined the group, and it wasn't because he'd been running. With some effort, he smoothed his fur down and forced himself to stop shaking.

"Did you spot him?" Tazira asked, her tail lashing. "Did he spot you?"

"Oh, I saw him, all right," Pellar breathed, rubbing his forehead as if to ward off a coming migraine. "I know for a fact that he didn't see me, because I wouldn't be standing here babbling if he had. But I think you'd better come see this."

He led them back down the road, whispering quiet and creative curses, and Tazira added a few of her own as she followed him. She didn't quite know what she was supposed to be cursing at yet, but she knew it wasn't going to be good.

Chapter 14

FOR THE FIRST TIME IN THIRTY-FIVE YEARS of life, words failed Tazira Goldeneyes.

The dry, barren land below the ridge was chaos, teeming with life, with writhing and misshapen flesh, a sea of restless motion and malevolence. A living nightmare more violent and terrible than anything that had ever set her thrashing in a cold sweat. The valley was filled with thousands upon thousands of monsters, of every possible size and description.

Vesh had an army, and it wasn't human.

Tazira spent a full minute absorbing that fact before she could force herself to conduct a more intelligent assessment.

She looked to her men first, to see how they were holding up. Pellar was the calmest of any of them, mostly because he'd already worked through his initial fear reaction. But his tail was still spiked out stiffly, and his claws were digging deep unconscious furrows in the earth. Jain was wild-eyed and breathing unevenly, and he couldn't seem to stop looking around him, as if he expected more monsters to come pouring out of the dense forest behind them. Najendra was lying stock-still, looking over the ridge with all the rest of them, but plainly not seeing anything in front of him. His dark eyes had glazed over in what might have been catatonic shock. It seemed genuine, though you could never be sure with him.

Even the eternally calm and even-tempered Raf was staring at the valley beneath them in stunned disbelief, hissing to himself over and over, "This can't be real; no human would do this . . ."

Tazira realized she'd better rein them all back in, and quickly. Her own fears left her completely, as they tended to do in the face of her people's needs.

"At ease, gentlemen," she snapped softly, not wanting to catch the attention of anything down in the valley. The nearest of the monsters were at least a hundred feet away, but there was no sense taking chances. The simple normality of the command accomplished everything it needed to, and even Najendra managed to rouse himself sufficiently to give her his nervous attention.

"The bad news," the captain whispered, "is that this is much, much worse than I expected it to be, and I'm about as pessimistic as they come."

"No kidding," Jain hissed, still wild-eyed and hyperventilating a bit. Tazira gave him a quelling look, and for once he took the hint and lapsed into silence.

"The *worse* news," she continued, "is that nothing is going to stop them from entering Tycor. Vesh destroyed the wards at Illana's keep, and we have to assume he'll be able to do the same to the wards that protect the city. Right now, all that's standing between Tycor and disaster is a ten-foot rubble barricade."

"And us," Pellar added, lightly teasing even in this situation.

"And us." She nodded with the ghost of a smile.

"What are we going to do?" Najendra began to babble hysterically. "What can anyone do against *that?*"

"For a start, we're going to calm down," the captain growled quietly. "If we fall apart at the seams and do nothing, thousands of people are going to die, hideously."

"They'll die anyway," the wizard hissed. "There's nothing we can do but save ourselves!"

"For how long?" she asked him, her eyes boring into him. "Where would we run? Where could we ever be safe? The more cities Vesh destroys, the stronger he'll become. And there aren't that many cities left on Delos. Where were you planning on going, wizard?"

Najendra lowered his eyes, unable to answer that.

"The more cities Vesh destroys," she repeated softly, "the stronger he'll become. He'll have their resources to add to his own. Legions of fallen humans resurrected as undead soldiers. The power, the spellstones, the magic centers of every city he takes, his to use, to turn against his next intended victims. Tycor, Amar, Nashira, Illain, he'll sweep across them one by one. We have to stop him here and now, before he succeeds in taking anything."

"But what can I do?" Najendra asked wildly, of

the heavens as much as of the mrem. "Vesh alone is stronger than I am. I'm ashamed to admit to you how much stronger he is. If we could get him alone, all of us, we might have a chance of killing him if we were willing to die ourselves. But he's currently surrounded by just a few close friends," the wizard muttered with a trace of his old sardonic humor.

"Actually, that might be a plan," Raf admitted, calmly considering his claws. Najendra looked ready to protest, but his expression slowly changed to one of grim thoughtfulness.

"It might," Tazira agreed, "with two amendments. First, Najendra's not coming with us. Najendra, we need you to go home to Amar and raise an army there. Join my forces at the Golgul Pass in Southmarch if you can. Vesh will need to take his army through it to get to Tycor, and it's an unchanging bit of terrain that'll let me bottle him up for a while."

"How long?"

"A day. Two if we're lucky," Tazira admitted. "Not long. Do you think you can make it?"

"I don't know," the wizard said quietly. "Amar is about three days away, and at least three days back, depending on how long it takes to assemble an army. But I'll try."

"That's as much as I can ask. And if you fail, you'll at least be able to warn Amar. That's something. Remember, too, that this is a large, slow-moving force. It'll probably be another four or five days before they reach the pass. As far as he's concerned, Vesh has the luxuries of time, surprise, and vastly superior numbers, and I doubt he'll be in any particular hurry."

Najendra nodded hesitantly. "If I'm to warn Amar, and try to whip up an army, I'd best get to it." He sighed. "Do you think you'll be able to take out Vesh without my help?"

Tazira shrugged "It's possible. It's always possible, though I won't know that until I've *studied* Vesh's army, rather than staring at it," she said with an amused arch of her whiskers. "What about you? Will you be able to make an unescorted journey across the Badlands?"

"I think so," he said, though doubt was plain on his face. "After all, Vesh managed it somehow . . ."

"Yeah, and look what happened to him," Tazira snorted softly. She loosed the money pouch from her wide black leather belt and handed it to him, along with his spellstones.

"You'll have to pass the village of Na'shir on the way home," she whispered. "Hire yourself a few adventurers, and don't take any chances you don't have to. Good luck."

"And to you."

The wizard took one final disbelieving look at the army ahead of them, crept quietly and carefully away from the ridge, and took off in the opposite direction at a light run.

Tazira sighed and closed her eyes in thought for a long moment, after which she forced her attention back to the sprawling horror below them. Before she decided which one of her men was going back to Tycor to raise the army there, she wanted a good, solid look at this one. She borrowed Raf's spyglass and studied the field intently.

The monsters were organized into orderly battalions. They weren't milling about or sniping at each other. Each battalion was staying in its assigned place, perfectly disciplined. *As if they were conducting a lesson in deportment.* Tazira wanted to laugh at that, shards help her, she wanted to laugh. But she was afraid that if she started, she would never stop laughing—or screaming.

Something had to be controlling them all; monsters simply didn't act with that degree of thought or purpose. The valley was a bristling hive of activity, but it was intelligent, organized activity.

Nearest the ridge was a group of seventy-six giant spiders. They sat, their massive legs folded around them, and waited with mindless patience for the order to move out. There was a small cloth-of-purple tent before them, and Tazira began to notice similar tents in front of each battalion. The flap of the nearest one flew open, and she turned her attention back to it.

Another wizard emerged. Too short to be Vesh. Female, by the way she moved. Another light-blasted wizard, willing to betray her own kind for the promise of power. Tazira spat and hissed sharply, unable to help herself.

"Do you see that?" she whispered, handing Raf the spyglass. He peered through it and swore softly, passing it to Pellar after a brief hesitation.

"Shards and ashes!" The light-furred mrem bristled. Jain snatched the spyglass away from him, but not before getting an earful of curses he thoroughly intended to memorize and file away for future use, assuming he would have a future to use them in.

"How many damned wizards are there?" Pellar hissed at last. "How many humans are capable of selling out their entire race to these things?"

"At least five," Tazira snarled. "And that's if there's only one to a tent. Five wizards, besides Vesh, willing to take part in this abomination."

"Why?" Jain whispered. "Why would anyone do this?"

"I dunno, kid, but you could always go down there and ask 'em," Tazira suggested, not helpfully.

"No, thanks," he growled. Tazira smirked half-heartedly, took the spyglass back, and peered through it.

The supposedly human wizard below them lowered her hood, glanced around a bit absently, and headed for the center of the camp. Her wide, flowing black robes weren't significantly different from any other wizard's, but that was where the similarity stopped. Her skin was an appalling shade of gray brown, covered with what looked like bristles. Tazira took in a short, sharp breath.

"What in the name of the Triune Suns is *that*?" the captain murmured to herself. Jain looked a question at her, but she was too distracted to notice. Her spyglass followed the wizard as she made her way to a large white pavilion tent in the center of the camp. That one would doubtless belong to Vesh, unless he wasn't in charge of the army at all. There was always the remote possibility that he was just another battalion commander.

On the way, the gray wizard passed other battalions. To the left of the giant spiders, there was a group of about five hundred Lizcanth, dark green lizard beings about fifteen handspans in height, with massive, powerful hind legs and wickedly sharp claws and teeth. They'd be dangerous. They were fast, extremely intelligent, and accustomed to attacking their prey in groups. The gray wizard entered the tent at their head, then emerged after a moment with another human. If he could be called a human. His skin was a shade of green only slightly paler than his wizard's robes.

"Can you make out the wizards from this distance?" Tazira whispered to the others.

"Barely, but yes," Raf replied over her right shoulder. "Their skin, it's—"

"Discolored," she finished for him, grimly. "I have no idea why. I suppose it's possible that they aren't human, either. They may be monsters themselves, some mutated form of intelligent monsters Vesh has managed to create."

"Shards and ashes," Jain whispered, and Pellar cursed very, very quietly. There didn't seem to be much to say beyond that, except of course for Pellar's soft and subtly crafted curses, which truly were works of art in their way. Tazira smiled in spite of herself and went back to watching the grotesque play before them.

Other wizards began to stir from their tents as if summoned. A gaunt, cadaverous soul at the head of about a thousand ghoul warriors . . . a short, bent, wiry woman commanding countless thousands of tiny, vicious, hairless gray nits . . . a frail-looking, gray-skinned man at the head of eighty-seven gargoyles. From all over the camp, they converged on the white tent in the center.

Vesh emerged to greet them all and began to give them their instructions. Whatever he was telling them couldn't be heard from this distance, and Tazira clenched her jaw in mild frustration.

"Raf, I don't suppose you might have built in a sewer tunnel under this valley?" she whispered with a wry grin.

"Not the last time I looked." He shook his head with mock sadness. "I could start one, but it might take a while."

"Never mind, dear," she said with a soft chuckle. She watched for a while longer as the wizards talked, telling each other the shards knew what. After a few minutes, the leaders of the ghoul warriors, the gargoyles, and the Lizcanth went back to their tents with a handful of human guards each. They decamped and headed east in a small group. The earth was damp and browning where their tents had been, suggesting that they'd stayed there for two days, three at the most. The grass wasn't dead enough for it to have been any longer than that.

"I should order one of you to follow that group out, but I don't think we can spare the manpower," Tazira murmured thoughtfully. "One of us definitely has to get to Tycor. If the other three split up, it means one person has no protection while he sleeps."

"Not a good idea, especially with this many monsters around," Pellar agreed. "I'll find a way to mark their trail, so that we'll be able to follow it back if we need to. I think that's simply the best we're going to be able to do."

Tazira nodded reluctantly and turned her attention back to the camp for a moment.

Vesh and the other wizards disappeared inside the pavilion, presumably for an extended war council. Tazira led her men quietly back to their original hill position so that they'd be able to have one of their own. They sat down, perched against their packs, and made themselves as comfortable as they could. A long silence ensued while Tazira frowned and closed her eyes in thought.

"I don't see any way to get at him," she finally hissed. "He's pretty redoubtably fenced in by his legions, and I don't imagine he has much reason to leave the center, there. If we're lucky, he might be stupid enough to march at the head of his troops, and we can pick him off that way before we're overwhelmed ourselves. But there's no way to sneak into that camp in broad daylight, and we don't have the ability to disguise ourselves. Quiet intrusion and deception are both out of the question."

"What about distraction?" Pellar asked. "One of us starts firing spells off at their rear, and the other three insert from different points in the camp. One of us might just live long enough to be able to take him out."

Tazira shook her head. "He's too deeply ensconced for that. We couldn't create enough of a distraction to faze an army this large; we don't have the firepower. I doubt Najendra would have had it, either. Vesh would lazily point a finger and dispatch a single unit, and whatever he sent would be more than enough to take out the distraction. If we have to die, I want to die knowing

I've accomplished something. There has to be another way. We'll find it."

She hoped she sounded more confident than she felt about that.

"You three might not be able to disguise yourselves as humans," Jain said slowly, "but that's not something I need to worry about. I'm already dressed as a mercenary; I could probably get close to Vesh before anyone found me out."

"Son, if you were a little further along in your training, I'd pounce all over that idea like a kit on string," Tazira said with a grin. "But you're not quite up to taking out a wizard yet, and I'm not willing to throw you away. I'm not willing to throw any of you away if I have a choice. Too many commanders throw bodies at a problem, casually, and I don't ever intend to be one of them."

She paused, closed her eyes again, and leaned her head back against her pack. Time was burning away on them, and she knew it, but she couldn't resist the temptation to savor the moment. It was probably the last time they'd all be alive together, the end of twenty years of shared adventures. Shards and ashes, she couldn't believe she was even thinking it, not after all they'd been through together. But she had to think it. She was a realist.

With her eyes closed, she allowed herself the luxury of feeling them without seeing them. Feeling them breathe, almost listening to them think. Feeling them, there, and alive.

She found herself irrationally glad she'd cooked that dinner last night.

The moment stretched on as long as she dared to let it, and a little longer, and finally she said what all of them were thinking. "One of us has to go back to Tycor to raise the army."

"It should be you," Raf said quietly. "You're the captain."

"I know," she sighed. "I've spent the last hour or so trying to find a way around that, but there isn't one. It's my job. I have to go. But I could take the rest of you with me . . ."

"We should stay," Raf disagreed, shaking his head. "We might still find a way to take out Vesh, maybe even end the war before it begins."

"No suicidal gestures," Tazira said, favoring him with a piercing gaze, which he returned calmly.

"Tazira, if we can find a feasible plan to kill Vesh, it's worth all three of our lives to execute it, and him," Raf said firmly. "You know that. It's why you want to order the three of us back to Tycor while you stay behind. And you're not doing that, for the same reason we're willing to contemplate a suicidal gesture. We all have a duty to Tycor that's higher than our duty to ourselves, or each other."

"Raf, you're pontificating again," she growled, but there was no real anger in her words.

"I know." He shrugged. "I thought it might help."

"I could *order* you back to Tycor with me."

"You could. But you won't. You're too good a commander for that."

Tazira climbed to her feet and started pacing. Her tail lashed in impotent frustration, and hot, unwelcome tears burned behind her closed eyelids. She grimly forced them back. There'd be plenty of time for that nonsense later, when her men weren't around to see the weakness.

"Private Riordan, I seem to recall telling you that killing was the hardest, most hateful part of what we do. I lied," the captain said tightly. "Now, you've got a decision to make. You can stay here with the lieutenants, or you can come back to Tycor with me. I'd take some comfort in knowing Raf and Pellar had a healer with them, but I leave you the same choice I'm leaving them. Staying here is too dangerous to put on anything but a voluntary basis."

"I'll stay," Jain said without hesitation. "If I'd wanted 'safe,' I'd be in a monastery."

"Good man." Pellar grinned, clapping him on the shoulder.

"Thank you, son," Tazira nodded, smiling faintly. "I doubt you'd be any safer with the army, really, but thank you. Raf won't put a young healer lightly at risk," she grumbled with a warning glare at Raf that said he'd damned well better *not*, "and I suppose I'm hoping that in his anxiousness not to waste you, he won't waste himself or Pellar, either."

"I hadn't thought of that," Raf admitted quietly.

"I didn't think you had." Tazira smiled, lightly teasing. Her heart wasn't in the banter, though, not now. Her smile faded, and her tail stiffened. "I'm serious, Raf—no suicidal gestures. You've got about an eightday to sniff out Vesh's weak points. Don't rush into a half-formed plan out of desperation; there's no need. I'll make that an order if I have to. If the worst comes to the worst, and Tycor falls, someone will need to warn the other city-states about Vesh. That's probably going to be more important than anything three men can do against an army."

"If I see my opportunity—"

"Then take it. Take it, and good luck. Just . . . I don't know . . . try not to die or anything." She laughed, turning it into a feeble quip for the sake of her sanity.

"We'll try," Pellar assured her lightly. "I like my life. Besides, I can't die until I've succeeded in seducing Sergeant Rlirr at least once."

"Sergeant Snarl?" Tazira laughed, a bit shocked at that. "Are you still on about that? I thought you would have given up by now."

"She hasn't torn his ears off yet," Raf pointed out calmly. "I think she likes him."

"Well, if she gives you all a reason to survive this, I'll bless every one of her claws." Tazira smiled. "And maybe I'll stop calling her Sergeant Snarl, though that's more of a stretch."

They lapsed into silence, none of them wanting to say good-bye. Tazira wanted to find a way to leave them on a laugh, but it just wasn't what she was feeling.

"Raf, I'm leaving you in charge of the mission," she finally said crisply, ignoring the painful tightness in her throat. "If you see a way to eliminate Vesh, do it, but not at the cost of all of your lives. Someone has to survive long enough to get word out to the neighboring city-states, to give them a shot at defending themselves."

Raf nodded, suddenly unable to speak.

"You be careful, too," Pellar said quietly, handing Tazira the Great Seal of Tycor and the ruined wardstone to take back with her. She tucked them away in her pack without really looking at them.

"I'll be as careful as I can." She hugged Pellar tightly, took a deep breath, and willed herself not to fall apart. "This'll just get harder the longer I take. Time to be gone." She let him go after a moment, turned to Jain, and caught him in an affectionate bear hug.

"Don't let them do anything too noble, son." She laughed to keep herself from crying. He nodded, not trusting himself to say anything. *Too much color will go out of the world when she's gone,* he thought to himself. He wanted to tell her that, or something like it, but he couldn't think of a way to phrase it that didn't sound stupid or effusive. Finally she released him and turned to Raf.

"I'm not saying good-bye." She shook her head stubbornly. "I refuse to say anything that sounds that final. I'll see you again in Tycor, at the victory celebration." It had the hollow, unsteady ring of a lie, but they needed to hear it as much as she needed to say it.

"No good-byes," Raf agreed. Tazira hugged him fiercely. After a long moment, she nipped his ear in a mrem gesture of affection and pulled away to leave. He turned to glance back at Pellar and Jain, but they'd both disappeared. Raf laughed softly to himself at that; Pellar was discretion's own soul, wrapped in fur.

"Subtle, aren't they?" Tazira smiled up at him, and her smile was brilliant and forced and heartbreaking.

"I'm sure Pellar has lured Jain into the Guards' betting pool by now." He shrugged lightly.

"They've all got their pet theories on when I'll finally bite the back of your neck again, and where, and how . . ."

"The dangers of life in an extended family like the Guard," she agreed ruefully, shaking her head. "Extended families gossip shamelessly, and there are no secrets. I hear the betting's gotten so involved even a bookie couldn't follow it. And now, when we probably won't see each other again . . . I'm not sure whether we'll be more miserable if we satisfy their bets, or if we don't."

She looked at him, her expression an odd, endearing mixture of longing and uncertainty. After the space of a breath he drew her into his arms and kissed her, gently at first, then urgently, making the choice for both of them.

Chapter 15

SERGEANT DANO GAPED WHEN HE SAW HIS captain. She was running down the wide white corridor toward him, and she looked like a cohort of monsters had done a wine-making dance on her. Her clothing was in tatters, and her black leather boots had literally been run through; her blistered feet were poking through them in places. That doublet might have been light gray originally, but it was so badly stained with sweat and dried blood that its original color had become a faint memory.

Tazira shot him a wan smile and a vague salute as she ran past him. Horrified that he'd forgotten, he hastily saluted her retreating form as she headed into the . . . *She's going into the great hall looking like that?* The other Guards on duty opened the broad, heavy creothwood doors before he could say a word. And in she went, holding her head like an empress, though her curious fashion statement and the rapid heaving of her chest did a bit to dampen the effect.

"Lady Tazira, Captain of the Tycor Guard!" a

herald's voice announced. The herald had apparently gotten a short, sharp warning, because he looked and sounded perfectly nonplussed. The court was less so. A shocked, rumbling murmur greeted her as she entered, and she dismissed it with a contemptuous flick of her left ear. She actively disliked courtiers and did nothing to conceal the fact.

"Tazira, thank the shards you're back!" Romney beamed. "Welcome home, my girl!"

He bounded down off the high wooden dais, greeted her with an affectionate bear hug, and did his best to ignore her dishevelment. "What about Raf and Pellar?" he asked her more quietly, expecting the worst.

"They were alive when I left them, though I don't expect them to survive the mission," she admitted quietly, unable to meet his eyes. He drew her into his arms comfortingly, but for once she was stiff and tense in his embrace. "Lose the parasites, Val," she hissed in his ear, still breathing heavily. "We have to talk, now, before I pass out, and I don't want to start a panic . . ."

He nodded and let her go, and she nearly collapsed before he managed to catch her again. "The court is dismissed," he announced sharply. The courtiers stared at him for a second or two before they began to file out, with the rustling of silks and the whispers of malicious tongues echoing in the cavernous hall. Romney ignored them all, drew Tazira over to the dais, and sat her down gently on the steps. She rested her aching head against the side of the massive, elaborately carved bloodwood throne and closed her eyes for a second, waiting for the last of the courtiers to wash out. Romney fetched her a glass of wine from a sideboard, but she shook her head at him.

"Thank you, Val, but all wine will do in my condition is get me drunk. I don't have time to be drunk, as much as I might enjoy it," she said, slurring a bit in her exhaustion. Romney looked down at the glass, contemplated downing it himself, then pushed it aside.

"I'll try to pull myself together and give you as tight a sit-rep as I can," Tazira started. "Please bear with me. First off, I have a present for you." She smiled wanly as she fished the Great Seal out of her pack.

"Woman, have I asked you to marry me lately?" He grinned at her.

"Not in at least an eightday, unfaithful one. Now, here's the bad news: Taran Vesh engineered the theft."

"Vesh! That son of an unnamed . . . I should have—"

"Yes, you should have killed him when you had the chance," Tazira cut him off quietly, without sympathy and without heat. "But it's too late to worry about that now. He's summoned an army of monsters. Thousands of them. And they're marching on Tycor as we speak."

Romney paled visibly before he could collect himself. He narrowly managed not to say anything stupid in his shock. He couldn't believe any human would sink to that depth, but if Tazira saw it, it happened, and that was that. Babbling platitudes about it would have been a waste of time.

"The wards should hold them out of the city itself," he murmured with more hopefulness than actual conviction, "but they'll decimate the marches."

"Oh, Val, it's much, much worse than that," she said gently, almost laughing at the impossibility of it all. "The wards aren't good for anything anymore; they won't hold out a brognab. I think I'd better tell you the whole story, from the beginning. Get comfortable, and slap me awake if I start to drift off."

"The wards won't . . . oh, shards . . . I think I want that damned drink after all," he muttered, resting his forehead against his throne. The smooth coldness of the dark red wood did nothing to forestall his coming headache.

Jain sighed and stretched as much as he dared, trying to relax a bit. Over the course of the last two days, he'd come to think of the small mound of sweetgrass on the south ridge as his spot. He felt as if he'd had time to memorize the exact pattern of every branch and leaf around him. Raf or Pellar would have told him, probably with some exasperation, that he'd be better off memorizing the army below them. But he'd already done that, well enough to start giving pet names to some of the more distinctive monsters. It hadn't helped him find a way to take out Vesh.

That was the problem, really. After two days of quiet, intent study, they still didn't have any answers. They'd picked off a few strays and set a few traps in the path the army would have to follow, if it ever finally moved, but that was all they'd managed to accomplish so far. Their food supplies were running low, and the army was stripping the land bare.

That alone would probably force the monsters to move within a day, two at the most.

"Vesh seems to be taking his sweet time about moving out," Jain whispered to the others. "I wonder why he's hesitating."

"Probably because he *can*," Pellar hissed back ruefully. "Nothing in this world is likely to stop his advance or even slow it down much. It doesn't matter if scouts encounter the army and report it back to Tycor. He's not counting on surprise or speed. He doesn't have to."

"But the longer he delays the march, the more time we have to bring in reinforcements and engineer defenses." Jain frowned. "He's already lost the element that was supposed to be taking over the city from the inside, and he knows it."

Pellar shook his head "Doesn't matter. You're forgetting Vesh. You've never actually met him, but Raf and I knew him reasonably well, when he was still a court wizard. Even when he wasn't particularly powerful, he was overconfident, and that clearly hasn't changed. He'll take his time about arriving in Tycor. He'll luxuriate in a long, slow kill, because he's convinced his victory is inevitable and unstoppable."

Something stirred in Jain's mind, uncomfortably. The image that had haunted him for days returned again. The Dark, the creature. Emotions and vague impressions crashed over him in rough waves, as they did every time he dared to think about it. Arrogance. Cunning. Lavish cruelty. Other feelings, less easily defined. Some he had

Send me the free Online Shattered Light CD-Rom.
(Disks will ship in April, 1999).

_____ Email me on updates, upgrades and expansions.

Name _____

Address _____

City _____ State _____

Zip _____

Email Address _____

Modem Speed _____ Online Game Services used (if any) _____

Optional: Age: _____ Computer Type _____

Please Print

PB039901

no names for at all, and he was almost grateful for that.

"He'll luxuriate in a long, slow kill," Jain murmured, almost to himself. "He will, and something else will." A bone-deep shudder forced its way through his skin. Raf turned to him and raised a single eyebrow, the most animation he'd shown in two days.

"You mean that thing Najendra mentioned," Raf whispered, more stating a fact than asking for confirmation of it. "The entity Vesh encountered in the Badlands, the one that gave him all this power."

Jain nodded wordlessly, afraid even to say its name, though he involuntarily thought it.

"You know something about this," Raf hissed a bit sharply. "Something you haven't told us yet. I think it's past time you did, young man."

Pellar looked at him askance, but his eyes stayed locked on the human. Raf had been uncharacteristically grim and short-tempered for the last two days, and no one needed to ask him the reason for it.

"I don't actually know anything," Jain admitted. "But I believe Vesh did encounter something real. More than that, I believe Vesh isn't the real danger. He's a puppet of something much more powerful, just like Illana Osska was his puppet while she lived. She . . . I don't know . . . this all sounds crazy . . ."

"No, it doesn't," Raf shook his head, managing something more like his usual even-tempered gentleness. "Go on. What makes you think the Dark, or whatever it was, is more than the product of a lunatic mind?"

"Well . . . this sounds really stupid, and I can't help that . . . but I had a dream, the day I healed Najendra. It was just before he woke up himself and told us about the Da—the entity." Jain corrected himself hastily. "I dreamed that monsters were coming to devour us all, teeming, murdering legions that stretched as far as the eye could see. And behind them all, there was another presence, more inhuman than any of them." The boy closed his eyes, and his brow furrowed with concentration as he struggled to find words for his impressions.

"It was like . . . well, I guess it was more like a spider than anything else. Patient, cruel, subtle. Unimaginably old, and in all its long life, it's existed for the joy of causing pain. I don't know, not quite that. More than that, much worse. As if its existence has been a study in the nature and degree of terror. As if it's developed emotions beyond our comprehension, and all of those advanced and subtle grades of emotion have some root in monstrous cruelty. I felt all that, my mind brushing over its own like a . . . I don't know . . . like a dull knife on the skin of a soft fruit, grazing it without breaking it. And the thing became . . . aware of me," he finished in a dull whisper. It was too unreal to make him afraid.

"I told you it was stupid." He shrugged apologetically. "But I can't seem to get the images out of my head, any more than I can shake the feeling that it's there, watching me with mild interest but no real concern. It's the same feeling I get off

Vesh, the unshakable arrogance, the feeling of complete invulnerability."

"Possible," Raf admitted, a bit shaken. "It's possible. An intelligence behind the monsters, directing them like pieces on a farak board . . ."

"I wonder if it hasn't killed us all yet because it doesn't have quite that much power, or if it simply wants to draw this out as long as possible," Pellar whispered grimly. "It might not even be coincidence that we've been suddenly clued into its existence."

"Also possible," Raf agreed. "And Tazira's going to be leading an army against that. Shit," he hissed fervently, his claws splaying into the earth.

"Raf, it's equally possible that Jain was just dreaming," Pellar said firmly. "We have no proof of any of this, as Tazira would be the first to tell you. The best thing we can do for her is to keep studying the army, with that creature in mind. We may find a way to break its link with Vesh, or break whatever hold he may have over the other wizards. Anything might help."

Raf nodded slowly, unwillingly, and forced himself to calmness. With a renewed sense of urgency, he picked up the spyglass and scanned the army below them, looking for its weak link. A lazy sentry, a careless wizard, an insubordinate subordinate, anything. He was going out of his mind with worry, but that wouldn't help Tazira now.

He secretly feared nothing would.

Tazira and Romney had adjourned to the presence chamber next door, and they'd spread a large cloth map of the southern provinces over the center table. Tazira was sprawled comfortably in a burgundy velvet chair, mostly to hide the fact that her legs were refusing to hold her up anymore. If she could just make it to her quarters unaided, it was as much as she'd ever ask of the wide world again.

"I've got the beginnings of a battle plan," she said, slurring her words from exhaustion. "We've got to take and hold the Golgul Pass, fortify it before Vesh can reach it. There's no easy way around it, and Vesh will try to take his army through it if I know him at all. We can bottle him up there, take his army out in sections before we mount an offensive."

"Why?" Val asked her with a raised eyebrow, purely to draw out the course of her thoughts.

"Vesh might be cunning in his politics and magics, but I suspect he'll prove decidedly unimaginative and straightforward as a commander in the field. The Golgul Range rises nearly a quarter league above the surrounding plains, straight as an arrow for more than a hundred leagues, and that pass is directly in the middle of the road between him and us. He'll make straight for it."

Val said nothing for a moment, thinking it through.

"He'll have gargoyles. I'd send them forward to secure the pass, then move beyond that to harass us as we come up."

She shook her head. "Old friend, think more like him. He believes he is terrifying, he's so damned convinced of it he expects that even now we are cowering like rabbits trapped in their warren as the snake crawls down the hole. He'll think we'll hide here, maybe pile some more rubble up on the walls and stick more beams across the gates. Our moving up to the pass will be the unexpected, and therefore the essential, move."

"The flanks, though. The Vaduska River is but a dozen leagues to the north. It's a wide-open path around us. The old road there is wide enough for twenty ogres to march through side by side, and the river's shallow enough that a hundred more could be on their flank. It's indefensible. I can't split our forces and cover both."

She laughed, shaking her head.

"I'll only whisper this to you, my love"—she leaned forward, whiskers brushing his cheek— "cut out the damned drinking!"

She snarled the words so loud that he recoiled in shock, a flash of anger sparkling in his eyes.

"Think like Vesh. He's so confident of the kill that he'll drag this out slowly," she said, smiling mischievously, "like two lovers who go slowly because the night is still young."

He grinned back.

"He wants to soak every moment of pleasure out of it. He'll advance with all proper pomp and ceremony. He reaches the lower plains of the Golgul Heights; advance scouts report that we are there. He'll be surprised, but then, in his mind he'll laugh at *our* arrogance.

"For him to try fancy maneuvers after that would be an affront to his precious dignity. That would mean concern, that in some small way we had matched him and now forced effort. No, once we meet at the pass it will be a straight-out frontal assault."

"And then he attacks and overwhelms us," Val sighed.

"It's time we're after now," she snapped angrily. "Time to evacuate this city because until we've put him down, this place will be the magnet and, if he reaches it, a death trap for everyone inside. But I think we just might turn it around with luck and some damn hard fighting. I want to suck him into the pass where superior numbers simply won't matter, but skill and cunning will. I can't win this battle on the defensive. Strategically this will look like a defensive fight, but in the nuances of each moment we maneuver within the narrow space—the eight-sided circle, if you will—we may succeed in exhausting his strength."

"You speak so casually about what seems to me to be one hell of a risk."

"My love, if the art of war consisted solely of not taking risks, glory would be at the mercy of the mediocre." Tazira winked with a rakish salute.

She paused just long enough to adjust one tattered boot so that it wasn't rubbing against the worst of her blisters.

"A pass action will seriously limit the ground mobility of his nits and Lizcanth. His giant spiders, which would be devastating on an open field, will be virtually useless inside a mountain pass. His gargoyles will be the most effective thing he has left, and we'll have an easier time taking them out with firepower along the ridges than we would taking them out from the ground.

"The pass also gives us the opportunity for a

flexible response," Tazira continued, gaining strength as she went. "We can slowly draw him through the pass, making him pay for every step. Fortify the crest so that if he does try a direct sweep up the flanking slopes we turn that into a slippery bloodbath. Remember, the deeper he gets in, the more fire we can pour down from either side as well. Let him get in, weaken him, then counterstrike and drive them back out. He's so bloody single-minded that he'll take a deep breath and charge straight back in again."

"One thing, though."

"And that is?"

"He has infinite power; he can but flick his finger and regenerate hundreds, thousands if need be. Eventually we will wear down."

"And do you have a better suggestion then?" she asked casually, eyes arching up.

There was a moment of painful silence, then at last he shook his head.

"Hell of a fight it'll make."

"It buys time."

"Time? For what?"

She glowered at him affectionately, as if he were a recalcitrant kit, and rattled off all the reasons she'd come up with in the last day of hard running. "Time to get reinforcements here. Time for your daughter to complete the evacuation of Tycor and get the noncombatants settled in the northern marches fortifications at Haymarket and Warton. Time for one of your wizards to figure out how to counter what Vesh did to the wardstones. Time to find and exploit the enemy's weaknesses. Need I go on?" the captain asked with a wan smile.

"We need time, Val. We'll have to sacrifice a great deal to buy ourselves that luxury."

"That's defeatist, girl," he rumbled. "I never taught you that."

"You're calling me a defeatist? You taught me to be a realist, Val." She shook her head, too exhausted to take umbrage at his words. "We have a little over twelve hundred soldiers we can muster immediately. Perhaps eight hundred more, if all the reinforcements from the other provinces make it in time to join the battle. Amar may or may not send anyone, and I'm certainly not counting on help from that quarter. Those soldiers will be fighting easily six or seven times their number, and that's assuming Vesh hasn't had more forces arrive since I left."

Romney nodded wordlessly and glowered at the map, as if he expected it to give him a better answer. He sighed after a moment and slumped into a chair next to hers.

"It's a realistic approach," he admitted after a moment. "Conservative, but we have no choice about that."

Tazira smiled at him. "I know. I'd love to sweep in there with banners blazing, myself. And as soon as we've worn him down sufficiently, that's exactly what we'll do. But in the meantime, we'll take and hold the pass and the high ground on either side of it. Barricades inside, every two or three hundred paces. Wards," she said slowly, with the beginnings of a truly wicked smile. "Wards will allow our soldiers to fall back point to point, but any monsters trying to come through will be fried. Vesh will have to waste time and magical resources burning out every one of them. It'll wear him down, slow him down, and hopefully frustrate him into tactical errors," she finished triumphantly.

"Brilliant!" Val crowed. "Tazira, my girl, you're a genius!"

"I know," she teased.

"So when are you going to come to your senses and marry me?"

"When your mother finally passes on, dear," Tazira drawled lazily, giving him a low-lidded sideways glance. "I don't know how we'd ever explain to her that your second wife was a giant cat."

He shrugged. "She'll get over it." The two of them looked at each other for a second and burst out laughing. When Tazira's punch-drunk laughter melted into a yawn, Romney looked at her askance.

"Just how far *did* you run?" he asked her, raising a suspicious gray eyebrow at her.

"Close to a hundred leagues," she admitted. The thought alone made her tired.

"In a *day*? And you're still awake, and talking tactics?"

"Barely. In fact, I'm not quite sure how I'm getting out of this shardblasted chair and back to my quarters, to be perfectly honest."

"I'll carry you. Damn it, woman, why didn't you say something?" he groaned, somewhere between anger and tenderness. In that moment he reminded her so much of Raf that she found herself suddenly blinking back tears.

"There was too much that needed to be done,

Val," she replied quietly. "There still is, but I can't manage it anymore. I need to sleep, *now*. Do you think you can handle things for a few hours?"

"Yes," he said emphatically. "Yes, of course I can handle it. I'll start with the wizards; they'll need time to start mass-producing wardstones for the pass. We'll arm and ready our own troops, then we'll call for conscripts."

"Better send runners out to the provinces just after you talk to the wizards. Those units will need time to get to the Golgul."

"Good idea. Got any others?"

"Tower shields and longspears for the companies inside the pass. We'll form them into forward phalanxes, turn the lack of mobility into a tactical advantage. Get Sergeant Dano or Sergeant Rlirr to help you with anything you need; they're the best I've got, in the absence of both my lieutenants . . ." The captain found herself unable to continue that thought. "War council at green dawn?" she asked him, a little more sharply than she needed to.

"Tazira, green dawn only gives you a four-hour sleep shift."

"It'll have to do, Val. None of us has time for more."

"You do, my girl. You've done what you really needed to; you got word back to Tycor in the space of a single day, and you've given us the beginnings of a very solid battle plan. Now it's time to let the rest of us handle things for a while. You've got competent subordinates and—dare I say it?—an absolutely brilliant predecessor." Romney winked. "And before you have time to argue with that, I'm carting you next door to that legendary place, my bedchamber."

"What *will* your mother say?" she mumbled blearily, shaking her head. Romney lifted her as easily as if she were weightless and started to carry her inside.

"I'm not worried about my mother. I'm worried about every other woman in Tycor. When word gets out that I carried you to my bed and actually let you sleep, my reputation will be in shreds."

The only answer he received to that sally was the soft, even sigh of her almost-snoring.

Tazira's bath the next morning was a hurried affair, not at all the scented luxury she'd promised herself on the road. But after so many days of nothing, hot water and plain lye soap seemed deliciously decadent.

Besides, she was still in the private chambers of the lord of Tycor Keep, and it didn't get much more luxurious than that, or much more decadent, for that matter. They were magnificently appointed, and clearly decorated by one of Romney's predecessors. Romney had little time and less patience for ostentation, and this had to be the most ostentatious place she'd ever seen.

The walls above the wainscoting were covered entirely with paintings of a pre-Fall cityscape, and the mural extended all the way to the vaulted ceiling, which was painted to look like a vaguely cloudy sky. An elaborately carved four-poster bed with pale yellow hangings dominated the rest of the chamber. Not that the other furnishings were plain, by any means; the bath she was hastily scrubbing in was a heavy lilanthwood affair, with gilded designs carved around the edges.

Nice, Tazira supposed, but she couldn't help feeling vaguely edgy in places like this. Too rich, too clean, nothing touchable or human. Too good for the likes of a mrem soldier, maybe . . . though that couldn't have been it, either. Pellar would have made himself right at home here, and so would Raf, for that matter, which left her with the uncomfortable conclusion that it was too good for the likes of Tazira Goldeneyes.

The heavy door creaked open, and Tazira splashed a little water onto the pale gold carpet as she started. Varral Romney sauntered in, nudged the door closed behind him with his foot, and set a pile of clothing on the bed.

"Right, you lazy kit!" he snapped in his best drill-sergeant bellow. "Up you get! Look at her bathing, when there's a war to be won! Getting soft, my girl!"

"You're a fine one to talk, old friend," she snorted softly, finishing up with the soap and starting to rinse out her fur. "Look at this place! Living in the lap of luxury, while my men and I sleep on the hard, cold ground . . . How *do* you manage to sleep in that soft bed every night?"

"I truly don't know." He shook his head. "I'd redecorate, but it doesn't seem worth the bother."

She smiled; that was typical of him.

"I had a healer visit you last night; I didn't think you'd mind," Val said dryly.

"I had a feeling," she admitted ruefully. "And, no, I don't mind. If you hadn't, I would have broken down this morning and sought one out. Something about needing to be able to walk . . ."

"Something like that. Now, I've brought you a change of clothing, and had another packed for the march, along with your armor," he informed her crisply, obviously turning his mind to the business at hand. "I assume you'll want to pack your own weapons. The wizards, my daughter, and your junior officers are gathering outside in the presence chamber for a war council. Is there anything else you need before you join us?"

"My pack," she said, grabbing the towel he handed her and drying off. "Any idea where it went?"

"It was damned tasty."

"Cute. Where is it?"

"Right there at the foot of that soft bed you took umbrage at."

"Do me a favor and dig out the wardstone while I throw these clothes on. Let's see, what did you bring me?" Tazira sorted through the pile, finding a crisp linen shirt, candlelight yellow edged in amber, a woven amber jerkin, and black breeks and boots. "These are lovely, Val, but they're not mine," she murmured.

"Of course they are! I owe you that much, at least; your own clothes were ruined by the journey."

"Val, my clothes weren't nearly this . . . I mean, I can't . . . Does everyone in Tycor have better taste than I do?" she finally inquired plaintively of the indifferent ceiling.

"Yes!" Romney guffawed, unable to resist a good opening. She threw a pillow at him in eloquent response and shrugged into her clothing.

"Thanks," she muttered, though as usual she

couldn't suppress a grin as she said it. She snatched the ruined wardstone away from him, mostly to keep him from dropping it in his uncontrolled mirth.

"I love you," he gasped, barely able to force the words through his laughter.

"I love you, too," she growled, fixing the ornate silver clasp on her jerkin.

"And then there's now," they chorused in one of their older in-jokes. Tazira smiled at that, but she didn't laugh as she normally would have. The easy, wonderful mundanity of the moment seemed suddenly out of tune, and she couldn't help wondering how many more moments like this they'd have before Vesh annihilated them. She'd never say as much to Val. She'd never say as much anywhere but in the privacy of her own thoughts.

Romney hadn't quite finished snickering when his daughter, Taziralendra, burst into the chamber, looking fully ready to commit murder. She slammed the heavy door behind her, which wasn't easy to do, then marched up to Romney and folded her arms meaningfully across her chest.

Poets and minstrels commonly hailed Taziralendra as the most beautiful woman in Tycor. Any lord's daughter might have been treated to that hyperbole, but in her case it was the simple truth, Romney thought with no small amount of pride. She had her dark skin and black hair from him, but those incomparable pale green eyes had been her mother's. Just at the moment, of course, those eyes were flashing unholy death at him. He brought his laughter under control, took a breath to steady himself, and got ready for one more argument with a daughter who seemed to live for the purpose.

"Yes?" he asked her simply. It almost set him laughing again.

"Darling father," the girl began sweetly, "whose bloody shard-blue-blasted idea was it to have *me* run the evacuation of Tycor?"

"Watch your language, young lady," he shot back, folding his own arms across his massive chest. "Who taught you to use words like that?"

"You did," came the impeccable riposte.

"I'll be going now," Tazira said sweetly, sketching Romney a hasty salute and making for the door.

"As a matter of fact, your *Aunt Tazira* came up with the evacuation idea last night," Romney said with a broad grin.

"Coward," Tazira growled. "I only mentioned it in passing! It was you who—"

"Aunt Zira, you of all people!" Taziralendra cut her off, wide-eyed with disbelief. "*Him* I could see, but *you*?"

"I guess I'm in it now," the captain sighed. "Thanks a lot, Val."

He beamed. "Anytime."

"All right," Tazira said sharply. "I don't know about your father, but I had two reasons for recommending it. First off, you're the heir apparent. If your father doesn't survive the battle, it's going to be your responsibility to lead those people, and hopefully to rebuild the city."

"My . . . but my . . ." the girl began, and found herself unable to finish the thought. Tazira waited patiently for her objections; she'd long since found that a valuable tactic. The seconds ticked on uncomfortably while Taziralendra absorbed the full and terrible weight of her responsibility and her loss, and the crest of anger she'd been riding faded off and left her foundering. She felt the sharp sting of unwanted tears, and she cursed sharply under her breath as she blinked them away.

"Second," the mrem continued gently, "leading troops into battle is hard enough without secretly worrying about how your only daughter is faring. I thought your father would have a much better chance of surviving and making it back home without that distraction. Does that make sense?"

Tazira's namesake nodded slowly, hating to have to admit that. Now that the worst of her anger had washed away, she was back to being reasonable, though she didn't particularly want to be.

"It makes sense, and I see why you recommended it," the girl sighed after a moment. "But I *still* want to go with you," she finished with a belligerent glower at her father.

"I know." Tazira smiled. "That, I can safely leave up to the two of you to hash out, while I escape to the presence chamber." Her eyes flashed lazy golden fire at Romney as she turned to go.

"Chickenshit," he chided her.

"Never said I wasn't," his captain grinned, reaching for the cold iron door handle. "I'll cheerfully take on an army of monsters for you, but teenage daughters are out of my jurisdiction. Have fun, dears, and try not to be too long about it."

"Thanks," they shot back in icy chorus.

"Don't mention it," she replied cheerfully.

Chapter 16

TAZIRA STOOD ALONE ON THE SUMMIT OF the left ridge, overlooking the rocky, narrow pass and the dry golden plains beyond it. In a day, perhaps less, an army the likes of which the world had never seen would trample every blade of grass in that still and quiet valley. But for now, at least, it was beautiful.

"Enjoying the view while it lasts?" a voice behind her asked her dryly. She turned, and Lord Romney stepped up to join her on the summit.

"Something like that," Tazira said quietly, feeling strangely subdued. "It'll end around green dawn, according to the report I got a few minutes ago. I sent that scout on to inform the company commanders, with instructions to let the men know. Accurate information is probably the best gift I can give them all right now."

"You're giving them a brilliant defense, my girl, and that's more than I could say for most commanders. A lot of them are going to die in the next day or two, but not one of them will have been wasted."

She nodded pensively, not saying anything for a moment. Her eyes narrowed. Romney could almost hear her thinking over her defenses, every trap, every barricade, the placement of every ward.

They were inspired, he thought. The pass, which stretched for nearly half a league before breaking open behind them into a lush open pasture far too wide to defend, was flooded with twenty-three separate wards. Barricades of felled trees, covered with dirt, were spaced every two hundred paces, just far enough apart that if the enemy gained the first one, it could not provide cover for archers to rain fire down on the next. They'd have to get out into the open space between the barricades, where they would be swept away. In front of each barricade a dry moat several feet deep and a dozen feet across had been dug. The sides of the moat were studded with sharpened stakes, and caltrops by the hundreds were concealed in the loose dirt at the bottom. The moat most certainly would not stop an ogre, but it would still drop it several feet down, so that a man standing atop the barricade could then get a good swipe at its midsection or go for its eyes with a polearm.

At fifty-foot intervals narrow sally points were cut into the barricades and marked with pennants. The troops had been drilled how to fall back quickly through the ports, push a cart across to block it, and then, on a trumpet signal, to clear the port and race back out. The enemy would have to fight through twelve such defensive barricades to gain the far side of the pass.

On the steep slopes leading up to the mountain crests, strong points for small units had been dug in and cunningly camouflaged. Archers would have a field day picking off those who were stupid enough to try to claw their way up the slopes. The crests might actually prove to be the weak point. Entrenchments and barricades had been constructed for nearly a mile out on either flank. A direct frontal assault would be suicide, but even someone as narrowly focused as Vesh might consider sending a flanking force out *two* miles, have them climb the slope, then pivot and roll up the flank, thereby gaining the heights. Therefore, the end of each line of trenches snaking along the crest was anchored with a fort that had been hastily but solidly constructed with piled-up boulders and logs. The forts were backed up with powerful wards, catapults, and the best of the archers.

Small units of light troops would be deployed farther out on either flank. These were play actors in reality, boys who were expected to appear for a moment, scurry back down the reverse slope, move a couple of hundred paces, then pop up again for a moment, thus giving the appearance that the mountaintop was lined for miles with troops who would occasionally get too anxious and stick their heads up for a quick look.

The first two checkpoints in the pass, one in the center and one on the far end, were double-warded; when the first ward cracked, the second could either be put up immediately or held in reserve, to trap groups of monsters and crush them in turn. The wizards had spent the last three days mass-producing wardstones, and Tazira had managed to double their supply by collecting every Catseye from the walls of Tycor and all the neighboring farms and homesteads. After all, if the army failed here, those stones wouldn't do anyone else any good, ever again.

Now who's being defeatist? Romney chided himself.

"We've got maybe half a day to fill in the gaps in our defenses," Tazira frowned, breaking into his thoughts. "Half a day to spot anything I've missed."

"All right," he said evenly. "Sit-rep, Captain. Wards."

"Twenty-three inside the pass, and a few more I'm saving for emergencies," Tazira said crisply. "Five concentrated on each end, thirteen randomly spaced in the center. Unless Vesh or his monsters have some way of sensing them, the random spacing will make them completely unpredictable. With any luck, the enemy will have to stumble into each one to discover them, and they'll lose a few to disintegration each time.

"The secondary wards can be fired off to trap enemy groups in the center, a minimum of five and a probable maximum of nine times. We'll get at least nine if Vesh has to burn them out one at a time, but he may have the ability to fry multiple wards in one shot. That's why I've only got the one at the mouth of the pass activated. We'll fire them off as we need to, as the soldiers fall back point to point. That should give them a chance to get their breath back, get back into formation, and hopefully retake the ground. I may decide to let Vesh through eventually, but I want every handspan of that pass sold dearly before that happens.

"And if the worst comes to the worst," she concluded, "and the wards fail completely, there are other traps. I dislike relying on magic; I don't trust it. If Vesh blows out the wards, there are still no less than five avalanche points drilled into the ridges on either side of the pass. If I can't ward it, I'll seal it, and hopefully trap a few thousand monsters under the falling rock. It won't stop Vesh, I'm sure, but it'll buy us a few hours. And as a brilliant former captain of the Guard once taught me, the advantage of time is as essential in battle as it is in single combat."

"My, that *was* a brilliant captain," Romney sighed lavishly.

"Yeah, he was," she agreed. "Damn shame he got so old and senile."

"Thanks."

"Don't mention it." She grinned.

"I won't. To anyone. Ever," he said sourly.

"In addition to the avalanche points," she continued, rolling her eyes at him teasingly, "I've got catapults deployed along the crests of each ridge, to give us heavy firepower from an elevated position. My longbows and crossbows are entrenched along each crest as well; it would be a waste to put them down in the pass when shortbows will do better in that terrain.

"I'll also be holding two wizards in reserve with you. Mbata will be cranking out Catseyes, and Shadir will be responsible for producing food for the army and maintaining the structural integrity of the Golgul. If Vesh summons an earthquake or destroys the mountains, I want someone available to thread an air shield through the pass, just long enough to get my men out of it."

"Good idea," Romney agreed emphatically.

"Got any others?"

"Have you thought about hot oil vats along the rim?"

"I thought about it, but there are more arguments against it than for it. First off, those canyon walls are a good two hundred handspans high. Hot oil damage would be negligible from that height, and it would take four soldiers to work every vat. I just don't have the manpower to waste, and that, my friend, is the real problem. No matter how well we plan these defenses, we just don't have enough damned defenders."

"You've done everything you could to even the odds, my girl," Romney said, somewhat inadequately.

"I hope so, Val, I really do. Every time I go into battle, I find myself wondering how many of my kits, mrem and human, I'm going to lose today. Never gets any easier, does it?"

"No, it never does. At least we kept Taziralendra out of it."

"At least we did that," she agreed quietly, with a solemn arch of her whiskers. And Raf, and Pellar, and Jain, she added to herself silently. If they still lived.

"I'm not eating that," Jain insisted stubbornly, for the twelfth or thirteenth time. Raf was at his wits' end. They'd been following Vesh's army through the same forest terrain for four long days, and in that time their food supplies had dwindled steadily out of existence.

"You don't have a choice, son," Raf drawled, leaning back against an enormous tree. "It's grubs or empty air." He started a bit at the sound of his own voice; he'd sounded damnably like Tazira just then. Maybe that wasn't a bad thing; she seemed to have a way with recalcitrant kits.

He thought about that but decided to try simple logic first. He was Raf Grayfur, damn it. He'd argued his way around councils and kings. And he could damned well talk an Uppervale farm boy into eating a few grubs.

"Look, it's like this, Jain," he sighed, settling into pontification mode. "We're stuck behind Vesh's army, right?"

"Right," Jain agreed suspiciously.

"And they've been stripping the land bare, right?"

"Right."

"So there's nothing left to hunt. We've foraged all we can, and it isn't enough. If we're going to have even a remote chance of nailing Taran Vesh, we'll all have to be in top form to do it. And that includes you, my boy. So eat."

"No way." Jain shook his head stubbornly. "I'm not eating worms, I don't care how hungry I am. I don't care if you beat me for it. I'd rather be soundly thrashed by the both of you, twenty times a day."

So much for logic. Logic is dead, Raf thought unhappily, holding his aching head in his hands for a moment. *Tazira, make the boy eat his grubs.*

"Let me try," Pellar said helpfully, stepping off

the road and into the small clearing. He picked an asaba leaf, rolled a few grubs into it and tied it off with a purely decorative sprig of red arnow. "There!" the mrem said proudly. "Half of good cuisine is presentation. See, isn't that nice? It looks like something Tazira would make you."

"Except that it's moving," Jain grumbled.

"Just eat the leaf, and don't think about the grubs."

"I . . ." Jain breathed, beginning to falter. Just then, Raf got a really evil idea. He forced the grin off his face and turned to his reluctant private.

"Well, I suppose it's not the boy's fault, if he's just not cut out to be a Guard," Raf shrugged laconically, slouching back against his tree. Pellar narrowly managed to keep a straight face as their eyes locked in understanding.

"Now, Raf, that's not fair at all," Pellar protested, slipping into the role of good Guard with the ease of a born actor, or a born liar. "I think he's done very well for a human."

"Yeah!" Jain agreed with some heat, choosing to ignore the latter part of that statement. Pellar draped a protective arm over his shoulder, and they both glowered at Raf. If Pellar's glower turned into a broad stage wink for half a second, Jain seemed not to notice.

"I'll grant you, his fighting skills are improving. Somewhat. And he's managed to keep up with us, for the most part."

"He certainly has!" Pellar nodded firmly. "It's not his fault if he had a few romantic illusions about what life in the Guard would be like."

"Yeah," Jain frowned, not sure he should be agreeing with that.

"Really, Raf, where's your sense of compassion?" Pellar orated magnificently, beginning to chew the scenery for all he was worth. "Until he joined us, he'd had a soft life. A warm bed to sleep in. Good country breakfasts. I can just imagine it: hot biscuits, fresh out of the oven, lavished with sweet butter . . ."

"Ham steaks, scrambled eggs with just a dash of charrh . . ." Raf agreed dreamily. Then he seemed to snap out of it. "Stop it, you're making me hungry."

"Clean clothes, hot baths . . . a soft and pleasant life, one any of us would envy," Pellar nodded, waxing rhapsodic. "Then he joins the Guard, and what does he find? What, I ask you! Four-hour sleep shifts on the hard ground. Gnawing, desperate hunger. Long days of running and combat training. Any of us could run seventy leagues in a day and subsist indefinitely off grubs and root grass if we had to, but we're Tycor Guards. The best of the best, the warrior elite. It's not Jain's fault if he can't keep up." The mrem nodded firmly. "He's only human, and a farm-boy healer at that! We've been expecting entirely too much of the lad."

"Hey, wait a minute! Stop helping me!" Jain started to protest, but as usual his mentors ignored him.

"Pellar, if he wants to be a Guard, he's going to have to get used to that," Raf argued calmly, folding his hands behind him. "Guards are trained and conditioned hard. We have to be, in order to survive the life."

"Yes, but why subject Jain to that misery? To fulfill a boyhood dream? To defend humanity?"

"Yes," Raf said, arching his whiskers forward in agreement. "Particularly now, when his skills are needed more than humanity will ever need them again. Suffering tests you. Life tests you, and you can't be found wanting," the older mrem said emphatically. "Especially not when so many lives are in the balance." He tossed back a nut-sized grub to hammer his point home, crunching it indifferently.

"You're good," Jain admitted after a moment. "You're both really, really good at this. Especially you, Raf. Pellar overacts a bit."

"Oh," Pellar said, crestfallen.

"Sorry, Pellar."

"Oh, that's . . . but . . . What's wrong with my acting?" The mrem suddenly bristled.

"Not now, Pellar," Raf shook his head quietly. "Jain, all kidding aside, what I said was absolutely true. The future of both our races may be riding on our ability to sniff out Vesh's weak points and nail him."

"I know," Jain sighed. "Give me that leaf sandwich thing." Pellar handed it over with just a shade of petulance, and the human bit into it. Unpleasant didn't begin to describe the sensation. The taste wasn't all that bad—a little nutty, a little bland—but the unexpected rubbery hardness of their skin, the squish of them between his teeth as they writhed to get away, was so nauseating he almost lost it. His eyes watered, and he forced himself to keep chewing.

"I'm serious, what's wrong with my acting?" Pellar demanded. Jain swallowed the sandwich and took a long pull off his waterskin before he dared a reply.

"There's nothing wrong with your acting," Jain said, with his best pastoral-sincere face on.

"But you said—"

"Enough, both of you," Raf growled in exasperation. "Vesh and his army are getting close to the pass. The battle should be starting in a couple of hours at most. I'd like to be *in* it, if you don't mind. Now eat up, Private. We're moving out as soon as I'm convinced you've had enough."

"Yes, sir," Jain said unhappily, forcing himself to swallow another fistful of wriggling desperation cuisine.

Taran Vesh surveyed the ridge above the narrow pass. This promised to be amusing.

In all, there were probably forty or fifty catapults lining the ridge. The entire Tycor army seemed to be waiting for him inside the pass, behind neat little barricades. *How cute*, he sneered. Someone had gotten a warning back to Tycor, and instead of fleeing before him like the vermin they were, they'd actually chosen to meet him. A harsh bark of laughter burst out of his throat, startling his honor guard.

The humans looked at each other a bit nervously, then turned their attention forward again when they realized their leader was watching them. Before he'd revealed the scope of his plan to them, they'd followed him out of loyalty. Now, of course, they followed him out of fear. A nobler emotion, vastly more enjoyable. He could smell their fear, and he savored it for a moment before he turned his attention back to the ridge.

His icy gaze scanned the position for weak spots. Though a wizard, he knew he was also a supreme general, for in intelligence he had leaped far beyond the thinking ability of mere military minds. The position actually looked rather good, he thought. *One I wouldn't need, but in their desperation a final fearful effort. They're like rats in a hole futilely trying to build a barricade as a torrential flood pours down upon them.*

He spied out the forts on either flank, paused for a second to contemplate, then saw a flash of armor farther on. Seconds later another flash of armor several hundred paces away as someone stood up for a moment then, as if sensing his gaze, flung himself back down. He smiled. *An amusing little subterfuge, forces spread farther out than they want me to believe.* His attention fixed again on the center.

No sense bothering to study the enemy defenses, he thought with a smile of cool derision. *They'll be insufficient. Troops spread for a league or more on either ridge, therefore the center is weaker than they want me to believe. And I do nothing but delay my own pleasure.* Vesh felt a stirring of some barely remembered emotion, something vaguely akin to lust. If he were still capable of such human frailty, he might be inclined to think it was lust.

This moment was good, very, very good. It was power, the raw power which meant that every action he performed—the merest flicker of a finger or nod of his head—would cause something to go forward, and some human would face it, know terror, and then die. There was no power finer than that, except when the killing was done with one's own hands.

He ordered his army forward with a nod to his commander of the nits. They were the most expendable of his creatures. It was amusing: a nod of the head, a flicker of the eyes toward the pass. No word needed to be spoken, but the command was understood. Send them forward, make those who waited die.

They rushed forward in a great wave, over-whelming, flooding the dry-grass valley with gray flesh and chilling shrieks. After only the barest hesitation, the catapults high atop the crest opened fire first, flaming bolts that soared heaven-ward, seemed to hang in midair, then come racing down. As the bolts struck, the dry grass quickly ignited into flames.

If the nits had been unguided, they would have broken and fled at the sight of the fire as more bolts rained down, then arrows from the barricade across the floor of the pass joined in until the sea of dried grass was an inferno. But there was no chance of that, Vesh thought, smiling to himself. His Zara, one of his Created, controlled them as absolutely as he controlled her.

Vesh watched her as her battalion poured forth across the open field. Humans had once consid-ered her beautiful, before he'd shaped and molded her into his own image of beauty. A small, dark, twisted thing she was now, a human image of the nits he'd so carefully and lovingly bonded her to. His Created. His Zara. His magnificent Zara. Her eyes were tightly closed, the harsh planes of her face straining with intense concentration as she guided her battalion forward.

The forward edge of the wave of charging nits reached the spreading wall of fire and for a brief instant actually hesitated. His will, slashing into Zara, drove them blindly forward. They fell into the flames, dozens, hundreds, and then thousands. As they fell in their agony, rolling back and forth, kicking and screaming, their flailing about gradually extinguished the fires, creating gaps in the flames so that those coming up from behind leaped through. He could hear a murmur arise from the defenders and smiled. To see thousands die thus, even the noisome nits, was a terrible thing to behold. Their suicidal rush served merely to extinguish a fire. It was the first move in the game, and it went to him for the power it displayed.

Those passing through the flames, many of them smoldering, some actually covered with flickering flames, staggered forward straight for the barricade. Well over a thousand pressed in.

A loud crackling, then a sudden scream rent the air. The shocked scream of his Zara. It was echoed by the shrill shrieks of hundreds of nits, pouring themselves into a disintegration ward at the mouth of the pass and unable to stop themselves for the compulsion their wizard had laid on them.

She was as powerless to stop it. She collapsed and writhed in agony, screaming, sharing the pain of her Bonded. Some commander must have noted that, because a wave of long-range crossbow fire was directed at her. Vesh blocked it with an irritated wave of his hand, throwing up an air shield to protect her. With an equally dismissive gesture he shattered the humans' feeble ward, and the hundreds of surviving nits seemed to fall into the dry moat, many of them dropping onto impaling spikes, their feet torn apart by caltrops, but even as they fell those coming behind leaped upon the backs of the fallen and scrambled up to the top of the barricade.

Now, finally, the screams would be human.

Raf strained his eyes and his spyglass to their utmost limits, watching the battle from the cover of a deeply wooded hill just behind the enemy rear. He took the luxury of glancing at Tazira for just a moment as she commanded the battle from the east ridge. Her armor glinted with a painful brilliance in the light of the green sun, and for once her tail wasn't moving. She was holding it carefully and rather woodenly still behind her, to keep from betraying her agitation to the men, and Raf smiled wryly at her attempt. For the moment, at least, Old Lash wasn't lashing.

A wall of gray suddenly blocked her from his view, and the mrem's heart leaped into his throat. Vesh was sending his gargoyles against her, with the obvious intention of taking the high ground. While the catapults were effective enough against the ground forces, they weren't nearly fast or mobile enough to take out individual flying monsters. A few tried, with only marginal success, and the wave of gargoyles pressed forward, concentrating on Tazira and the east ridge. Their enormous wings seemed to swallow the sky itself.

He could barely, briefly catch glimpses of Tazira between them. Her long tail never even twitched, as far as Raf could tell. She raised a yellow signal flag, brought it down with a slashing motion and bellowed an order he couldn't hear. The first line of gargoyles shrieked and plunged to earth. And the second. As their ranks began to thin, Raf could make out thick volleys of arrowfire coming from what must have been trenches on the ridge.

The ranks of gargoyles continued their relentless advance. Vesh threw up another air shield to protect them from the arrows, and the next volley bounced off it. Tazira quickly signaled a cease-fire, to save ammunition, and the gargoyle advance picked up speed. They shrieked with the fierce joy of the kill, and Raf's hackles rose at the sound.

The first wave of them crested the ridge with a resounding crack, and the shrieks of the others rose to a terrified, bloodcurdling pitch. *Another disintegration ward?* Raf wondered, unable to tell from that distance. The gargoyle ranks swiftly thinned enough that Raf could see them bursting into powder as they hit an invisible wall. It had to be a second ward! He almost had to clamp down his jaw to keep from cheering.

The ward decimated dozens of monsters before Vesh could burn it out. They were felled, one row after the next, almost too swiftly to see, the speed of their attack dive playing into the trap. But when the killing barrier finally collapsed a few seconds later, the last line of gargoyles managed to dive through it and land on the ridge. They closed on

Tazira with blinding speed, and Raf had to turn away at that, unable to watch anymore. He turned just in time to see Jain nock and draw back an arrow, and he grabbed it before the boy could fire the longbow.

"No! You can't help her, Jain," he rasped. "She's out of range, and all you'll do is give away our position."

"I can't just stand here and watch!" Jain stammered. Raf didn't bother to argue the point; he knew exactly how the boy felt. Helpless, like him.

A sudden sharp gasp from Pellar made Raf look back in spite of himself. A tight flame shield shot out around Tazira and swept outward, searing the monsters instantly to ash as it expanded to enfold them. They were too closely packed to run or to take off into the air again, though a few tried. Their bright outlines burned against the shield for the space of a breath, then were gone as quickly.

Tazira dissolved the spell with a flourish after a few seconds. A lusty cheer sounded over the ridges as she bowed to her men, waving her white-tipped tail at Vesh in a vulgar and broadly comic gesture of contempt. Raf sank to his knees and shook with relief, and Jain and Pellar pounded each other on the back impulsively, barely resisting the urge to cheer out loud themselves.

Vesh snarled with rage and hurled a fireball at her, and Tazira dove into the nearest trench. The fireball hit the ridge with stunning impact, but missed its target. She sprang to her feet, waved to her men, and licked her shoulder at the wizard. Her mrem soldiers yowled delightedly at the gesture.

"That's our Tazira," Pellar laughed softly. Raf wasn't nearly so amused.

"What in the name of the three blasted suns does she think she's doing?" the gray mrem hissed tensely, wringing his tail in his anxiety. "Is the woman *trying* to make my fur fall out?"

"I'd say she's trying to keep Vesh distracted, and doing a good job of it," Pellar whispered back. "He's completely lost focus on the action in the pass."

Raf spared a reluctant glance at the ground battle, realizing he'd done the same. The humans had been pushed back to the second barricade, but they were fighting ferociously to take back the lost ground. The front line of the phalanx was keeping the nits at bay with their longspears, if barely, and thick volleys of arrowfire were felling the monsters in droves. But the hundreds that died were simply replaced in seemingly inexhaustible waves.

"I wonder how many hours or days she'll have before all those dead monsters start to resurrect," Raf whispered. Jain started visibly, turned, and stared at him for a moment.

"Shards, I hadn't thought of that," the boy admitted. "How are you supposed to defeat an enemy that won't stay dead?"

"You're not," the mrem replied flatly, turning back to scan the battlefield. "The only possible way to disperse that army permanently is to kill Vesh, and that's probably going to be impossible. Until that happens, Tazira's best bet is a holding action. She'll have to keep him and his army bottled up here while we or her wizards find a way to take him out. Shards and ashes!" he cursed sharply, and Pellar and Jain turned quickly back to the battle.

The gargoyles were resurrected already, all of them, and they were taking to the air for another attack on the left ridge.

Jain went dead white. If the monsters were resurrecting this quickly, there was no force on Delos that would be able to stand against them, no strategy cunning enough to do anything more than delay them for a handful of hours. He would have prayed, if there was anything left to pray to. As it was, all he could do was watch.

Raf lifted the spyglass, almost unwillingly, and peered through it. Tazira was standing calmly at her place on the ridge, and Thodorus, one of Romney's older and more powerful court wizards, was standing at her shoulder. The wave of gargoyles shrieked toward the ridge, flying faster and faster. Not a single arrow arced through the air. The knot in Raf's stomach tightened.

"Tazira . . ." he hissed, unable to help himself. "Do something, damn you . . ."

He could catch only the occasional, fleeting glimpse of her behind a nearly solid wall of gray flesh. She nodded coolly to the man behind her, who held up a large spellstone and fired it. The wave of gargoyles disappeared, replaced by a horde of useless nits—useless, falling nits, suddenly deprived of their wings and their power of flight in the same moment. They shrilled in terror as they plunged to the ground, and cheers and laughter echoed along both ridges.

Laughter, Raf thought, so wild with relief that he barely mastered his own. *Shards, they're laughing at*

Taran Vesh! Their eventual defeat might have been written in stone already, but there was an odd sort of victory in the humans' laughter. Vesh screamed with incoherent rage and started firing random spells in Tazira's direction, and Thodorus hastily stepped in front of her and moved to counter them with his own. Another wizard joined Thodorus, and the rest concentrated on the battle in the pass below them.

With a sharp wave of his arm, Vesh sent his Lizcanth rushing into the pass over the bodies of his own nits, and went right back to blasting the ridge. The monsters moved with unnerving speed and a desperate hunger, and the nits shrilled in agony as the reptiles ran over them in waves of hundreds. Zara screamed, and was ignored.

Tazira grimly threw the next signal. Her soldiers lining the barricade turned and ran. They sprinted across the open ground, falling back to the next defensive line. Archers already deployed at that line fired high, arcing their shots over their retreating comrades. From up on the steep side slopes concealed skirmishers stood up, kicking over small boulders that plunged and bounced down the sides of the pass and crashed into other boulders, setting them rolling, so that by the time the rocks reached the bottom they were an avalanche.

The Lizcanth charge swarmed up over the abandoned barricade, hundreds of them, bellowing with blood lust as they leaped over the wall and sprinted after the fleeing humans, the sight of their running prey's backs triggering the instinctive lust of the hunt and the kill.

On either flank scores of the deadly creatures were swept under by the avalanches; yet in the center of the pass a solid wall of them were coming on fast. As the forward wave dropped from hissing arrows raining down, those following simply leaped high over their writhing companions and charged on.

The retreating line was back to the next barricade, but here was the moment Tazira had feared. She had designed the choke points of sally ports cut at intervals of fifty feet. If the men panicked and started to push their way in, dozens might fall into the dry moats. Pride swept through her as discipline held. The first warriors to reach the ports actually turned, forming defensive perimeters, while those lagging behind, dragging along the wounded, were pushed through first. As the last of the wounded cleared the barricade, sergeants shouted off sections to fall back in turn while the archers who lined the barricades poured out a steady stream of fire over the heads of the warriors.

Still it was turning into a near disaster. She looked back at the abandoned barricade. The lizard phalanx was still pouring over. Hundreds had yet to get into the killing ground, but the forward edge of the charge was getting too damned close to the last of the men who were grimly holding the sally ports and waiting their turn for escape.

She hastily threw another signal, and the second ward in the pass went up. The lizards began pouring themselves into it, obviously under the same compulsion the nits had been. Waves of arrowfire assisted by a mass sureshot spell now slammed into the charge from the archers as the last of their comrades gained the sally ports and the carts were dragged across behind them to make fast the barricade. Lizards died by the hundreds.

After a moment, the monsters broke and fled, their compulsion apparently lifted. Tazira fired off a third ward, concealed just behind the abandoned barricade, thus trapping the remainder of the assaulting phalanx.

Thick volleys of arrowfire continued to fell the creatures without mercy. Their shrieks reached an unearthly crescendo of rage and terror that gradually died off to low plaintive moans of pain from the wounded and dying. There was no need to expend a precious mass fiery death spell from the heights above, so she ordered them to be finished off with a burning spell of disposal. It was an act of mercy, which one should extend even to such loathsome things. The blue flames ignited, flared, then died away, so that not even the creatures' charred remains were left. There was a moment of stunned silence and then wild cheering for a remarkable victory in which barely a man had been injured while well over a thousand of the enemy had died. The carts blocking the sally ports were pulled back, and companies of fresh reserves sprinted out, racing back to the abandoned barricade and reclaiming it before Vesh could send in the next wave.

"Has either of you been watching the enemy wizards at all?" Pellar whispered, glancing back at Raf and Jain with a raised eyebrow.

"Honestly? Not really," Raf admitted bluntly. "I've been a bit distracted for some reason."

"Understandable enough." Pellar smiled at him. "What about you, lad?"

"Well," Jain began a bit hesitantly, "I noticed that the one who's leading the nits can feel their pain. The monsters and the wizards seem to be linked in some way."

"Very good," Pellar nodded, talking swiftly in his excitement. "I noticed the same thing when the nits ran into the first ward. The wizards can feel their creatures' pain, and they seem to be able to compel them to charge. Monsters don't attack in organized groups, and generally speaking they're pretty easy to frighten off. The sight of fire or a large group of humans should have been enough to break them and send them packing, but it wasn't. They have to be acting under a powerful compulsion. But what happens to that link if we manage to eliminate the wizards?"

"Interesting," Raf murmured, glancing down the field at the two wizards who'd come with Vesh. The giant spiders' wizard was redoubtably fenced in by her creatures, and unassailable from the pass or the ridges. But a few good shots from behind the lines just might suffice to take her out. The nits' wizard had fared much worse; the woman was lying alone and untended on a bare patch of ground behind the forces of her slowly resurrecting creatures. She was moving, if barely, seeming to grow a little stronger with the rebirth of each of her Bonded. She looked like nothing so much as a charred and broken doll, one Vesh temporarily had no use for.

"I seem to recall Vesh putting an air shield up around the nits' wizard in the beginning of the battle," Raf frowned, plucking Jain's longbow out of his hands. He nocked an arrow without looking at it, considering the woman thoughtfully. "I wonder if he's been able to keep that up, with all the other spells he's been throwing."

He drew back the bow and fired at her, experimentally. His arrow bounced off her still-active shield, but she apparently felt or heard it. She lifted her head with obvious effort, scanning the trees behind her with suspicious dark eyes. She knew there were human assassins behind the lines, whether or not she could actually see them. Jain shied like a nervous animal and prepared to bolt, but Raf's gentle hand on his arm stopped him. All the world seemed to hold its breath.

She might have screamed, alerting her troops, and Vesh. She might have set the entire forest ablaze, or worse. But she didn't. With all the strength she had left, the wizard pulled herself painfully to her knees, and then to her feet, and staggered almost blindly out of the protection of the air shield.

Her black cloak flowed around her like a live thing, a stark, oddly fragile silhouette against a sea of blood and flame. Her thin dark arms spread wide, a gesture of supplication, a last hushed embrace of the wind and the light. There was no trace of fear in her eyes, or resignation either. She wanted this.

"Do it, shards damn you," she rasped hoarsely, just loud enough to be heard over the din of battle. "Kill me while he's distracted and I'm free of him. Do it, and when I see you on the other side, I'll bless you for it."

The woman smiled in sharp-toothed self-mockery and waited. Raf drew the bow back, hesitated for the space of a breath, and fired. The arrow took the woman clean through the heart. She crumpled silently, a dark unsettling puppet whose strings had been suddenly sliced through, and her resurrecting nits began to shrill in confused terror.

Raf drew out another arrow and turned to fire on the other wizard, but Pellar was well ahead of him. The tall, graceful woman behind the line of giant spiders fell beneath their combined barrage of arrows, screaming. Because she'd been behind her giant spiders, Vesh apparently hadn't seen the need to protect her with any sort of shielding at all.

Her master turned back to her in irritation, and paused in obvious shock as he got a truly good look at her. He broke off his attack on the ridge and turned to scan the forest behind him, a grimace of inhuman and terrifying rage marring his brutal features.

"*Now* you should run," Raf assured Jain tightly, pulling him along as he hastily took his own advice. The trees erupted behind them, row by row, the shockwaves propelling the Guards along ever faster as they fled. Jain stumbled on the uneven ground, scrambled up again, and a gray-furred hand pulled him down roughly into a shallow bank to wait out the explosions.

The human curled into a ball against the narrow wall of earth, covered his head with his arms, and shook. His breath was coming in short, shallow gasps, and the thunderous explosions drowned out everything except the sound of his own wild and erratic heartbeat. He couldn't even hear himself choke, though he knew he was doing it. The suddenly scorching air was filled with debris and flying splinters, making each breath an agony.

Finally, the explosions stopped, suddenly and seemingly for no reason. Jain started to look up over the ridge, and Pellar pushed his head gently back down. He held up a small polished silver handmirror with an intricately carved backing, and he used it to scan the forest, or what was left of the forest.

"Where on Delos did you get that?" Raf hissed tightly, biting back a cough and struggling to normalize his breathing.

"Oh, I stole it from the castle," Pellar whispered back a bit hoarsely. "Nice, isn't it? I just knew it would be useful for something."

Raf shook his head with a sigh of exquisite martyrdom, not bothering to reply to that. Pellar turned his attention back to the mirror and the blasted ground behind them. Almost half a league of forest was a decimated tribute to Vesh's rage. The trees were reduced to charred kindling, and the ground was a mottled gray-black that stretched all the way back to the burning battlefield.

"It's safe to look up," Pellar murmured softly. "Vesh and his minions seem to be a bit distracted at the moment." Raf and Jain peered over the bank, and the human let out a low whistle, partly for the forest around them and partly for the chaos on the field. It was a sheet of flame, one long brushfire that had caught and apparently refused to let go.

Vesh's monsters were burning, reanimating,

and burning again in a vicious and terrible cycle. The giant spiders and nits had slipped the control of their dead masters, and those that weren't fleeing were mindlessly preying on each other and anything else they could find. The humans were taking full advantage of the situation, raining arrows, heavy catapult bolts, and mass confusion spells onto the field below them. Vesh alone seemed to be unaffected; he was surrounded by a glowing red nimbus, and the flames slid away from its surface like oil, slick and tainted.

Seeming to gather a measure of calmness from the chaos around him, the wizard surveyed the utter rout of his forces. If he felt anything at having been outwitted, even mocked by the humans, his face showed no sign of it. The terrible rage, the absolute loss of control of the last few minutes might never have happened at all.

Vesh held up a cool white hand, and the flames died swiftly away. The nits and giant spiders disappeared, and his Lizcanth, ghoul, and gargoyle battalions reformed, along with a stone giant and twenty ogres. The ground was black beneath them, but it was the only evidence that that hellish vision hadn't been an act of collective imagining. The humans had done their worst, and it wasn't enough.

The wizard gestured again, and his ghouls shambled forward. The humans in the pass braced themselves for another charge.

"Light," Jain whispered to no one in particular. "We can't lose; we can't afford to. Death would be a welcome release from what we'll suffer under Vesh."

"Especially Tazira," Raf murmured softly, staring at the battlefield without really seeing it. "She baited him on purpose, you know: one more way of protecting her own. When Vesh wins, and she knows he will, she's the one he'll seek and focus on, possibly to the exclusion of all else. She'll sacrifice herself for them, do everything she can to keep his twisted attention on her for as long as she can stand it. That damnable martyr complex of hers is going to be the death of her. If she's lucky." Anger and hopelessness warred across his face, and anger won.

"We *have* to find those other wizards," he hissed. "The ones controlling the remaining battalions."

"Raf, we have no idea where they've gone!" Pellar shook his head emphatically. "Tracking takes time, even if we're able to find them at all—"

"We have to try," Raf insisted. "We're the only ones who have a chance; we saw them leave Vesh's base camp and head east. We know where to start, and that's more than anyone but Tazira knows. She's a little busy right now. That leaves us."

"But Vesh—" His friend started to argue, then stopped himself. "We have no shot at taking Vesh out, do we? Not with half a league of decimated forest for cover. If we couldn't get near him before, we're never going to do it now."

"Right you are," Raf arched his whiskers forward in agreement. "But killing the other wizards will tear his army apart, and it's about the only thing that will."

"Looks like we're the only Guards in the neighborhood again," Pellar smirked. Raf barked a short, astonished laugh in spite of himself. Jain thought it might be another of their inside jokes, because he didn't understand it.

"Looks like," Raf agreed equably. "Let's get ready to run."

He cast one final look at Tazira, burning every line of her into his memory, bristling as a shot of ball lightning came much too close to her for his comfort. *Hold on, love. Hold them off as long as you can, and we'll find a way to do the rest,* he promised her, and himself.

Chapter 17

"THE BASTARD IS INEXHAUSTIBLE!" TAZIRA snarled under her breath, glowering at the wizard in the center of the charred and blasted field. "Ordinarily, I'd consider that a fine quality in a man."

She smirked in spite of her mood, and shook her head. *Bad Tazira. Must pry my mind out of the sewers one of these days, and up into the gutter with my friends.*

That brought another smile, followed shortly by the painful remembrance that those friends had surely died two days ago, when Vesh blasted out half a league of forest around their last known position. She wouldn't think about that, not until the battle was over. She could stand it then. Most likely she'd be dead herself, and she wouldn't have to worry about it.

The Tycoran wizards on both sides of the ridge had kept Vesh under a steady bombardment of spells, hour after hour without ceasing, for the last three days. Vesh was the key to everything; if they could kill him, exhaust him, or strip him of his power, the monsters could be driven away. But the court wizards were tiring, as Tazira and her men were tiring, in spite of the healers' best efforts to keep them awake and working at full strength. And Vesh and his constantly resurrecting troops seemed none the worse for wear.

Twice her troops had been forced to retreat back to the center of the pass, where the enemy was stopped by the double wards, and once the monsters had broken through even that and pushed nearly to the far end before being driven back. What was so damnably frustrating was that in that final charge Vesh had, for all practical purposes, been annihilated. Not one stone giant, not one ogre, and a mere handful of lizards and gargoyles had managed to survive the blistering counterattack, which had swept all the way back to the first barricade. In any other war, it would have been over, the defeated wizard crawling away to hide or more likely to be torn apart by his slaves, who would finally break free of his bonds and turn on him in their frustration and agony.

But this was a war against Vesh.

In the last countercharge, her warriors cheered as they advanced, believing that victory might be at hand, but they reached the first barricade and then stopped. For out on the plains they could see it. Her numbed, exhausted warriors watched as inexorably Vesh drew back his minions from death, resurrecting them yet again, rank upon rank, column upon column, by the hundreds and the thousands, as if his strength in magics was inexhaustible, which in fact it was. She knew it was a taunt, a game, a perverse act like that of a sick, disturbed child who tortures a mouse, letting the tormented thing believe it might actually slip away and live and then, at the last second, dragging it back for another round of pain.

For one of the few times in her long years of command she saw comrades weep, not from the anguish of losing a friend or even from sheer exhaustion, but rather out of frustration and rage, knowing that their victory of the moment was hollow and that soon it would start yet again, and continue this way, perhaps forever if Vesh in his sickness wished it so.

Behind her own lines, in the hospital area established in the valley beyond the pass, the precious healers worked as well, but now for every man they saved, five or more were simply falling into the final abyss, not as a result of wounds, but from what appeared to be a final woe, a belief that to struggle to live had become a gesture of futility, and the silence and peace beyond were now preferable.

Shards, I knew it would be this bad, if not worse. No sense whining about it. At least she was goading herself in her own voice, this time; no need to summon Romney to her mind when he was so close to hand.

Mostly for the sake of her already raw nerves, she'd put him in charge of the reserves at the north end of the pass. He was training conscripts, ordering their few reinforcements around, and staying mercifully out of her fur. This battle was hard enough without her old mentor staring over her shoulder; with him, it would have been impossible.

Focus, girl, his voice came unbidden into her mind, and with irritated effort she dragged her wandering attention back to the battle. *If you lose focus, so will they.*

The ghouls, with their shambling slowness and inferior weapons, had been no match for the long-spears and tower shields of her phalanx. Tazira hadn't bothered firing any traps on them; she needed to save those for the Lizcanth. Having withdrawn his ghouls in frustration, Vesh would send the Lizcanth in next, if he was running true to form.

She glanced out at the army beyond the ridge. The Lizcanth were preparing to charge. *What a surprise,* she thought ironically. *Of course, if he actually* does *decide to try something new, it'll come as such a shock that I won't be able to cope with it.*

The stone giant chose that moment to resurrect, again, and Thodorus groaned from his vantage point beside Tazira.

"This is getting tiresome," he growled. "Any other army on Delos would have broken ten times over by now." She wasn't sure whether he was referring to Vesh's army or their own, but either way, she found herself in agreement.

"Your turn to deal with the stone giant," Tazira shrugged. "I got him last time." Finding clever ways to kill the monsters had become an elaborate game between them, a farak match with deadly implications, a way to keep their wits sharp through an increasingly prolonged and difficult siege. Thodorus frowned thoughtfully for a moment, brightened, and started fishing through his pouch.

"I've got one," he smirked. "A simple spell, one of the first I ever learned. Create-water."

Tazira grinned back, instantly grasping the course of his thoughts. "You're a sick man, Tho, and I respect that."

"Thank you, Captain," he drawled with a mock salute.

As the Lizcanth rushed forward in a great, glittering, malevolent wave, and the stone giant made another hamfisted grasp for the ridge, Thodorus held up a small stone and fired it straight into the open mouth of the monster. The giant paused in its tracks, howled in pain, and clutched impotently at its rapidly expanding stomach. A geyser of water shot out of its open mouth with such force that it fell over backward, so that a fountain then soared a hundred feet into the air.

In all the madness it was actually a rather lovely sight. Some of the soldiers lining the ridge broke into appreciative applause, until the stomach of the giant ruptured from the pressure. Massive chunks of stone bombarded the ridge and rained over Vesh's army, and Tazira braced carefully to keep her balance, holding Thodorus up as well.

A light breeze carried a mist of water over the line. It felt refreshingly cool, and she nodded her thanks to Thodorus, who was obviously proud of the show.

The first line of Lizcanth charged into the mouth of the pass below them, and wizard and warrior exchanged a quick glance.

"Fire the next ward?" he asked her.

"No, the stone door," she snapped with a

wicked grin. "Time to really start annoying Vesh; when he gets angry, he stops thinking."

The aging wizard nodded wordlessly and complied, setting the door squarely in front of the rapidly advancing line of reptiles. A few of them ran headlong into it and were stunned, but their compulsion was swiftly taken off, and the rest stood and stared at the new, unpredictable barrier. With a look almost of intelligence, they started to scan the walls of the pass, searching for a way around it. A silvery, feminine voice spoke to them in soothing tones.

By the Triune Suns I speak it: I can hold but never touch it, the door informed them softly. The lizards looked at it, mystified, and a handful of them began to sniff at it suspiciously. The door repeated itself politely, and the monsters stared in blank, uncomprehending consternation. Behind them, Vesh howled with lathering fury and sank to his knees. The Lizcanth shrilled and started to explode.

Frantic, incoherent with rage, Vesh rummaged through his spellpouch. He tossed stones aside thoughtlessly, looking for the one he wanted. The earthquake spell. The one that would end this and bring the mrem bitch to her knees, where she belonged. There, it was there, he felt it fire in his hand . . . and he stopped it.

No, he thought, something like lucidity coming back to him. *No, an earthquake will kill her, kill all the humans in the pass, kill them all when I want them alive. I want her alive, I want her to taste the deepest humiliation, age after age without ending, I want her to service me in front of her own soldiers . . .*

UNIMAGINATIVE, TARAN, a vast, familiar echo sounded painfully in his head. Vesh clutched his skull, as he always did when the Master spoke to him.

UNIMAGINATIVE AND CRASS, it said, amused and disapproving all at once. RAPE LACKS FINESSE. THERE ARE FAR SUBTLER PLEASURES, BUT I SUSPECT MY TEACHINGS WOULD BE WASTED ON ONE OF YOUR ILK. NOW, THE "MREM BITCH," AS YOU CALL HER, SHE HAS POSSIBILITIES. CUNNING, AND A STREAK OF PRAGMATISM THAT COULD EASILY BE TWISTED INTO RUTHLESSNESS. WHAT WOULD HAPPEN, I WONDER, IF SHE WAS TURNED? SHE WOULD OUTSTRIP YOU AND A HUNDRED LIKE YOU.

PERHAPS I CHOSE THE WRONG VESSEL, it continued almost thoughtfully after a moment. AT ANY RATE, THAT ONE INTRIGUES ME.

Master? the wizard thought into the sudden silence, terrified as he'd never been, even as a child. Silence was his only answer, and his fear grew.

"Attack!" Tazira cried, her tail lashing in her sudden excitement. Vesh was down, writhing on the ground for no apparent reason, and his troops were milling in growing confusion. She would have been an imbecile not to take advantage of the moment. "Fire catapults! Switch out the pass defenders and fortify with reinforcements while we've got a moment's breathing space! And for Light's sake, Thodorus, do something about those spellstones Vesh dropped on the ground! Move, people!"

Her orders were carried out with more than the usual alacrity, and if looks alone could have decimated Vesh, the intensity blazing in her eyes would have gone a fair way to doing it.

SUCH A BLOODTHIRSTY CREATURE, a vast and terrifying voice suddenly filled her mind. Tazira could feel the echo of it even in the marrow of her bones, and her black fur spiked out as she clutched her head in pain.

"What . . . who are you?" she hissed, afraid.

A KINDRED SOUL, LITTLE MREM, it thought at her with what felt like amusement. Its mind slid over hers, probing, violating, leaving a slick trail of tainted thought everywhere it touched.

"Vesh, you son of a bitch, get out of my mind!" she screamed, clutching her head ever tighter in a fruitless attempt to crush him out.

"Captain, what's wrong?" one of her adjutants asked urgently, wanting to grab her and shake her out of it, but suddenly afraid to approach.

NOT VESH, MY PET, it answered her, half laughter and half impatience. I CREATED VESH. I AM CALLED THE DARK.

"I don't care if you're called the Winterfest Bunny," the woman snarled, trying to keep any trace of fear or desperation out of her voice. "I said get out, and I mean it. Get out! I have a war to fight!"

I AM YOUR WAR. AND I CAN GIVE YOU THE POWER TO WIN THIS ONE. SUCH POWER, it sighed, and a dark wind echoed through the pass below them, IF YOU OBEY ME.

Tazira remembered those words coming out of

Vesh's mouth just after he'd punished Najendra, and she shivered.

I WILL GIVE YOU THE POWER TO DEFEAT VESH, THE POWER TO CLAIM TYCOR FOR YOURSELF. YOU WILL BE THE GREATEST WARRIOR QUEEN IN THE HISTORY OF THIS WORLD. HUMANS AND MREM ALIKE WILL FALL AT YOUR HEEL AND PAY YOU HOMAGE.

"I don't *want* that." She shook her head vehemently. "Why would I? Power brings responsibility, and I've already got enough of that to last me three lifetimes!"

"Captain?" Thodorus asked her, touching a gentle hand to her forehead. There was a moment's silence as the Dark pondered its next move. "Captain, can you hear me?"

"There's something . . . inside my mind, I think," Tazira admitted quietly, in a dreadfully calm, detached voice. "That, or Old Lash has finally lost her wits. I think you'd better stay back. Sergeant Rlirr is in charge until I can—"

She cut herself off with a sharp gasp as an agony more intense than anything she'd ever felt ripped through every limb. She sank to her knees and curled into a tight ball, trying not to scream. She'd bite her own tongue out before she gave this bastard the satisfaction.

OBEY ME.

"Kiss my ass!"

SUCH LANGUAGE, it chided her. OBEY ME, AND THE PAIN WILL STOP. OBEY ME, AND I'LL GIVE YOU THE POWER TO DEFEAT VESH AND SAVE THESE PEOPLE.

"So you can rule them through me, make everything I ever fought for meaningless?" Tazira raved, barely managing coherence through the pain.

THEY WILL SERVE US, AND LIVE, AS YOU WILL LIVE.

"Healer!" Thodorus cried, clutching Tazira's shoulders.

"Don't touch her!" the familiar, whip-sharp voice of Sergeant Rlirr snapped. "I think she's about to frenzy!"

POOR TAZIRA. POOR KIT. IT DOESN'T HAVE TO BE LIKE THIS. YOU CAN STOP THE PAIN WITH A SINGLE WORD. YES, it simpered in a grotesque parody of compassion. YES . . .

The pain continued, increased, if such a thing were possible. Tazira gritted her teeth and took in short, sharp gasps of air, fighting back tears. Rlirr looked at her for a long moment and finally came to a decision that clearly pained her.

"I'm truly sorry for this, Captain," the sergeant whispered, her claws splaying, glinting dull red in the suns' light. "More than I think you'll ever know. You were a talented commander, and I respected you, and I hope someday I'll be worthy of the honor of having killed you." Her powerful, ginger-furred arm rose to strike the ritual death-blow that the mrem used to put a comrade out of agony, for it was obvious that her commander and friend was possessed and would die a horrid death once the being that had seized her was done with its play. "Die well, Tazira Goldeneyes," she said softly, regretfully. "May you always be remembered with honor."

"No!" Thodorus cried, grabbing her arm and trying to pull her away from Tazira.

All at once the pain stopped, and a numb, heavy warmth spread through Tazira's limbs. She gasped in pure shock and tried to move. Slowly, achingly slowly, she managed to raise her head. Rlirr and Thodorus were engaged in an undignified tussle a few handspans away, and Rlirr was lunging for her with teeth and claws bared.

"At ease, both of you!" Tazira snapped, unable to do anything else to defend herself from the sudden, unexpected attack. Her voice was shockingly weak, but it carried. The two of them stopped dead in their tracks. Rlirr looked ashamed of something, and Tho looked insanely relieved. "Sna . . . Sergeant Rlirr," Tazira corrected herself with acid precision, "I assure you, I'm in no danger of frenzy. Now quit screwing around and get in charge of this battle! Thodorus, do anything she tells you to! Move!"

The pair literally jumped to do her bidding, and Tazira slowly began to force herself to her feet. Limb by limb, a bit at a time, she willed her body to obey her. Private Hallir stepped forward to try to help her, and she warned him off with a shake of her head.

"Not safe to come near me yet," she grunted to him, taking her first step and biting back a gasp at the pain.

IMPRESSIVE, TRULY, the Dark crooned. ALL THAT NOBLE DETERMINATION.

"Thank you," Tazira growled icily. "Now, if you'll excuse me, whatever you are, I intend to beat your puppet wizard into the ground."

SO SPIRITED, it mocked. SURELY YOU'VE RE-ALIZED BY NOW THAT YOU'RE GOING TO LOSE. ALL THE DETERMINATION IN THE WORLD WON'T CHANGE THE OUTCOME OF THIS BATTLE.

Tazira looked down into the pass, expecting the worst, but what she saw was enough to hearten her. The stone door was still in place, and it was currently blasting the ogres apart. Vesh hadn't yet guessed the answer to the riddle.

NO, OF COURSE HE HASN'T GUESSED IT. BUT I HAVE. DO YOU HONESTLY THINK THERE'S A RIDDLE I HAVEN'T KNOWN THE ANSWER TO SINCE BEFORE THIS WORLD WAS CREATED? I'M OLDER THAN THESE MOUNTAINS, LITTLE MREM, AS OLD AS HATE ITSELF. IF I WILL IT, THE DOOR WILL OPEN, AND YOU AND YOURS WILL BE DE-STROYED. BUT YOU COULD SAVE THEM ALL WITH A SINGLE WORD; YOU'D RULE THEM MORE GENTLY THAN VESH.

"The shards I would," Tazira laughed softly. "Do you really think I have no inkling of just how terrible I could be, if I let myself become anything like you and your pet wizard? I'd be worse than Vesh, much worse. I've chosen not to walk that path, and I continue to choose my own way. Not yours, and not his.

"Whoever you are, whatever you are, you're absolutely right that nothing can change the outcome of this battle. We're going to win it," she spat with a sudden gleam in her eye. "It doesn't matter how many riddles you know the answers to, how many stone doors you open, how many of us you kill. We've fought your invincible army to a standstill for three days! Who would have expected that? With minimal warning and minimal preparation, we're holding you here. We may die to a man, but in every meaningful sense of the word, we've won already."

WHAT PRICE VICTORY, KIT? WHAT WILL ANY OF IT MATTER IF YOU DIE? AND IF DEATH IS YOUR ONLY OPTION, WHAT DOES IT MATTER HOW YOU EMBRACE IT?

"When death is the only option, how we die is *all* that matters," the woman responded with quiet intensity. "If we die, we die well, and the other human cities already rising to crush you will remember us with honor. You think you know the answers to every riddle in existence? You don't. The human spirit clearly eludes you, and I think it always will. Now get out of my mind, because I've got work to do."

For a long, jarring moment, Tazira's skull echoed with the creature's laughter. Her tail lashed in irritation, and she started to force herself to walk back to her place at the front of the ridge.

SUCH A STUPID CREATURE, SO TYPICAL OF YOUR KIND. YOU GENUINELY SEEM TO BELIEVE YOU HAVE A CHANCE WITHOUT ME, it sighed in what felt like amused astonishment. LOOK LONG AND HARD AT ALL THESE PEOPLE YOU LOVE, CITIZENS AND SOLDIERS YOU'VE SPENT YOUR LIFE DEFENDING. THEY'LL DIE, ALL OF THEM, FOR NOTHING BETTER THAN YOUR PRIDE.

AND YOUR FRIENDS, RAF GRAYFUR AND PELLAR LONGCLAW, WILL SUFFER AGES OF

AGONY BEFORE I TIRE OF THEM AND LET THEM SLIP OFF INTO THE VOID. THEY'RE VERY MUCH ALIVE, MY KIT, AND I CAN KEEP THEM ALIVE FOR A LONG, LONG TIME. CENTURIES. AEONS.

"No . . . No, they died two days ago," Tazira murmured in growing horror. She'd thought they were safe, at least, untouchable in death. The creature's mocking laughter echoed in her skull again, painfully.

STILL ALIVE, it gloated, scenting triumph at last. STILL ALIVE, AND MINE, WHENEVER I WANT THEM. MY CREATURES, MY PETS.

"Like Vesh?" she bristled, somewhere between rage and sickening fear, a fear she'd never felt in combat, and never would have felt for herself. She sensed the thing's power, godlike to her, sensed malevolence and madness and cruelty beyond imagining. And it would lavish all those things on Raf, Pellar, and Jain, to punish her for her defiance. She was condemning her friends, not to death, but to tortures she probably couldn't begin to imagine. Shards and ashes, there had to be another way.

"Take me instead," Tazira insisted desperately, as close to pleading as she'd ever come. "Call off this attack and do anything you want with me. I imagine I could keep you entertained for a long, long time."

TOO EASY, TAZIRA. TOO EASY A CHOICE, AND MUCH LESS INTERESTING THAN WATCHING YOU RACK YOURSELF OVER THIS ONE. YOUR RAF IS ALWAYS MOUTHING PLATITUDES ABOUT CHOICE AS THE DEFIN-

ING POWER OF SELF; LET'S SEE IT PROVEN IN YOU, NOW. YOUR FRIENDS, OR YOUR CITY? HONOR, OR LOVE? SURRENDER, AND SOME OF THESE PEOPLE WILL LIVE, BROKEN UNDER YOUR CLAW. YOU'LL HAVE YOUR FRIENDS WITH YOU ALWAYS, AGELESS AND IMMORTAL.

"I can't do that," Tazira said slowly, forcing herself to speak every damning word. A breath caught in her throat, almost a sob. "I owe it to these people to defend them. Raf and Pellar would understand that better than anyone. I think even Jain would understand. They're Guards . . . and I always knew I might have to sacrifice them," she said, doing her best to sound cold about it. "It's a risk we all accepted, long ago. Now, for the last time, get out of my mind and stay out. If by some strange chance I survive this, I swear by their blood, I'll hunt you to the ends of Delos. And I'll find a way to destroy you, no matter how many lifetimes it takes me."

SO BE IT.

With a great and terrible rush, the thing was gone from her mind. Tazira felt sick. She'd condemned three of her closest friends. She'd killed them. Worse.

No, she realized, correcting herself sharply. This had to be exactly what the creature wanted her to do; this might have been its entire purpose in tormenting her. Perhaps it hadn't wanted to corrupt her at all, not really. It had done something worse, after all, much worse. It had made her responsible for the agonized deaths of her loved ones, thus striking at her in the deepest way anything could.

That might have been the thing's purpose, but it didn't change what she'd done.

Tazira looked out over the ridge at the battle below. The Stone Door was still holding, though she doubted that would last much longer. Tears pricked at the back of her eyelids, and she willed them not to fall, knowing half the soldiers on the ridge had to be watching their captain out of the corners of their eyes.

More than anything, she wanted to lay her head in her paws and howl like a lost kit for what she'd done, for what she would never have again, for the love she'd lain like a sacrificial offering at the altar of her conscience. But she couldn't, not yet. Not until it was over, and she'd given every last pathetic scrap of her soul to the battle. There would be time to grieve later, when she was no longer needed, if she was unfortunate enough to survive.

She held everything, every shred of grief and physical pain behind a tight, brittle mask of self-control as she made her way to the front of the ridge.

TARAN.

"Master?" the wizard answered in a quavering voice, looking wildly around him. It had never helped to look; no one ever saw the face of the Dark. "Master, have I displeased you?"

YES.

The rush of pain began, as Vesh knew it would,

and he thrashed and howled in its grip even as he secretly reveled in the abasement.

YOU HAVE FAILED ME, TARAN. FAILED. I HAVE GIVEN YOU THE GREATEST ARMY EVER ASSEMBLED ON THIS WORLD, POWER BEYOND ANY HUMAN'S IMAGINING. HOW IS IT POSSIBLE THAT TYCOR STILL STANDS TO MOCK US?

I WOULD FEED ON THEIR SOULS, TARAN, AND YOU ARE MY LINK TO THEM. YOU SHOULD BE WADING IN THEIR ENTRAILS BY NOW. BREAK THEM. REND THEM TO BITS.

"Master . . . forgive . . ." the wizard sobbed brokenly. "Forgive me . . ."

EARN THAT FORGIVENESS BY WHAT I WILL TEACH YOU NOW. FIRST, THERE IS A SPELL I WANT YOU TO LEARN. A TRANS-PORT SPELL. The Dark sighed, luxuriating in the thought of the blood to come.

"Lizcanth!" a soldier screamed, collapsing as the thing raked out his stomach and began to devour him. Suddenly they were everywhere, inside the pass, popping into existence all the way back across half a dozen barricades. Within seconds her careful deployment of heavy infantry, light infantry on the flanks, and archers manning the barricades disinte-grated as Lizcanths by the hundreds simply ap-peared out of thin air, pivoting, turning, and slashing.

Tazira cursed loudly over the fray. "Can you do anything about that?" she snapped at Thodorus.

"Nothing that won't also harm the soldiers," he shouted back. Her entire plan was melting into chaos. Even if she fired every ward, it would only kill the handful of monsters that happened to stumble into them. Unless . . .

"This is impossible!" Thodorus shook his head, panic beginning to clip his voice. "No creature should be able to do what we're seeing!"

Horrified, she saw men and women who had stood through three hard days of combat finally come unglued. Troops at the next barricade to the rear were actually beginning to break and run, while those caught in the tangle simply ran blindly, some trying to scramble up the steep slopes, only to be pulled down and torn apart by lizards who now raced about, leaping upon the backs of their prey.

"Impossible or not, they're doing it!" Tazira growled tersely. "Can you cast softfall on a spellstone?"

"I suppose, but—"

"Then do it! My men are dying down there!" she shouted, holding up the last Catseye in her pouch. The wizard was clearly mystified, but he hastily complied, and Tazira dropped the pale green stone into the pass.

It touched down gently, and she fired it, desperation giving her spell added strength. The ward ran along the ground for half the length of the pass, disintegrating every monster it touched. They might not stumble into perpendicular wards, but they couldn't help but touch the ground.

"Clever," Thodorus murmured admiringly. "Very clever." He added his energies to hers, and the ward stretched through the pass and out a few hundred handspans into the battlefield, obliterating the ranks of ghouls gathering at the entrance.

A ragged cheer rose in the pass as the Lizcanth abruptly vanished. Tazira let out a slow, tense breath. The wizards flooded the defenders with mass healing and mass determination spells, but too many of them failed to rise. By the look of it, she'd lost over a hundred soldiers in that one action. Worse though, it was evident their confidence had been sorely shaken by the terrifying attack. She cursed savagely under her breath and turned to face Vesh with cold rage written in every line of her body.

The wizard screamed, a long, agonized howl as he was lifted off the ground. He writhed and spasmed like a badly manipulated puppet, surrounded by a sickly nimbus of green flame.

"You're not doing that, are you?" Thodorus quipped, only half joking.

"No." Tazira shook her head, and her voice was soft with venom. "I'll have to settle for the vicarious thrill."

"So, that's your Dark, or whatever you called it—"

"Must be," she murmured, a bit distracted. Her mind was already turning to all the things that would need to be done during this shardblessed lull in the fighting. With any luck, it would be enough.

"Private Karstan!" she called to the nearest soldier. Shards, he was young, too young to be here. The short, dark-haired boy snapped to earnest attention, and Tazira shook her head affectionately.

"Never mind that now, son. I need a few things. First, you'll find the wizard Mbata waiting with the reserves at the north end. He should have a few extra wardstones created for me by now, and I'll need them as quickly as you can bring them.

While you're down there, make sure the reserve forces are getting the bodies out of the pass, giving them a decent funeral, and burning them immediately. None of us wants to come back as a ghoul," she said grimly. "Once all that's done, ask Lord Romney to join me up here. Tell him it's time to start the shift to the offensive; I don't think we're likely to see any more reinforcements."

Karstan paled at that thought, but Tazira wasn't about to leave him any time to absorb it.

"Hurry," she said softly, with a faint undercurrent of urgency lacing the word. It was enough to send him bolting for the north end.

Thodorus walked over to join her, frowning. "Shifting to the offensive before we've worn them down is going to cost us everything, Captain. It's suicide."

"We're not *going* to wear them down, Tho," she corrected him ruefully. "We're not going to live that long. Taran Vesh has to die, no matter what it costs to accomplish that. He's more than a deranged wizard, much more. He's a physical link to this world for something more powerful than he is, something I'm willing to sacrifice myself and every soldier in my command to keep out. Our wizards have been trying to get through his defenses for close to eighty hours, and nothing's worked. I've sent out scouts and assassins, and no one can get near him. I can't just sit here in the pass while he whittles away at my troops. I can't surrender and I can't retreat without making my position even worse than it is right now. What I *can* do is run the remaining wards along the ground to take out as many of his creatures as possible, and launch an attack before they have time to resurrect and reorganize."

"We'll do our best to keep Vesh occupied for you, but a lot of your men are likely to die in a frontal assault," the wizard muttered. "He'll probably decimate them in waves before anyone can reach him; you saw what he did to the forest behind him."

"Yes," Tazira nodded grimly. "And I'll be right there on the front lines, my friend, taking my chances with my soldiers. It's our last option, and we're down to it, unless you can honestly tell me you've got a brilliant spell that'll polish him off and pull our tails out of the fire."

"I wish I did, Captain," the old man shook his head miserably. "I truly wish I did."

"Not your fault, Tho," she arched her whiskers at him in the ghost of a smile. "Don't you *dare* start blaming yourself. No commander could have asked for better support, I mean that. You've done everything you could, and now it's up to us. And you know something? In spite of the facts, in spite of the odds, I'm going to find a way to beat this bastard hollow." The mrem clapped a companionable hand on his shoulder and turned away to study the ravaged field with a new eye.

Thodorus watched her for a moment. She stood on the crest of the ridge, absolutely unmoving, with the cool determination of a huntress considering her prey. A generation of young Guards had been raised in the shadow of her legend. Tazira Goldeneyes, they called her, and Old Lash. A military mind without equal, it was said, and he believed it. He almost believed she had a chance against Vesh.

Almost.

Chapter 18

THE WIZARDS' KEEP WASN'T MORE THAN A league from the trampled and denuded valley where Vesh had established his original base camp. It was a squarish and rather sterile white stone building covered by dense vegetation, almost invisible beneath layer upon layer of rot and greenery.

"Looks like a pre-Fall ruin," Pellar whispered from his vantage point between Raf and Jain. "I wonder how long Vesh knew about this place."

There was no road that led to it as such; there was a bit of trampled ground that did no more than suggest the recent passage of a handful of men.

"The real question is, why didn't they clear away any of this brush?" Jain frowned. "The heavy concealment is nice, but it's going to make it almost painfully easy for us to sneak in."

"You're getting rather good at this," Pellar winked at the boy. Jain brightened visibly, but Raf's next words deflated him just as quickly.

"The concealment kept this place hidden for a

long time," the older mrem whispered, "and it's not going to give us much of an advantage, because we're going in as soon as we've charged our spellstones. We don't have time for stealth."

"No time for stealth?" Jain hissed disbelievingly. "What do you mean, no time for stealth? What are we gonna do, knock on the door and ask 'em to set three extra places for dinner?"

"It's a thought." Raf shrugged with a wry tilt to his whiskers. "I'll figure it out when I get there."

"You've always been the one who wanted to go in with guns blazing, Jain," Pellar smirked, clapping him on the shoulder affectionately. "Here's your golden opportunity!"

"What's a gun?" Jain blinked.

"Pre-Fall tech— never mind," Raf shook his head irritably and started loosening the fastenings on his throwing knives. "Just get ready to move. Spellstones first, blades as backup."

"Spellstones first?" Pellar cocked an eyebrow at him. "Won't they just alert the wizards inside that much faster?"

"I'm counting on it," Raf grinned fiercely. The other mrem nodded and started checking his weapons. Jain followed suit, not that there was much for him to do in that department. He strung his longbow, fished out his jolt stone, and proceeded to feel largely inadequate beside his two companions.

He watched Raf for a moment before they began. The mrem's movements were agitated, and there was a ragged and feverish edge Jain wasn't at all used to seeing there. It worried him, frankly. The cool, contemplative Raf was letting his heart do his thinking for him. Raf, of all people, who never lost control, who'd so often been a steadying influence on the rest of them. After a brief bout with indecision, Jain decided to risk saying something.

"Raf, why can't we afford stealth? Why are we rushing into this?"

"Because there's a chance that the army might still be holding out against Vesh," Raf replied shortly, firing up the last of his spellstones. Even the flare of his stone seemed agitated.

"It's been three days since the battle began," the boy said as gently as he could. "Do you honestly think they've held out this long?"

"It's Tazira leading them," Raf glared at him, unable to keep his tail from switching. "There's a good chance. Believe me, Jain, I've already had this argument with myself. I know we're the only ones who know about this keep, and I realize that if we fail, there'll be no one left to take these wizards out. I know Tazira's probably dead by now, and Vesh is probably sacking Tycor as we speak. If she were here, she'd be ordering me to study the keep's defenses and take the time to enter by stealth, sacrificing her and Tycor and anything else I had to. I'm not going to do that, because there's a chance, however nonexistent, that they're still alive."

Jain nodded; that was reason enough as far as he was concerned. "Understood, Lieutenant," he saluted smartly. "And thank you for explaining."

Raf nodded and managed the shade of a smile as he ruffled Jain's short brown hair. "I'm dragging a seventeen-year-old healer into a dangerous situation with a low probability of survival," he admitted, shaking his head. "An explanation is the least of what I owe you. Are you both ready?" he asked, fitting a red spellstone into a ring on his right hand.

Jain and Pellar nodded, and Raf started to move quickly and silently through the dense growth of the rain forest. And suddenly there was no more time for arguments, or panic, or anything at all.

There was a small contingent of four guards at the front gate, and Raf paused and flashed an elaborate series of hand signals back at Pellar. The light-furred mrem nodded, fished out a small white spellstone, and fired it. The guards collapsed.

"Mind riven," he explained to Jain in a quiet whisper as they ran forward and dragged the unconscious men into the brush. "Nothing that would get blood on their uniforms, because we'll need them." Raf and Pellar started stripping their downed opponents, and Jain followed suit. "Raf and I won't pass as guards for very long, but the sight of these uniforms might make some of the other guards hesitate for a second or two."

"Hesitation is fatal, Jain," Raf added. "Don't hesitate if you want to live."

The human pursed his lips and nodded, more than a little reluctantly. He would almost certainly have to kill again, and he tried to resign himself to that as best he could. It wasn't easy, but the black mark was already on his soul, if you believed in that sort of thing.

Killing gets easier with time, though it's never easy,

Tazira's unanticipated ghost sounded in his mind.
*After the first time, there's so much less of yourself
to lose . . .*

"Come on, Private, wake up and suit up," Raf
whispered sharply. "It's time to move out."

"We're just going to leave them here? Like
this?" Jain whispered back, gesturing down at the
naked and semiconscious guards as he hastily
tugged on a uniform.

"The mind riven will hold them for about two
hours," Pellar shrugged, "easily long enough for
us to finish what we have to do here. But if for
some reason it doesn't, they'll probably waste time
looking for something to wear before they come
after us. Nudity seems to present a serious psy-
chological disadvantage for most humans; I'll
never understand why."

Jain grinned at that, remembering how embarrassed he'd been the one time he'd tried to bathe
in the river with Tazira there. He fastened his
newly appropriated dark red half cloak over his
shoulders, and they walked out of the brush and
into the compound.

The inside was dark and imposingly silent. The
front doors opened into a vast, crumbling front
hall with dark green floor tiles of no material any
of them could name. Dampness from the rain forest outside was bleeding down the cracked and
corroded walls, and the torchlights flickered and
hissed with the occasional spatter of moisture.
Heat and rot blended with the acrid smell of lush
decay. Jain had never set foot in an ancient ruin
before, and he found the feeling of desolation a

decidedly uncomfortable one. The ghosts of a dead world lined every crack in the walls.

There were four large corridors off the entryway, and Raf decided to start with the ones that led toward the back. He walked forward, keeping his footsteps perfectly normal, allowing nothing to suggest that the group might not belong there. No guards rushed out to meet them; either the wizards were too preoccupied with the battle to notice the intruders, or the corridor was so heavily trapped that human guards were unnecessary. Raf made sure he was on point, just in case, and he held his spellstone in front of him as if to ward off the darkness.

He threaded his way through the rear right corridor, determined to check them all quickly and systematically. Jain and Pellar kept pace with him, spread out into the same widely spaced triangle they'd always used with Tazira. Raf tried to ignore that ache of familiarity as they moved from room to empty room, each looking very like the last, revealing nothing of the keep's occupants.

A rat bolted across the corridor in front of them, and the sudden movement startled Jain into a gasp. Raf turned and grabbed his wrist before he could fire off his jolt stone, and the human locked eyes with him for a second and let out a tense, explosive breath.

"Nervous?" Raf silently mouthed at him. Jain nodded a bit sheepishly. "Me, too," Raf mouthed with a wry grin, and headed for the last door in the corridor. Somehow, that simple admission was enough to let the boy relax a little.

The last door was an imposing creation of solid

metal, rusting, but obviously functional. Raf reached out a single experimental claw and drew it almost delicately across the surface. Nothing happened.

"No traps," he signaled to Pellar, mouthing the words for Jain's benefit. He tried opening it gently, but it was either rusted shut or locked. Forcing it didn't work either, and he had to stop himself when his attempts began to make too much noise.

"Locked, I think," he mouthed, frustrated. In wordless answer, Pellar drew a long, slender pick out of his boot and inserted it into the badly rusted keyhole. Raf's eyes widened in shock, and after a few seconds he shook his head ruefully. Where in the name of the three bloody suns had Pellar Longclaw of all people acquired a picklock, much less such obvious expertise with it? He almost laughed out loud. Even after twenty years of friendship, Pellar still managed to surprise him more than occasionally, and more than a little.

Jain nocked an arrow, raised his longbow and set himself to watching the long, torchlit corridor behind them. Pellar worked at the lock for a minute, maybe two, and it finally clicked softly. He opened the door a fraction of a claw's length, and Raf readied a spellstone behind him in case something on the other side was waiting for them. A blast of stale, sour air came from the chamber within, and Raf's hackles rose. The place smelled very faintly of other mrem. Raf and Pellar exchanged a quick glance and burst through the door, spellstones raised to fire.

They swept the room coolly and thoroughly. It was empty, at least for the moment, but it showed signs of recent use. The white walls were absolutely bare and had recently been scrubbed clean, possibly even plastered and whitewashed. Three long tables were covered with an array of tubes, glass beakers, computers, and impossibly odd machines. And the distant, lingering scent of mrem was stronger here. Mrem, and monsters.

Raf growled in the back of his throat, unable to help himself. Something terrible had happened in this room. It was written in the neat array of glass, plastic, and metal, in the pristine, faultless cleanliness of everything, in the scent of fear that mingled with the other scents. It filled him with an irrational horror that grew in the breathless silence.

Pellar seemed to feel it, too, that sense of nameless dread and bone-deep familiarity. This was home. Raf didn't know exactly what he meant by that thought, but he intended to find out.

"Watch the door," he hissed at the others as he worked his way through the room. He sniffed at the tables, the instruments, the mingled scents cloying in his nostrils. Sterility, terror, exultation. Power and helplessness. Experiments had been performed here, before the Fall and again, more recently, and not all of the test subjects had been willing ones. The fur on Raf's thin tail began to spike.

He moved into the next chamber, a long, narrow, cramped collection of iron-barred cages. Row after row of skeletal remains lay in varying states of decomposition, and the scents of fear and decay were stronger here. Human skeletons. Humans, or what looked like humans, in cages. *Shards and ashes* . . . Raf shuddered and moved down the row. Monsters, dead, rotting, and apparently unresurrected. A Lizcanth, a nit, something that looked like it might have been a gargoyle. That one was fresh, and the stench of it nearly overwhelmed him. He turned to look at the cages on the other side, and retched when he realized what he was seeing.

This place was one of the original breeding centers for mrem.

Every phase of the experiment was written in the bones of the specimens. Failed attempts were labeled, dated, and otherwise discarded and forgotten. Others, apparently more interesting, had been dried by a taxidermist in an attempt to preserve them. Raf shuddered and retched again, reeling with horror. These creatures, and others like them in breeding centers all over Delos, had been his forebears. Sentient test subjects.

Shards . . . this was home . . . familiar, every inch of it . . .

He held his head in his hands, and his breath started coming in short, ragged gasps. His eyes watered. This was home. And Vesh had used it to create his hybrid wizards, using the same techniques, the same equipment, with the monsters in the other cages.

Voices crowded into his mind, and he squeezed his head tighter in an attempt to shut them out. The nits' wizard, the one who'd wanted to die because of what she'd become . . . *When I see you on the other side,* she'd smiled, *I'll bless you for it* . . . the mercenary they'd captured in the Southgate, spitting her venom at them . . . *You're not humans, you're mrem! You're animals, freaks, genetic constructs!*

"Raf?" a voice hissed from the outer chamber. "Raf, are you all right?" *Pellar,* he thought. *Another mrem, another freak.* Raf howled, and a jet of white flame burst out of his spellstone almost of its own accord, blasting the specimens to powder and searing their cages. He stood in the center of the flames and watched the things burn, as if burning them would make them unreal.

"Raf!" Pellar shouted, bolting for the other room. "Jain, watch the door!"

Jain nodded, closed the door, and started moving a table in front of it to brace it; he knew he couldn't hold off a fist of guards by himself, and it sounded like Raf was already under attack from the other direction. He knocked another table on its side and took cover behind it, raising his longbow and waiting for the guards to come through.

"Raf!" Pellar called again, trying to see through the smoke and ash. "Raf, answer me! Are you all right?" He hastily fished a create-water stone out of his pouch and flared it, giving it just enough energy to douse the flames and damp down the smoke. Raf charged past him, growling low in his throat, and Pellar instinctively shied and hissed at the rage contorting his features.

Frenzy? the light-furred mrem thought wildly, freezing in a moment's indecision. *Oh, suns, no, not Raf, it's not possible . . .*

Another searing jet of flame poured out of Raf's spellstone, and the table in front of him exploded, spraying shards of glass, wood, and metal everywhere. Jain froze in place in the far corner, afraid to move a muscle. Raf began to tear through the room, smashing what he couldn't burn, bloodying his hands on the breakage, and raising the ring to fire again.

"Raf, what are you doing?" Pellar shouted, grabbing him and trying to hold him back. "Stop, now! Jain is behind one of those tables!"

"I would never hurt Jain." Raf shook his head, the dreadful calmness of his voice contrasting with the unnatural gleam in his eyes. "But this place has to be taken apart. Every stinking, miserable handspan of it," he snarled, letting loose with another burst of flame. A group of guards arrived outside and started trying to pound down the door. Jain drew back his bow and waited.

"Raf, stand down!" Pellar snapped at him, readying a spellstone and aiming it at the door. "We're about to have company, and we need you functioning!"

"You didn't see the inner chamber, Pellar," Raf growled, scorching the walls as if to cleanse them of their complicity. "This place was an abomination! One of the original mrem breeding centers! And Vesh restored it somehow, used it to infuse his wizards with the genetic codes of the monsters he set them over!"

The guards pounded on the door, rhythmically, ominously. Finally one of them blasted through it with a flame strike, sending the table in front of it flying apart. Pellar hit the first three men to come through with a mass-confusion spell, and they hesitated in the doorway for a few seconds. Jain started peppering them with arrowfire, trying hard not to notice the bewildered look in the first one's eyes as he fell.

Another guard pushed her way in past the first three, aimed a stone and fired ball lightning in Jain's direction. The table in front of the boy exploded, and he dove away from it as it shattered. One of Raf's throwing knives took the guard down before she could fire again, and Pellar breathed a quick sigh of relief. Raf was back, thank the Light . . .

Jain scrambled hastily to his feet. His longbow cracked when it hit the ground, and all he could do was toss it at the oncoming guards as they poured through the door, rushing over the bodies of their fallen comrades. Pellar hit them with another mass-confusion spell, and Jain took the opportunity to snatch up the ball lightning stone from the ground where the woman had dropped it. He set it off, a clipped edge of panic lending force to the spell. Six of the guards collapsed, screaming as he laced them with white fire.

The others kept coming. Raf burned out a handful of them with his flame strike, and then the rest of them were inside the room, too close for spells. Pellar hissed at the nearest one and kicked debris up into his face, and the human screamed as shards of glass and metal stung his eyes. The mrem's next spinning kick left him mercifully unconscious.

Jain hissed as he swung his short sword. The guard facing him was so startled that he barely managed to block the cut, and Pellar's eyes widened as well.

"We may just make a mrem of you yet, lad,"

he smirked, sending the next guard across the room and into the opposite wall with an open palm strike to the sternum.

"Shards, I *am* starting to sound like one of you!" Jain laughed, rather pleased with that. He parried the next cut and smashed the hilt of his sword into the other man's head. The guard collapsed like a stone.

Another came up behind Jain and swung at him with an axe. Raf managed to catch the tip of it with his quarterstaff, barely deflecting it. Jain felt the impact of the blow behind him, and he turned and clipped the guard savagely across the jaw with the hilt of his blade. Raf finished the man with a solid blow to the head.

"You have to be prepared to kill them, Jain," the mrem warned him. "No half measures in a situation like this; you don't have the luxury of mercy at this point in your training."

He's pontificating! Jain thought, wild with relief, and almost startled into laughter by the thought. If Raf was in lecture mode, he was definitely back among the living, as Tazira always put it.

"*You* manage to put them down without killing them," Jain pointed out, purely for the sake of prodding Raf into argument. He blocked another strike in prima gardia, using the momentum of the blow to snap into a head cut. But a moment's guilt and hesitation washed over him, and he pulled the cut, bringing his sword hilt crashing down on the woman's skull instead. Raf nailed her in the temple with a short, sharp thrust of his quarterstaff, and she reeled backward.

"I'm an old man, Jain, and I've been doing this

for an awfully long time," Raf said calmly, scanning the room for his next opponent. All the guards seemed to be down at this point, and Raf and Pellar exchanged a glance of relief and started stripping them of their weapons and spellstones. "That training gives me advantages you can't expect yourself to have yet. You have the talent, believe me, but the rest takes time. And right now, you don't have that luxury." The mrem paused to scan the outer corridor. It was empty. He nodded to Pellar, and the two of them continued to rifle the bodies, swiftly and methodically.

"Mind riven, Pellar," Raf interrupted himself sharply. "I don't want them coming around until we're long gone." Pellar fished the soft white stone from his pouch and complied with a nod.

"Killing is easy, Jain," Raf murmured thoughtfully as they worked. "No matter how difficult it might be to live with afterward, the actual act is terrifyingly simple. It's a lot harder to render someone unconscious without killing them. If we both survive this, and you really decide you're set against killing, I'll teach you to use a quarterstaff. It's less brutal, and more effective in a lot of situations."

Jain nodded pensively, sheathed his short sword, and moved to stand guard by the door. "I'd appreciate anything you're willing to teach me, sir," the boy said quietly. "And I'll try not to hesitate."

"That's all I can ask," the mrem responded calmly. "And I honor what you're trying to do, believe me." He sighed and surveyed the impressive wreckage of the room before he set himself to breaking the weapons they wouldn't be taking with them. "Speaking of honor, it seems I owe you both an honorable apology for my behavior. I lost control, at the worst possible time. I honestly don't know what made me do that."

"Raf, we all have our limits," Pellar murmured, shaking his head. He raised his create-water stone and started damping down the fires in the chamber. "We all have our limits, and we've all tested them sorely over the last couple of weeks. My weakness is dire wolves. Tazira's is enclosed spaces, as hard as she tries to hide that. And you were already running the ragged edge because of your anxiety over her, and this place just happened to push you over that edge. I'll admit, you had me worried. It occurs to me that in twenty years, I've never really seen you angry. What was it about this place that got to you?"

"A lot of things," Raf admitted darkly. "But we don't have time to sit here discussing them." The sharp snap of one of the swords in his hands betrayed his agitation.

Pellar shrugged. "I dunno, I think we've probably put down most of the guards in the building at this point."

"Probably," the gray mrem concurred, glancing over the carnage. He didn't seem willing to say anything more about the incident, though, and Pellar decided to let it drop, at least for now.

Raf set the last of the broken weapons down and started bandaging his bleeding hands. Jain healed them without even turning to glance at him, and Raf stared at the boy for a moment, unnerved by his perceptiveness.

"For the record," Pellar said evenly, extracting one last throwing knife from a downed opponent and cleaning it, "I think you did the right thing. This place needed to be gutted out. I smelled something here that bothered me more than the mrem or the monsters. I think some of the test subjects were forced into the experiments."

Raf's head snapped up at that. "I smelled that, too."

"The mrem, or the wizards? Could you tell?" Jain asked them both with an urgent gleam in his eye, glancing in from the doorway.

"At least one of the wizards," Raf said evenly, searching his memory for other clues. "Beyond that, no, I couldn't tell."

"Wonderful!" Jain gasped. "Come on, we have to go!"

"Wait a minute! What's so wonderful about involuntary test subjects?" Raf quirked an eyebrow at him.

"I think I might be able to heal the wizards!" he explained, talking so quickly in his excitement that he was tripping over the words. "You have to *want* to be healed in order for anything to work, and if the change was involuntary . . . there's a chance, and I want to try. Can we?"

"What is this, Be Nice To Enemies Eightday?" Pellar quipped. "Wasn't Najendra enough for one lifetime?"

"Nope," Jain grinned. "As a matter of fact, he wasn't."

"Delos, beware!" Pellar teased, as melodramatic as a stage actor. "We've birthed yet another votary to the moral high ground!"

"It's a drug," the boy admitted cheerfully, leading them out, his short sword in one hand and his healing stone in the other. If either of the mrem saw any irony in that, they managed not to say anything.

Jain's heart was pounding, and a thin trickle of sweat slipped down his forehead. He was moving too quickly in this place, and he didn't care. He was going to heal those shardblasted wizards or die trying.

The power flared with his determination, filling him, overflowing, and spilling out into the dark corridors. There was so much of it he wanted to scream, or laugh, so much he almost couldn't breathe with it.

His consciousness expanded through the stone, and he began to feel all the life around him as intensely as if it were his own. Raf and Pellar behind him, nervous, as he should have been nervous. The unconscious guards behind them, and those outside. Two wizards and a small cluster of guards, belowstairs. And another wizard, alone, in a room at the end of the next corridor. The wizards were a stronger presence, twisted and unnatural motes on the psychic wind. There were no other guards on the ground floor, he was certain of it. He broke into a run, the healing stone suddenly flooding the corridor with light.

"Jain, what are you doing?" Raf hissed, catching up with him and rooting him firmly in place. "What's wrong?"

"Nothing's wrong," he whispered. "There are no other guards on this floor, and the wizards aren't expecting us. They're preoccupied," he frowned, turning his consciousness inward to feel them. "They're concentrating on something else . . . some other place . . . I can't tell you any more than that without attracting their attention, and if they weren't hard-pressed to do what they're doing, they would have noticed me already. They're stronger than I am."

"How are you sensing this?" Raf frowned, looking at the boy with concern.

"I don't know," Jain admitted. "But I'm sure it's got something to do with my healing stone. I'm not crazy, Raf. I just need you to trust me. Come on, ahoy for adventure!" he teased, and Raf visibly relaxed at that.

"Yes, Jain is still Jain," the mrem whispered and shook his head, amused. "And, yes, I trust you. Lead on."

Jain paused and frowned for a moment with a sudden thought. "Does either of you have a spell that'll hold a wizard for a few minutes?" he whispered. "Pellar, what about your mind riven?"

"I seriously doubt it," Pellar grimaced. "It's fine for ordinary humans, but I don't think it'd put a dent in a full-fledged wizard."

"All right, we'll have to do this the old-fashioned way," Jain growled, sounding for all the world like Tazira. The mrem blinked at him in astonishment. "A wizard without his spellstones is utterly useless, right? Right," the boy agreed with himself firmly. "So while they're distracted, we sneak in, steal their spell pouches, and *then* Pellar hits them with the mind riven. Would that work?"

"It might," Pellar said rather guardedly after a

moment. "But I can't guarantee that. None of us knows enough about wizards or their capabilities."

"Then we'll wing it," Jain shrugged. "It's a good enough plan for what we know, and if the circumstances change, so can we. Ready?"

Raf and Pellar exchanged an amused nod, a silent agreement not to tell Jain he'd suddenly shifted into the lead. If they teased him about it, or even mentioned it to him, he might freeze. But if they saved it for later, it might just give the boy some confidence. *Not that he seems to be lacking in that department*, Raf thought to himself ruefully.

"Let's go," the gray mrem said quietly, positioning them so that he and Jain were on double point, with Pellar behind and between them.

Jain edged into a slight lead, his enthusiasm getting the better of him again. They crept soundlessly to the end of the opposite corridor, to a small room lit by a profusion of rank, guttering tallow candles. The half-open, rusting metal door groaned slightly as Jain tried to squeeze through it, and something inside the room shifted and stirred feebly in response to the sound. Jain gasped, flung the door open, and dove at a small, shriveled figure lying on a white pallet in the center of a chalk circle.

The wizard tried to raise an arm to defend himself, but he'd been out of his body for a considerable time, and his movements were sluggish and awkward. Jain ripped the pouch of spellstones off his belt and tossed it back to Pellar, and Raf launched a vicious kick at the wizard's head. It connected, full force, and the old man went limp.

"Effective. Inelegant, but effective," Pellar shrugged laconically, studying his claws.

"You're lucky you didn't break his neck, Raf," Jain chided him, taking the wizard's greenish, hairless head in both his hands.

"*He's* lucky I didn't break his neck," Raf corrected him with a growl, lashing his tail. "Whatever you're planning, son, do it quickly. The next two will probably have some sense of what's coming. Keep an eye on the door, Pellar."

"Yes, my liege."

"Not now, Pell."

"Oh. Sorry."

Jain ignored their banter and concentrated on finding some spark of the wizard's animate intelligence to work with. *Who are you, my friend? Or better still, who were you?*

No answer; not that he'd really expected one. He closed his eyes, deepening the search. A scrap of memory, an emotion, something . . . there. A small, bright spark, flickering and fading. Jain grasped it, held it, pulled it closer to consciousness. He sensed humor, oddly enough. An old, old man with a dry, delightful wit. And he sensed darker things. Chaos, terror, discipline, obedience. The impressions flew over and past him like bats suddenly released from a chest. They tore at his spirit: hunger, lust, power, wanting, blood, the taste, the sweet warm feel of blood . . .

Jain shuddered and cried out incoherently, and Raf instinctively reached out a hand to pull him away.

"No, Raf!" Pellar hissed from the doorway. "Whatever he's doing, let him do it."

"But he—"

"Let him try," the younger mrem insisted calmly. Jain's features contorted with rage and terror, and Raf bristled and forced himself to watch.

"Two minutes," Raf whispered sharply. "If he doesn't manage this in two minutes or less, we're killing the wizard and moving on. I won't risk losing Jain for this."

Pellar nodded agreement and went back to watching the corridor.

Jain brushed aside the darkness and his own horror, forced himself to delve deeper, to find again that faint, bright spark of dry humor. A sea of black, chaotic thought rushed around him, drowning him, and he fought down his own panic. Made himself breathe. The thing was so much stronger than both of them . . .

He almost screamed. Almost. But he knew that if he did, Raf would cut the old man's throat. He already felt the knife in the mrem's hand, along with a faint, damning sense of anticipation. Calling on a well of strength he hadn't known he possessed, Jain forced the darkness back, created a reservoir of light, and made it brilliant and painful. The darkness shrank away in almost sentient fear, and the healer renewed his search for the wizard. If he'd had a name to call, he sensed it would have been easier, but he had what he had.

The wizard became conscious with a sharp gasp, and the light and the darkness swirled together for an instant, threatening to obliterate everything. Jain held on to the edges of the light and pulled the wizard inside with him. His hands trembled on the old man's head, and Raf moved to strike with the knife, fearing that Jain might be weakening.

"Do you remember your name?" Jain asked, not sure himself whether he spoke in reality or thought. Raf hesitated, holding the strike; it must have been both. The name was everything. If the wizard could remember enough of himself to connect with his own name, it would make everything else possible. He knew it. And he suddenly knew how to win.

"Tell me!" Jain roared, filled with a sudden rush of determination that instantly translated itself into energy. "Tell me your name!"

"Oriann," the old man croaked, "Oriann Jarnel." Tears seeped from his eyes, and Jain wiped them away gently.

"Do you want me to heal you, Oriann?"

"Yes," the wizard whispered, barely audible. It was enough. Power rushed through the healing stone and into them both, and they gasped at the sheer force of it. Their energies met and merged. The room was suffused with light. The old man howled as every cell in his racked and withered body erupted, rewriting his genetic codes in a single, blindingly painful moment. Unconsciousness came swiftly, mercifully.

Oriann's skin paled, losing its greenish tinge, and his scales faded back into wrinkled flesh. Sparse, short white hair and a close-trimmed beard grew back in, and the healing light around him flickered and dimmed.

Jain let out an explosive breath, closed his eyes for a moment, and concentrated on healing all the damage to the wizard's body, including what Raf had done with that kick.

"Shards, Raf, you really did break his neck," Jain chided him. The sound of his own voice was strange to him, as if he'd never really heard it before. "We'll have to be more careful with the next two."

"Jain, you've got to be joking! You were lucky enough to succeed with this one! Do you honestly want to go through *that* again? Twice?"

"Honestly? I'd rather have all my teeth pulled by an ogre with a pair of rusty pliers. But I have to try, Raf. If there's a possibility that I might succeed, I have to try."

"The boy *wants* me to tear my fur out worrying," Raf muttered. "Are you listening to this, Pellar?"

"You might look good bald," the other mrem quipped from the doorway.

"Or not."

"Darling, you'll always be pretty to me," Pellar batted his eyes teasingly.

"I'm immeasurably relieved," Raf drawled.

The old wizard's black eyes opened a crack, and he glanced around him. Fear, pain, and relief flickered across his weathered face as thought and consciousness returned to him in a rush, for the first time in an endless age.

"Welcome back to the world, Oriann," Jain smiled down at him. The wizard grinned back, a weak but delighted grin in which his few remaining teeth were no longer ferally pointed.

"Thank you," Oriann said hoarsely, and his voice cracked with age and emotion. "I can't ever thank you enough."

"This, Raf, is why I feel compelled to try again," Jain said quietly.

Chapter 19

ANYTHING WORTH DOING IS WORTH DOING well. She'd said it thousands of times to thousands of recruits, and it was never more vital than now, when so many of them would be called upon to die well.

Anything worth doing is worth doing well, and suicides require exquisite planning, Tazira thought bitterly, furious with the world and with herself. All their savage fighting and clever stratagems had still come down to this, and she could see no better way. It was a way that virtually guaranteed their victory, but the price of that victory sickened and shamed her. How many of them were going to have to die to take down one ambitious wizard?

What a waste, she thought, her tail lashing savagely in spite of her best efforts to control it. *What a pathetic waste. Damn Vesh, damn the Dark, and damn my own impotence, for not finding us all a way out of this that would let us keep our skins intact.*

Strain and exhaustion were plainly written on the faces all around her, all of them familiar. She'd practically raised them. Most of them were in their teens or early twenties; few warriors survived to see the age of Old Lash.

I was twenty-six when they started calling me that, she thought. *Old, at twenty-six.*

With a growl of irritation she mastered her wandering thoughts. The captain had put Sergeant Rlirr back in charge of the battle, to give herself a few minutes to think, but that was no excuse for this kind of woolgathering. She had to focus on her battle plan, to make sure that it was everything it should be. She owed her men that much and more. With some effort, she shut out the din of the raging battle, the singing and fizzling of spells, the incessant shrilling of the creatures in the valley below. And after a moment, the world narrowed to the tiny tactical map in her head.

The plan had simplicity in its favor, at least. In an hour—less—the wizards would clear the pass of monsters and obstacles with one great fireball that would roll through it all and out onto the battlefield, destroying everything it touched. Next, they'd start throwing every offensive spell in their arsenal, all at the same time. Nothing would be held back; there wasn't any need. Once Vesh was sufficiently distracted with that, the last of the wardstones would be catapulted onto the field, spelled with softfall to keep them from breaking.

Thodorus would wait until the last possible minute to fire them. Tazira and her army had to cover as much ground as they could before the monsters disappeared en masse; it might keep Vesh from aiming any spells at the wave of soldiers until it was too late. At any rate, it was the best chance she could give them, and herself. *A*

mass haste spell should put the odds more in our favor,
she thought, and made a mental note to ask Thodorus or Sema about it.

It would make a difference to a few of them, at
least, and that was something. The irony of it was
exquisite, really: Tazira had always prided herself
on not throwing bodies at a problem, and this last,
expensive action was the one for which she would
undoubtedly be remembered.

"Captain, are you sure you ought to be doing
this?" a voice murmured quietly behind her. Startled, Tazira spun and hissed, one paw raised to
strike. Thodorus stumbled backward and tottered
on the uneven escarpment, and she caught him
by the belt and reeled him back in before he
could fall.

"Sorry." The woman shook her head ruefully.
Her lips managed laughter, if her eyes didn't
quite. "You've had a bad day with mrem, my
friend."

"I have, haven't I?" the wizard laughed, breathless and babbling with sudden relief. "Remind me
to feel terribly sorry for myself when this is all
over. Speaking of which, my question remains.
Why are you putting yourself on the front lines,
Captain? It's not necessary, you know."

"Yes, it is," she corrected him firmly, turning
back to her assessment of the field. "I've never
asked my men to do anything I wasn't willing to
do myself, and I'm not about to start now. It
would kill the last of their morale. Look at them,
Tho," she said quietly, studying them from the
corners of her eyes. "Look at them and tell me
I'm wrong."

He couldn't, of course. They looked young and haggard and ready to break, most of them. The only thing holding them together was the will of their commander. Leading from the front lines would be a spectacular gesture, worthy of Tazira Goldeneyes, and the best way she had of giving them courage at the last. She was undoubtedly right, but that didn't mean he had to like it.

"You're wrong, woman," Lord Romney called over to his captain teasingly as he made his way up the precipice. "What are we talking about?" Light, but the man had good ears.

"Morale, eavesdropper," Tazira rolled her eyes at him with lazy good humor. "And you're supposed to tell your old housewife she's right! Thodorus, what are my two favorite words?"

"I'm sorry?" he asked vaguely, not quite following her.

"No, the other two."

"Oh!" the wizard nodded in sudden understanding. "Yes, dear."

"Yes, dear," Tazira purred, loving the simple sybaritic feel of them on her tongue. "They have such a lovely ring, don't they? I could listen to them all day long. Anyway, Val, it's good to see you." She grinned with all the bravado she could muster, punching her liege lord lightly on the arm. "Thanks for coming."

"Don't thank me too soon, my girl," he objected. "I've come up here to talk some sense into you."

"No, you haven't." She smiled at him affectionately. "You came up here to say good-bye. You know that, and I know that. This offensive is all the hope we have left, my love. It has to succeed. I have to lead that charge."

"What do you really think you're going to do out there?" Romney growled. "Win the battle all by yourself? Save the day?"

"I wish," she snorted. "Val, this isn't bravado or a death wish. Look at my soldiers. Look at them! For days now, they've been bombarded with healing and mass determination spells, and they're exhausted and disheartened. How long did you really expect magic to stay effective, considering the odds they're facing? Happy spells aren't going to hold my units together. That's my job. I have to be there. As an individual, I won't do much on the field, and I have no illusions about that, believe me. But as a figurehead—"

"Tazira, will you listen to yourself!" He cut her off impatiently. "A figurehead? I'm supposed to let my captain lead a suicidal offensive so she can serve as a *figurehead?*"

"Yes," Tazira answered him calmly, folding her hands behind her consciously in the same way Raf tended to. A devastatingly effective weapon, calmness, and Raf Grayfur was its guildmaster. She could learn from him. She had. Thodorus raised an eyebrow at her in surprise, but didn't say anything.

Romney purpled under that cool and calculated assault, exactly as she'd intended he should. He opened his mouth to deliver a suitably scathing reply, but Tazira cut him off.

"Val, I know this is hard, believe me," she said quietly. "I know. I don't want to sacrifice these children. I don't especially want to sacrifice myself. But the facts are inescapable. It's been three days, almost four, and the reinforcements from Amar haven't shown. We're going to have to find a way to win this with the soldiers we've got. That means doing it soon, because the odds are going to get steadily worse the longer we wait. My men are ready for this, Val, and so am I. We need you up here, to sound the charge at red dawn, when Vesh will be facing into the harshest light of the day. Less than an hour, my love. And when that charge sounds, you'll be here to signal it, as you should, and I'll be on the front lines with my men, as I should."

"I could order you to stay up here, you know," Romney growled.

"You could," Tazira nodded. "But you won't. As Raf recently said to me in very similar circumstances, you're too good a commander for that. I appreciate the sentiment, Val, believe me, but we both know this has to happen. We both have our parts to play, and we'll play them."

"To the bitter end?"

"I don't see anything so bitter in that." She smiled softly. "At least some of my men will survive long enough to swarm Vesh. We'll win this, Val, no matter what price we have to pay for it."

They locked eyes in challenge, and the battle raging on the field behind them seemed to become distant and insubstantial. Romney tried desperately to think of some more compelling reason to hold her back and keep her safe. The moments passed, though, too many of them, and nothing came. Finally he looked away and nodded, unable to say the words that would condemn her, or even to give her the "yes, dear" that would have made her laugh. He hugged her tightly instead.

"I love you," he said, and his voice was rough with unshed tears.

"I love you, too. I always will. Light go with you, my old husband."

"Suns illumine you, my girl." Val kissed the top of her head, turned from her quickly, and walked over to join Sergeant Rlirr on the peak of the ridge. When red dawn cast its pitiless brilliance over the bloodstained field, he would be there to signal the charge, ordering Tazira and Light knew how many of her men to their deaths, for the sake of his oaths to his people and a wordless promise to an old friend.

Romney never looked back, but Tazira watched him for a moment as he walked away, a darkly glittering armored silhouette illumined by the first faint rays of red dawn. It was time. She nodded to herself firmly, ran a hand over the already loosened fastenings of her weapons, and pulled her helmet on. Thodorus shifted uneasily next to her, still obviously wanting to talk her out of going.

"Tho, I need to ask one last favor of you," she said before he could manage it.

"Anything," he said, and he meant it.

"The wizard Sema has a mass haste spell. I need her to use it on my troops. It'll give us a better chance against Vesh."

"Yes, it will," the old man admitted. "But I wish you'd reconsider—"

"I know, dear," the captain cut him off, grinning at him affectionately. "You don't have to say it. I know. Thank you, for everything."

"Thank *you*, madam," the old man shook his head gruffly. "Light go with you."

"And you," she said, kissing his weathered cheek and starting down the steep precipice toward the north end of the pass.

She should have been nervous, should have felt something, at least, but oddly enough she didn't. She'd already said her good-byes to everything that mattered, and the rest would be easy enough. One final charge and the thing would be ended at last, one way or the other. As calmly as she'd ever done anything in her life, the captain made her way down the precipice, down to the valley where her troops were massing for the charge.

Her soldiers began to cheer her as she approached. The hoarse voices chanting Tazira's name spread like brushfire along the ranks, swelling, wilder, as if they would never stop. She was stunned; it was the last thing in this world she'd expected. She'd thought to have to brace them against the inevitable, to feel resentment and hopelessness at her back in this last desperate course. These half-licked kits were being ordered into a charge that was virtually guaranteed to kill hundreds of them. And they were cheering her in a voice to startle the heavens.

There in the front ranks were Tazira's Hellriders, her elite infantry, hard and reckless, the natural choice to lead the charge at her side. Some of them, the veterans, she'd known and served with for half her life. Gruff and honest Lainn, brilliant and funny and utterly tactless, smiling at her and laughing as they'd laughed together over dozens of wineskins in as many campaigns. Beautiful Fasine, with her parti-colored coat, soft voice, and deadly hands. And the loud and boisterous Balyar, her brown-furred husband, always the one to make them laugh, even in the darkest times. There had never been a darker time than this, but there he was, lifting his helmet on his spear and waving it at Tazira like the rawest of recruits, purely to see her whiskers arch in amusement.

And then there were the young ones: Trafsi, Jikar, tiny red-haired Allende with her fierce temper and easy laughter . . . so many others, her kits, grinning at her, their armor glinting dimly in the hazy morning sunlight. The sound of their chanting voices rang in her own armor, buzzed in her fur.

No commander has ever been blessed with finer troops than these, Tazira thought with breathless pride, and she was awed and humbled by the knowledge.

At that moment, when she'd all but convinced herself there was nothing left to feel, she was stunned and a little shaken by that pure, fierce testament of their love. It flowed, it echoed off the canyon walls, it embraced her where she stood. A single tear slipped down her cheek, and she brushed it aside almost absently as she made her way down into the valley to be with them.

Tazira walked along the front lines, touching palms with every mrem and human she passed, every one of them painfully familiar. She expected to hate herself at this last moment, when she looked into the eyes of her soldiers, knowing how many of them wouldn't see another red dusk because of her. But oddly enough, she only found herself proud to be one of them, among them, about to die with them.

In her pouch there was a clear spellstone she'd borrowed from Thodorus, a wizardstone that would project her voice across the entire valley. Originally she'd thought she might need it to try to hearten her troops, and she laughed now at the thought. The stone wasn't for them; it was for her, to let her give them some small measure of what they were bringing back to her.

The cheers finally softened to a rumbling murmur, and she spoke into it.

"My loves," she said, her lazy Haymarket drawl echoing off the mountains and visibly startling her troops, "you make me wish I were Raf Grayfur, or Pellar Longclaw, or Varral Romney. If they were in my place, they would give you words of wisdom, fire, and unimaginable eloquence. I have nothing to give you but my heart, and myself." Weapons, ears, and whiskers bristled along the ranks as her kits settled in to listen, and Tazira smiled quietly to herself.

"I know you're afraid, and I know what you fear. It isn't death, or monsters, or magic; it's worse. You're afraid to fail, and so am I, because of what's at stake if we lose. You're afraid you'll somehow prove unworthy of the moment. Well, forget the issues, my kits. Forget humanity. Forget tyranny and terror, forget your families. Taran Vesh and the man at your shoulder are all that exist. Kill the one and protect the other. That's all I can tell you. That's all I know. That's all Old Lash ever had to teach you.

"Forget the future, forget humanity. Let them

remember us. And they will remember, I promise you that. They will remember that for three long days we held back the most terrible army in the history of Delos. And then we turned to charge them! And we destroyed them and the man who would have set them over us! Let them remember that!" Her tail lashed a fierce semicircle, its white tip glowing red in the light of the raging dawn. Her soldiers roared their approval, and veterans like Lainn and Balyar grinned openly at that familiar gesture.

"And I want all of you to remember how proud I am to be one of the men at your shoulder," Tazira said more softly as they quieted. "Such as I am, I'm here to lend you my spells and my arms, and to live or die amongst you all, to lay down my life and my honor in the knowledge that if I don't destroy Vesh, someone I love will do it for me. There's nowhere on Delos I'd rather be. I'm home, and you are all the family I could ever want. You have had, and may have again, wiser and better commanders than I have been. But none of them, I promise you, will ever love you more. Suns illumine you. Suns illumine you all!"

Tazira's whiskers quivered with barely suppressed emotion as a thunderous cheer erupted across the valley in response. Her soldiers chanted her name as she walked to her place in the front line, with the eternally restless Yulish on one side of her and lanky, gorgeous Toelle on the other. She warmed her spellstones and unstrapped Black Bessie, and as she tested its familiar heft in her hands, the captain closed her eyes and savored the warmth and love of her people.

In this last moment of relative peace, it gave her something truly worth dying for. It was enough. It was more than enough.

Romney stood with Sergeant Rlirr on the crest of the east ridge. They were silent, a state both of them seemed to prefer, for the moment. The red sun was dawning in a clear sky, and Romney knew he couldn't delay the moment he'd been dreading. He swept a long, careful glance over the field. The wizards were currently focusing most of their efforts on holding the monsters at the mouth of the pass; the human soldiers had been pulled out of it half an hour ago to clear the way for the charge.

The Lizcanth were preparing to attack. Thodorus hurled a fireball at them, and Vesh forked it so that it impacted harmlessly around them. The flames chewed into the black earth and died quickly; there wasn't much left to burn on that field.

Vesh raised a fist and held it in the air, and his lizards crouched in their tight formations, ready to spring forward with all their terrifying speed. A ball lightning spell came crashing down on them from somewhere along the west ridge, and the creatures didn't even flinch as it forked around them. Vesh brought his fist down, and they leaped forward into a long-gaited run, fierce and swift and utterly mindless. There was no fear in them, and no hope of mercy for any mrem or human caught in their claws.

They poured forth across the blasted field as spells fizzled harmlessly around them. Faster,

hungering, shrilling. Romney raised the red flag
that would signal the beginning of the last assault
on Vesh. Red dawn crept over the ridge, flooding
everything with ominous brilliance.

"My lord, there will never be a better moment
to strike," Sergeant Rlirr said in her rumbling,
purring growl. She looked at him expectantly
and waited.

It might have been that simple for her, but he
was condemning an old friend, and scores of her
soldiers and his. It was the best course, the best
time; it was expected of him. He knew it, but
knowing didn't make it any easier. It never did.

Romney took a deep breath to fortify himself.
The blood was pounding in his head. *Light protect
them all*, he thought, *because I can't anymore.* He
started to lower the signal flag, as grimly as the
master of the gallows.

A hideous screeching from the field made him
freeze instinctively. The Lizcanth broke formation
inexplicably and started running in different directions, and Romney held the flag in a trembling
hand and waited to see what would happen.

One of the creatures stumbled and lost its footing, and three of the others leaped on it and tore it
to shreds. All over the field, the Lizcanth suddenly
turned on each other and their allies with spectacular brutality. A pack of them burst into the ghoul
ranks and started ripping them apart, and another
group of them rounded on Vesh himself.

Vesh hurled a fireball at his creatures as they
charged him, but he didn't lace it with enough
energy to incinerate them on contact. They staggered, burned, collapsed, shrieking more and

more feebly as the flames consumed them with agonizing slowness. *That could have been the first few ranks of the charge,* Romney thought, sickened.

Vesh gesticulated wildly in the middle of the field, trying to restore his fraying troops to some semblance of order. The Lizcanth continued to devour each other and everything else in easy reach of their claws, and two more packs rounded on their leader.

There was always the possibility that one of his own Lizcanth might get through the wizard's defenses, and Romney pounced on that thought and signaled a hold to the charge. Signal flags began rippling down the line of the pass behind him, and he allowed himself a small, grim smile. At the very least, this was a Lightblessed opportunity to watch Vesh cope with purely physical attacks, and it would give them all a chance to find some weakness in him without having to risk their own soldiers.

"Let's see if we can't give 'em a little help," Romney muttered to Rlirr with a sudden, wicked grin. He snatched a blue signal flag off the ground and waved it emphatically. His wizards started blasting Vesh with offensive spells, with such alacrity that he knew they must have been waiting anxiously for the order. The human's eyes narrowed thoughtfully as he watched Vesh's every move, every spell. Anything he learned now could save lives or win the battle.

A tremendous roar surged up from the valley on the other end of the Golgul. The soldiers were cheering. *They've done a surprising amount of that, for a group of people about to embark on a desperate*

thirteenth-hour charge, Romney smiled to himself.
I wonder what Tazira found to say to them.

"The soldiers must be hearing something about
the Lizcanth," Rlirr murmured absently, still concentrating her attention on the field.

"Lord Romney!" a young woman shouted,
breathless with running and excitement. "Lord
Romney!"

Rlirr hissed instinctively and rounded on the
intruder. Romney whipped around to find a messenger bearing down on him, her eyes wild with
joy. Apparently she hadn't noticed the sergeant's
bared claws. The girl saluted them both hastily,
and her report came tumbling out in a rush.

"Milord, Sergeant, the Amarans are here, their
whole army by the look of it! The wizard Najendra is with them! The reinforcements are here!"

The stone-willed Lord of Tycor Keep looked
ready to faint with relief, and his stoic and battle-
hardened sergeant looked ready to join him.

Chapter 20

ORIANN JARNEL SHOULD HAVE BEEN DEAD
by even the kindest stretch of logic. He was a
corpse with a broken neck and the genetic signa-
ture of a Lizcanth. A *dead* Lizcanth. Deceased. De-
funct. Summarily dismissed from the tragic run
of life. Raf knew that, even if the astonishingly
ambulatory Oriann Jarnel didn't seem to.

Jain didn't seem to, either, and that was worse.
The two of them were skulking down the moist
and rotting hallway as if it were the most natural
thing in the world that they should both be doing
so. The wizard was moving with the ease and
lightness of . . . Raf would have said a man half
his age, but a man half Oriann's age would still
be old. Oriann Jarnel had been another of Romney's court wizards, and it was said that he wasn't
a young man when the world fell.

Jain's talents were developing at a rate Raf was
beginning to find unsettling. He was performing,
instinctively, miracles no healer should have been
able to accomplish. Oriann should have been past
all hope, and any of the healers Raf had ever

known would have agreed. The man should be dead, according to everything the mrem knew. And here he was, walking quietly alongside them.

Raf shook his head and cast a worried glance at Jain's back. The boy had stepped into the lead again; he was trying to sense the other lives in the keep, the way he had before. One more talent no healer should have had. There was tension in the set of his shoulders, silent desperation in every step. Raf had seen its like before, in men who'd pushed themselves so far beyond their own limits that they'd finally left limits behind. Jain had their look, their scent, the manic energy of a man who was running on sheer adrenaline and not much else.

"It's happening," Jain whispered back to them, breaking Raf out of his thoughts. "I'm getting confusion from the wizards. One of them is in pain. The guards know something's wrong. Three of them are headed this way to investigate."

Raf nodded and stepped into the lead, loosing a throwing knife from his boot.

"Mind riven, Pellar," he hissed. They couldn't afford anything more spectacular, not here. The corridor was so badly rotted that it looked ready to fall apart at a breath. The guards rounded the corner, and surprise registered on their faces as they caught sight of the intruders. The shocked expressions stayed frozen by the mind riven spell that hit them before they had time to react. They sank to their knees, their eyes wide and unseeing.

The mrem let out a slow breath. If Jain hadn't warned them about those guards, the guards might have gotten the drop on them. Not a pleasant thought.

"Any more on this level?" Raf hissed.

"No, just them," Jain whispered back. "There's a cluster of five more gathered at the bottom of the stairway, waiting for these three to report."

Raf nodded, and Oriann snorted soft laughter behind them, startling them a bit.

"So they want a report, eh? Well, I hate to disappoint such earnest young people," the wizard smirked, "but it just so happens I'm an illusionist. I can make you look like the three of them, temporarily."

"How long?" Raf asked him.

"Four or five days, I'd say."

"More than enough. What about you? Did you happen to see yourself while you were . . . umm . . ."

"Green?" the old man finished for him, his small black eyes sparkling with mirth. "There's no diplomatic way of putting it, sonny. Don't try. Yes, I saw myself. I know what I looked like, and I can include myself in the spell."

"Do it, then," Raf nodded, and Oriann started to work the illusion on all of them as the mrem continued, "Pellar, will your mind riven take out all five of them?"

"Not likely, no. I've overused it a bit on this trip," Pellar admitted.

"What about you, Oriann? Anything that would put them down for a few hours without killing them?"

"Not really, son," he muttered absently as he worked. "All wizards have specialties, and mine happens to be illusion. Works a little differently than your friend's mind riven. I can make those five guards see or hear anything you want 'em to, but I can't actually diminish their faculties in any way. Sorry, boys; you woke up the useless wizard first."

"Hardly that," Raf shook his head, and his whiskers arched wryly. "What about the other wizards? What can you tell us about them?"

"Well, let's see. Delag, that's the wizard in charge of the gargoyles, he specializes in air magic. Kinda fits, don't it? And Tam—that's the one who runs the ghouls—his specialty is life. Don't ask me how it helps him with ghouls, but that's his specialty."

" 'Life' as in healing?" Jain whispered.

"Naw, he grows stuff. Plants, trees, crops, you name it. He's a glorified farmer, really. I think that should do it," he said at last, looking them all over carefully. "You're ready."

"Let's go," Raf nodded, not even bothering to glance down at himself as he led them forward. Pellar, always the more curious soul, fished the polished silver mirror out of his pack and winced as he looked at his human face.

"I looked better as a mrem," he whispered.

"So what?" Raf hissed back. "You'll only have to look like that for the next hour or so. Who cares what you look like?"

"Well, he could have made me an *attractive* human, at least—"

"Shut up."

"But—"

"Shut up. You're a plug-ugly human. Live with

it," Raf whispered. Jain clapped a hand over his mouth to keep from laughing out loud, Pellar subsided into sullen muteness, and they moved on.

There was a stairway at the end of the hall. The ruined part of it led upward, to a floor that no longer existed, and the rest led down toward the sleeping wizards and the waiting guards. Raf continued to lead them forward at a normal pace, as if they had every right to be there.

"Halt! Who goes there?" a voice snapped up at them. Raf glanced back at Oriann to prompt him; the old man's voice would hopefully be somewhat familiar to them.

"Who goes there?" the wizard mocked, in a somewhat more gravelly voice than his own. "What kinda threadbare cliché is that, son? Did your grandpappy teach you that? Heh! Who goes there, indeed!"

"Lizcanth," one of the guards volunteered, disgustedly. "Come on down."

"That doesn't sound like Lizcanth," another whispered.

"It's Lizcanth, imbecile," Oriann shot back as he began to limp down the dark stairwell. He gave his voice more hauteur, and it was apparently enough to convince them. Jain felt faintly ill. They didn't even refer to the man by his name. They probably didn't know it.

"What happened up there? What was all the noise?" the first guard asked. The four of them continued to make their careful way down the slick tile staircase.

"An unexpected series of complications." The wizard frowned, giving his tone an icy formality that clearly didn't belong there. "The Tycorans were actually waiting for us in the Golgul Pass. The battle is continuing. I've been instructed to assist the other wizards. As for you, the Master wants you all to join the battle. You'd better go, quickly."

"What about the rest of our unit?" the one who seemed to be their captain asked.

"Already on their way," Oriann lied after a moment's awkward pause. Clever, but not quite quick enough, or smooth enough. The guards eyed each other and the wizard suspiciously.

"They left without notifying us?"

"Yes, you see, it was like this," Raf bluffed pleasantly, taking a single step forward. It was all he needed. His quarterstaff snapped out in a blur. The right side smashed into the face of the nearest guard, and the left smashed into the next in the blink of an eye. He rammed their heads back into the wall, and they collapsed. In a single smooth cast he whipped the staff around and butted the end into a third guard's temple before anyone had time to react.

The other two turned and started to draw their weapons. Raf dropped his staff and lunged; the quarters were too close for any more staff work. Pellar leaped into the fray, disarming the nearest guard, sweeping him, and smashing his head into the tile floor.

Jain tore the jolt stone out of his pouch and raised it to fire at the last guard. Raf took her down with a flying axe kick before she could unsheathe her sword, and she reeled and dropped to her knees. One more kick took her out completely. Jain hastily pulled his energies back in before his spell could fire, and he breathed a shaky sigh of relief. The mrem seemed to be undamaged, and the humans were down for the count.

Pellar fired his mind riven slowly over all the downed guards. "That was abrupt," he teased Raf. "Remind me never to upset you."

"It worked," Raf shrugged a bit absently, turning back to Oriann with an urgent gleam in his eye. "Oriann, did I just hear you tell that guard the battle was still going?"

"That's right, son," the wizard nodded. "The Tycorans have held the monsters off for the last three days. It's nothing short of a miracle."

Jain and Pellar looked ready to shout exuberantly, but they managed to contain themselves. Raf sucked in a sharp breath and held himself rigidly immobile with all the self-control he possessed. "Do you know if the Tycoran captain, Tazira Goldeneyes, is still alive?"

"I've lost contact with my . . . with the Lizcanth," Oriann corrected himself a bit irritably. "I can't see what's goin' on over there anymore, and I don't want to try, 'cause I might just get sucked back in. But when I left, your captain was still alive."

Raf closed his eyes and slowly let out the breath he'd been holding. The other mrem clapped him on the back.

"Of course, you realize that when we see Tazira again, I'm going to have to tell her all about that stunt you just pulled with the flying kick," Pellar teased him. "She'll have you in retraining sessions for at least an eightday over that one."

"You'll have all the time in the world to tell on me later," Raf beamed, unable to wipe the stupid grin off his face. "For now, let's move. Jain, lead on."

Jain shot him a wry smile before he closed his eyes to pick up his concentration again. It came more easily this time, as if he'd only momentarily dropped the thread of that other awareness. He could feel anxious impatience gnawing at the clipped edges of Raf's self-control, and for the sake of that he hurried on without pausing to feel out Pellar or Oriann. It probably wasn't right, anyway. It probably wasn't right doing any of this, but he had to find the wizards.

He latched onto the first, a stronger, darker presence than either of the other two. Perhaps he'd been under Vesh's sway longer, or perhaps he'd been drawn into the plot for reasons of his own.

Only one way to find out, I guess, the boy thought. *And best to deal with him first, while I might still have the strength.*

His thoughts felt odd in that slightly shifted otherworld, the skinless inner skin of not-quite-physical existence. The thoughts ran together with other thoughts, other feelings, his and not his. He sought out that darker presence—Delag, the gargoyles' wizard—and started off in that direction, only dimly aware of the more tangible physical realm around him. It didn't matter. There were no more guards, no more physical threats. The rest would be up to him, he supposed.

The healing stone began to fire in his pouch, and he pulled it out and felt the warm glow of it in his hand. He started seeking out the edges of Delag's consciousness, weaving his own into it subtly. The wizard stirred, became dimly aware of him. Jain felt rage, hunger, and the consuming darkness again, and he realized that he was more than a little afraid. He took one last look back at Oriann, and that steadied him somewhat.

With all the suddenness of a dream, there was a door of some light, undefinable metal in front of him. The door to Delag's chamber, he knew. He reached out a hand to open it, and Pellar caught his wrist before he could complete the motion.

"It's trapped," the mrem hissed. "I can almost smell it." He moved Jain away from the door, and the boy went easily, without resisting. He was already in the pull of the wizard's mind, unable to resist the joining. Raf shot him a concerned glance; Jain felt it, but couldn't quite respond to it.

Pellar backed everyone else away and ran a single claw tip over the door. It began to glow a dull, ominous red, and it sounded a riddle in a gravelly male voice.

A thousand thousand were stolen from us by three.

Pellar frowned, trying to think. He'd heard this one, somewhere. The Amaran court . . . he'd been visiting . . .

The door began to repeat the riddle, and the red glow began to pulsate. The mrem frantically gestured for the others to get back, and he racked his brain trying to remember . . .

"The stars!" he and Oriann exclaimed together breathlessly.

"Heh!" The wizard shook his head. "That one's

older'n dirt! Took me a minute to remember it, though."

The glow around the door dimmed and faded off, but the door didn't open as expected. Pellar tested the handle and found it locked. With an irritated sigh he pulled the picklock out of his boot and went to work.

"Trapped *and* locked? Some people are just *beyond* paranoid," he muttered to himself.

"You never know," Raf shrugged. "The Furies might try to break into this chamber with a promising young healer in tow or something."

"Impossible," Pellar scoffed. "This hallway isn't wide enough to hold those monumental egos."

"Especially that Pellar Longfang, or was it Flapjaw . . ."

"I believe that would be the brilliant, amusing, and fantastically sexually attractive Pellar *Longclaw* you're referring to," Pellar muttered absently, lifting the third pin in the lock. "The one who carries that useless Raf Fleafur along with his wit and talent . . ."

Jain felt the reassuring rhythms of their usual banter, but couldn't quite make out what they were saying. Words meant nothing where he was. Voices meant less. He felt the wizard stirring to consciousness, probed at the frayed edges of the soul within the black wall. Reaching down into that reservoir of sheer determination that was the only real strength he had left, Jain plunged ahead into the darkness.

He tried creating that same small, painfully brilliant sea of light he'd created with Oriann, but this time everything shied away from it, and nothing but rage and terror answered him. He forced the brilliance outward, farther, straining against his own limitations and the overwhelming evil that surrounded him without pervading him. *I should be terrified*, he thought, surprised by the words. *I was, and I should be . . .*

Nothing in that blackness answered him, nothing in it sought the light. He was simply unwanted here. The small sea of light began to shrink back in on itself, and Jain found himself powerless to stop it. He cried out, and Pellar glanced back and hastened his efforts on the lock. *Shards and ashes, we're not in the room yet . . .*

Delag, Jain thought, straining to reach some human consciousness in the dark. *Delag, do you understand me? Do you want to be healed?*

No, a thousand voices seemed to whisper, to howl. The hair stood out on the back of Jain's neck as an icy wind flooded the corridor. *It promised us power,* the voices crooned, *and power we shall have. It promised us blood, by shards. It promised us . . .*

Jain screamed and sank to his knees, and Delag came fully awake in the body. The healer tried to pull away, and the darkness clutched at him, whispering sweet promises of blood and power and pain. Pellar turned back to Jain and took an instinctive step toward him, and it was probably all that saved the mrem's life. The metal door flew off its hinges and out into the corridor, hitting him from behind and stunning him. The wind in the corridor grew stronger and colder, howling with malevolent life and a thousand voices.

"It promised us power, it promised us blood," Jain moaned almost incoherently, fighting for breath, drowning in a sea of black thought. "Promised us, by shards . . ."

Oriann hastily created an illusion of flame and sent it spinning into Delag's chamber. The room seemed to go up in a blaze. Delag stumbled weakly toward the door, still awkward in his body after all the days spent out of it.

"Old fool, do you honestly expect me to believe this?" he laughed, blasting the other wizard back into the opposite wall. "All you are is an illusionist. You're nothing! Unworthy of the Master's love!" He lifted Oriann off the ground, slammed him into the ceiling, held him there for a moment, and dropped him. The old man collapsed and didn't move.

Raf threw the first of his knives, and an unnatural gust of wind snatched it up and turned it back on him. He dodged it, and it missed him by inches and embedded itself in the wall behind him.

The wind in the corridor lifted Raf off the ground as easily as if he'd been a dead leaf. His dark red cloak flapped around him wildly, choking and entangling him, and he hastily ripped away the fastenings and forced the thing awkwardly away from him. He bared his claws and managed to sink them into one of the soft and crumbling walls as he was propelled into it.

He held on for dear life, digging his claws in deeper, and risked a glance up at Delag. The frail-looking gray wizard was only a few paces away, easily close enough to hit with a spell or a thrown weapon. But either would just get blown back at the caster, and would probably kill everyone else in the room as well. No, only a physical attack would take him down. Somehow, he had to get close enough to do it.

Groaning with the effort, he pulled himself arm over arm along the crumbling wall, the loose white fabric of his shirtsleeves billowing in the fierce wind. The winds blew cold, hot, harder, and Raf clung tightly to the joints in the walls, edging forward cautiously. Two more paces . . . The light metal door flew off the ground and hit him across the back, and he grunted with the pain and held on. One more pace.

Sweat began to shine on the wizard's leathery gray forehead, and he began to tremble with the exertion.

So close, Raf thought, gaining strength from that. *A few more handspans, and I'll have him . . .*

The wizard spotted the loosely sheathed blades in Raf's boots and along his belt, and he smiled to himself. Four razor-edged knives flew out of their sheaths, flipped, and plunged into the mrem's back before he had time to notice the move—not that there was anything he could have done to stop it. First he felt the dull, heavy weight of them inside him, cold, alien, tearing. His muscles tensed and spasmed around the blades, and then the pain hit.

Raf gasped, too shocked to scream, and his eyes watered. His claws slipped along the wall, and the world faded to a white haze of agony. By instinct alone he tightened his grip around a rusting metal pipe, and it crumbled dangerously under his fingers.

He risked a breath. At least two of the knives had pierced his lungs, and they tore further as he tried to breathe. *I'm dead,* he thought dully. *I just haven't fallen down yet.* Digging his claws into the pipe, he willed himself to stay conscious for a few more seconds. He might be dead, but he could still send the bastard on ahead of him.

Blood began to fill his lungs, and he shoved the pain aside, using the last of his strength to propel himself off the wall and spring at the wizard. Delag screamed. The sound was cut off abruptly as the mrem ripped out his throat with an illusioned hand that still seemed human. The winds died away, and Raf collapsed on top of his kill.

Delag's dark energies shriveled away, faded off into the cracks in the floor and along the walls, and Jain came back to himself with a sharp gasp. He looked up and saw Raf and Delag go down in a bloody heap, and he scrambled a bit awkwardly to his feet and raced over to the mrem's side, the healing stone flaring with his panic.

Jain's power sharpened instantly into an almost unbearably tight focus, a single, brilliant point of light anxiously seeking out the last of Raf's swiftly fading life force. Blood poured out of the mrem's mouth with his body's last rattling attempt at a breath. He was slipping silently over the edge into oblivion, falling. Jain caught at the last of his essence, latched onto it tightly, and began to pull, weaving tendrils of white energy around him with a haste born of desperation.

"Raf!" he cried, hurling the name out into the void, trying to wake his spirit. In the physical world, it came out as a feeble moan, but on that gray featureless plain between life and the Summer Lands, it had all the force of a psychic scream.

Raf's spirit stirred slightly, but in response to the scream, not to the name. All Jain felt was a faint sense of polite curiosity from the fragile soul he held to existence by a thread.

"Raf, it's Jain Riordan. Do you recognize me?"

Nothing. No words. His spirit was beyond them, but his curiosity began to extend to his surroundings, and he began to stir slowly to awareness. The pull of Death became more relentless, and Jain reached out with all his strength and pulled back. The bright, bemused spark between them evinced no sense of horror at either the darkness or the light. Both were wondrous adventures to be admired, recorded, and analyzed by that vast, logical intellect.

"Raf! You have to fight this and come with me, now!" Jain tried to fill the other man with his own urgency. Raf's curious, utterly fearless appraisal began to extend to him. "That's right," the healer thought at him soothingly, pulling him a little closer, easing him back up to the edge. Death howled in its mindless hunger, pulling, beckoning with soft cold fingers of black entropic energy that tugged and tore at the fraying edges of the mrem's spirit.

"Come with me, Raf Grayfur," Jain insisted. "Do it for Tazira and Pellar if not for yourself." He forced his own recollections of them into the soft, malleable stuff of that other half-conscious mind, forcing the darkness away with images. Tazira, glancing up at Raf and smiling before she turned back to finish braising her hens. Tazira, setting her axes down on the ground, saluting cheerfully, and starting off down the escarpment to take out pairs of sentries with nothing more than her knives.

Something in Raf started to stir, a small, faint spark of wordless longing, and Jain fanned it with desperate eagerness and a barrage of other memories. Tazira and Raf, lounging idly on Raf's blanket after their bath in the river, absolutely at ease with each other, as mated in spirit as fire and ash. That thought steeled Jain's determination even more, and the power flowed in him as never before. Death wasn't going to separate them. Not yet. Not for a long, long time.

The memories flowed faster, easier, and Jain began to realize that some of them were starting to come from Raf. He watched their story unfold with fascination, watched Tazira grow from a brash, arrogant kit to a seasoned commander, sometimes his lover, always his friend. And Raf, calm, efficient, logical Raf was always at her side, promoting her career above his own, partly for love and partly for the sheer potential he saw in her.

More images came of Raf, Tazira, and Pellar, inseparable almost from the time they met, and Jain was reminded of an old, old saying that behind every great soul there are other souls of equal greatness . . .

"Raf!" Pellar's voice penetrated Jain's consciousness. "Oh, shards, Raf . . ." He sounded almost hysterical, and Jain wanted to comfort him, but Raf was too close to the borderline.

The healer continued to pull Raf up with all the strength of his spirit, and the mrem's thoughts and memories flowed in a tangled stream unlike their usual well-ordered procession. Tazira, telling Jain she was going to give him to Raf to play with . . . *he's a lot meaner than I am, and he doesn't like humans much* . . . Jain laughed out loud, seeing his own pale, scared face reflected back through Raf's eyes. Tazira arching into his caress, sighing, the softness of her . . .

Jain almost pulled back in embarrassment at that, but he forced himself to stay put. *This is no time for your farm-boy morality, son,* Tazira's lazy, good-natured drawl sounded in the boy's mind, as it had more often of late. *This is just one more aspect of physical existence, no more shocking or shameful than any of the rest of it.* It really did sound astonishingly like something she'd say if she were here.

Raf came fully awake at the imagined sound of Tazira's voice, bristling a bit with his own embarrassment as he realized the depth of the memories he'd just shared with the boy.

"Don't worry about it," Jain said cheerfully. "It's nothing I haven't done myself."

"Have you? We had a bet on about that," Raf admitted, starting to look around him. His ethereal body was resting on the edge of a deep, colorless chasm, and Jain had one arm around him tightly.

"Who won?" the healer asked lightly, laughing as he dragged Raf back to a safer distance. Of course they'd bet on his virginity; Guards bet on everything under the suns, especially when it came to each other's personal lives.

"I won, Tazira and Pellar lost. They both owe me ales. Where are we?"

"I'm not sure how to describe it, especially without sending you into shock," Jain hedged carefully after a brief hesitation. "I think we should probably just leave as quickly as possible."

"Is this death?" Raf asked, fascinated rather than afraid.

"Sort of. Not quite. It almost was. Are you ready to go back? It's going to be excruciatingly painful, at least until I can get those knives out of your back and heal the wounds."

"Doesn't matter," Raf shook his head after a last, curious glance around. "I'm ready."

Light, pain, and physical consciousness returned in a rush. Raf gasped and choked on the blood that had half filled his lungs, and he struggled desperately for air. Jain pushed him down gently onto his stomach and set to work as quickly as he could, pulling out the knives while Raf vomited blood and struggled to breathe. The healing stone flared in Jain's hand. It was weaker than it had been, but it was enough. Raf's wounds closed with a rush of warm energy, and he shuddered and breathed in ragged gasps.

"Raf," Pellar whispered hoarsely, clasping one of the mrem's hands in both of his. Pellar looked like death himself; his head wound had bled profusely. Jain started to turn his attention to healing that, but Pellar caught him up in a fierce bear hug first.

"Thank you, lad," he said quietly, fervently. "How can any of us ever thank you enough?"

"Truly," Raf arched his whiskers weakly in agreement and coughed a little more blood. "Thank you, Jain."

Pellar ran a hand over Raf's forehead and mussed his fur affectionately. "Looks like we clapped hard enough," he quipped. Raf laughed softly, though it was obvious it hurt. And Pellar nearly fell apart with a laughter that was closer to tears, and was more healing in its way than anything even Jain would ever do.

As usual, the boy had absolutely no idea what was so funny, and he promised himself that when this was all over, he was going to sit all three of them down and grill them for every inside joke and pre-Fall cultural reference in their respective arsenals. For now, though, there were wounds to be healed, and he turned his attention to those.

"Rest for a few minutes, both of you," Jain said quietly, firing the healing stone again and holding it a few inches over Pellar's head wound. "You've earned that much, at least. And while I'm patching you both up, you can explain that flying kick to me, Raf. I thought you were never supposed to let both feet leave the ground."

Pellar laughed, shook his head, and stopped the motion when he realized it hurt.

"It's usually not a good idea," Raf admitted sheepishly. His voice was faint and blurred with pain, but he realized Jain was trying to get him to focus on something else. With a bit of effort, he managed to force himself into what even he had come to call his pontification mode. "It's important to know the rules, and in the early stages of your training, it'll be important to follow them. But for every rule we teach you, keep in mind that once in a while you can break them with impunity. Sometimes it's even the best choice. You can risk a high kick, let both feet leave the ground and even turn your back on your opponent if you've got sufficient time on them."

"Time? As in timing?"

"Something like that. I think I'll save that lesson for another day, when I'm less delirious." He closed his eyes in sheer exhaustion, and Jain's energies flooded him, warming him. A groan from Oriann startled him into opening his eyes again, and he saw Jain shake his head.

"Don't move, Oriann," the healer warned. "Your back is broken; I can feel it from here."

"Oh, Light," the old man moaned fearfully. "Can you—"

"Yes," Jain said reassuringly. "Yes, you'll walk again, I promise. I'll be right there." He ran a hand over Pellar's head wound, probing it gently, and he nodded to himself after a moment, apparently satisfied with the job he'd done healing it. With a slight, muffled groan he raised himself to his feet and started off across the room.

"I owe you all two apologies," the boy muttered. "The first is for not being able to handle Delag. He was stronger than I was, and he didn't want what I had to offer him. I'm sorry."

"Jain, no one expects you to be as strong as a full-fledged wizard," Raf argued, and his voice already sounded stronger than it had. "Someday, maybe, at the rate you're going. But not yet."

"No, not yet, and it almost cost you all your lives. Worse, I'm going to ask you to stand watch while I try it again with the last wizard."

"No," Raf said sharply. "Absolutely not. I'm

sorry, son, but we can't go through this again. You're not strong enough, and neither are we."

"I'm strong enough, Raf. I have to be. Tam deserves a chance, if I can give him one."

"No, and no. And again I say no. One man's second chance at life is insufficient reason to put Tycor and all of us at risk."

"Ho boy," the wizard sighed as Jain settled in to heal him.

"I feel the grandmother of all pontifications coming on," Pellar smirked, shaking his head.

"Oh, yes, you do," Jain and Raf chorused.

The two men locked eyes in what promised to be a titanic clash of wills.

Chapter 21

THIS IS POSITIVELY MADDENING, DAMAN Najendra thought irascibly as his dark eyes swept the vast expanse of cheering Tycoran soldiers. *How is one supposed to pick Tazira out of that mess? If I could get one of them to shut up just long enough to tell me where she is, I'd kiss the trampled ground in thanks. And if I could get all of them to shut up, maybe, just maybe, this sudden, splitting headache would go away . . .*

He glanced behind him at the reinforcements he'd brought from Amar. They were grinning equally foolishly, he was sad to say, and were obviously on the verge of breaking ranks. They were unlikely to help the situation, and if both armies broke ranks and milled into each other with fond hellos, he was going to get caught in the middle of it. The wizard sensibly exercised the better part of valor and made a hasty and somewhat undignified beeline for the safety of the escarpment.

"All right, my kits, stand fast!" Tazira's voice echoed across the valley, chiding and cheerful.

"We've still got a charge ahead of us. Fall in, and the first one of you to break ranks will be cleaning latrines until the next Harvest Festival!"

Her men laughed and moved to obey her, but not too hastily; that wasn't one of the threats their captain made when she was serious. The Amarans glanced around unconsciously, trying to figure out where her voice was coming from. She stepped off the front line and strode back to greet them, unable to keep the grin off her face.

"Daman Najendra, I see you brought me a present!" she drawled delightedly. "And it's just my size!" Soldiers in both armies laughed, cheered, and pounded on their shields, perhaps a bit too loudly for the jest, but the excitement in the air was infectious. And Najendra, the confirmed cynic, laughed harder than any of them and walked over to greet her. *Like a terrier bringing a fat rabbit back to its master*, he supposed ruefully. Well, it *was* a bit like that, and he was honest enough to admit it. He needed Tazira to pat him on the head and tell him he'd done a good job. He needed that irritating bastard Riordan to tell him he'd been worth saving, after all.

He reached Tazira's side, and she threw an arm around his waist and kissed him on the cheek affectionately. "You did it," she whispered, laughing softly. "You really did it."

"I did, didn't I?" He grinned cheerfully, looking around him at the units he'd managed to wheedle away from Queen Rowan. He looked so delighted with himself and the world that Tazira laughed again.

"Daman, if we both survive this, I'm giving you

the biggest bottle of nolok anyone's ever seen, I swear it."

"Just the scrap of dog bone I was looking for," he admitted with a sardonic laugh.

"Sorry?" the woman frowned, utterly mystified.

"Nothing." He shrugged with a practiced expression of beatific innocence. She frowned at him for a second or two longer, gave up with a sigh, and turned to welcome the Amarans. For a few seconds she let her eyes wander over them, aging veterans and raw recruits, mrem and human, some of them familiar faces from other battlefields. Tazira took a deep breath, fired her wizardstone, and spoke into the rumbling murmur of thousands of excited voices.

"Fellow soldiers . . . Amarans . . . you know, I can't think of anything to call you that doesn't sound pretentious," she admitted, and soldiers from both armies chuckled appreciatively. "I thank you from my heart for joining us on this field. You've no doubt heard by now exactly what we face, and I salute the courage of every one of you." The Tycoran soldiers added their own cheers at that, and the blue-cloaked Amarans grinned and slapped their swords against their black hide shields. The dull, rattling sound of that pounded in her sternum like an echoing heartbeat.

"You've come in a good hour. I'm just about to lead the final charge against a mad wizard and whatever else we find out there. Once the wizard dies, the battle and the day are ours." She said it simply, quietly, but both sides roared their approval.

She remembered a fragment of an old war tale

from before the Fall, loved by Romney, who would recite the lines when too deep in his cups.

"We few, we happy few, we band of brothers, for he who sheds his blood with me this day shall be my brother . . ." She paused, struggling to remember the lines. Somehow, "to be or not to be" was next, but it didn't seem to fit so she let it pass. "Once more into the breach and we'll fill the plains with the monster dead."

The cheer at that was ferocious. *Good,* Tazira thought, smiling to herself. *They'll need that ferocity. Now, at least, I have the comfort of knowing that Vesh won't survive this day, either.*

Tazira moved out to take her own place in the front, with cheers and good wishes sounding on both sides of her.

"Good speech," a male voice boomed cheerfully behind her. "Someone should write it down. It was nice and short."

"Best kind," she murmured, turning back to look at the largest human she'd ever seen. Fossergrim, the Amarans' warlord. Ten solidly muscled handspans of blond, fur-clad barbarian, with the great axe and the temper to match. The two of them had a less-than-glowing history together, to say the least, and she'd wondered when she'd have to deal with him. In a few long strides he was walking beside her. Najendra was clearly doing his best to stay invisible on Tazira's other side.

So, what do I say to him after lo these many months? Tazira asked herself a bit wildly. *How's the old wound? Been in any kitchens lately?*

Najendra started into a catchy tune about two

inebriated captains and an epic battle conducted with various cooking implements, and Tazira glowered him into silence, spanking him sharply with her tail. The wizard's song ended with a pained and startled yip.

"Good song," Fossergrim boomed. "Short song."

"Best kind," the mrem agreed sourly. Najendra blinked innocent protest at her.

"Good fight," the barbarian opined.

"Short fight," the wizard couldn't resist finishing for him. Tazira smiled with a few too many teeth and wrapped a friendly, claw-tipped arm around Najendra.

"Isn't it nice that we've been having weather lately?" she sighed beatifically. "And so much of it?"

"Good weather," Fossergrim agreed politely.

"Short weather?" the other man asked in a tiny voice, gasping as Tazira's claws dug in.

"What short weather?" The warlord frowned. "Fossergrim say good weather, and *is* good weather. Good for killing monsters, or for fighting, like Fossergrim and little Tazira fight. Tazira fight good. Fossergrim respect Tazira." He nodded enthusiastic agreement with himself.

"Of course," Tazira drawled with lazy amusement, spearing him with a sideways glance. She raised a single eyebrow at him and smirked, turning her amused contemplation to his spotless and rather impeccably arranged furs. Entirely too neat for the big, mindless barbarian act he'd always cultivated. And it was an act, she was sure of it. Her smirk widened, and their eyes met. His lit with sudden amusement.

"You're not buying this, are you?" Fossergrim grinned back at her.

Najendra frowned in open astonishment and risked a glance in his direction.

"My dear lady, could you possibly be implying that my barbaric ferocity is less than convincing?" the warlord sniffed teasingly, glancing down at his flawlessly manicured fingernails.

"I didn't say it, you did." She shrugged, turning her innocent attention to the red-streaked clouds overhead. "I would never imply that such an august and esteemed guest might be exaggerating his barbarian persona, and rather painfully at that."

"You . . . but you . . ." Najendra sputtered in shock.

"I *was* laying it on a bit thick, I suppose," Fossergrim sighed.

"But . . . but he . . . big words . . . I don't understand—"

"A bit," Tazira winked up at him, ignoring the wizard's obvious confusion. "Not that I wasn't enjoying it, especially that part about respecting little Tazira who fights so good. How *do* you manage not to laugh when you do this?"

"Who said I wasn't laughing? But I protest, madam, that my admiration of you is entirely sincere," he said, raising her gauntleted hand to his lips and bowing over it. The three of them drifted to a halt at the foot of the escarpment.

"Well, gentlemen, this is my stop," Tazira sighed, glancing over at the reassembling front line. "You'll both get a good view of the battle if you join Varral Romney up on the crest of this ridge."

"What?" Fossergrim boomed, his barbarian persona firmly back in place. "Fossergrim not come to watch! Come to fight, kill many monsters! Fossergrim go with Tazira!"

Najendra shot him a low-lidded glower and sighed.

"You realize, the risk—" Tazira started, not bothering to finish the sentence. The two warriors locked eyes, and Fossergrim nodded.

"I know," he said simply. "And it's where we both belong."

"I'll just, umm . . ." Najendra started, gesturing uneasily toward the relative safety of the ridge.

"We know, you'll be up there." Tazira shook her head, smiling. "And that's where *you* belong. Now get going, and good luck."

"And to you," the wizard said quietly, taking her hand and pressing it to his lips. He turned and started up the steep embankment before anyone could call him back, and Tazira smiled to herself and shook her head. Najendra's courage was tidal at best; it came and went, and often unpredictably.

"Shall we?" She motioned Fossergrim toward their place in the front line with a graceful bow and the hint of a smile. A messenger came bolting down the escarpment, stopping the two of them in their tracks. One of the conscripts, obviously, a human boy just a little too young to be joining the charge.

"Captain Tazira!" he saluted, wild-eyed with barely suppressed agitation, or excitement, Tazira couldn't quite tell which. "Captain, there's been a reverse on the field!"

"What?" Fossergrim bellowed. "What sort of—" Tazira held up a quick impatient hand to silence him, and her eyes narrowed. She nodded wordless encouragement at the boy, and he plunged back into his report.

"The Lizcanth and the gargoyles have rebelled! Or gone ineffective, or something! They're turning on Vesh!"

Tazira gasped, unable to keep herself from reacting, and Fossergrim put a large, gentle hand on her shoulder to steady her. She barely felt it.

More of Vesh's creatures were turning against him, just as the giant spiders and the nits had. Someone was killing his other wizards; that had to be it! Raf, Pellar, and Jain were still alive and free, at least one of them had to be, and the Dark didn't have them yet. It was almost too much to let herself hope for . . .

"Why hasn't Romney sounded the charge yet?" the woman asked as soon as she could find her voice again.

"I don't know why he's waiting, ma'am. But he could signal it at any moment."

"Thank you, son." She nodded quickly, her decisiveness returning in a rush. "Come on, Fossergrim, let's get ready to move out!"

The messenger saluted her crisply, and Tazira hastily returned the salute and started off toward the front line.

"Oh, goody!" Fossergrim beamed, trotting along dutifully beside her. "Fossergrim get to smash monsters now!"

"So, tell me, how does this barbarian routine of yours work with women?" she asked him wryly, loosening the straps on her axes a bit as she moved. He smiled evilly down at her in reply, and she laughed. They made it to their place in the front of the line and settled in to watch for the signal to charge. The murmurs around them faded to restless whispers, and the air became electric with tension, anticipation, even eagerness. They were ready.

They were ready, and there was the faint, wonderful possibility that one or all of her friends might not have fallen into the Dark's clutches yet. It was almost too good to be true, too sweet to let herself believe. A trap, a trick, a final bit of self-delusion. But it was enough. It fueled her growing determination to survive the charge. Somehow, she would. She would see them again, and Vesh and the Dark be damned.

His hold over his creatures was disintegrating, and he felt it, felt victory slipping inexplicably out of his grasp. Taran Vesh—the great Taran Vesh—was failing.

Tycor should have been his by now. The humans should have fallen at his heel in terrified submission. Should have. His plans were brilliant. Flawless. His legions were powerful, his Created, obedient—until now, when everything was starting to fall apart. There were no answers, no more voices in his head to tell him what to do. The Master was ominously silent. Gone, perhaps.

The ghouls erupted before his eyes, turning on each other and the remains of his creatures, breaking the ranks they'd maintained flawlessly for days. His Created, his chosen, his beloved, turning on him as all Delos was turning on him. But he was still powerful. He was the greatest power in this world, save the Master alone, and even the Master needed a willing human host to effect anything in the physical realms.

Vesh looked around him nervously, afraid of the Dark's displeasure. But there was nothing left to punish him, nothing powerful enough to touch him, in truth. He would take back his creatures and bring Delos to its knees, now and forever.

Drawing his terrible power around him like a veil, he reached inward to draw on the links with his created wizards. Tam. Delag. Oriann. They were his, body and spirit, and they would remain his . . .

Oriann felt something cold probing at the back of his mind, a hateful and familiar presence. It spread its dark and loving tendrils around the edges of his consciousness. *Oriann*, it whispered. *Lizcanth* . . .

"No," the old man whimpered, clutching his head in his hands. "No, not again!" He looked wildly around Tam's damp and comfortless wizard's chamber, looking for a spellstone, a weapon, anything. But there were no weapons to fight this. Nothing he could do. He moaned in terror, and Jain glanced up at him from the damp tile floor, where he was kneeling beside the hard white pallet of the newly healed Tam. He'd won that argument, surprisingly.

"What's wrong, Oriann?" The boy frowned, a

sharp and surprising tone of command infusing his words.

"Vesh," the old man whispered, and his breath started coming in short, fearful sobs. "I won't go back, I can't go back . . ."

Tam moaned deliriously and thrashed on the ground next to Jain. He'd been healed, but he wasn't quite conscious yet. Jain realized that he might yet lose them both, and he spat out an oath so harsh it impressed even Pellar.

"You're not going back, either of you," the boy insisted. "Come here and give me your hand; I want to see if I can link the three of us."

"You want to see if you *can?*" Oriann asked wildly. "You mean you haven't tried it before?"

"That's exactly what I mean, my friend. If a healing link works with one, it might work with more than one. Now get down here, unless you've got any better ideas."

Oriann stumbled to the center of the chamber and lowered himself a bit painfully to his knees.

Lizcanth . . . my own, the voice called him, softly beckoning, almost seductive.

The old man shivered convulsively. Before he knew what was happening, Jain took his hand and placed it over Tam's cold one, and their minds began to fuse in that nameless otherworld. Raf and Pellar joined the circle and placed their hands over Tam's as well, determined to add whatever they could.

The slick and graying chamber walls seemed to melt around them all, and the room seemed to shimmer instead with a faint greenish light. The edges were softer, here, and there was a moisture, an ichor to everything they touched. There was a darkness in this place that no sun's light would ever banish. Jain placed both his hands over theirs. The white glow around them all increased, became brilliant and warm and a little painful, and the lines of their ethereal bodies faded and became indistinct in that light.

Lizcanth . . . Ghoul . . . come to me, Vesh commanded, cajoled. *Come to me . . .*

They're no longer yours to command, wizard, a voice among them said sharply. Jain's voice, perhaps, or Jain's and Raf's together, or else Pellar's. It didn't seem to matter, in this place. The voice spoke for them all, and echoed itself with a chorus of denials. Vesh's pull became stronger, the dark tendrils of his controlling thought weaving in and around the group's consciousness.

You are mine. You will always be mine. You will all be mine. And you will pay for this insolence.

The light suffusing them all became brighter in response, burning, and the darkness retreated with an inhuman shriek and returned again with a rush of overwhelming rage.

You are mine! I created you! I gave you everything! You will obey me!

There was a distant rumble of terrible laughter, from nothing inside this chamber, and Vesh seemed to shrink back inside himself a little in fear. The light around them wavered, and a painful and powerful voice filled the crackling air around them.

ENOUGH, TARAN, it chided, sounding almost amused. THIS EXPERIMENT IS OVER. YOUR TIME IS DONE.

Master? Master, don't abandon me, I beg you, its child pleaded, desperately, brokenly. *You promised me power—*

AND I GAVE IT TO YOU, it said coldly. I ALWAYS FULFILL MY PROMISES. YOUR FAILURE IS YOUR OWN.

Master . . . forgive me . . .

NO MORE, CHILD. NO MORE. THE PLAY IS FINISHED, AND YOU HAVE ONE LAST PART TO FULFILL. YOU WILL DIE, AND YOU WILL KILL, AND YOU WILL LEAVE THIS WORLD WITH A LEGACY OF TERROR. THE TALE WILL END WITH THE HOT FLOW OF BLOOD, DESTRUCTION, SEPARATION, AND GRIEF, AND THE CURTAIN WILL CLOSE.

But . . . Master, I've—

LEAVE US. NOW. YOU HAVE THE DESTINY YOU CREATED FOR YOURSELF, AND THE DEATH YOUR VANITY HAS BOUGHT YOU. GO. MY NEXT CHILD IS HERE, AND I WILL NOT MOURN YOU. GO.

With a great dark rush, Vesh faded out of the otherworld, his screams echoing more and more dully on the psychic winds.

JAIN RIORDAN, it said, and its great and terrible voice was suddenly filled with all the love and warmth of the world, YOU WILL BE MY CHILD.

Tazira's heart leaped into her throat as the signal flag dropped at last. The charge was on. She sprang into a full run, her armor rattling and heavy around her, bouncing a bit painfully on her shoulders with every step. Her legs blurred beneath her with the flush of a mass haste spell, and she could feel the quickening rush of two armies behind her, the heat of their bodies, the mass and force of them, their determination feeding her own. It made her run faster, and her heart was pounding with energy, fury, fear, and delight. Tazira kept a careful eye on the ground beneath her, knowing that a single misstep in that narrow and blackened pass could be her last.

They were roaring behind her, the great, full-throated battle cry of thousands. The yowls of mrem blended into the wordless bellows of humans and the high, chilling screeches of her front ranks, the Hellriders. There was no sense in going quietly; there would be no stealth or subtlety about this last action. The captain added her own war cry to the din and grinned ferociously at Fossergrim, who ran beside her.

The rest of the world narrowed and faded, as it always did for her in those moments, and the roar of her soldiers muted to a faint humming note in the back of her mind. She and Fossergrim seemed to be alone, after a fashion, and everything seemed to slow in spite of the mass haste spell. The Amaran threw his own war cry out to the winds and sped up, and Tazira found herself racing with him through the pass, laughing and loving it all with the intensity of a madwoman. This was what it meant to be alive, she thought. This moment was everything.

The mouth of the pass opened in front of them, and the air around them crackled with spells and spent magic. This was it. With a last, deep breath she braced herself for the sweeping charge across the field, and she yowled with all the lust, joy, and rage in her soul as she ran.

No, Jain thought with a frisson of pure revulsion. *I won't follow you, and I won't replace Vesh for you.*

YOU DO NOT YET REALIZE THE HONOR I DO YOU, OR THE NATURE OF THE GIFT, the Dark crooned. I HAVE WATCHED YOU GROW, BOY. YOU HAVE A POWER THAT IS STRANGE TO YOU AND EVERYONE AROUND YOU, ABILITIES YOU DON'T YET UNDERSTAND. YOU'RE NOT A HEALER, JAIN. YOU WEREN'T MEANT TO BE, AND YOU ARE NOTHING LIKE WHAT YOU FEAR. I WILL TEACH YOU TO BE THE GREATEST WARRIOR THIS WORLD HAS EVER KNOWN. I WILL TEACH YOU TO USE YOUR TALENT TO HURT. YOUR GIFTS CAN BE TWISTED TO CAUSE PAIN. SEARING, UN-IMAGINABLE PAIN. NO MERE HEALER'S GIFT COULD DO THAT.

You're lying, Jain said, his heart sinking at the thought. *You have to be—*

NO, CHILD, the Dark laughed, the false warmth in its voice sickening Jain almost as much as the sudden realization that it was right. I NEVER LIE. ANYTHING I TELL YOU IS TRUE. ANYTHING I PROMISE YOU WILL BE GIVEN TO YOU. RULES OF A GAME FAR OLDER THAN THIS WORLD, JAIN. YOU DON'T UN-DERSTAND YET, BUT YOU WILL. BELIEVE ME, YOU WILL.

You'll always tell me the truth?

ALWAYS, I SWEAR IT.

Who gave me this power? Was it you?

The creature hesitated for a long moment, and the silence was damning. If his gift had come from this thing, if it had been meant to harm rather than to heal . . .

You have to tell us, you know, came a dry, amused voice that could only have been Raf. *Rules of the game. 'Anything I promise you will be given to you,' followed shortly by a promise to always tell Jain the truth. Kindly note that you left yourself no provisions for choosing not to answer any or all questions he puts to you. Now that the question's been asked, by your own rules, it must be answered, and truthfully.*

WONDERFUL, the Dark sighed, infusing the word with unimaginable irony. MY CHILD HAS MELDED WITH A RULES LAWYER.

You do have to be so careful with your child's little friends, Pellar commiserated. *They can be such a bad influence—*

Not now, Pellar, Raf and Jain thought in tense chorus.

Oh. Sorry.

The silence stretched on for a spell; there was really no way of knowing how long it lasted. They could almost hear the Dark thinking, and the longer it took, the more encouraged Raf became. And suddenly, a truly devious idea occurred to him. His wry amusement flickered across their joined minds, became the others'.

Jain, while our new companion is considering the answer to your current question, you might want to think up a few more for it, Raf murmured aloud for the Dark's benefit. *You might consider asking it how a band of humans would be able to defeat it, where we might be able to find it if we decided to look, how it manages to keep its creatures in a continual cycle of resurrection—*

SIMPLE NATURAL SELECTION CREATED THE POWER IN YOU, AND I WAS IN NO WAY RESPONSIBLE FOR IT, the thing snapped, its words coming out in a hasty and irritated rush. THAT WHICH I PROMISED HAS BEEN DELIVERED.

With a fantastic rush of energy, the dark glamour lifted from the chamber. The creature was gone, and they were alone. There was a brief moment of stunned silence before the group fell apart, laughing.

Shards, Raf, you did it! the part of them that was Jain thought exuberantly. *You out-pontificated the Dark!* The boy eased them gently out of their link, and they found that they were still laughing as they came back into their bodies.

"He bored it away," Oriann howled, wiping away tears of glee.

"I miss it already," Pellar quipped. "Perhaps we should send it a fruit basket." They erupted at that mental image, and their laughter was nervous and cleansing and genuine all at once. It was over. Thank the Light, the worst of it was over.

Vesh's ogres and a single stone giant were all that was left to him out of an army of thousands. The field was littered with the bodies of his chosen: ghouls, gargoyles, Lizcanth. His human guards had died days ago, not that he could have expected any loyalty from them. Even the Master had left him to his fate. He continued to hurl his spells at the other wizards on the ridge, but with no real sense of anger or desperation. He was dead, and he knew it, and he'd accepted it. If he could bring most of them with him, if he could just bring Tazira Goldeneyes with him, it would be enough.

"If" was a dull, hammering echo in his mind, the only company he had in these last hours. If the Furies had died in that ambush in the Southgate, if his allies hadn't turned on him, if he'd succeeded in killing Varral Romney a year ago . . . better still, if he'd never assisted in the creation of wards at all . . .

Then again, he supposed, if he'd never done that, he wouldn't have known how to disable them. Not even the Master knew that. He alone possessed the knowledge, and it would die with him.

A choice irony, that. His last bargaining chip, if he chose to use it.

The front ranks of the human army burst onto the field with a roar, and the spells of the Tycoran wizards redoubled in an effort to keep Vesh occupied. The charred field began to glow with magical strikes, counterstrikes, and explosions.

Tazira pulled Black Bessie off her back in a single fluid motion, tested its familiar heft in her hands as she ran. She'd named it that because too many other warriors gave their pet weapons pretentious names like Demonslayer and Dark Fire, and she couldn't resist the implicit mockery of a name as unterrifying as Black Bessie.

I wonder if Fossergrim has a pet name for his great

axe, she smiled to herself. *He probably does, and it's probably something ridiculous like Bloodbringer. It would do wonders for that barbarian persona of his.* She laughed out loud, and Fossergrim glanced down at her. Tazira shook her head in rueful amusement and kept running. If they both survived the next few minutes, she'd have to remember to ask him about it.

Vesh was surrounded by a protective ring of about twenty ogres and the stone giant, the last remnants of his army. The stone giant moved forward to intercept the seemingly endless wave of humans, and the ground shook with its every step, making their footing suddenly precarious. Tazira dodged the thing's enormous fist, sped under its tree-trunk legs, and kept moving. She didn't have time to deal with the petty distractions; she wanted Vesh.

Fossergrim hurried through after her, taking a swipe at the giant's ankle as he went. His great axe bounced off the creature's stone skin and rang in his hands, and he shook his head and kept running after the other commander.

Tazira's Hellriders screeched their war cries behind her as they swarmed the giant, taking it apart limb by limb with their spellstones, sacrificing prized weapons to drive wedges into its flesh. More than one of those chilling battle cries turned into screams, but Tazira forced herself to keep running. The best thing, the only thing she could do for them now was to kill Vesh. She felt the massive rush of thousands of soldiers behind her, dispersing across the field in well-organized units, and she took just enough energy from that force to keep going herself.

The smoke and haze of wasted spells was fanning out around the wizard and spreading slowly across the field, obscuring everything, and the din of battle made it impossible to distinguish one sound from another. Lights flickered inside the growing fog, spells, counterspells. Dark shapes were barely visible inside: the rough-hewn and brutish outlines of ogres. The stone giant collapsed behind Tazira, shaking the wasted ground, and her Hellriders surged forward again. The ogres came out to meet them.

The wizards on the ridges began to slow down their spells; the soldiers were getting too close now to risk them. They'd done what they needed to, anyway; they'd kept Vesh from blasting the army apart, row after row, as he'd done to the forest behind him a few days ago.

The humans continued to pour out of the pass in a seemingly endless wave. Some engaged the ogres, while other units held up in reserve and watched for their chance at the wizard. One of the ogres rushed out of the mist and dove at Fossergrim and Tazira, and the Amaran swung his pet axe viciously.

"Ogre want fight Fossergrim?" he bellowed as the axe connected, nearly severing the creature's left leg. It roared and swung its club wildly as it toppled over. "Bad, foolish little ogre! Fossergrim strong!" the warlord snarled with a quick wink in Tazira's direction. She didn't see it, though; she was peering through the hazy glare of smoke and fading spells, desperately trying to find the wizard. Fossergrim shrugged and continued his performance in the absence of an audience, berating the ogre in a spate of enthusiastic monosyllables as he finished it off.

The haze was thick and still glowed faintly, and Tazira raised a paw and fired a short, controlled flame strike out of one of her rings. It flickered around a dark shape inside, illuminating it without seeming to damage it. Without hesitation she hurled Black Bessie at that shape, full force, and she heard it connect with a wet, sickening smack.

"Tazira Goldeneyes," Vesh said mockingly, seeming to savor the name on his tongue. "You come like the answer to a dream." The dark shape in the mist raised a single hand, and there was suddenly an air shield around the two of them, shutting them in together. Tazira could hear her Hellriders running into it and bouncing off, and she knew they could no more reach her than she could them. She was trapped inside, with a mad wizard, trapped . . .

"Oh, yes," he purred as if he were able to sense her thoughts. "Your soldiers can't help you. In fact, they'll see everything that's being done to you, every humiliation I'll heap on you before I finally allow you to die."

Tazira consciously kept her fur smoothed down. This was the sum of all the worst of her fears. She wondered if he knew it, if he knew her well enough to know how much enclosed spaces terrified her. Her breath wanted to come in short, sharp, panicking gasps, and she had to force herself to breathe evenly.

The mists inside the air shield lifted like a shimmering veil, and Vesh stepped out of them. Black Bessie was buried in his skull, its shaft sticking out at an odd, unnatural angle. One of his eyes was gone, and the other glared at her in delighted malice, like a scene out of one of her nightmares.

Tazira thought quickly, forcing herself to stay calm, forcing back the frenzy that was starting to take hold of her. He was immune to her flame strike, her most powerful spell. Black Bessie hadn't felled him, or even fazed him particularly. Decapitation might be worth a try, if she could get her axe back . . .

She screamed as the first of his attacks hit her, a dreadful slow flame that felt as if it could easily take hours to kill her. It was all over her, oozing inside her armor, working slowly through her fur. She dove, rolled, trying to smother the flames and her own screaming, and she let the rolls take her toward Vesh. The flames wouldn't die, and she felt her panic rising.

The mrem pulled herself to her feet, grabbed Black Bessie's hilt, and pulled it free. With a single great swing she decapitated the wizard, and he made no move to stop her. His head hit the ground and rolled, but it was still laughing. He lifted her off the ground with a single arm, choking her slowly. She dropped her axe and flailed in his grip, kicking at sensitive spots, looking for some weakness in him.

The head laughed wildly, and the flames continued to lick at her with agonizing slowness. In a final, desperate attempt, Tazira reached down, ripped his heart out, and crushed it in her claws. Nothing, no effect. His eyes, head, heart, all invincible, apparently. She'd exhausted all the old legends, and there seemed to be nothing left to try.

She heard her soldiers pounding on the air shield, Lainn and some of the others sobbing openly as they watched her die, and there was nothing any of them could do. Fossergrim was swinging his axe, firing spell after ineffectual spell and roaring curses, as if curses or anything short of wizardry could slice through a shield. They sounded terribly far away, she thought, almost delirious with the pain. She wished there was something she could say to comfort her kits, but there seemed to be no way to kill the bastard. She'd tried everything she could think of.

Her struggles lessened, and she allowed herself to go limp, and the flames died down abruptly. Apparently, Vesh wasn't finished with her yet. A jolt spell laced her with searing pain, and she jerked like a puppet on the end of a string, spasmodically. She managed not to scream, but it was faint comfort. Death, unconsciousness, anything would be a blissful respite from this, but the merciful blackness refused to come. She thought over every spellstone in her limited arsenal, looking for one she could use to kill herself if she got the opportunity. And it was then that she seized on the wildest, most impossible hope of all.

With a shaking hand she fumbled through the charred and ruined pouch on her belt and pulled out the wardstone she'd brought with her. Vesh was human, but he was also the vessel of something that wasn't. It might work. It might . . .

All the hatred she had for the man came rushing out of her in a great burst of desperate, manic energy, no doubt the last she would ever have. She fired the pale green Catseye and shoved it down into the cavity where his heart had been. The head on the cold ground screamed as Vesh's body began to shrivel and blacken. The human soldiers cheered wildly, a dull roar in Tazira's fading consciousness.

The hand that had been holding Tazira in the air let her drop to the ground, and she collapsed and didn't move. Vesh's body staggered and fell beside her, writhing as it phased in and out of existence. The air shield weakened and ruptured, and the first line of soldiers rushed in.

"Master!" the wizard sobbed wildly. "Protect me, protect your child, and I will give you the secret . . . of . . . the . . ."

He never completed the sentence.

Chapter 22

"THUS A TALE IS TOLD OF A CAPTAIN BOLD *and a warlord most irate, who learned to eschew pots and pans and kettles, too, but, alas, he learned too late! And the evils of drink are thus explained to the listener's benefit; Old Lash won the day, the Amaran went away, and the treaty went to—"*

"Must you, Pellar?" Raf asked him in a pained tone, slicing across the last of his song and speeding up their run. The dusty road seemed to stretch on through endless miles of golden forest, with no sign yet of the mountain range where the battle took place. Raf was hoping they'd find the army—and Tazira—still there. Pellar and Jain glanced at him and each other in astonishment and picked up their paces to match his.

Raf was tense, so worried about whether they'd find Tazira alive or dead at the end of their journey that he'd insisted on leaving the wizards behind to make their own best pace back to Tycor. They'd be fine, he was sure, but he still felt awkward and guilty about it, and his building tension and Pellar's constant singing were slowly making him insane. He realized he was being somewhat unfair, snapping at them, and he did his best to turn it back into banter for their sakes.

"Jain is such a nice young man, and your lewd songs are corrupting him," he sniffed, teasingly indignant.

"That, my friend, is precisely the point," Pellar replied dryly. "He *needs* corrupting. He practically *begs* to be corrupted. Just look at that innocent face of his! Why, with a face like that, I could steal half the world!"

"I'm not *that* innocent," Jain growled in protest.

"Nonsense, my boy!" Pellar contradicted him cheerfully. "Why, I'll bet you've never *once* gotten so stinking drunk that you've come to your dulled and groggy senses in the bed of a woman you don't even remember meeting."

"Well . . . no," the human admitted, somewhat shamefaced.

"You see? I'm performing a public service," Pellar shrugged. He slowed his run long enough to pluck a purplish berry off a branch on the roadside. "And I'll bet you've never taken a pair of twin sisters and—"

"No, he hasn't, and that's a good thing," Raf muttered, cutting him off. Pellar popped the berry into his mouth and caught up with them in a few long strides.

"In fact, I'll bet you've never—"

"Pellar? Why don't you sing something?" the older mrem suggested helpfully.

"I was only going to suggest that he'd probably never played verity or penalty."

"What's verity or penalty?" Jain blinked, confirming Pellar's guess.

"Well, we ask each other questions, and if someone refuses to answer, he pays whatever penalty the questioner deems appropriate. Questions like—oh, I don't know—have you ever been with a woman?"

"Yes," Jain replied. Pellar lifted an eyebrow, waiting expectantly for more, and finally he sighed with exasperation.

"Yes?" he asked, disappointed. "That's it? No bragging, no details? We have a series of bets on about this, you know. It's important."

"You didn't ask for details," Jain said innocently. "Is it my turn?" Pellar nodded and grumbled reluctant acquiescence, and the human pursed his lips in thought for a moment. "I've got one. Raf, why did you blast that lab apart back at the wizards' keep?"

"Ooo, that's a good one," Pellar admitted.

"I never said I was playing," Raf protested.

"Aw, come on!" Jain badgered him. "I just told half the world I'm not a virgin."

"We're not half the world," Pellar sniffed.

"Pellar, by the time you finish sharing it with the regiment, I will have told half the world."

Raf actually broke into laughter at that, in spite of himself. "He's got you there, I'm afraid. Are you sure you want to know why I destroyed the lab?"

"Definitely," Pellar and Jain chorused.

"You owe me an ale," Jain muttered before Pellar could.

"He's getting good at this," Raf pointed out with a smirk.

"Yes, he is," the other mrem admitted. "Now quit stalling."

Raf sighed and glanced down the road ahead of them. Still no sign of those shardblasted mountains. No sign of the battlefield, no distractions, and no excuse not to begin.

"It was a lot of things," he admitted at last. He didn't really feel like talking about it, now or ever, but the question probably deserved an answer. "The lab was one of the original breeding centers for mrem, and everything about it suggested the unnaturalness of our roots, the coldness of our creation—"

"Raf, we're not unnatural," Pellar shook his head, cutting him off a bit impatiently. "We're a viable species. We've been procreating without the help of a single test tube for more than a century. However we got here, we're here, we're alive, and, yes, we're natural. We're better adapted to this new world than the humans who created us, and we're surviving. That's nature in action, my friend."

"We're better adapted because we were bred to be warriors. Do you know why, Pellar? Jain, do you?" Raf asked, his tail lashing in his agitation. Jain shook his head and frowned sympathetically. "I'll tell you why. About a hundred years ago, humanity reached a point of democratic prosperity where there was no real underclass left to exploit. No underclass left to draw their own soldiery from, but there were still political agendas to be advanced, and wars to be fought to advance them. So they came up with the ultimate diplomatic, democratic solution. They created a new underclass. Mrem. They gave us a genetic predisposition to protect them, to do their fighting for them, and they made it almost impossible for us to rebel. No more humans would have to die bloody. They had mrem to do that, now."

"*Then*, my friend," Pellar corrected him gently. "Then. A century ago. Times have changed, obviously. It's a different world. It's not a perfect world, it never was, but it's still a world I'm glad to draw breath in. And if my purpose is to protect humanity, fine. They have so much potential, Raf, for good, or for evil. Look at Vesh, willing to summon monsters to subjugate and destroy his own kind. And then look at Jain, who's kept up with us step for step so far, and who's so unwilling to kill that he puts his own life at risk to try to be merciful. Look at Romney and all the good he's done. If our species exists to preserve the potential of theirs, to weed out tyrants and teach the young, it's not a bad reason for continuing to breathe. Could you have chosen a better one, honestly? Could you?" He fell silent, and Raf glanced over at him after a moment.

"Probably not," the older mrem admitted quietly. "But that choice was never mine to make. If choice is what makes us human, the lack of choice is what makes us mrem."

"Raf, I'm sorry, I really am." Jain shook his head. "I wish there was something I could do to change things."

"Not your fault, son. It's not the fault of anyone who's still living. I don't resent humans for this, believe me, and I certainly don't blame you. I just regret a set of bad choices made by a handful of humans a long time ago. There was no love in our creation, not even the vaguest consideration of ethics. *That's* why I burned out that lab."

"You don't hate us for it?"

"No, of course not!"

"Good, because that was going to be my next question." Jain grinned with relief.

"Actually, I think it *was* your next question," Raf pointed out dryly. "But it just so happens that it's my turn, and I've got a good one. Pellar," he smiled evilly, "where did you learn to use a picklock like that?"

"In Tycor," Pellar hedged after a moment.

"In Tycor? That's it? No bragging, no details?"

"You didn't ask for details. Ho, look at that!" Pellar exclaimed cheerfully, with a distinct note of relief in his voice. "The mountain range is just ahead! We should be able to make it in two or three hours if we keep up a decent pace."

"Good," Raf grinned. "That gives me two or three hours to pry all the sordid details out of you."

"Let's sing, shall we, Jain?"

"Why? I want to know, too." The human shrugged.

"Because it seems to me that there was another little matter you weren't willing to give us any details about—"

Jain launched into a heartwarming rendition of "The One-Legged Reaver and the Farmer's Daughter" with haste and feverish brightness, and

Raf rolled his green-gold eyes, shook his head, and kept running.

There were other songs being sung in camp when the three of them arrived. The valley on the north end of the Golgul had been transformed into a festival grounds, with an explosive array of banners, bonfires, and multicolored tents. The party looked like it had no intention of ending anytime soon. There were sentries ringing the camp and two skeleton detachments of guards along the ridge, but they seemed to be the only concession left to military discipline.

The first rays of red dawn were casting a soft glow over the tents, glinting off carefully discarded and stacked bits of armor and weaponry. Thousands of revelers seemed cheerfully exhausted, but unwilling to quit. A group around the nearest bonfire was singing "What Do You Do With a Lusty Brognab?" in various clashing keys, and Pellar hummed softly along with them, his tail lashing with excited anticipation.

The victory must have been a decisive one, he thought to himself, grinning. *Who would have imagined that?*

The sentries saluted and bowed them through, and a cluster of female Guards eyed Jain somewhat covetously as he entered the camp. One of them smiled and approached him before the others had a chance to act. Raf and Pellar exchanged a glance at that and shook their heads ruefully. Tazira was right, the boy had women falling all over him already, and he'd barely arrived.

"Do you dance?" the soldier purred, taking

both Jain's hands and starting to draw him over
to their bonfire. Her eyes, he noticed, were an extraordinary shade of blue.

"Not now, Toelle, they don't have time," a
woman's voice chided her gently from behind Raf
and Pellar, startling Jain out of his rather innocent
appraisal. A petite, pretty blonde woman walked
up and saluted them a bit nervously. "Lieutenants, Private Riordan, I'm Private Jenna Dold, and
I've been ordered to watch for your arrival."

Oh, no, Raf thought, his heart sinking. There
was only one reason someone would have been
sent to meet them as they came in. Tazira was
injured, or dead. The compassion in the woman's
eyes was proof enough of that. *Light, no . . .*

"She's dead, isn't she?" he asked, steeling himself for the worst. Jenna hesitated for a second or
two; there was no need to ask who "she" might
be. All the pretty, comforting speeches she'd prepared flew out of her head, and she suddenly had
nothing but the bald truth to give them.

"No, Lieutenant, the captain's still alive," Jenna
stammered, and Raf let out a slow breath of relief.
"But the healers don't know how long they
can . . . it's bad, I'm afraid. I think she's been
waiting for you—"

"Oh, shards. Where is she?"

"Come with me, I'll show you," she offered
gently, not quite noticing in her nervousness that
she'd just given an order to two superior officers.
She turned and headed quickly toward the center
of the camp. Raf and Pellar followed her in grim
silence, not even daring to look at each other, as if
it would make the moment too real. Jain dropped

Toelle's hands like hot coals and took to his heels after the three of them. Toelle sighed and walked back to the bonfire and the good-natured ribbing of her friends.

"How did it happen, Jen?" Pellar asked before Raf could gather enough presence of mind to form the question.

"She fought Vesh herself, sir," Jenna said softly, and her voice was filled with admiration. "The captain led a charge, and the two of them found each other on the battlefield. I think he might have been waiting for her. He put an air shield up around the two of them and trapped her inside. We couldn't get to her; all we could do was watch. It was awful. He burned her terribly. Most of her fur is gone." Raf bristled at that, and the woman continued quickly, trying to dispel that image. "But she's still alive, and she managed to kill Vesh. She fired a wardstone into him, and he was susceptible to it. And if she hadn't thought of it, I don't know how many of us would have survived, to be honest. Vesh seemed to be immune to everything else under the suns."

Pellar kept up a steady barrage of questions all the way back to Tazira's tent, but Raf didn't hear any of them. The mental image of his lover being tortured in front of her helpless soldiers had him somewhere between tears and breathless fury, and completely unable to speak. And not a little of that anger was directed at her. She had no business leading a charge, no business putting herself in that kind of danger when she knew perfectly well how badly Vesh would want her. It was that damnable martyr complex of hers, and he'd always said it would be the death of her.

She'd finally found the perfect opportunity to sacrifice herself for her soldiers, and it was going to cost her everything. Her life. The life they might have had together.

Maybe Jain would be able to do something. Maybe, but Raf just didn't have anything left to invest in that hope. More experienced healers had clearly tried already, and it didn't sound as though anyone expected her to live.

He remembered the last time they'd made love, with tears and tenderness and infinite knowledge, and he realized that was all there would be to warm him through a long life without her. He'd wasted years, always thinking they'd have time, and she'd thrown everything away with idiotic heroism, and it was over.

The Dark hadn't lied. The play would end with death, anguish, and separation, and the curtain would close.

Raf felt his fur bristling, and he realized his ears were laid flat against his skull. He smoothed them and took a few deep breaths to steady himself. It wouldn't do for Tazira to see him upset. There was one final battle to get through, one last exquisitely painful act, and for her sake it had to be played well.

Jenna showed them to Tazira's tent and bowed herself off, and Raf realized he'd missed most of what she'd said and had no idea what to expect inside. Tazira would look bad, he'd already steeled himself for that much. She might not be sane, either, he realized, and he had to force his

fur not to bristle at the thought. She'd been
trapped inside a small space with a deranged wizard, she'd been tortured, and under those condi-
tions she might well have snapped . . .

"Stop worrying," Pellar whispered at him
sharply, mercifully cutting the course of his
thoughts. He tugged at Raf's worn and bloodstained doublet, trying to make him look present-
able. "This is Tazira we're talking about. She'll
be fine."

"Of course she will," Raf lied, trying to summon enough false enthusiasm to make the words
sound less hollow. He almost succeeded, and Pellar smiled and clapped a hand on his shoulder to
steady him.

"That's good," he approved. His smile was as
false and forced as Raf's sudden enthusiasm, Jain
thought to himself as he watched the pair of them,
but only someone who knew them both extremely
well could have seen that. Unfortunately, Tazira
knew them better than anyone.

They lifted the flap of the white canvas tent and
ducked inside, and Jain followed them and hov-
ered in the doorway, not wanting to intrude too
much on their time with her.

Raf glanced around the pavilion out of old
habit, giving his eyes a second or two to adjust to
the darkness. It was plainly Romney's tent, not
hers; Raf remembered those lightwood furnishings
and soft fur blankets from campaigns they'd
fought with the man twenty years ago. Tazira's
tent was probably too small to accommodate the
parade of healers and visitors who must have
been tracking through the place hourly. Several of

them were with her now, watching as a white-robed healer worked over her.

Tazira was lying in the far corner of the tent. A shallow immersion bath had been hastily dug in the dry earth and filled with water for her, and she was soaking in it. Pellar gasped at the sight of her, but Raf had already prepared himself for it. Jenna was right; most of her fur was gone, and her skin was charred and cracked, and bleeding in patches.

She was mercifully unconscious, and the healer was doing his best to tend to her while a small group of friends looked on helplessly. Varral Romney was there, and they'd expected that, but Daman Najendra was there as well, and that was a lot more surprising. Raf recognized the wizard Thodorus, all four of Tazira's sergeants, and Lord Fossergrim, of all people. What in the Light was he doing there?

If Fossergrim looked as if he'd been gloating over her, Raf would have killed him on the spot. He was in the mood to kill something, and the stupid and arrogant warlord would have served nicely. But oddly enough, the man seemed to be watching Tazira with genuine concern. Raf couldn't figure out why, for the life of him. After a few seconds of scrutiny had revealed nothing, he sighed and turned his attention to what the healer was doing.

The healer's spellstone glowed a weak, flickering blue as he held it over Tazira's body and chanted soft, indistinguishable words. He seemed to have been at it for quite a while, judging from his apparent exhaustion and the fading attentions of most of his audience. They all looked nearly as exhausted as he did, and Raf suddenly wondered just how long they'd all been at this.

Jain's spellstone didn't seem that weak even after all the rites he performed yesterday, he thought, trying not to let hope run away with him. *Must be something about the resilience of youth . . .*

Jain watched the healer as he worked, studying his aura and the play of his energies through the stone and over Tazira. It was so different from what he knew how to do. The end result might have been the same, but the techniques involved were as alien to him as they would have been to Raf, or to any other non-healer, for that matter. The Dark was right, he wasn't a healer. That wasn't what he did; it wasn't even close. Light alone knew what he was, but he wasn't a healer.

Shards, he might never know exactly what he was, or what he was supposed to be doing with his talents. Tazira was right, there were a lot more questions than answers out there . . .

The healer paled and strained, his chanting growing more desperate, almost pleading. It made almost no difference to the woman slowly dying in the bath; it was just too little, and her injuries were too severe. The worst of it was that she might live on for months like that. Helpless, in agony.

The old man finally broke off his chanting, and the stone flickered and dimmed out. His breathing was labored, and his unadorned white cotton robes were drenched with his sweat. He glanced up at the three newcomers, and there was an apology in his pale gray eyes even before he spoke.

"You must be Raf Grayfur, Pellar Longclaw, and Jain Riordan," he nodded, rising to greet them. "I'm Allain Sintar, grandmaster of the Healers' Guild. The captain's been asking for you; thank the Light you all made it safely."

The old man offered each of them his hand, in the Old Way, and as he did so he continued to speak, mechanically, by rote, as if he'd been dispensing the words for hours. "She's unconscious more often than not, I'm afraid, and even when she's conscious, she's barely aware of her surroundings. We're having to feed her oil of poppies just to keep the pain at a bearable level."

"Will she die?" Raf asked, and his voice sounded calm and terribly distant. He couldn't take his eyes off her. Pellar put a comforting hand on his shoulder.

"I honestly don't know," the man admitted. "She's a fighter, that's obvious. She's been holding on, waiting for the three of you to arrive, and you have. But I can't be sure whether her strength of attachment is to life or just to you. If she truly wants to live, she might just pull through this, though it's going to take a long time, and she's not likely to recover completely from these injuries. We're doing everything we can, I promise you, but the battle against Vesh seems to have weakened us all a great deal."

"Have you tried linking?" Jain asked him. The words were out of his mouth before he thought about them, and he clamped his mouth tightly shut and paled visibly. Pellar shot him a warning glance, but it was much too late already.

"Linking?" The healer frowned, too busy

scouring his memory for the term to have noticed any of the byplay. "What's linking, exactly, and why would we try it?"

Raf turned and locked eyes with Jain, and Jain froze as he realized his entire future rested on his next words. He might not be a healer, exactly, but he could still be shut away for his talents.

And it was the only choice, he realized. He didn't have the strength left to pull Tazira through injuries like these, and even if he did, there would be a lot of unhealthy questions asked about how she'd suddenly recovered. There would be no way to hide his abilities then, and in truth, it was probably wrong to try. As badly as he wanted a life in the Guard, he would have sacrificed it to save a stranger. Saving Tazira Goldeneyes wasn't even a question.

"I should have known it would catch up with me eventually." Jain shook his head ruefully. He looked at Raf and Pellar with regret. "I don't think I have any more of a choice about what I am than you do about what you are. I suppose none of us gets to choose, not really. We just do what we have to. But it has been the honor of my life, serving with the three of you for as long as it lasted."

Raf frowned, trying to think of something to say. It was a terrible choice, Jain's future against Tazira's life. It was a sacrifice Tazira never would have asked him to make, but Raf couldn't find the words to argue him out of it. He wanted Jain to save Tazira if he could, as selfish as he knew that was.

"You're another healer, aren't you?" Sintar asked Jain, his eyes widening in surprise. "Look at that aura, for Light's sake! How did I miss that?" he murmured to himself, eyeing Jain almost covetously. "What's linking, my boy? It must be some new spell you've discovered."

Jain shook his head. "It's not exactly a spell, and I'm not exactly a healer. I just watched what you do, and I don't think I could recreate it if I tried. It's nothing like what I do."

"But that aura . . . You can heal, boy, I see it in you."

"Yes, I can heal," Jain admitted, "and I've done it."

"You can't have healed anyone yet." Sintar shook his head a bit smugly. "No one's taught you the chants yet."

"I don't chant."

"You can't heal without chanting."

"Yes, I can. I have. Your chanting is no part of what I do."

"But it has to be."

"It isn't, I swear to you," Jain insisted, trying to keep the clipped impatience out of his voice. If he succeeded, it was only by the narrowest of margins. He knew it had to be exhaustion and stress working on them both, but he couldn't help it, the man was just irritating him. Shards help him; if he and the guildmaster were quibbling like infants after less than two minutes of conversation, what was a life of this going to be like? *Too late to worry about that now*, he supposed.

He shook his head and started speaking before the other man could open his mouth again. This Sintar seemed to find himself an expert on what was and wasn't possible, and in this case, the man had absolutely no idea what he was talking about.

"Linking," Jain offered up before the healer's lecture could begin, "is a technique I discovered very recently. Yesterday, actually."

Sintar hesitated for a moment, clearly wanting to lecture, but finally he rose like a fish to the bait. "And what did you discover, exactly?" He smiled, folding his hands in front of him placidly. The possibility of discovering a new technique, and a healer of Jain's raw power, was worth a few minutes of listening, he supposed.

"Well," Jain hesitated a bit, not liking this sudden show of interest much, "we had a bit of an emergency on our hands. I'd managed to break the psychic link between Vesh and two of his wizards, and he was trying to take them back, and I linked all our minds together. Raf's and Pellar's, too. Together, we were strong enough to resist Vesh."

The small knot of people at the back of the tent broke into open murmurs at that, and one of them stepped forward. He was a muscular, impeccably dressed man with dark skin, short gray hair, and shrewd, piercing black eyes. Raf and Pellar bowed to him, and Jain hastily followed suit, though he had no idea who the man might be.

"You must be Private Riordan," he said. "Tazira told me a bit about you. I'm Varral Romney."

Varral Romney . . . the Lord of Tycor Keep . . . Jain's jaw dropped a bit in shock; he'd expected Romney to be much older. In all those pleasant dreams Tazira had blasted him out of, the lord of Tycor Keep had been a doddering old wreck,

ready to hand his throne and his daughter over
to the brave young hero of countless battles . . .
Jain shook himself out of that thought and saluted hastily.

"It's an honor to meet you, sir," he managed to
say. And he managed *not* to say anything stupid
about doddering old wrecks with beautiful daughters, or the handing over of thrones, and he congratulated himself for that.

"Tazira seemed to think you three had been responsible for killing all of Vesh's wizards," Romney murmured.

Shards, that gaze of his could pierce lead, Jain
thought to himself. "Was she right?"

Jain glanced over at Raf and Pellar, and they
grinned, but didn't say anything. This was Jain's
moment, and they wanted him to have it.

"Well, actually, we only had to kill three of
them," the boy admitted. "I managed to heal Tam
Alamar and Oriann Jarnel, and they'll be making
their way back to Tycor soon. It's an awfully long
story; would you be offended if it waited until
after we've healed Tazira?"

"No, son, of course not," Romney laughed,
shaking his head. The boy definitely had an eye
for priorities, and right now, bragging to his liege
lord about his accomplishments and trolling for
favors weren't among them. *A refreshing grain of
honesty in a cynical, self-interested world*, he thought.
Tazira's right; I'm going to like this one.

"Do you think there's really a chance you *can*
heal her, Private?" Val asked, bringing his own
priorities back in line.

"By myself, I don't think so, not yet, anyway.

If I was at full strength, I'm pretty sure I could, but the last two days have taken a lot out of me."

"You're not at full strength?" Sintar gasped, stunned by the potential implications of that. What *was* this boy's full strength?

"Not anymore, and I have no idea how long it would take me to recover, if I could recover at all," Jain admitted ruefully. "I don't know enough about how it works. It's only been about a month, maybe, since I discovered I could do this."

"A month?" the healer repeated weakly. A month, and he was manifesting abilities no healer had ever had. A month, and he was already stronger than the next three or four healers the guildmaster knew, and he was at less than full strength, apparently . . .

"About a month," Jain said a bit distractedly, turning his attention to Tazira. The healing stone flared in his pouch, and he took it out and knelt beside her. The light pouring out of the stone was extraordinary. Several of the onlookers gasped in shock, and Thodorus's shaggy white eyebrows lowered in a thoughtful frown.

"I've never seen any healing stone do that," the old wizard murmured, and Sintar shot him a look of sour displeasure. He'd never seen any healing stone do that, either, but there was no sense telling the boy anything of the sort. Jain Riordan was an arrogant whelp, but that arrogance could be tempered into humility, once he was safely behind the walls of Ishtys Monastery in Tycor. And that strength had to be properly harnessed.

Jain missed the look that passed between the two men; he was oblivious to everything now but the subtlest signs from Tazira. She was deeply unconscious, and that was undoubtedly for the best. He sensed her there, hovering just at the twilight fringes of awareness, and he did his best to work without waking her. The burns were terrible, agonizing, and almost every inch of her skin would need to be regrown. Best to lay the groundwork now and do the rest later, when he would have the strength of the other healers to draw on.

The faint hope flickered through his mind that they wouldn't all be as irritating as Allain Sintar, but he quickly dismissed that thought and got back to work. He didn't have to like them, as long as they were competent healers and willing to help Tazira. They didn't have to like him, either, as long as they let him do what he needed to.

Jain started by trying to stimulate new growth in the layers of skin beneath the surface, but layer after layer was too badly burned to work with. This would be more difficult than he'd imagined. There was no completely undamaged skin tissue left on her body, nothing on which to pattern the rest. There was some tissue that was slightly *less* damaged, and he found that, stimulated it, and finally got a decent layer of new skin knitting beneath the injured tissue. It was a start, anyway.

Jain kept working, feeling out all the separate nerve endings that carried pain or burning messages back to the brain. There were thousands upon thousands of them, and he blocked them all with a single wave of energy. It was something he'd have to go back in and undo later, when Tazira was healed, but for now it would kill the pain much more effectively than the poppy oil they'd been giving her. Oil of poppies was addictive, and he decided to heal the physical addiction while he was there.

"Sintar, why didn't you just block the pain nerves while you were here?" the boy asked out loud as he worked. "Why feed her a dangerous addictive substance when it was so unnecessary?"

"How are you blocking her pain nerv . . . never mind," the healer stammered, shaking his head. "Oil of poppies is the strongest painkiller we have. It's addictive, we know, and she'll have to break the addiction after she's had sufficient time to—"

"Already done," Jain muttered somewhat tersely. So far, he was less than impressed with the Healers' Guild.

The new layers of skin seemed to be coming along nicely; Tazira would even recover her fur eventually. He'd been worried about that. The groundwork was set, and that was as much as the boy dared to do on his own severely diminished power. He'd have to gather those healers and get to work quickly; Tazira felt like she was still weakening, in spite of the fact that he'd taken the pain away. Her strength was fading a little more with every ragged breath.

She'll fight a lot harder if she's conscious, he realized. The pain had been dealt with, so there was no other reason to keep her under. *Tazira?* he called out, trying to spark her into awareness. She felt very faint, unfocused. He decided to try something he knew she'd recognize.

Wakey waaaaakey time, my lovely! he thought, and he felt a vague stirring of amused irritation. Jain laughed out loud and tried again. *It's another beautiful morning in the Guard! I love the Guard! Every meal is a lord's banquet, unless the captain isn't around, in which case they tend to make me eat grubs . . .*

They made you eat grubs? she asked groggily, laughing as she started to come around.

Tazira! Jain cried. He would have hugged her, if there'd been anything to touch, or any visual manifestation of her spirit. But that was the odd part of this kind of ethereal healing; it was all feeling, and words flowing back and forth through a shared link. There wasn't much to see beyond your own closed eyelids, unless the person was actually dying.

You mean I'm not? Tazira thought at him, and he flushed when he realized she'd been able to read his unstructured thoughts in their shared healing trance.

No, you're not dead, and you're not dying, either, Jain said firmly, to convince himself as much as her. She still felt shockingly weak, for all her good humor.

Oh, shards! came her sudden, explosive thought as reality, memory, and full consciousness returned to her in a rush. Tazira came awake in the physical realm, and she drew a sharp, panicked breath as her eyes popped open.

"Raf! Pellar!" she rasped, looking wildly around for them. Her friends gasped with shock as she came suddenly awake.

"Don't move, Tazira," Jain said sharply. "They're alive and well, and they're here."

Raf and Pellar rushed forward and knelt beside

her, and weak tears of relief coursed down her ruined cheeks.

"I knew it," she struggled to say, "I knew I'd see you again. I promised myself . . ."

"So did I," Raf and Pellar admitted in chorus.

"You owe me an ale," Pellar said lightly.

"Let's just move to a vineyard together and get it over with," Tazira rasped, with the ghost of a smile. "Shards, but I've missed you both."

Their friends erupted in soft cheers and embraces, and Varral Romney clapped Jain on the back and grinned down at him.

"Well done, my boy," he said quietly.

"Well done, indeed," Allain Sintar murmured, considering Jain with an unfathomable expression.

Chapter 23

"THAT BOY HAS ALL THE MAKINGS OF A TY-rant," Romney muttered, shaking his head. Jain had gone off to wake up the other healers and get them moving, but not before he'd left his patient and her visitors with a full set of stern, explicit instructions. Most of the visitors had been terrified into leaving the tent. Only Val, Raf, and Pellar remained inside, and none of them had any intention of going anywhere for any great length of time.

"Jain is either a budding tyrant or a country doctor," Tazira rasped in agreement. "They're similar creatures, I seem to recall. Oh, sorry, I'm not supposed to talk much. Or smile. And if I laugh, I suppose I'll be setting the entire course of Nature on its ear," she concluded wryly.

"Speaking of talking too much, don't," Raf shook his head at her. "You're starting to sound like Pellar."

"Thanks," Tazira and Pellar shot back in chorus. "Don't mention it."

"Ohh, don't make me laugh," Tazira moaned,

her face cracking and bleeding as she smiled. "Jain'll come back and abuse me."

"Well, he'll have to come through me, my girl," Romney grinned down at her. She really did look terrible, but he managed to keep any hint of that thought off his face. "Nobody abuses my old housewife."

"Except you," she rasped, smiling with her eyes.

"Except me," he nodded. His eyes filled with sudden tears, and he turned away before she could see them. This was his fault, and he knew it; if he'd had Vesh executed last year, Tazira wouldn't be lying there now, dying by inches in front of them all . . .

"Val, don't you dare take responsibility for this," Tazira spat sharply. "I can almost hear you thinking it. Don't. I insisted on leading that charge, I took my own chances, and I killed the bastard. And I'd do it again. This was my responsibility, not yours and not anyone else's, do you hear me?"

"Tazira—"

"My responsibility, Val. You don't get the guilt for this one. You try to take it on your own shoulders, and you'll diminish me and damage yourself to no purpose . . ." Her voice started to weaken, and her breath became more labored.

"Tazira, stop talking," Val said gently, turning back to her. "I understand, my girl. I know. It's all your fault," he teased.

"I love you." Tazira smiled.

"I love you, too."

"And then there's now?" she teased him with

a catch phrase they'd been using for years. Her voice had never sounded so weak when she'd said it.

"Always," he said gruffly, turning away from her. "I'd better go see what's keeping the healers." He strode out of the tent, and Tazira shot a bemused look at Raf and Pellar.

"Boy, I always could drive the men away in droves," she drawled, keeping her own emotions tightly in check.

"It's a gift," Pellar admitted, lightly teasing. They all fell silent for a moment, and then Pellar brightened somewhat forcibly and forged on. "Oh, Jain settled a bet for us on the road, Tazira," he said, too cheerfully. "Turns out he's not a virgin after all, though we couldn't get any more details out of him than that. He's a shockingly reticent boy."

"Looks like we both owe Raf an ale," Tazira sighed. "I figured there was a fifty-fifty chance either way. He's awfully good-looking, for a human, at least, but he just seemed too innocent to me . . ."

"Ha!" Pellar laughed down at her. "That innocent-looking boy was singing songs and spouting words on the road that would have made even you blush."

"You taught him all those songs, and easily half those words, Pell," Raf chided him.

"Oh, of course he did," Tazira rolled her eyes at them both. Her eyes, at least, were undamaged and still beautiful. "This is Pellar we're talking about."

"Thanks."

"Don't mention it. So, speaking of bets, what kind of odds are they laying on me, out there?"

"They'd better not be," Raf said grimly. "I'll gut the first one of them who dares."

"They'd never be that tasteless," Pellar assured them both lightly. "Besides, you're much too stubborn to die, and Jain is much too stubborn to let you."

"I just hope Jain's stubbornness won't be the death of him, now that he's being forced into the Healers' Guild. I never wanted that for him; I feel awful . . ."

"Nothing's written in stone yet," Pellar shook his head, though his eyes told another story. "He's still a free man. Who knows? Maybe we'll find a way to smuggle him out of here when he's finished with you." He said it lightly, but Tazira's evil mind started to fire around the idea.

"Maybe," she murmured thoughtfully. "Maybe. Why not?" She took them both in with her eyes, and Pellar's joking suggestion started to become a serious prospect.

Raf frowned. "It wouldn't be easy. If Jain were less talented, an appeal to Romney might work. But Allain Sintar was practically drooling as he watched the boy healing you, and I doubt he'll be willing to let him go—"

"We'll find a way," Tazira insisted, cutting him off. "We have to. I'm not going to see Jain thrown to the proverbial Lizcanth because he tried to pull my tail out of the fire. Pellar, I'm putting you on this. If you have to, take a leave of absence and spirit the boy off to the keep at Blackstone for a few weeks."

"Done, madam," Pellar bowed with an elegant flourish. "Don't you worry about it; I'll take care of the lad. I'll think of something."

He glanced up at Raf, and decided to leave the two of them alone for a few minutes. It might well be the last time they'd ever have. It might well be his last time with her, too, but he set that thought aside. He looked down at her, wishing he could touch her in some way. A kiss good-bye, something, but she looked too fragile, too damaged.

"Well, if I'm to find us all a way out of this, I'd best get to work," the mrem said cheerfully, tossing his cloak over one shoulder with aplomb. "I'll be back as soon as I'm able." He blew her a kiss, and she smiled at him softly.

"I love you," she whispered.

"I love you more," he replied. And before she could argue the point, he was gone.

"And I've succeeded in driving another man off," Tazira sighed after a moment. "What is the secret of my charm? Can't be that I don't bathe, 'cause that's all I've been doing for the last day or so."

"It's our private test of manhood." Raf arched his whiskers at her teasingly. "I was something of a dark horse. All the real money was on Romney."

"My two old husbands, locked in mortal combat for control of my sickroom . . ."

"Well, you notice who won," he said proudly, licking one gray paw with mock dignity.

"My hero," she drawled, rolling her eyes at him.

"Of course, you realize, now that I'm Lord of the Sickroom, you have to do whatever I say . . ."

"Oh, good. With Jain and Val gone, I needed another tyrannical man to tell me what to do." Her eyes laughed up at him, and she looked away after a moment. "Shards, Raf, I'm so tired," she whispered, unable to keep up the act anymore.

"I know," he said softly. "I know."

"I would have asked you to marry me, you know."

"And I would have said yes. And I will say yes, when Jain pulls you through this."

"Of course," she said, though neither of them quite believed it. "Hey, look at that spot on the floor over there!" she rasped after a moment, too cheerfully. "It's the tiniest acting troupe on Delos, and they're playing out our lives as an ancient tragedy!"

Raf drew in a sharp breath that was somewhere between a laugh and a sob, and he turned away from her for a moment and collected himself.

"Raf, it's all right," Tazira said quietly. "Whatever happens, I'm not afraid."

"I am."

"I love you, Raf Grayfur."

"I love you more."

Tazira sighed, amused, and pretended irritation. "Why are all the men in my life suddenly convinced they love me more?"

"I don't know," he admitted. "I just thought it was a great line."

Before she could formulate any response to that great line, the cavalry entered the tent en masse. Jain coughed politely, pulled back the tent flap and ducked inside, followed by Allain Sintar and five other white-robed healers. Pellar, Romney, and a small group of well-wishers gathered just inside the mouth of the tent to watch.

"Are you both ready?" Jain asked Raf and Tazira. They looked at each other and nodded, and Raf moved around the bath and knelt down on the other side of it, wanting to stay near her. Jain sat beside Tazira and stretched out his left hand somewhat awkwardly behind him, so that the other healers could take hold of it. They did, tentatively, one after the other, and Jain glanced down at Tazira and smiled.

"This is going to be weird, you know," he admitted. "You're the first patient I've ever had who wasn't unconscious, dying, or possessed. I almost don't know what to do with you, you're in such good shape by comparison."

She smiled weakly, glanced up at Raf one last time, and closed her eyes, waiting. Jain's right hand moved a few inches above her charred and ruined skin, and she felt it, felt her skin itching and tingling wherever his hand passed. She had to fight to keep from squirming.

"I should have knocked you out for this, lady," he chided her. "Anybody got a brick?"

"That head's too hard for a brick," Romney called from across the tent.

"Thanks," she growled faintly.

"Don't mention it."

"I won't. To anyone. Ever," she said sourly, though she couldn't help smiling a bit as she said it.

Jain felt her strength growing in response to the good-natured banter, felt her heart beating more and more steadily as he worked. His healing stone flared, suffusing the tent with warmth and a soft light, and he smiled to himself as he felt a ripple of shock from the other healers. Tazira's new skin knit faster and faster, and the damaged tissue sloughed away.

"Wait," Sintar protested faintly. "What are you . . . I don't understand . . ."

"Just trust me," Jain said, "and keep giving me your strength, all of you, please. I'm too weak to do this alone right now."

"But . . . what are you doing, exactly?" the guildmaster asked a bit plaintively, shaking his head in pained confusion.

"Healing Tazira, the only way I know how, damn it," Jain muttered distractedly. "I told you, I'm not a healer. I can't begin to do what you do."

He'd been too diplomatic to say openly that he didn't think any of them could do it his way, either, but in the healing link they couldn't help but hear the thought. He felt everything from confusion to indignation coming out of them, and he didn't have time to care. Diplomacy and explanations would have to wait.

The power flowed through him and out of him, and Tazira's new skin warmed, glowed a brilliant white, started growing fur. The healers gave a collective gasp and erupted with questions.

Jain ignored them and kept working with a short, sharp sigh of irritation, severing his link with them as gently as he could and deepening his link with Tazira. The healers began to protest their sudden exclusion even more loudly than they'd been protesting their confusion. Raf Grayfur silenced them all with a look.

The appendages that had been burned off began to grow back; ears, tail, toes, and three fingers on her left hand knit, lengthened, darkened with the velvety growth of new fur. Jain's breath started to come in sharp, labored gasps as he neared the end of his strength, and he trembled uncontrollably. The last thing he did was remove the blocks on her nerve endings; she wouldn't need those blocks anymore, not if he'd done his job right.

"That's it," he breathed at last, collapsing. "I don't think I can do anymore, not for a while, anyway."

"Son, I don't think there's a whole lot left to do," Tazira chided him softly. She risked moving each of her limbs. They were painless. Perfect. Gingerly she pulled herself to her feet, ignoring the excited protests of her friends. She took a few experimental steps, moved her arms, lashed her tail and laughed out loud with the purest joy she'd ever felt.

Raf took off his cloak and threw it over her shoulders, and she turned around and kissed him, purring. Her friends laughed, surrounded her, embraced her. Sintar and the other healers poked her, prodded her, and made a general nuisance of themselves until Tazira politely but firmly banished them from the tent.

"All right, Val, we need alcohol," Tazira announced cheerfully as soon as the last of them filed out. "Where do you keep the good stuff?"

Romney barked a delighted laugh and made his way across the crowded tent. He fished out a large, thin metal flask of nolok and tossed it over to her. Tazira snatched it out of the air with her tail, leaped gracefully over her immersion bath, and shot her liege lord a graceful bow.

"Show-off," he chided her.

"I'm not the only one in the family." She smiled, shaking her head ruefully down at Jain. The boy had managed to prop himself up in a sitting position—more of a slouching position, really—leaning against a lightwood chest. But he still seemed exhausted and a little dazed. Tazira knelt beside him and offered him the bottle, and he took it and drank without bothering to ask what it was.

"World's best healer, son," she teased him, "next to you. Thank you." She kissed the boy on the cheek, took the bottle back, and drank some herself.

Can you still hear my thoughts? Tazira projected at him experimentally. She handed him the bottle again, and he downed a bit more.

Yep, he replied. *We can drop the link whenever you need, but—*

Oh, never mind about that. Can anyone else hear us? she thought, casting a quick, surreptitious glance at the tent flap.

No, I booted the healers out of the link because they were being a pain in the ass.

Tazira laughed out loud and took the bottle back to cover the slip as best she could. *You have changed, son. You went and grew up behind my back, didn't you?*

Jain ducked his head and grinned.

Seriously, though, Tazira thought, *stay next to Pellar and be ready for anything. We're getting you out of here, unless you've suddenly changed your mind about the monastery.*

"I love you," Jain said out loud, laughing softly and shaking his head.

"I love you more," Tazira said smugly, climbing to her feet.

"How do you know?" he grinned up at her.

"I don't. It's just a great line." She held out a hand and helped him to his feet.

"Speaking of great lines," Raf drawled from across the tent, "I'm waiting." He folded his arms across his chest and tapped his foot impatiently.

"Waiting for what?" Tazira frowned.

"Just before Jain healed you, you said there was something very important you were going to ask me."

Tazira searched his eyes for a moment, trying to figure out what on Delos the man was talking about. Something very important . . . She mentally replayed their conversation, and her jaw dropped. Raf smiled knowingly.

"Well," she hedged, "we both thought I was dying—"

"And I don't plan on waiting until the next time we think you might be dying, madam. Ask me now, or I swear to the Light, I'm running away with Pellar."

"Darling," Pellar batted his eyes teasingly, "I thought you'd never ask me!" Raf and Pellar looked at each other for a moment before they broke into comic shudders. Their friends laughed and looked at Tazira expectantly. She glared at Raf, and his grin widened.

"In front of all these people?" she asked almost

plaintively, gesturing at them with the tip of her tail.

He nodded. "It's time. It's long past time."

"You could always ask me, you know," she growled.

"I could, but it wouldn't be nearly as much fun as watching you try."

"Oh, all right," she grumbled. "If everyone is going to insist."

There was a cheerful chorus of assent from all the onlookers, and Tazira started to pace. "Raf, do you . . ." she started, and her voice died out. "Umm, you . . ."

Romney howled with laughter. "The woman can take on an army of monsters and kill a deranged wizard—"

"I'll show you who else I can kill," she growled, and her tail thumped an ominous tattoo under Raf's cloak. That, of course, only made everyone laugh harder. She took a deep breath and a heady swig of nolok, and forced the words out in a hasty, terrified jumble. "Rafwillyoumarryme? Ha! There!" the woman beamed, looking extraordinarily pleased with herself. "I did it!"

"You did, and I will." He smiled, catching her up in his arms. "You were so brave . . ."

"I was, wasn't I?" she preened, kissing him.

"Now, be honest, Tazira," Pellar drawled. "Was that as bad as the sewer tunnel?"

"Worse, infinitely worse!" she laughed. He came over, licked her cheek, and hugged them both, and then he moved into position beside Jain. The light-furred mrem and the human exchanged a small smile and settled in to wait for their chance to escape.

"You mean to tell me you're actually leaving me for this loser?" Romney called over to Tazira with mock disapproval.

"I'm afraid so, my love."

"About damn time." He grinned, catching them both up in his arms. That started a flood of embraces, jibes, and good wishes, and more than a little money started changing hands. Tazira watched with more and more interest, and her jaw dropped as Romney grudgingly reached over and handed Pellar five gold pieces.

"Val, you bet against us?" She rolled her eyes at him in disbelief.

"I thought you'd never stop arguing long enough to ask each other," Romney teased her, and she spanked him with her tail.

"Ow," he complained. "Jain, did you really have to grow her tail back?"

"I'm afraid I did, sir." The boy grinned. "She might not love Old Lash as a nom de guerre, but it's better than Stumpy."

"Careful, Grayfur," Thodorus said to Raf as he shook his hand. "It seems your future wife's two favorite words are 'yes, dear.' She told me so herself."

"And she'll have plenty of time to get used to saying them, I assure you," Raf said smoothly.

" 'Yes, dear'? 'Stumpy'?" Tazira growled, and as usual she couldn't keep from grinning. "When did I sign on for this abuse?"

"You asked for it." Raf shrugged, wryly amused.

"I did that, didn't I?" She nodded, still quite delighted with her show of courage. She yawned, and her claws splayed as she stretched.

"I think it's high time we let you sleep," Raf murmured, nuzzling the top of her head affectionately.

"Yes, dear," she agreed. Her visitors took the polite hint and began to file out. Sergeant Dano paused on his way through the tent flap and glanced back at Raf and Tazira.

"Permission to tell the men that the captain's been healed, sirs?" he asked. "They've been anxious, and they're not happy about the fact that we ordered them away from the tent."

"Denied." Jain shook his head firmly. "I'm sorry, but I want Tazira to sleep right now, and sleep won't be an option once the soldiers know about this."

"But—"

"Five hours at least. Give her and everyone else a chance to sleep, and we'll make the announcement this evening."

Dano frowned thoughtfully for a moment. The healer made sense, though he hated to admit it. He nodded, saluted his superiors, and smiled at last.

"Welcome back, Captain," he said quietly.

"Thank you, Sergeant," Tazira grinned back at him. "So, when are you going to satisfy all our bets about you and Sergeant Lira?"

Dano winced visibly. "Is nothing sacred anymore?" he inquired of the wide world.

"Nothing under the suns, my boy," his captain

shook her head cheerfully. "It's a hard and piti-less world."

Raf laid out a soft white fur blanket over Rom-ney's pallet and patted it insistently, giving Tazira a meaningful look.

"Yes, dear," she grumbled. "I consider my point made."

Dano ducked his head to hide a quick grin. "Good night, Captain, all," he saluted and bowed himself out, leaving Jain, Raf, Pellar, and Tazira alone for the moment.

Pellar quickly and quietly lifted up the back of the tent. One of the healers was waiting there; they were clearly expecting Jain to try to make a break for it. The mrem cursed quietly to himself and started racking his brain for alternatives.

He crossed over to the pallet where Tazira was settling down to rest. "The healers have the tent surrounded," he whispered, taking them all in with his eyes. Jain paled a bit.

"Of course they do," Tazira sighed irritably. "Never easy, is it? And if we all go out there en masse, they'll know we're all up to something, and they won't let any of the three of us near you, ever again. Best if we leave it up to Pellar. Play for time, do whatever you can, and if we have to, we'll find a way to smuggle Jain out of the monas-tery. We will get you out, son," she said firmly, locking eyes with Jain. "That's a promise. Good luck, and just yell if you need us."

"We will," Pellar assured her. "In the mean-time, try to get some sleep, finally. You've earned it. And don't worry, I'll think of something. I al-ways do." He hoped he sounded more confident than he felt about that. Tazira winked at him and closed her eyes, and Pellar blew her one last kiss and was off in a bound. He cast one final glance back at Raf. "Are you coming?"

Raf shook his head. "The already suspicious healers will only be that much more suspicious if I do. Besides, you don't need me, Tazira does. Call out if you get yourselves in trouble, and we'll be there."

Pellar nodded, and he and Jain stepped out into the light. Thodorus and the sergeants had all gone, but there was still a small group talking in front of the tent, and it was largely composed of healers. Allain Sintar moved to stand on Jain's left, and two of his followers took up positions close to him.

Pellar managed to appear nonchalant about the whole thing, but inwardly he was cursing a blue streak. He couldn't attack any of the healers without bringing the death penalty on himself, and they clearly weren't going to make it easy to slip away. He tuned back in to the somewhat heated conversation Romney was having with Daman Najendra, looking for something that would serve as a distraction.

"So, Najendra, what am I supposed to do with you, exactly?" Romney was saying, and he was clearly somewhere between amusement and genuine anger. "On the one hand, you brought us reinforcements, but on the other hand, you're an Amaran spy. Am I supposed to let you just walk away with whatever secrets you might be taking with you?"

"I was hoping so, milord," the wizard admitted.

"After all, you've sent your fair share of spies into Amar. Isn't that right, Pellar? Or should I say, Lir?"

"Your name is Lir?" Jain frowned in confusion.

"No, my name is Pellar," the mrem hissed tightly, starting to glance around in search of his own escape route. "Once again, Najendra, I have no idea what you're talking about."

"Really?" Najendra purred. "Do allow me to refresh your memory. It was, oh, about ten years ago, I'd say. Queen Rowan had a mrem court bard who just happened to look exactly like you. He stole some very important documents, along with a spellstone for mass confusion which we still haven't recovered, last I heard."

"Fascinating," Pellar said innocently. "He sounds perfectly heroic to me."

"Oh, yes, he's very brave, and very clever, and there's a very fat price on his head. Perhaps we might all agree that spying is a dirty but necessary part of life, and let bygones be bygones?"

"Fossergrim let bygones begone," the Amarans' warlord nodded thoughtfully. Romney was ominously silent, and Fossergrim got a truly wicked light in his eyes for just a moment before he spoke again. "If Romney agree to let little wizard go, maybe Romney and Fossergrim reneg . . . renegate . . . discuss trade agreements?" he suggested innocently.

Romney considered him for no more than a second. "Done," he said sharply. The two men started talking earnestly as they walked off, and Romney was smiling broadly. Fossergrim, if possible, looked even stupider than usual. The two spies were left outside the tent with the healers and Jain, utterly forgotten.

"Well, I guess that's that," Najendra sighed. "Sorry about that, Lir. Just saving my own skin, as usual."

"You're good at it," Pellar murmured, and his inscrutable expression gave no clues as to how he felt about that talent.

"I'm a spy." The wizard shrugged indifferently as he wandered off in search of his tent and a soft pallet.

"Are you, Pellar? A spy, I mean?" Jain asked him, fascinated. The mrem hesitated for a moment, thinking.

"Promise me you'll never tell Raf or Tazira? They'd never let me hear the end of it."

"I promise. Not that it'll matter, where I'm going," the boy said glumly, glancing around him at the white-robed healers.

"I was a spy, on and off for a few years. I've been a lot of things, in my time."

"And the lock picking?"

"Is a story for another day, young man." Pellar winked. "Never tell all your best tales in one sitting."

"Just as well." The guildmaster shrugged indifferently. "We've wasted enough time in this place. Are you ready to come with us, Jain?"

"No." The boy shook his head, surprising himself and everyone else. "I'm sorry, but no. I'm not a healer, and I'm not going with you. I doubt I could ever learn to do what you do. I thank you for the invitation, but I already have a place in the Guard."

"It's not an invitation, young man," Sintar said coldly. "You have a terribly rare gift, and we need to protect you while we study it."

Pellar suddenly laughed out loud at the absurdity of the situation. They hadn't realized it yet, any of them, but they were about to. Everyone turned to him, and their expressions ranged from incredulity to annoyance.

"You can't touch him." The mrem shook his head, still smiling. "You can't lay a shardblasted finger on him."

"He is ours," Sintar pointed out irascibly. "He is one of us."

"Is he?" Pellar asked ironically. "Is he a healer? Because if he is, he's protected by Tycor's strongest laws. The penalty for attacking a healer is death, and that law doesn't make any exceptions for other healers. If Jain is a healer, you can't touch him, and if he isn't, you have no right to."

Sintar's jaw dropped, and his frown deepened at that unanticipated wrinkle. The other healers exchanged uncomfortable looks, and Pellar's grin widened.

"Either way," the mrem sighed with mock regret, "Jain's a free man."

Jain took that in for half a second and cheered loudly. He and Pellar caught each other up in an enormous bear hug, laughing, and Tazira swept open the tent flap and charged out with Raf right behind her. The four of them looked at each other in momentary confusion.

"I'm staying in the Guard!" Jain shouted, laughing in his excitement.

"Well, of course you are, boy!" Tazira agreed with

a lopsided grin. "We knew Pellar would think of something; he always does. Now quit waking the neighbors!" She threw a companionable arm around him and turned to face the disgruntled healers. "Guildmaster Sintar, gentlemen, I thank you truly." She smiled, all graciousness and teeth. "I thank you all, not just for myself, but for my men. We couldn't have won this battle without you."

"That's true enough," the old man grumbled sourly. He locked eyes with Tazira for a long, tense moment before he looked away. "You'd protect this boy if I tried to take him, wouldn't you?"

"You know I would. We all would." The Furies casually surrounded Jain in their old, protective triangle, and Jain did his best not to smile.

"And I suppose an appeal to Varral Romney would be a waste of my time."

"Probably," Tazira agreed politely. The old man sighed after a moment and shook his head.

"Well, you all seem to have me dead to rights," Sintar concluded with the best grace he could. He didn't seem terribly graceful. In fact, he looked like a man with a toothache. "Jain, my boy, I won't force you to join us. But you'll always be welcome if you change your mind. I don't suppose you'd be willing to visit us from time to time, share a few of those techniques with us?"

"Gladly," Jain said, and meant it.

"Well, then, I suppose that's as much as I can ask," the guildmaster grumbled. "And now, if you'll all excuse me, someone around here has to get some sleep!"

He stalked off in a huff, and his followers did what followers do: they followed. Tazira smirked and mussed Jain's hair, not quite able to keep herself from licking her shoulder irreverently at the departing figures.

"Tazira," Pellar shook his head with mock sadness, "was that absolutely necessary?"

"Yes, dear, I believe it was," she replied cheerfully.

"Right. Just checking."

"Speaking of sleep," Raf interposed, looking at Tazira meaningfully, "weren't you supposed to be doing that?"

"Ha!" she boomed, throwing her head back in challenge. "I scoff at sleep! Sleep is for weaklings! It is not the way of a warrior!" Jain laughed, Raf sighed, and Pellar shook his head and glowered at her affectionately.

"Captain Tazira? It's the captain!" a man's voice cried out behind them incredulously, and her name began to buzz through the camp with wilder and wilder enthusiasm.

"Uh-oh." Pellar rolled his eyes at her with a lopsided grin. "It seems the kits have spotted you."

"The chaos begins." The captain winked back at him.

"You love it and you know it," Jain chided her.

"Never said I didn't, son," she drawled laconically.

"No rest for the wicked, it seems," Raf sighed in amused resignation. "Captain, gentlemen, shall we?" He flicked a single gray eartip in the direction of the nearest bonfire, and off the Guardsmen walked together, arm in arm in arm in triumphant arm.

Epilogue

One Year Later:
The Red Tower in Tycoramar

WARM SUNLIGHT FILLED THE COURTYARD, casting a bluish haze over the red building around them and the soft earth under their feet. The sergeant felt the new recruits' eyes on him, dissecting every move he made. His opponent circled him warily, looking for her opportunity, her staff poised to strike.

For almost a full minute, neither one attacked. The tension in the courtyard heightened as the seconds ticked on, and the Guardsman felt it and smiled to himself. Finally he feinted high and struck low, sweeping the girl off her feet. She rolled with the blow and leaped back into a standing position, and he had to curb a delighted smile at that.

J'Deera rushed him with a series of elegant feints, finally committing to a thrust aimed at his midsection. Nonlethal, but enough to knock the wind out of him. Her sergeant thwarted the blow, spun, and snapped his staff out with flawless control, stopping it just short of connecting with her head. J'Deera blinked at him for a few seconds and burst out laughing, and his students applauded. The fighters bowed to each other, and J'Deera went to sit with the others.

The soldier paced back and forth for a few seconds, gathering his thoughts. His recruits sat respectfully, waiting for him to speak.

"According to everything I've taught you up to this point, you should never, ever turn your back on your opponent. But I just did, and I got away with it. Why?"

"Because you were faster?" Rahel volunteered hesitantly after no one else spoke. That was her way, filling in silences, eternally transforming herself into whatever the situation needed. She'd make a fine Guard, one day.

The man shook his head. "Not quite, but you're on the right track. I could risk that move and get away with it because I had time on J'Deera. She'd overextended herself, and I knew I could get in the next blow before she could recover."

"And you were showing off," J'Deera drawled.

"And I was showing off," he admitted, and his students laughed. "Time is a judgment call, and you'll have to make the call in the blink of an eye. Less. You'll have to hone your instincts, to know your body and your weapon, to know what they're capable of and what they're not. Every opponent you'll ever face will have a rhythm of his own. Sound out his rhythm, and you'll know whether or not you've got time on him. You'll develop a sense of exactly what you can afford to risk to deliver the next blow. That's why I knew I could afford to turn my back on J'Deera for half a second, and the spin I risked would have added a lot of power to the blow if I'd connected with it. Do you all understand?"

They nodded, and the sergeant smiled to himself.

"Good," he murmured. "Let's see if you do. On your feet!" They groaned a little in protest, and he grinned to himself as he tossed them their practice staves. "Listen to them whining! Up, you lazy kits! Suffering tests you! Life tests you, and you can't be found wanting! It's a beautiful morning, the red sun is dawning, it's the start of another wonderful day in the Guard!"

He heard a light, musical laugh behind him, and he turned to see who'd come in. A tall, elegant black mrem was walking toward him with a dancer's grace, and he could have identified her as much by movement as by sight. Tazira Goldeneyes. The new recruits saluted her hastily, and she waved a breezy arm at them and shooed them back to work.

She was decidedly out of uniform today. Her gown for the victory celebration was a flowing black silk creation with narrow gold trim, and the sergeant thought to himself that he'd never seen her more beautiful. She'd acquired better taste, or at least a husband with better taste.

"Captain!" He grinned delightedly, saluting her. The two of them came together in a great bearhug, ignoring the proprieties completely. "I thought you were taking the day off?"

"Hello, Jain." She smiled, kissing him on the cheek. "Yes, I'm officially on leave today, and I'm here to suborn one of my junior officers. Pellar's coming over for breakfast, and I was hoping I could drag you along."

"Wait a minute—if you're here, and Pellar's coming over, who's cooking?"

"Raf."

"Seriously?"

"Seriously. He's teaching me staff forms, I'm teaching him to cook. We never stop learning."

"He's not going to feed us grubs, is he?"

"He damned well better not."

"In that case, I'm all yours." Jain grinned. "I'll be right back." He let go of her hands and turned to his students, who redoubled their attacks on each other as soon as they felt his eyes on them. He bit back a smile and strode through their ranks, correcting positions and postures, demonstrating blocks and strikes.

"Getting soft, my kits!" He shook his head at them. "Today might be a festival, and you might be getting out early for it. But there's no excuse for ever giving anything less than your best effort; I don't care if it's sparring, healing, or tying your bootlaces. Anything worth doing is worth doing well."

"Where does he come up with such wise things to say?" Tazira wondered aloud. Jain shot her a mock glower and turned back to his students.

"Now, I'm leaving early for Festival, because I've earned the break. What you do with the rest of your day is up to you. I'd suggest finding something to do that'll leave you better off at the end of the day for having done it. If it's reading or sleeping, or spending time with friends, that's fine. But if it's more sparring, do it and do it well, and make sure you go to sleep tonight knowing more about your capabilities than you did when you woke up this morning. Never waste a single day, my kits. They're all life is. Have fun today, but don't have too much fun," he growled, unable to keep from grinning.

His students laughed and saluted him, and he turned and started to walk out of the courtyard, arm in arm with Tazira. To a man, the students kept sparring, and the two warriors shared a smile at that.

"You're becoming more like a mrem every day," she decided, nodding in pleased agreement with herself, and Jain laughed and kissed the top of her head as they walked out into the newly cobbled streets.